Praise for Louise Hare

'The perfect escape – evocative, smooth prose'
HARRIET TYCE, *Sunday Times* **bestselling author**

'I was glued to the pages of this sophisticated historical crime drama ... Mystery, drama, murder, all wrapped up in a story sublimely told'
LOUISE FEIN, *People Like Us*

'A brilliantly seductive mystery set against a glamorous backdrop that completely comes alive'
FRANCES QUINN, *The Smallest Man*

'This is evocative historical crime fiction at its best with an intelligent, classy voice. Utterly fabulous!'
VICTORIA DOWD, *A Smart Woman's Guide to Murder*

'Hare beautifully transports us to 1930s Harlem with a story which oozes class and intrigue. I loved it!'
CHARLOTTE LEVIN, *If I Can't Have You*

'This atmospheric snapshot of 1930s New York is utterly unputdownable'
WOMAN'S OWN

'Entertaining'
THE SUNDAY TIMES

'[A] tightly plotted adventure that brims with atmosphere'
BEST

'Louise Hare writes so effortlessly. It was a joy to read'
WOMAN'S WEEKLY

'Atmospheric ... a mystery with characters you can't help but feel drawn to'
WOMAN

Louise Hare is a London-based writer and has an MA in Creative Writing from Birkbeck, University of London. Originally from Warrington, she has found inspiration in the capital for much of her work. Louise was selected for the *Observer* Top 10 Best Debut Novelists list in 2020, securing her place as an author to watch.

Louise's debut novel, *This Lovely City*, was featured on the BBC Two TV book club show, *Between the Covers*, shortlisted for the RSL Ondaatje Prize, and longlisted for the HWA Debut Crown Award. *Miss Aldridge Regrets* was shortlisted for Historical Novel of the Year in the Fingerprint Awards 2023, and *Harlem After Midnight* was shortlisted for the CWA Historical Dagger Award 2024.

Also by Louise Hare

This Lovely City
Miss Aldridge Regrets
Harlem After Midnight

THE HOUSE OF FALLEN SISTERS

LOUISE HARE

ONE PLACE. MANY STORIES

HQ
An imprint of HarperCollins*Publishers* Ltd
1 London Bridge Street
London SE1 9GF

www.harpercollins.co.uk

HarperCollins*Publishers*
Macken House, 39/40 Mayor Street Upper
Dublin 1, D01 C9W8, Ireland

This edition 2026

1

First published in Great Britain by HQ,
an imprint of HarperCollins*Publishers* Ltd 2026

Copyright © Louise Hare 2026

Louise Hare asserts the moral right to be identified as the author of this work.
A catalogue record for this book is available from the British Library.

ISBN: HB: 978-0-00-849500-8
TPB: 978-0-00-849501-5

Typeset in Bembo Std by HarperCollins*Publishers* India

This novel is entirely a work of fiction. The names, characters and incidents portrayed in it are the work of the author's imagination. Any resemblance to actual persons, living or dead, events or localities is entirely coincidental.

All rights reserved. No part of this publication may be reproduced, stored in a retrieval system, or transmitted, in any form or by any means, electronic, mechanical, photocopying, recording or otherwise, without the prior written permission of the publishers.

Without limiting the exclusive rights of any author, contributor or the publisher of this publication, any unauthorised use of this publication to train generative artificial intelligence (AI) technologies is expressly prohibited. HarperCollins also exercise their rights under Article 4(3) of the Digital Single Market Directive 2019/790 and expressly reserve this publication from the text and data mining exception.

Printed and bound in the UK using 100%
Renewable Electricity at CPI Group (UK) Ltd

For Rob, my favourite brother.

✷ DECEMBER 1765 ✷

Miss Daisy Gardner, Drury Lane, Covent Garden

This young lady is not to be confused with the elder Miss Gardner, for that wench is nothing compared to her comelier sister. This young lady is still learning her way in the world, but for those who value youth and vitality, she comes highly recommended. A fine girl with good teeth and an admirable figure.

1

London is the greatest city in the world. That is what they say, and, for some, I suppose it must be true. If you have money. Power. If you perch on the higher rungs of the ladder that makes up the city's society. For people like me, London is just a trap. A place where so many of us struggle to survive. A place full of darkness and danger and . . .

But I should try not to think about what might be lurking on these streets. I am huddled in a doorway, shivering. The street is pitch black, else I know I would see my breath clearly, a white wraith of heat leaving my body, every inhalation bringing more freezing air into my lungs. It is well after midnight and there are few abroad at this late – or early – hour. The distinction, I find, depends on your circumstances, on your place in the world. I push my body back into the night, knowing how vital it is to keep going.

I think I know where I am. After all, I can't be more than a mile away from Covent Garden, the place I have called home over these past few months. I don't belong there. I'm just a girl from a country town. A place where you could walk from one end to the other in less than the time needed to eat an apple. A girl who grew up thinking that she would live out her days in that place. Who knew everyone's name and never felt unsafe. Now here I am, alone and cold in the dark. I have done something foolish. Something desperate. I have run away.

It's too early to know if I have made a terrible mistake. I didn't have time to contemplate the consequences. An impulse led me to dive out into the street when a slim opportunity presented itself, my gaoler having left his post temporarily. I'd slipped back the bolts on the heavy front door to Mrs Macauley's house, wincing at their creak, but the raucous singing in the room behind me had drowned out any sound that I could make and, for once, I was grateful for their festivities.

My absence will, by now, have been noted. Emmy will have been the first to miss me, and I try to quell my guilt over leaving her behind. Would she have kept quiet, or would she have been first to raise the alarm? I'd have tried to bring her with me only I know she would never leave. I don't blame her. She has her reasons for staying put, just as I have mine for leaving. If I can get far enough away, they might not find me. They might give up the search after a day or two and think me gone the same way as Daisy Gardner.

Daisy disappeared from her own home, on Drury Lane, a fortnight ago. She hasn't been the only one. At least three others have gone missing from the Garden since the end of summer when I arrived in London. At night, as Mrs Macauley's girls sit in the parlour and wait for a knock at the door, they tell stories to scare one another. *The Pied Piper took her*, is their favourite. *He says he'll save you but if you follow him, you'll never be seen again*. Mrs Macauley scoffs and says that there is no such thing, but it suits her to let them tell their tales. Better her girls see life under her roof as the safe option rather than looking to a saviour elsewhere. Some of the men who come to her door are less than gentle with her girls, but what is the odd slap or punch compared to the legend of a terrifying ghoul?

A flash of light blazes suddenly from an alleyway up ahead and my heart thuds against my ribs, my back grazing the wall in hope that the shadows will keep my secret. My terror abates only slightly as I see a young boy emerge, leading his bewigged gentleman home from an evening at the coffee house. He is a tiny thing, his torch weaving an angel's halo from his golden hair. He looks innocent but I know better than that. Mrs Macauley keeps several such lads as pets, and they feed her titbits of knowledge in exchange for her coins. Boys like this, they get everywhere and see everything. Word travels as fast as the fleetest foot and the first thing she'd do is set her little spies on my trail. I have no money for bribes and these boys have no care for anything but coin. They drop to their knees before the foulest of men for a penny. Why would they hesitate to claim the finder's fee for a runaway girl? The boy glances in my direction and I forget to breathe, but he hasn't seen me. He has only turned to say something to the gent, and I drop to my haunches in relief.

The pair pass on and I am alone once more. What is my plan? Unfortunately, I have none. My preference would be to find a fine house, to knock at the kitchen door and enquire if they had any positions available. I can do the work of a maid, have been doing it for most of my life, but in my current state it is no good. Any housekeeper would take one look at me and kick me off the doorstep, maybe even call for a constable. Good, respectable maids, girls of good standing, honest and reliable, do not look like me – half frozen, uninvited, dressed up in an obviously cheap version of a gown that a grand lady might wear. Beneath the woollen cloak, which thank goodness I had the sense to grab before fleeing, the bodice of my dress is scandalous. They would know exactly where I've come from.

There is no point worrying about that now, I tell myself. I need to be safe first, away from Covent Garden. At the break of dawn, these streets will be bustling once more. Crowds to disappear into but more eyes looking out for me. If I head east, I might be safe. I am a sensible girl. Educated. I can read and write. There will be something I can do to earn money, just for long enough to survive until I can think of something better. If such a thing is possible. For how can I think straight when I am having to concentrate on basic functions? My breathing is fast as my heart races, I perspire even though I am freezing. London is not the greatest city in the world; it is the most terrifying, and I have not the first idea what I should do.

I am so close to giving up, to turning back and facing my fate in Covent Garden, when I trip and fall. Misery upon more misery! A bundle of rags on the floor, carelessly discarded, and I fly over it with the grace of a drunkard. I sit there on the ground, stunned, my palms burning where the skin has been grated away. Sobs rise up within me, pressure building until, just before the dam bursts, I hear a sound. A whimper, like that of a dog who is used to getting kicked in the ribs by his master and knows there's little sense in making a louder fuss. The rags shift, one corner falling away to reveal an arm. A sliver of moonlight peeps out from behind a cloud above, its glow illuminating an ear.

I push myself up from the ground, grimacing as I realise too late that this poor soul has pissed himself and I have planted my palm in the puddle he has made, recently enough that it has not yet frozen. He stirs a little and the stench of urine and blood hits me with force.

'Are you all right?' I ask. A stupid question. I prod the bundle with a fingertip and look around, but the street is still deserted. He has likely been here a while. Did he lose money to the wrong person? Pick a fight with a stronger man while over imbibing gin in a local tavern? 'Can you hear me?'

The body slowly unfolds. A man, I guess, from the cut of his hair close to the scalp. But wait – I peer closer. He is beaten badly, blood staining his face, but I can see that his skin is dark, even darker than my own. One eye is closed, swollen out of all proportion, but the other stares up at me and I can see the desperation there. He is young, only a little older than me. Perhaps seventeen or eighteen years of age.

I dare to reach out a hand – the unsoiled one – and he lets me touch his face, though he cannot help but jerk back a little in pain. My fingers are marked with his blood when I pull them back. He is real then, flesh and all the rest of it.

'Who did this to you?' I ask, and he shies away a little. 'Don't be afraid. I only want to help. My name is Sukey. Will you tell me your name?'

His breath is laboured, and he can only croak out a sound that makes no sense. Perhaps he doesn't speak English. Either way, it pains me to watch him try to speak.

'Hush,' I tell him. 'I reckon we can do proper introductions later on.'

In the distance I hear laughter, the off-key singing of drunken men. We should leave. We aren't safe. *I* am not safe. I consider the boy in front of me, he who is nothing to me. I could easily leave him. No one would know and few would blame me, yet I waiver. I hear the voice of the Reverend Ashley in my head. A voice of reason and compassion at all times, though his actions often proved to the contrary. *Therefore, all things whatsoever ye would that men should do to you: do ye even so to them.* Many times, I'd wished the good reverend and his wife had lived the Gospel of Matthew as fervently as they'd preached it. I had just as often wished to leave their care. Look where foolish dreams can lead you.

An idea occurs to me. I have heard mention of a doctor, one who cares for the poor and does not charge for the privilege. Maria, one of Mrs Macauley's girls, told me about him. He treated her nephew for a fever, and, against all odds, he survived. Perhaps he can also save this boy. Perhaps he can also help me.

Mincing Lane, I remember. That is where his surgery is. So strange it had seemed to me when Maria told me of this man, that there is real goodness in this city as well as bad, that it has stuck in my head where to find him. My knowledge of the local geography is still limited but I will try to find it for I have no better idea, and the boy seems incapable of any decision.

He seems to trust me when I tell him of my plan. It takes us both some effort but, once on his feet, our arms around one another, he is able to hold himself upright. On we stagger until I see St Paul's, its dome a welcome companion. We are just past that grand building that I will later come to know as the Mansion House, home to the Lord Mayor of London, when our situation worsens. The boy suddenly loses his strength, and my hands – so numb in the cold that I cannot recover my grip – let him fall. I drop beside him, exhausted. It is still dark, but I can sense the city beginning to wake. A wagon passes us by, and I turn my head away, but I needn't worry. We are just two more desperate people abroad on the city streets. I feel tears sting the corners of my eyes as I consider how close we must be to our destination.

Somehow, I get to my feet. The boy lifts his arms and together we stand. I do not know how we manage it. Some modern miracle. Fatigue plagues me but suddenly there is a young girl before me, heading out to work, and when I ask for the doctor, she simply points to the next street. We have found it. Hobbling, we turn down that street, my spirits reviving, then sinking as we see a queue of people ahead of us. A sorry congregation of sickly and sad people. This is the place, but we are not the only ones in need. A woman carrying a crying baby hurries past, shooting us a suspicious look as she joins the queue.

We take our place behind her, and I gladly let the boy sink down until he comes to rest against the wall.

'This is the doctor's house?' I check with the woman in front.

She looks at me and sniffs, clears her throat and spits into the gutter, turning her back on me.

'Don't worry, miss, you're in the right place. Doctor Sharp's surgery.' Behind me an old beggar man has arrived, leaning heavily on his stick, probably his only possession of value. 'He's a saint he is, the good doctor.'

'Thank you, sir,' I say. Looking ahead I see at least six people waiting. 'Does he see everyone who waits?'

'Tries his best but even he can't work miracles. He has his work at the hospital, see, and he must be on time there else he won't earn the money to look after his own family, let alone the rest of us.' The man smiles, showing me his two blackened teeth.

There must be something I can do. To have come all this way for nothing . . . I step out into the street and survey the prospective patients. None look full of health but then who does in this city? Certainly, none look as close to death's door as my companion. Would any of them give up their place for someone less fortunate? My gaze falls on the vile woman and her sickly babe. She is watching me, eyes narrowed. I look away in time to see the door to the house swing open and a man step out into the street.

'Sir!' Without thinking, I dash forward.

He holds his hands up to ward me off. 'I'm sorry, my dear girl, but I'm not the doctor. You will have to wait. He will be opening his surgery soon.' He may not be the doctor, but he is well-dressed, well-groomed, well-spoken. I follow him as he begins to walk away, desperation erasing the manners I was brought up with.

'Sir, please. Perhaps you can still help me.' I have to run to match his long-legged pace. 'Sir, I found a boy. Lying in the street, beaten to within an inch of his life.' I sense him slowing down. 'He is gravely ill. I managed to bring him here, to the doctor, but there are so many in front of us that I . . . that I . . . ' I pause to gasp in air and a sob emerges. I had not meant to do it, but it is then that the man stops and gives me his full attention. 'Sir, I fear that without treatment he will die.'

He looks back at the waiting crowd, every pair of eyes watching us, then sighs. 'Who beat the lad?'

'He was alone when I found him. He hasn't been able to say a word to me. Not even his name.'

Another sigh. 'Let me see him.'

We walk back past hostile stares to where the boy lies, looking just as close to death as I have claimed.

''E's in a bad way,' the old man says, unnecessarily.

'Don't worry. My brother will help him.' The doctor's brother lifts the boy easily, the woman with the baby squawking in fury as she realises what is happening. In the presence of a gentleman, she doesn't dare say a word and I follow closely behind my saviour as he stalks towards the front door of the house, leading me inside and ignoring the complaints of those we leave in our wake.

2

Doctor William Sharp resembles his brother Granville greatly; they both possess a nose that brings their surname to mind. His expression, like his brother's, is kind. He has a short discussion with his brother, allowing me the privilege of learning my rescuer's name, and then bids Granville farewell. He will be late to his work, whatever and wherever that is, and I am equally sorry and grateful.

We are in a room at the back of the doctor's house, along a narrow passageway from the front door. The fire roars and I can feel my fingers slowly unfurl like the first leaves of spring. I edge closer to the flames as the doctor attends his patient, laid out upon a battered chaise longue to the side of the room. All of the furniture looks well-used and comfortable. I wonder if the rest of the house is furnished so, or if this room is kept safe for even the foulest of patients to be cared for without fear of ruining a fine brocade or a rich wool rug. The back wall is lined with books while a large cabinet stands against another, filled with a cornucopia of bottles and strange instruments that I assume are associated with the doctor's practice. On the mantelpiece above the fire stands a wooden clock, advising that the hour is just past eight o'clock. Seven or so hours then since I first left Little Wild Street.

'Was he in this same state when you found him? Unconscious?'

I drag my attention back to the doctor. 'No. He was able to walk a little, but I have not been able to talk with him. I don't even know his name.'

A woman bustles in then, the housekeeper I presume, and the room seems to shrink in comparison to the vast cloud of ill-feeling she carries in with her, aimed entirely at me though I am sure she would share some of it with the boy were he in any position to notice. In her large, chapped hands she carries a tray with a pot of coffee, its inviting aroma teasing me as I see that she has brought only one cup to drink from. 'This'll wake you up, sir.' She deposits the tray on the cluttered desk, balanced across two weighty-looking tomes.

'Thank you, Mrs Day.' Doctor Sharp pours out the coffee and adds a generous lump of sugar. He waits until the door has closed behind the housekeeper before passing the cup to me. 'Drink that down. It'll warm you up.'

He turns back to the boy, and I watch him work in silence, my back to the dancing fire, trying not to wince at the stabbing pains that attack my body as it thaws. I hold the cup behind me as Mrs Day returns with a basin of steaming water which she leaves on a low table beside the chaise longue. Thank goodness she doesn't even glance in my direction, but I can see the effort it costs her in the straining of her fat-ringed neck.

The doctor dips a cloth into the water and wrings it out before applying it gently to his patient's head, the water turning red the instant that the cloth returns to the bowl, like some cheap magician's trick.

'It took rage to wreak such damage,' he says, to himself more than to me. 'What sort of man does this to another?'

I dare to take a step closer towards that still body, unmoving as the doctor presses his cloth to wounds that look deep and painful. His eyes are frog-like in their swelling and the knuckles of both his hands are split and ruined from the fight he lost.

Doctor Sharp goes to his cabinet and retrieves two glass bottles, the smaller of which he holds below the boy's nose. The boy makes a sound, unintelligible words followed by a groan of pain as his senses awaken.

'You're in the surgery of Doctor William Sharp. You've been hurt quite badly. Can you tell me your name?'

The boy struggles but finally manages to eke out one word: 'Jonathan.'

The doctor smiles at me, satisfied with this small progress. 'Pleased to meet you, Jonathan. Are you able to tell me what happened to you?'

'I can' see,' comes the reply, muffled through his poor broken lips. 'I can' see, I can' see, I can'—' Tears stream from his ruined eyes.

'Calm yourself, my boy.' The doctor's face belies his words, his voice remaining tranquil even as his face crumples in concentration. 'Let me wash your eyes. It may be that it is only dried blood that glues them together so. This will sting but it will be bearable.'

The patient disagrees vehemently with this verdict, his body convulsing as Doctor Sharp applies first his warm water and then a liquid from the second bottle to Jonathan's eyes and face.

'Now, isn't that better?' Doctor Sharp turns to me and lowers his voice. 'This is all I can do for him here but – I'm so sorry, I didn't even ask your name.'

'Sukey, sir,' I stammer. 'Sukey Maynard.'

'Well, Sukey Maynard, it may well be that you have saved this young man's life. Be proud of yourself.'

Mrs Day interrupts us once more. 'Doctor, the rabble are roused. I dread to think what will happen if you don't admit the next patient soon.'

Sharp groans and looks at Jonathan. 'I shall go and talk to them. Sukey, would you mind staying with Jonathan just a few moments longer?'

I shake my head and the doctor leaves us, thankfully taking Mrs Day with him. The warmth of the room is making me feel sleepy and I sit down on the floor beside Jonathan, not wanting to sully the doctor's furniture with my filthy clothing.

'He's going to help us,' I tell Jonathan, hoping to soothe myself as much as him. 'I don't have a home anymore. I don't think you do either.'

I can see his chest moving slightly as he breathes but he doesn't show any signs of having understood me. I take hold of one of his hot, dry hands and feel an immense weight envelop me like a dark shroud. I am no closer to safety. I will have to leave here once the doctor returns, I do realise that. The past hours with Jonathan have been an ordeal but at least they gave me purpose. I could forget my own problems while I was forced to think about his. Now, no longer at bay, my miserable circumstances threaten to overwhelm me.

Just a few months ago my life was completely different. I grew up in a house that, while never loving, did at least have the appearance and sensibility of a home. My guardians gave me a rudimentary education, more than most girls received, and trained me in the carrying out of household tasks. This was how I repaid their charity, and I expected that eventually, once time came to leave that place, it would serve me in good stead. A life in service was secure. Safe. The best that someone like me could expect. I'd had no idea that someone else had set my fate in motion long ago. My old life had nothing in particular to recommend it but I had thought that I understood my place in the world. Now, I have no place at all.

'I can tell you a story if you like,' I say to Jonathan, looking for a distraction from my woes, and I take the squeeze of my hand as acquiescence. 'It has no ending yet, but I hope that in the future it will have a happy one.'

I begin to talk, telling him of my life before I found him. I tell him about the house in the small town and about the other little girl who lived there with me, my friend Emmy. The house belonged to her aunt and uncle, our guardians. We are almost the same age, her and I, only a month or so separating us. I think of her as my sister though we would never be mistaken as such. How could we be when she is a golden-haired princess and I am naught but a tangle-haired savage, referred to as such by my guardians? Though they are very good people. Everyone says so. Who else would take in two waifs without obligation? If I was expected to take care of the household chores, then that was nothing but duty and recompense for my lodging. If Emmy had no requirement to help me, even though of course she did, then it was due to her position as their blood relation. I am not bitter about my time with the Ashleys. If I had been told what was about to happen to me, I would have begged to stay.

Everything changed on the day of Emmy's fourteenth birthday in August. A carriage turned up at the house and although I recognised Emmy's mother immediately – Mrs Macauley – it was a surprise. She hadn't paid us a visit in three or four years.

When she appeared, dressed in her London finery, full of smiles, Emmy had run to her, overjoyed.

She took us away with her that very day. It was Mrs Macauley who had persuaded the Ashleys to take me along with Emmy in the beginning. She had loved my mother, who had died when I was still very small. The least she could do, she told me on that long ride back to London, was to make sure that I was taken care of. She didn't tell me then that my mother was a whore. That my father was – or is, who knows – one of any number of men who had lain with her. I found out quickly enough once we arrived at Little Wild Street, but I leave out any mention of my mother to Jonathan.

The doctor reappears. 'I've sent a boy to fetch a hackney. Jonathan can come with me to St Bartholomew's. I hold a position there as surgeon and I can make sure he gets good care.'

'So he will get better?'

The doctor glances down at his patient and sighs. 'Let me treat his fever and we will see then how he will fare.'

I hear Mrs Day call for the doctor. The carriage has arrived.

'That was quick.' Sharp looks relieved. 'Go ahead, Miss Maynard. I'll carry Jonathan.'

I grab my cloak and make my way out of the room and along the corridor. Mrs Day waits outside, scowling as she sees me. I ignore her and stand beside the carriage door, hoping the doctor invites me to go with them.

Jonathan is carried out and the driver helps to lift him into the carriage as Doctor Sharp turns to me. 'This young man owes his life to you, Miss Maynard. I shall ensure that he's aware of that fact once he's in a sensible state.'

'Thank you, sir,' I stammer, overcome by his praise. 'It's a great thing you do, sir. Helping these people, when so many don't care.'

'Ah, well, just think what the world could be if we all showed a little more kindness.' He laughs and shakes his head. 'Hark at how I go on! My brother teases me for it constantly. I am not so naive that I think all of our problems could be solved so easily. I just see no reason not to try.' He pauses then, and I see that he is formulating his words of departure.

'I should not go to the hospital with you, sir,' I say, trying to conceal my hopelessness. 'I don't suppose it's a place for a girl.'

'It is a place for the sick,' he agrees. 'Might I . . . Can I give you this?' He hands me a shilling and I have to take it though my face is burning. 'It isn't much, I'm sorry. But perhaps you can come back here in a few days' time. I can let you know how young Jonathan is faring.'

I manage a smile as he mounts the carriage step. 'That is most kind of you, sir, thank you.'

I step back as the driver flicks his whip and they set off. I turn to watch it go which is why I don't see the figure stalking across the road until it is too late. In the very second that I recognise my pursuer, I feel his steel grip on my arm and gasp at the pain as he squeezes harder. 'Gotcha!' He wheezes out a laugh, grinning in pleasure and showing off rotting teeth in blackened gums.

I try to scream but all I can manage is a yelp as he shakes me, hard. I twist and try to punch him and he rewards me with a slap to the head that makes my ears ring. I give up then. I always knew that he would be the one who found me, if anyone did.

Jakes has been Mrs Macauley's right-hand man for as long as anyone can remember. She pays him well to be her bully, but it isn't money alone that keeps him in her service; he is in thrall to her. Jakes has been by her side since before Emmy was born. He keeps trouble away from Mrs Macauley's door, his massive frame ensuring the peace, his well-used fists ready to teach a lesson to anyone too stupid or too far in his cups to take a hint. He knows London in a way I never will, but I hadn't thought he would find me here.

'You ain't as clever as you fink, girl.' The words whistle through the gap between his mis-spaced front teeth, answering my thoughts. Reaching into his pocket, he throws a few coins in the direction of the woman with the baby, and she almost drops her child in order to scrabble for them. She won't see the doctor today because of me and now she has taken her revenge.

I make one last attempt to break free, while he is holding me one-handed, but he's too strong. Jakes hoists me over his shoulder like a coalman shifting a sack of fuel and my only view for a minute or two is the back of his jacket, and the dirty cobbles beneath his feet. Then he is throwing me forward, my left palm picking up a splinter from the rough wood of a carriage floor. When I take too long to scramble up onto the seat, Jakes kicks me in the stomach before stomping in and slamming the door shut. I am bent over, hardly able to breathe through the pain, blinded by my tears. He strikes the roof with his cane and off we set at a fast clip. I recognise the dark-green leather of the bench that I finally manage to sit on. This is Sir Horace's carriage. A faithful attendee of Mrs Macauley's nightly soirées, he has often lent it to her, including on the day that she brought me and Emmy to London. I remember how excited I had been then to ride in such a fine vehicle. I know better now.

'Don'tchoo think about it,' Jakes warns, seeing my gaze fix on the carriage door. 'Mistress said not to mark your face. She never said nuthin' 'bout the rest of yer.' Sitting directly opposite me, he spreads his legs wide so that I am trapped between his knees. It would be some feat to vault over his body, wrestle open the door and disappear before he can catch hold of me. A miracle.

I hold my stomach, still feeling the tip of his boot where it struck me, and try not to think about the stories I've heard about the man. That he once killed a lawyer in a coffee house and escaped the noose because any witnesses present were too scared to speak against him. That although he never shows any interest in Mrs Macauley's girls, when a girl has committed some serious misdemeanour, she is handed to him for an hour or two, his to do with as he pleases as long as he doesn't leave a mark. That he has often been offered large amounts of money to go and work for one of the bigger bagnios of Covent Garden but loyalty to his mistress has led him to stay. *Don't mark her face.* I hear Mrs Macauley's words as clearly as if she were in the carriage with us.

My captor closes his eyes and leans back, arms folded. He begins to snore but still I am too scared to move. Instead, I sit there and listen to his untroubled sleep until the carriage pulls up at the end of Little Wild Street. Mrs Macauley's house is here, much to her chagrin. The environs of Covent Garden are not what they were. Debauched, falling out of favour, she would rather move us to a more fashionable address, but funds are lacking. Her great ambition is to open a large premises, with girls who speak well and will attract the gentry. Lords and dukes are her holy grail. Her current girls are not of the standard she would wish, but she works them hard in pursuit of her reward.

Jakes leaps down and reaches back to yank me out after him. I only just manage to keep my balance as he drags me along the street. He bangs on the door of our destination, and I am glad that it is Maria who stands there, smiling out at me, not the house matriarch. Maria Fawkes is the darling of Little Wild Street and, apart from Emmy, the only one of the girls I truly trust. She is a favourite with several gents, what with her unruly red hair and buxom silhouette, but she also has a heart of gold and a pleasant nature that makes her popular as well as keeping her in favour with Mrs Macauley.

'Thank the Lord!' Maria flings herself around me, pulling me close so that she might whisper in my ear. 'I'm so sorry, my love. At least he brought you back in one piece, though.' Louder she says, 'I can't tell you how grateful we all are that the Piper didn't get you.'

'Get 'er inside.' Jakes shoves me hard in the back so that we both stumble.

'Come on.' Maria takes my hand. 'You're bloody freezing. Cook'll have something to warm you up.'

Jakes grabs my arm once more and shakes us apart. 'Bugger off, tart. I got orders.'

I try not to show my fear. 'Don't worry, Maria, what's the worst she can do?' Maria looks worried and I feel my legs tremble. I walk ahead of Jakes, his hand resting heavy on my shoulder, a gaoler leading his prisoner to be judged.

The house's dimensions are cramped but the décor shows off its owner's ambition. Little Wild Street may not be the address that she desires but that doesn't mean that Mrs Macauley wants her premises to take on the appearance of a cheap bawdy house. The walls of the hallway are papered cream with red roses, at various stages of growth from bud to full flower, a perhaps less than subtle reference to the delights a visitor has to look forward to. We walk on, though, Jakes pushing me along the hallway and down the stone steps into the warm kitchen where Cook is busy at work, dismay creasing her face as she sees me in Jakes' grasp.

'Surely not,' she pleads. 'On a day as bitter as this? The child'll freeze.'

'Got me orders,' Jakes tells her, though I can tell he's not particularly unhappy about them. He heaves aside the solid kitchen table to reveal a large wooden trapdoor. Rattling his key ring, he grins at me as he bends to deal with the padlock holding it closed, yanking it open to reveal the space below.

Jakes made the Coffin himself, so I've been told. Dug it out like a grave with his own hands and re-set the stones around it. The solid door he salvaged from a wine merchant's cellar after the merchant himself was carted off to the Fleet over his gambling debts. I can easily imagine Jakes, lovingly sawing down the wood to fit his homemade torture chamber. In my few months at Little Wild Street I have only seen it in use once, when Hattie put her foot down and refused to see a rake who had blackened her eye on a previous visit. The state of her when she emerged the next day set it in my mind that I should endeavour never to end up in there. Yet now here I am.

Jakes does have the decency to turn his back as Cook helps me undress, off with that soiled gown, tight stays and ripped stockings. I step into the hole barefoot and shivering in my thin shift. I find a way to lie down, not much space to spare, knowing that once the door is closed, I won't be able to sit up.

'Don't you fret now,' Cook tells me. 'It'll be over soon enough.'

Jakes pulls over the trapdoor and closes me into the dark.

3

I brace my arms against the solid earth that forms the sides of the Coffin. My breath comes out in shallow bursts, ragged and uncontrolled. My fingertips find gouges in the earth that have been left there by earlier occupants. Other girls who have crossed Mrs Macauley. The only light comes from the thin gap around the door, just enough to emphasise the darkness within. I close my eyes and try to stop the rising panic. Before Hattie went in, I remember Maria telling her that the trick to the Coffin is to forget where you are. Close your eyes so that the darkness is a choice. Think of happy memories, of family and friends. Hers, she had said, were of her mother when she was alive. Of Sundays at church with her family.

Church. I went every day, ever since I can remember, right up until the day I came to London. I can see the Reverend Ashley up in his pulpit preaching, his wife pinching my arm if I didn't fall quickly enough to my knees to pray. Even so, I would give almost anything to be back in Dorking, in that safe home with a roaring fire and hot food on the table.

I feel something move against my ankle, a light tickle that makes its way up my calf in a scurry of legs. My scream catches in my throat, dry from terror, as I try to turn. Just a spider, I tell myself. A tiny spider. Harmless.

I still myself and feel nothing else move. All I think about, for what feels like hours, is remembering to take even breaths. It is an effort in the Coffin, the air limited and close. If I don't concentrate, I might forget to breathe altogether. At some point I hear Maria's voice above me, talking to Hattie. Breakfast, or what passes for breakfast in this house of late risers. My stomach groans as I think of the hot rolls that Cook will have put out on the table. I listen in to the conversation, hoping to take my mind off the hunger. The previous night had been good, despite my flit, from what I hear. I thank the Lord for it. Mrs Macauley's spirits are most affected by her income. Perhaps she will feel more benevolent towards me than if it had been a poor evening's worth of takings.

'I told you the Piper never took her.' Maria is talking. 'He's never taken a girl from inside her own home before.' I can tell from her tone that she hadn't been that certain though. The legend of the Piper must have felt very real to them last night, and for that I am sorry.

I press on the door above my head, knowing it will not move. There is the temptation to knock, to remind the girls that I am there; only they do know. They cannot help me, and it is better not to make them feel guilty over something that is not their fault. There is nothing I can do but wait.

Exhaustion shows itself not in a loss of consciousness but in a flood of shameful tears, silent sobs racking my body. Hope is on the verge of deserting me already before Camille drags her privileged limbs from her boudoir to the kitchen table, complaining loudly that there is nothing left but a heel of bread and a scraping of porridge from the bottom of the pan.

'The early bird catches the worm,' says Hattie, her giggle

changing into a shriek as I hear the sharp crack of a slap. 'You cow!'

'Girls, for the love of God.' Cook's plea lacks strength. She is well used to these antics and is tired by it. 'Wash them plates up, Miss Hattie, if you're done. And you, Miss Camille, it's first come, first served in this kitchen. Just as it's always been.'

'I shall dine out in that case. After last night I can easily afford a decently cooked meal, and it will be a nice opportunity to attract some new custom, perhaps. Maybe if the rest of you made an effort, you wouldn't be stuck making do with whatever walks through the door. And left with this stodge to eat. No offence, Cook.'

Camille de la Croix, to give her full name, said that she'd come to London from Paris, that she'd been enticed to cross the Channel when she'd heard that the bordellos of London were the place to make a fortune as a successful courtesan. She was less clear on how she'd ended up with Mrs Macauley, in a brothel that was hardly high class, rather than the truly elite establishments in St James's. It was Maria who shared the truth with me: Camille is just Cerys Ellis, a girl, like so many, who arrived on a stagecoach from south Wales and was swept up by a kindly looking woman who offered to look after her. All of these women, Mrs Macauley one of them, are devious bawds, keen to snatch up a clueless virgin and make money out of her. Some take to the business; others fall foul of it. Much as I can't stand her, I do respect how Camille embraces her profession. She even seems to enjoy it.

Camille departs the kitchen, and the others soon follow. I wait and I wait and am finally about to fall asleep when someone taps on the wooden door above me. 'Sukey?' My eyes fly open. It is Emmy. I haven't had time to think of what to say to her, how to beg forgiveness for having left her behind.

'You can come out soon. Mama wants to speak with you, soon as she's finished her accounts. I'll have a warm bath ready for you,' she says. I wonder at how she can be so kind to me after I have been so entirely selfish, leaving this place without her. Abandoning her. If she had done the same to me, I am not sure I would forgive her so quickly or easily. 'You haven't missed anything,' she says, to me, as if that were my greatest concern. 'And it's a miserable day outside.'

'I'm sorry,' I whisper.

I think that she has not heard me but eventually she replies: 'I know.'

Why did I desert the best friend – the only friend – I've ever had? Let me begin on the morning of my fleeing, a day that had dawned blinding, that winter sun that barely brings any warmth while at the same time stinging your eyes as it hangs heavy in an oppressive sky. Emmy and I woke at first light, as we did regardless of the season. At Mrs Macauley's, the hour itself doesn't matter so much as it does in respectable households. We are of the dusk; nightingales, not larks. Our trade is mostly done after nightfall, our clientele coming to us from the card tables, via word of mouth in the coffee houses or through chance of stumbling down our street.

Emmy and I share a mattress on the floor of an attic room. Not exactly a bedchamber, more an oddity of a room that is little bigger than a cupboard. Unsuitable for entertaining and therefore available to the two of us who were not yet ready for such activity, we were lucky to have any room to call our own.

Girls who didn't earn usually slept on the kitchen floor, so Mrs Macauley had told us. We should be grateful. The only benefit to the room is that it possesses a sliver of window, shared with the bedchamber next door. At some time or other no doubt, they were one, but now we have our glorified cupboard and each night we can listen as Hattie entertains.

It was Emmy who spotted it first that morning, the red stain on my nightgown that began as a bright scarlet and spread to a duller, browner shade where the blood had dried, like rings on a tree. The symbol of womanhood that we had been told to watch out for. Both Emmy and I had expected her to be first. She was the elder, even if by a matter of weeks. I saw the disappointment on her face before she could turn and run to fetch her mother. Mrs Macauley's lips pressed together as she saw the truth with her own eyes, but she was a woman of business after all. She had great plans for Emmy; she told us so often. I was forcing her to wait.

'Welcome to womanhood,' she said. 'Tonight, you'll have a chance to repay me for the care I have provided you all these years. A half-decent gown and a bit of rouge, who knows? Perhaps someone will want you. I daren't hope for ten guineas, but something is better than nothing.'

Her words had made my head spin. I was no longer shocked by what happened under her roof, but I had cloaked myself in denial. Mrs Macauley had spoken so often of Emmy's future, the golden girl who would make her mother a fortune and lift the Macauley name out of Covent Garden to some more desirable location. I had only ever been given orders, to clean or to help Cook, and that didn't upset me. I wasn't jealous that Emmy would one day be wearing beautiful gowns like Camille, or that soon I would be emptying her chamber pot and laundering her dirty bedclothes as we currently did for the other girls. To act as a maid, just as I had in Dorking, was all I had thought about. It had never crossed my mind that I would be joining the others each night.

'Tonight?' The word caught in my throat.

Mrs Macauley looked at me as though I were a simpleton. 'Even a Negro maid can fetch a nice sum of money these days, I hear. Some men like to try new things. It makes them feel worldly, apparently.' She sighed and her face told me what she thought of these 'worldly' men. 'Camille has an old gown that makes her look like a fat shepherdess, but it may well suit you.'

She went off to fetch the offending gown and, a few moments later, came a loud knock at the front door. 'Sukey!' I heard her bellow from the landing below. 'Door!' It was still morning, just, and Jakes would be asleep in whatever hole he called home. God forbid that Mrs Macauley should ever answer her own door. I quickly dressed and hoped that whoever it was wouldn't notice that I was barefoot. Still, this was Covent Garden. Expectations were low.

Or so I had thought, but the lady standing there when I swung open the door seemed not to realise that she was in the wrong part of town. A woman of quality, I saw, dressed in navy blue to match her cobalt eyes and with a grand, peacock-feathered hat covering ebony hair.

'Good morning,' she announced, her brow furrowing as I just stood there, my mouth agape. She was, I estimated, of a similar age to Mrs Macauley, though she was far more impressive. 'This is the house of Lucille Macauley?' There was an accent there, though her voice was refined. Both very English and not quite.

'Yes. Sorry, ma'am, yes, it is.' I stepped back to let her enter, wondering where to put her. I hadn't had a chance to clean the parlour yet, so it probably wasn't a suitable place for her to sit. But then where?

'Sukey, who is it?' The mistress herself saved me from making a hasty and horrendously wrong decision.

I opened my mouth to reply, then closed it again realising that, amongst my other errors, I had not asked the woman her name.

'Just an old friend, Lucy.' The woman winked at me as I heard a bang from upstairs. Mrs Macauley must have dropped something.

She emerged slowly from the floor above, her face paler than normal as she descended the staircase. 'Gisele Martin? That can't be you.' She looked as though she'd seen a ghost. 'I never thought I'd set eyes on you again. Word was that you were dead.'

'You are not so fortunate, I'm afraid, Lucy, for I'm very much alive. I married a man whose business was overseas, so I went with him. You're now talking to Madame Gisele Vernier. My poor love is no longer with us, but he was kind enough to leave me with a respectable name and a comfortable amount to live on. Wasn't that what we always dreamed of?'

'I suppose so.' Mrs Macauley hesitated at the foot of the stairs before Madame Vernier stepped forward to embrace her old friend.

'My God, Lucy, it's been so long! And you're still here. Right where I left you.'

Mrs Macauley drew herself up tall and proud. 'I may still be in Covent Garden, but this is my own house now. We are well known to be the highest-class establishment on the street.'

True, but that was not saying much. Madame Vernier's face told me that she was not fooled.

'A woman of business then. Perhaps there is something I can learn from you, as I have some small ambitions of my own now that I am back in London. You have many girls residing here?' She put a light hand on my shoulder. 'This one is very young. Still a maid?'

Mrs Macauley smiled at me in a benevolent manner that made me tremble. 'For now, though I will be showing her off this very evening. I hope that my Sukey will fetch twenty guineas at least.' My value had doubled then, in a matter of minutes.

'Twenty, you say?' Madame Vernier tilted her head, assessing me. 'You know, Lucille, I should admit that I do not come here completely unaware of your circumstances. People have been talking about your Sukey. I have a proposition for you that you will want to hear before this evening.'

'A proposition? From you?' Mrs Macauley looked wary.

'Let us speak in private. I think you'll be keen to hear what I have to say.'

Mrs Macauley took a moment to consider. 'Very well. Come up to my office. Sukey can bring you something to drink if you wish. Tea. Something stronger?'

'That won't be necessary. Thank you, Sukey.'

Mrs Macauley led her guest up the stairs, turning to call down to me. 'Try that gown on for this evening. I shall be along to see it on you when I'm finished here.'

Mrs Macauley's private quarters were situated on the first floor of the house, the rooms where she slept at night but where, during the day, she conducted her business, totting up the previous night's takings and making plans for her great future. I waited until both women were safely inside before racing back upstairs, finding Emmy lurking on the top landing.

'Who was that?' she whispered to me.

'An old friend of your mother,' I whispered back, heading to our tiny room to carry out Mrs Macauley's command. I could see the gown laid out on the mattress.

Emmy pulled me back. 'Let's listen to them.'

'How?'

She pointed to the room next to ours. 'Hattie's room is right above Mama's.'

Hattie claimed to have heard all sorts by pressing her ear to the floor on the left of her bed where there was a gap in the uneven floorboards – though at that moment she was still fast asleep and snoring her head off.

Taking up our position quietly, so as not to wake her, an ear each up against the rough wood, we discovered that she'd been telling the truth. We might have been in the room with the two women, so clear were their voices.

Mrs Macauley was laughing. 'And I should trust you?'

'It's been well over a decade, Lucille. Still, you won't forgive me?'

'You tried to ruin me, Gizzy. And let's not talk about poor Eve, may her soul rest.'

I stifled a gasp. Eve had been my mother's name. She and Mrs Macauley had apparently been great friends, just as Emmy and I were. That was why Mrs Macauley had taken responsibility for me all those years ago. She never broke a promise, she'd told me, though she'd looked as though she was tempted to on my account.

'What's changed?' Mrs Macauley sounded suspicious. 'You

fled this city in fear of your life and now you're walking around dressed like a member of the quality, like you're better than the rest of us. Look at you! Real jewels hanging from your ears and everything. How on earth did you manage this, Gizz?'

Even the woman's laugh sounded rich. 'Darling, Lucy. Did you really doubt that I'd land on my feet? Come on, now. You know I never give up until I get what I want. And what I want today is your Sukey. I know who she is. Her skin may be a little lighter but she's still the absolute spit of her mother.'

'Eve would have slit her daughter's throat rather than let you get your grubby hands on her, never mind the fancy gloves you've got on. I know what you're capable of, never forget that.'

I could feel the burn of Emmy's stare on my face, but I was just as confused as she was. The bed creaked and I put my finger to my lips as Hattie sat up, rubbing the sleep from her eyes, confused to see us lurking there.

'I can make you both rich,' Madame Vernier was saying beneath us. 'I've got the perfect gentleman for Sukey.'

'Who?' scoffed Mrs Macauley. 'I know all the gents around these parts. I don't need to pay you for introductions.'

'You don't know this gentleman, Lucy, trust me, and he most certainly does not know you. He's not even in London yet, though his ship should dock any day now. I'm talking about a man who is travelling from the Caribbean. Son of a sugar baron. Not yet married and looking to enjoy himself. Need I say more?'

'I'm quite content with my match for Sukey, thanks all the same. Sir Horace has made it clear that he's willing to stump up a goodly sum for her.'

I heard Emmy gasp, and Hattie laid a hand on my shoulder for comfort as she joined us on the floor. Of all the men I had hoped never to have to go near, it was the ancient, hairy old Member of Parliament. Titled but with barely a penny to the fancy name. Emmy and I would hand out drinks on busy nights in the parlour and he'd certainly made a grab for me before but was usually quite drunk and easily evaded. He stank of sour wine and his wig was greasy. I felt sick at the thought of him touching me.

'That old goat's still alive? No, Lucy, come along. You can't subject the poor girl to that.' Mark this moment, for this is when Gisele Vernier won me over. The moment when I first saw her as my protector. Anyone who could save me from Sir Horace deserved my trust.

'Can you honestly guarantee me that this young rake from the West Indies will pay me more than twenty guineas?'

'I can. In fact, I will make you a promise, Lucy. You can have some fun with Sir Horace if you like. Show her off but save her innocence for Mr Drake. If, when he arrives, something goes wrong, and he doesn't like the look of her after all, then I'll pay you twenty-five guineas myself. Do we have a deal?'

There was silence for a moment, then: 'He's wealthy this gent? And youthful? Because you should see my Emmy. She's well taught, well-educated and hasn't been broken in yet. Skin like alabaster and soft hands. Brought up in a church family so she has a heart of gold, but she knows what's expected of her.'

'I'm sure she's a delight but alabaster isn't what this gentleman values. Trust me, you offer him Sukey, or he'll go elsewhere. She isn't the only Negro in the capital capable of lying back and spreading her legs. In fact, there are several bordellos specialising in the exotic. I only come to you because his preference is for a clean girl, untouched. Listen to me, Lucy, and listen well: I will guarantee you fifty guineas for Sukey. For one bedding, though I'm almost willing to gamble on it becoming a longer standing arrangement. You're a bigger fool than I remember if you don't shake on that.'

'What are you getting out of it?' The suspicion was back.

'I want twenty per cent of anything he pays over the fifty guineas. That seems fair, don't you think? Since you were only expecting twenty to start with.'

It seemed very fair to Lucille Macauley and the deal was made. She kept several good bottles of French wine in her room, and they toasted to their good fortune with one of them, never giving a solitary thought to me or what I might have to say on the matter.

'It'll be all right, Su. Mama won't let anything bad happen to you,' Emmy told me, but it was easy for her to say that. She wasn't the one about to be sold off to the highest bidder. Her mother would never have even countenanced the idea of her beloved offspring being handed over to Sir Horace.

I got up silently and walked to the room next door to try on the gown that had looked so offensive on Camille. This was what I was good for. Cast-offs from those who thought themselves better than me. I'd always known it, but I had never thought it would lead me here. Being handed over to a man I didn't know so that he might – well, I didn't even know the extent of it. I saw what went on in the parlour each night, but once the girls vanished behind closed doors with their quarry, I could not begin to fathom what went on though I bore witness to the aftermath. I had seen bruises around Camille's throat, though she wore them with a strange pride that made Maria look askance. I had heard Hattie grumble about the weight of one of her more corpulent cullies, that she had struggled just to breathe underneath him, let alone anything else.

But I had no choice. If I wanted to keep the roof over my head, then I had to do as I was told. I had to put on this ugly gown with too many ruffles, made of a brown-red taffeta that reminded me of the blood that had put me in this awful position. I would do almost anything to avoid this fate. I knew that if I stayed, there was a price to pay. But what if I didn't?

What if I left?

4

'Wakey, wakey!'

I open my eyes to the sound of Maria's voice, teasing but warm. 'C'mon then, get yourself up before you catch your death.'

The door has been pulled back and Maria and Emmy are both staring down at me, Emmy's hands reaching to grab mine. I let her pull me to sitting, my body stiff from the cold and the cramped conditions of the Coffin. Maria throws a scratchy blanket over my shoulders and helps Emmy to hoist me out of the hole, the pair of them half-carrying me to the fire where they drop me on a stool.

'There we are, nice and warm. You'll be good as new in no time, trust me.' Maria bustles off and leaves me alone with Emmy.

I feel as though my body is not my own, disoriented, as if I have emerged not back into the world that I used to know, but into a new one where everything is different and uncertain. I have lost all sense of time, only the lit candles telling me that the long winter night is back upon us, though if it is late afternoon or midnight I have no way of guessing.

'You must think yourself so lucky,' Emmy tells me. 'Mama said that half a day in there would be good enough, it being your first time.'

Half a day. I try to feel grateful, as I feel is expected of me, but I cannot. I look at Emmy and she is as cheerful as ever. As if my ordeal has been nothing. I want to put her straight, to get angry about what has been done to me, but my feelings are as numb as my fingers.

'Where are the others?' I ask her.

'Camille and Hattie went down to the Strand, to visit the haberdashery,' she tells me. 'Maria you just saw, she's taken over your housework duties since you were otherwise occupied.' I feel as though I'm being scolded. 'Mama said she'll talk to you later, once you're in a suitable state. It's my duty to look after you for now.'

'She must be angry.' I am not looking forward to finally facing Mrs Macauley.

'She was but she was more worried for you.' Emmy strokes my hair back from my face. 'We all were. Anything might have happened to you out there. You know it's not safe, not with the Piper about.'

The water has been heating over the fire and Maria returns to the kitchen with the tin bathtub, hefting the cauldron off its hook and pouring the steaming contents into the container before adding cold water to moderate the temperature. As I soak, Emmy sits on a stool before the fire, toasting muffins, and passes me the first. We eat in silence: I am too afraid to ask what happened last night after my disappearance was noted; she is perhaps sensing that I'm not in the mood for idle chatter.

'Another girl went missing. From one of the coffee houses.' Emmy is the first to speak, eager to fill me in. 'Word is that the Piper took her. Unless she just ran away. Like you did.'

'I'm sorry,' I say quietly.

'It doesn't matter now.' Her eyes shine with excitement, confusing me. 'Mama says that I can attend her soirée tonight. To be shown off, like you. It can't be too long now until my own courses come after all. She has high hopes for me, she said. For both of us.' She adds this last phrase quickly and I know that Mrs Macauley's lips have never mentioned me in such warm regards.

I don't know if she really is so eager to join her mother's profession or if it is just her love that she seeks. Perhaps it is as simple as the sight of Camille's finery, her jewellery, paraded in front of us daily. Emmy has always been a magpie. So bitter, my thoughts now, but I cannot stop them from flooding my mind, even though I swear I love her more than anyone else alive.

'What happened then, after I'd gone?' I stifle a yawn and wonder how I am going to stay awake into the evening. My body feels stiff and battered, and although Jakes did not mark my face, there are his prints on my arms, a blotch beginning to bloom on my bare stomach that shows his brutality.

Emmy speaks with her mouth full. 'Oh, it was madness! Camille would have been in the Coffin for letting you out of her sight.' I remember that I had been helping her to dress upstairs. It was on our way down, Camille ordering me to count to one hundred before following her into the parlour, allowing her the maximum attention, that I spotted my opportunity. 'It was lucky for her that Mr Percival turned up wanting to pay well for her company.'

Percival was Camille's latest target, a relatively humble Justice of the Peace who had somehow managed to inherit a nice amount of money from an uncle overseas. Mrs Macauley always put her income first. 'What about Jakes?'

'He was with Mama at the time so she could hardly put the blame on him.' Emmy kicks the side of the bathtub lightly with her stockinged foot. 'You know, you ought not to have left. Why did you? Mama promised me she'll look after you.'

Emmy's innocence is a thing of wonder. How can she look upon my bruised body, see me dragged out of the ground like an animal, and think that I am the one who has done wrong? 'But she won't be there. After we're chosen. We're supposed to take the gentleman upstairs once he agrees the price, but then what? Do you know? Has she told you?'

'Not in so many words.' Her cheeks flush. 'But it is a natural thing, Mama says. It is common behaviour between men and women, and it will become obvious once the situation arises. Goodness, Sukey, even Aunt Betsy and Uncle Edmund do it.'

I suppose that is true, though I cannot imagine that whatever it is that they do bears any resemblance to the goings-on at Little Wild Street. Besides, what little I do know includes the knowledge that children can be a result of such activity. The girls here take precautions to avoid any inconvenient situation and the Ashleys have no children of their own, so maybe they don't engage in those sorts of activities after all.

'What if one of us were to end up with a baby?' I ask Emmy.

'Mama knows how to avoid it. She'll show us.'

I'm sure that Mrs Macauley has her tricks, but they are clearly not foolproof. Emmy's very existence suggests so. And am I not also the fatherless child of a harlot? The tricks will have to suffice, I realise. For I cannot run away again. I rolled the dice, and they did not land in my favour. Perhaps Emmy is right. Convince yourself that this is a good thing, something that you want to happen, and it feels so much easier.

'Mama says that we do a great service for our gents,' Emmy tells me proudly, and I can hear her mother speaking.

'Do you not . . . do you not think that it is a sin?' I can see the doubt in her eyes as she thinks on what I have said. 'Listening to your uncle, in church every week. Emmy, can you honestly say that you don't think that all of this, what your mama does, what Maria and Hattie and Camille do – is a sin? Some, perhaps most, of these gentlemen are married. You hear them in the parlour talking about their wives even as one of your mother's girls sits in their lap. Are you going to be able to do that yourself so easily? Disregard everything that we have been taught?'

She does think carefully before answering. 'I don't know, Sukey. I really won't until I have the opportunity to do it.' She smiles at me, and I see that there is little saving her. She is a steadfast convert. 'At least here we can earn our own money. Be in charge of our own destinies. In Dorking, my only future lay in marriage, and isn't that just another form of what Mama does? Lying in bed with a man for the safety and security of his house, his money, having to provide him with children and acting as his servant?'

'So we renounce love and tradition and follow your mama into Satan's clutches?' I try my best to frighten her, to get her to think about what it is that we – that I – am being made to do.

Now she laughs. 'Don't be so silly, Sukey. You've never been one to quote scripture and it doesn't suit you now to pretend that it is the Bible or God who inspired you to flee.' She takes my hand in hers. 'I know that you're scared. I am too. But this fear, it will be fleeting. And as long as we're together still, does it really matter about those men or my mother?'

'I suppose not.' I manage to smile as she bends forward and

kisses my forehead. I realise that she has not needed to forgive me because she never believed that I would succeed. She knew better than I, that such an action was useless.

'Now tell me where you went. I want to know.'

So I tell her how scared I was; how I found Jonathan and then Dr Sharp; I show her the mark where Jakes kicked me, and revel in her shock and awe.

'You feeling better, Sukey?' Cook returns, her ancient slippers slapping against the stone floor, my usual day dress over her arm. She looks as tired as I feel. 'She wants to see you.'

Emmy squeezes my hand. 'Don't fret. It'll be all right.'

I nod but I am not so sure.

Mrs Macauley's room overlooks the street and has one of the few windows in the house that hasn't been bricked up to avoid the tax. Hand-painted bluebirds traverse her four walls, trapped in never-ending flight, and the fire roars. The room isn't big, but she has a separate bedchamber through a door behind her large mahogany desk. She sits behind that desk now, as she often does at this time of day, conducting her financial business.

I have heard many a male visitor, those guests who have patronised this establishment for years, speak longingly of her beauty. I see the truth in it, but to me her beauty is that of a January morning, her eyes the cold light blue of clear winter skies, her skin as pale as the watered-down milk that Cook serves us. That gaze of hers can freeze me to the spot. Besides, for all that these men might covet her, she rarely indulges their desires. I have been told that she has done on occasion, but in my short time in Covent Garden, I have never seen her take a customer herself. She doesn't need to. Her reputation is based on providing the best girls in Covent Garden. The cleanest and some of the youngest, for even Maria and Hattie, old hands in this profession, are not even twenty years of age.

She looks up and blesses me with that glacial gaze. 'Sukey.'

'Ma'am.' I bob a curtsey.

She puts aside the ledger in front of her. 'You should be grateful that Jakes found you before something awful befell you. Silly girl. What were you thinking?'

I shake my head and mumble an inadequate reply.

Her tone grows more brittle. 'Did you really mean to leave me? After all that I have done for you? Paying for your idyllic childhood in the home of none other than my own sister when I could have handed you over to the Foundling Hospital or worse. Is it not my hard-earned money that has kept a roof over your head, clothes on your back? And the fine gown that I gave you and that is now in rags.' She presses her lips together so tightly that they disappear. 'You arrived back here this morning looking exactly the savage that everyone else thought you to be.'

I feel hot tears sting my eyes and bite the inside of my cheek, praying for them not to fall.

'Nothing to say for yourself?' She waits but I know there is nothing I can say to defend my actions, at least nothing that would meet her satisfaction. 'I suppose I should be grateful that you do not waste my time with lies and excuses.' She takes her ledger back up and opens it. 'Let me speak plainly, Sukey. You are now a woman. Your own body has determined it so, and any woman under my roof must earn her keep. Your care with my sister was not given for free. I paid her expenses on your behalf but now your bill is due. You do understand me?'

'Yes, ma'am.' I understand very well. For all her words of

benevolence, this woman has never given me anything, simply invested her money in me, hoping to recoup her losses later on. She will sell me to the highest bidder, and I will be grateful to not end up in a debtors' gaol. I blink, my eyes still adjusting to the light outside of the Coffin. Is this what a man feels like as he waits to be walked to the gallows? Trying not to think about what is to come but knowing that it is inevitable.

She sighs as she picks up her pen, dipping the quill into her inkpot. 'That gown is ruined, and I must find you a replacement for this evening.' She inscribes a figure on the page. I wonder how many pages in that ledger belong to me. Over a decade's worth of entries and nothing paid back.

'And an additional ten guineas.' She looks up at me as she writes. 'For that was what was offered for you, Sukey. Not a bad sum at all, all things considered, and I may have been able to bargain for more had you not taken it upon yourself to run away. How do you think I explained away your sudden absence to the gentleman?'

'I'm sorry, ma'am,' I say, trying not to let anger seep into my voice. An outright lie! But she doesn't know that Emmy and I eavesdropped on her conversation with Madame Vernier. She doesn't know that I am fully aware that the gentleman I am to be sold to isn't even in the country yet, and that more than twice ten guineas has been promised.

She sits back in her chair and assesses me, unfavourably. 'You are not like your mother. She had nerves as strong as the oak they build ships out of. Can you at least try to follow in her footsteps? Do you not wish to make her proud, wherever she may be?'

I hope that she is in Heaven, but after years of the Reverend Ashley's sermons I know that to be unlikely.

'Now, you may think me harsh,' Mrs Macauley continues, 'but I counter that I am at least fair. This last ten guineas shall only stand if there is a repeat of your imbecilic behaviour. If you do as you are told, then I shall strike out this figure. In addition, you will also have your share of the payment made for you. An excellent deal under the circumstances, no?'

'Yes, ma'am. Thank you, ma'am.'

'One piece of luck is that news of your escape and subsequent return has spread beyond these walls. Your . . . concerns, shall we say, have convinced any doubters of your legitimate status as a maid and accordingly we have received several enquiries today as to your availability.'

I feel sick and forget myself. 'But am I not to wait for Mr Drake?'

'Mr . . . ' Her eyes narrow. 'Where did you hear that name?'

I think quickly. 'The French woman. Before she spoke to you. She patted me on the head and told me that Mr Drake would be very happy with me once he arrived. I don't know who he is, but she made him sound very important.'

Her smile was carved from ice. 'I'm sure she did. Well, yes, we shall expect Mr Drake in a few days' time. However, to celebrate his arrival I thought an auction might be fun. We haven't had once since Camille. You shall appear in the parlour each evening in order to charm and attract the attention of potential bidders. The sale itself shall wait for Mr Drake but I'm not willing to simply trust that he lives up to the promise of Gisele Vernier.' She closes the ledger and stands. 'Now come, I want to offer you some inspiration. The sooner you realise how lucky you are, Sukey, the better.'

I am made to take off my dress, replacing it with one made

of sack cloth, barely more decent than a shift. My woollen cape shields my indignity, and I am given thin slippers for my feet. Mrs Macauley calls for Jakes to come and bring a lantern as she bids me to follow her outside onto the street. We go at a brisk pace, Jakes barely an inch behind me so that I can hear his breath, heavy with effort. The sun is almost set, and the street sellers are packing up and heading for home. The crowd seems perfect for slipping away, but that would be a foolish thing to do. I am shivering terribly already on a day that is even colder than the one before.

We walk along Drury Lane and, as we pass a shop, I stumble, thinking that I see Jonathan. But of course, it is not him. Jonathan is in the hospital, at death's door, and this man is tall. Strong and solid but with skin as dark as Jonathan's. He gives me a curious look as he tips his hat in Mrs Macauley's direction and passes on by. She sees me watching him and grabs my arm, dragging me along faster.

We turn left and head into St Giles, Jakes taking the lead as he lifts his lantern aloft, cutting through the darkness. He stops outside a house that has seen better days. Barely a house, in fact, for it looks as though it is ready to collapse, slumped over in despair.

'You won't remember this place.' Mrs Macauley looks down at me, not unkindly.

I stare at the soot-covered brick. 'Was this where I lived before? With my mother?'

'I came here when your mother was on her deathbed. She used her last penny to send a lad over to Little Wild Street to fetch me. And you know what she said to me when I arrived?'

I say nothing, though she has told me this before.

'She begged me to look after you. To treat you like my own daughter.'

I have no memories, for I was barely big enough to walk when my mother died. And this is where it happened. I feel the tears as they spring up, but I blink them away. She would not want me to pity her for where she ended up. I know this because I would not, and we must be the same. I cling to that, I always have, the idea that if she had lived that we would have been close. That we would have loved one another fiercely and that she would have done anything for me.

'I made your mother a promise, and I kept it, though everyone said I was mad. Do you know how hard it was to convince my sister to take you, a mulatto child who would hardly pass unnoticed in a country town? I had to beg her husband, that damned man of God, and remind him of his Christian duty.' She grips my jaw in her hand. 'Your mother was a whore, and you are to be a whore just like her. There's no shame in that and you do a disservice to her memory by thinking that there is. Besides,' she says, releasing me and turning me to face the opposite gutter where a body lies, a man or woman, unconscious or dead, 'do you want that? Or will you let a nice young gent pay handsomely for a few hours of your time?'

When she puts it like that, there is no choice at all. It is time for me to embrace my fate.

5

Mrs Macauley lets me sleep for an hour or two before it is time to prepare. I am sleepy and resigned when she comes up to our tiny room and rouses me. Emmy is by her side, bubbling over with excitement.

'You must thank Camille for her generosity. She has been kind enough to donate another two of her old gowns for the pair of you to wear this evening. I needn't remind you, Sukey, that this is the last I shall give you until you start earning your keep. I do trust you are committed to remaining a part of this household.'

I see the concern on Emmy's face and nod. I'm not a fool. I tried to find a way out of this predicament and there isn't one. My only consolation is that perhaps my failed escape saved a boy's life, but it did not help my own cause. Better to embrace my fate with dignity, I decide. I look at Emmy, at her face aglow now that she knows that I won't leave her. I might have no living family, to my knowledge, but I have her. That has to matter, and I cannot disappoint her again.

'Emily, do you think it possible for you to do something with the hair of this heathen?' Mrs Macauley shoots me one last baleful glance before leaving us.

One of the gowns is a rich ruby silk, the other an emerald that I know will suit Emmy's complexion. I see her look at it, her fingers trembling slightly as she reaches out to touch. She looks at me. 'Which do you prefer, Sukey?'

'You choose.' It amazes me that after all I've done, she still thinks of me first. If I took the green gown, I know she would put on the red without a single word. I don't deserve her high regard.

'They're so beautiful.' She picks up her choice and holds it against her body. 'We shall look like princesses going to a grand ball.'

'Then it's a shame that the only place we are going to is the parlour downstairs,' I remind her. 'Just smelly old Sir Horace and a host of gents in their cups.'

'Don't be like that.' She looks annoyed at me for the first time since my return. 'Think what might have happened if Jakes hadn't found you. How were you going to survive, Sukey? What if the Piper had taken you?'

'The Piper isn't real,' I tell her. I refuse to believe in him now, for surely if he existed, he would have taken me as I ran away. Perhaps I would have deserved it.

'Then what happened to those girls?' she demands.

'They weren't spirited away like in a fairy tale. They probably ran away.'

'Like you did.' She puts down the dress carefully before dropping heavily on to the sagging mattress beside us. 'You left me.'

'I'm so sorry, love, I didn't think you would want to come.' I hate myself for not trusting her, but the truth, that I would never tell her, is that I hadn't been sure that she wouldn't run straight to her mother. 'I didn't have time to find you. There was an opportunity to leave, and I took it.'

'Would you have missed me at least?'

I laugh and bend down to stroke her hair back from her face. 'Of course. I love you, you daft girl. We are sisters, are we not?'

'I suppose.' Her smile is back, bright as ever. 'Come, let me arrange your hair before Mama comes back and shouts.'

She starts to plait my hair, the best method for taming its wildness in a manner acceptable to Mrs Macauley. 'Don't you miss home?' I ask her.

'We are home,' she says. 'You must stop thinking otherwise. Dorking is in our past.' She pulls my hair tight and pins it while I try not to wince. 'Besides, you didn't even like it there. You hated Aunt Betsy, and she hated you. Would you have been satisfied in being their maid for your whole life?'

'I might have been a maid elsewhere,' I mutter, though I had never wanted to be a maid. It was purely a better alternative to becoming a harlot. I alter the direction of the conversation. 'You said another girl went missing. Who?'

'I didn't hear a name, just that she worked at a coffee house a few minutes' walk from here. Maria knows her. Everyone's been talking about it apparently. She didn't turn up for work and no one's seen her since. And so soon after Daisy.' I can hear the excitement on her breath. 'Speaking of Daisy, Dotty Gardner's been worse than usual. They say she's gone mad trying to find her daughter.'

The first girl disappeared the week we arrived in London, when we were barely even familiar with the other girls in the house. A month or so later, it was a woman who worked in one of the taverns on the piazza, a flower girl a few weeks later and then a gap of at least six weeks until Daisy Gardner, the only girl I knew by sight. The Gardner women lived just around the corner on Drury Lane. Daisy, her older sister Rose and their mother Dotty. Daisy was still fresh of face but the other two were far from it, and their accommodation lacked the ambience and mock finery of the Macauley house. They do know how to strike a bargain though and they don't lack for persistence. More than once, I've heard the commotion of Jakes shooing, for want of a better description, Rose or Dotty away from our front door as they try to convince Mrs Macauley's customers that there is a better deal to be had around the corner. Daisy has always been less brazen, or should that be less shameless, than the other two.

'I hope Daisy found a wealthy beau to take her away,' I say. 'You know how Dotty is, always in her cups.' The old harlot is pox ridden, so they say, and Rose's last entry in Harris's List was less than complimentary: *A hussy already diminished in looks at such a young age, she is nevertheless open to varied requests for an incredibly cheap sum. Very agreeable when a pint of gin or more has been taken, which is most days.*

'Let's hope that she found someone to keep her safe,' Emmy agrees. 'Better that than the Piper.'

The parlour is the most important room in the house. Firstly, it has the width of two houses, this house having been at one time two, re-made with some creative building by a previous occupant. Every evening the fire is lit along with a glut of candles, the chief expense of the business. Cheap port is made ready in decanters alongside a tray of crystal glasses, donated to the brothel by Sir Horace, as he reminds us endlessly.

Mrs Macauley draws me and Emmy to one side as Hattie

carries the punch bowl in from the kitchen and Maria settles herself at the harpsichord, ready to fill the room with music in lieu of the talk and laughter that will hopefully arrive later on.

'Tonight, you are to be looked at. Nothing more,' she tells us. 'You may smile, and you may speak when spoken to but only use the words that are necessary. There will be a time for charm and flirtation, but I will tell you when that is. Understand?'

Excitement radiates from Emmy as she nods, her grin wide. I can only hope that she will not be disappointed too soon.

I am not sure what I expected this evening, but unrelenting boredom was not it. My previous times in the parlour, I was busy serving drinks, tidying away empty glasses and generally being as invisible as possible. Mrs Macauley had always wanted us to be in and out as quickly as possible, and back into the kitchen. I had always sensed a lively ambience. Now, Emmy and I stand in a corner of the room as instructed, observing events around us. Maria only has three tunes to her repertoire, pressing the notes out heavily, her eyes glazing over as she plays on to her unappreciative audience. Camille and Hattie do needlework on the sofa.

Emmy is stifling yet another yawn when the first of our clientele arrives. We hear the knock at the door and the embroidery disappears. Maria segues into one of her jauntier tunes and Mrs Macauley sweeps around the room making sure that the punch is well stirred, the fire stoked and her girls presentable. 'Sing, Sukey,' she barks at me as she pulls me by the arm to stand beside Maria.

I know the words to the song, but my throat is dry as bark. By the time the parlour door bursts open, our peace broken by four rowdy gentlemen who appear to have travelled to us via several taverns, my boredom has been entirely replaced by a sheer, burning terror. It is real, then. Now I am about to find out what actually happens in here most nights. What I will soon be expected to partake in fully.

'Gentlemen, welcome.' Mrs Macauley greets them with a wide smile. 'So lovely to see you all again.'

The men move into the room as though they belong there, the parlour shrinking in size as they take up space, breathing in all the air so that I struggle to fill my own lungs. I glance up and see that at least two of them have spotted me and Emmy. Camille has also noticed this and is glaring in my direction. She does not appreciate it when she does not draw all the attention.

'Good sirs, do you have any requests for a song?' Maria's voice is a soothing charm that breaks the tension.

'My only request is that I might take a step closer and inspect this new merchandise,' says the first gentleman, his gaze firmly fixed on me, the others distracted now that Hattie has begun to pour the drinks and shepherd them towards the gaming table on the other side of the room. 'Did you lay these two on especially for us, Mrs M?'

'Apologies, Mr Ford.' Mrs Macauley's laugh is a tinkle. 'These two maidens are not on offer to anyone this evening for they are a tad too young. This is simply a viewing in anticipation of exciting prospects ahead for this establishment.'

'Do you jest, Mrs Macauley?' Ford raises an eyebrow. 'You bring out two fine young – and exotic – fillies, only to tell me that I shall have to make do with the old mares instead?'

He waves his arm in the direction of Camille as he utters this devastating verdict on the three older girls. Maria stifles a snort of laughter, but I see Camille's jaw clench and she gives me a look of such incendiary hatred that I'm surprised not to burst into flames.

Mrs Macauley steers Mr Ford away and whatever she whispers in his ear seems to placate him. Camille forgives his insult and is quick to him with a cup of punch and a smile and he follows her like a puppy dog to the table where his friends are already laying out the cards.

Maria begins to play something new at last. A song that I have heard Cook sing often as she bakes. A folk song, she said, when I asked her on first hearing it. Cook has a rough voice, but she can hold a tune, and over the weeks I must have memorised the words for they come easily to my lips. I sing the first verse before the next knock on the door comes.

'Sir Horace, how wonderful to see you.' Mrs Macauley greets the newcomer warmly.

I hardly dare look at him, this man who I am so desperate to avoid. He walks in on bowlegs, well dressed but old enough to be my grandfather with almost as much white hair growing from his nose and ears as is sewn into his periwig. His heavy cloak, carrying with it an air of frost and ice wind from outside, is whisked away by Hattie before it can lower the temperature of the room. In mere moments he is seated with a full glass of punch, and I turn my back slightly as he leans awkwardly, trying to catch my eye.

As he gets bored and lets Hattie distract him, Maria segues into a song that I do not know but no one notices that the singing has stopped and so I can stand with Emmy and watch the tableau before us. Those at the card table are caught up in their game and I can see that Mrs Macauley is looking annoyed. Not a single coin has crossed her palm so far. An unsuccessful night so far with one bowl of punch already consumed. Camille, defeated by the cards, flounces over to join us in our little corner.

'Perhaps I should leave. I doubt any of these so-called gentlemen would notice. They would rather drink here for free apparently.' She has drunk at least two cups of punch herself.

'Hush your mouth,' Maria hisses, having stopped playing; not a soul was paying the music any attention either. 'If Mrs M hears you, you'll be for it. We're all supposed to be on best behaviour at the moment.'

'You can play the good girls over here,' Camille sneers. 'If I'm not going to earn anything this evening then I'm going to at least enjoy myself.' She heads to refill her cup.

'Ignore Camille,' Maria says to me and Emmy. 'She just isn't used to men who don't fawn over her and promise to buy her jewels, though not many of them actually honour those promises. This is a normal evening here, believe it or not. The hardest part of this job is looking as though you're pleased to be here. The gents don't like it when you look miserable. They want you to smile and say nice things to make them feel good. There are two things that make a successful whore when she's starting out: enthusiasm and a pleasing disposition. Camille relies on her looks, but they won't last. And if you can't look eager when you're in the parlour just conversing with a cull, you'll have no chance when he's taken you upstairs and shoved his pole in your mouth.'

Emmy's jaw drops and Maria pours us both a glass of ratafia from the bottle sitting on a side table. 'This will help but don't drink too much. You just want enough to make the jollity feel real. Get too much of a taste for it and you'll end up like Dotty Gardner.'

I want to ask her about the pole but there's another knock at the door and Maria disappears to prepare more punch.

'Ah, Tobias Kellett, is that you?' Sir Horace looks up at the new guest. I cannot tell if he is pleased or unhappy to see this man, so close is his smile to a grimace.

Mr Kellett is not alone. To my surprise, Madame Vernier is accompanying him, the Frenchwoman who came to the house only two days previously. She sees me and smiles, giving a nod in greeting which I return. Her companion, Kellett, is a little older than her though a good ten years younger than Sir Horace. His face is dominated by thick dark eyebrows, a deep frown between them bisecting his forehead. His nose is too small for his face, and he has no lips to speak of. Not handsome in the slightest, still he stands in the centre of the room as though he owns it. Madame Vernier's presence softens him a little. Again, she is dressed like a lady, in dark-green silk with gold stitching that looks very expensive. The bodice is dangerously low cut, with no handkerchief to maintain modesty, and more than one of the men present has his eyes fixed to her chest.

'Mr Kellett, come and sit by the fire? A drink?' Mrs Macauley clicks her fingers in Maria's direction. Under her breath she tells Emmy to move to the other side of the room, to keep watch over Mr Ford and his friends. Perhaps she thinks that Ford may be a good prospect after all.

'I would love a glass of champagne if you have any, Lucy,' Madame Vernier drawls.

'Of course. Maria will fetch it for you.' Mrs Macauley speaks through gritted teeth as Maria disappears in the direction of the kitchen. 'It's such a pleasant surprise, but what brings you both here this evening?'

'This is her?' Kellett points at me and my breath stops. This cannot be the man from the Caribbean. Please, no.

'Ah, you have heard of my Sukey?' Mrs Macauley's grip on my wrist is tight as she drags me before him. 'Untouched, unsullied. For now.'

His eyes begin at my feet, slowly taking in each detail of my new dress, my gloved hands, my powder-dusted visage thanks to Emmy who had told me that a paler complexion was fashionable, even on blacks, according to her mother. Kellett's gaze stops below the neckline of my dress, and I fight the urge to take a step back. I have been so fearful of ending up with Sir Horace that I never thought about the alternatives. At least the old man is harmless, not cruel. This man, Tobias Kellett, freezes me to the spot with one look. There is something terribly wrong about him, though I cannot say what exactly.

'You have proof that she is a virgin?' he asks. He removes his gloves to reveal soft, well-manicured hands. I try to shrink away, fearing his touch, but Mrs Macauley rests a heavy hand on my shoulder while moving forward to place herself between me and him. He does not look happy. 'I would prefer a physical examination if I were to put up the sort of money you talk of, Mrs Macauley. And t'would be better for you, as if I were to pay what you ask and then discover that this is no maid after all, I would be most unhappy. And my unhappiness is a malaise that tends to be contagious, especially for those who have caused me to feel so aggrieved in the first place.'

'Tobias, please.' His French companion scolds him as she takes her glass of cheap champagne from Maria. 'I assure you, Lucy, that I have vouched for your honesty with the esteemed acquaintance I mentioned to you. He will not require any such examinations. In fact, Mr Drake's ship docked just today.'

Mrs Macauley clears her throat. 'Mr Kellett, I would stake my reputation on the purity of this girl. She was brought up in a religious household, alongside my daughter, and only recently arrived in London. Besides,' she laughs, 'how many young Negress harlots are there in Covent Garden at this present time that you suppose I could sell her purity twice over without the great Tobias Kellett hearing of it?'

I see Madame Vernier watching me, her face unreadable. What is her place here? Is Kellett her keeper? I've been told that it's the holy grail for a harlot, to find one gentleman with the funds to keep a courtesan in the finest clothing, the nicest lodgings, so that she need no longer take the money of whoever is willing on a given evening. Madame Vernier's clothes are fine indeed but whoever her husband was before he died, she cannot be a real lady. Not when she looks so comfortable in a house such as this.

'Sukey's auction is to take place tomorrow evening,' Mrs Macauley informs the room. 'All interested parties to arrive by eight o'clock with the funds on their person. Bids will begin at no less than the fifty guineas that Mr Drake has already offered, and the highest bidder will win my Sukey.'

It is as though I am standing on a precipice, waiting to be pushed off into the abyss. Mr Drake is just the beginning of things. After that I will be passed around like a toy, to be played with until I am worn out or poxed like Dotty Gardner.

'Child, don't fret!' Madame Vernier walks towards me, though she is looking at Mrs Macauley as she does so. 'Why that face of yours has almost lost its colour entirely and that won't do.'

'She is going into the wrong profession to be so precious,' Sir Horace mutters, but Camille takes her turn to distract him, clearly grown tired of being at the centre of no one's attention.

Madame Vernier lowers her voice to talk to her old friend. 'Lucy, make sure the girl's face is not powdered tomorrow. Mr Drake wants her because of her complexion, not in spite of. And make her look her age.'

'I know what I'm about, Gizz.'

'But I know Drake. Just some friendly advice, that's all.'

It is almost unbearable to stand so close to the pair of them, the strain of their polite yet barbed words infecting the air around them. Maria, in her wisdom, starts up a rowdy ditty that the other two girls are also familiar with, lightening the mood considerably. Kellett sweeps Camille away from Sir Horace, striking a quick deal before they disappear upstairs, Hattie helping to soothe the outrage of the disappointed Member of Parliament. Eventually, even Hattie realises that the old man is not going to be forthcoming with his salary and goes with Maria to whisk away the almost forgotten about Mr Ford and one of his friends.

Emmy and I are kept separate for the rest of the evening but, where I am restless, wishing I was anywhere else at all, Emmy is acquitting herself well with the young men. They laugh and joke with her but appear to be respectful that she is not there for any other reason than that. She looks as though she was born to this life. Of course, she was. As was I.

6

The next day, I feel ill, dread festering deep in my stomach. I vomit twice in the afternoon and Emmy looks worried, but I know that she thinks me melodramatic. Her mother says as much as I rinse out my mouth and take a spoonful of honey from Cook to soothe the sting in my throat. Each time I pass the front door I reconsider my choice to stay, but it is pointless now. The door is locked and bolted; the keys hang around Mrs Macauley's wrist like a bracelet. She will pass them to Jakes once he arrives.

'You must rest,' Emmy tells me as I sweep the parlour floor, for everything must be spick-and-span for our esteemed guests. 'This is the beginning of everything, Sukey.' She lowers her voice. 'Camille is green with envy.'

Indeed, if there is one tiny grain of solace to be had, it is that Camille is furious over the whole business. Mr Drake, young and wealthy, is just the sort of gentleman she would expect to be hers. To add insult to Camille's injury, she has already been ordered to give up her bedchamber for the night. Hers is the largest and most luxurious of all the rooms, Mrs Macauley's aside, and our prestigious new customer is to have the best.

'I won't do too much with your hair,' Mrs Macauley tells

me that evening, pinning my curls by candlelight in her office. 'And no rouge. They're coming to see a girl, not a woman. They expect to have the honour of effecting that transition. This is why you're worth anything at all, Sukey. Remember that if you want to make life easy for yourself.'

My palms are damp as we gather in the parlour, and I feel light-headed from barely eating a scrap of food all day. Camille is glowering at me. It doesn't help that Maria and Hattie joined together in teasing her all afternoon, guessing at how handsome Mr Drake might be, and pretending to be envious that I would have him all to myself.

'Don't she look a picture, our Sukey?' Hattie winks at her partner in merriment. 'This young gentleman'll be over the moon when he sets eyes on her.'

'They say that in the West Indies the whores are all poxed and the men survive by drowning their sorrows each night in barrels full of rum.' Camille throws herself down on the chaise longue closest to the fire and clicks her fingers in Hattie's direction, demanding a drink. 'I'll pray for you, Sukey, for he'll likely give you the clap along with those fifty guineas.'

Hattie pours wine into a glass but instead of passing it to Camille, she gives it to me. 'Have a drink, Sukey, and pay her no mind. I'm sure he'll be a lovely young man. And Mrs M keeps a clean house. Don't be afraid to give a shout out if he don't look right down there.'

I know she means well but her words do the very opposite of soothing me. The thought of a naked male body, shucked of its finery, makes my stomach fold in on itself and my lungs constrict. I begin to see spots before my eyes, and it is lucky that Maria is there to hold my hand and shake me out of my terror.

'You ain't the first to feel this way,' she tells me quietly. 'My first cull, why I thought I was going to die on the spot from fright! He was so drunk he could barely unbutton his breeches. Won big at a card game and decided to waste his winnings on my maidenhead. The more eager they are, the better it is, love, for they cannot contain themselves for long, or else they cannot engage in the first place. Either way, there is little work for you to do.'

Camille sniffs, listening in. 'Honestly, I don't know why you look so terrified. Our job is the easiest there is.' I look at her and for once, her face softens. 'Truly, by tomorrow morning you will wonder why you ever felt this way. Men are simple beings. It takes very little to satisfy them. Even Hattie makes more money here than she would working in the market with her mother, and she has a visage that could only generously be described as plain.' She laughs and her old, spiteful expression returns. 'It's why she so often has to offer up her arse to them. So they don't have to look upon her face.'

'Oh, you're only jealous.' Hattie is totally unbothered by this attack on her looks. 'Gents want to look at a pretty girl for hours on end before they get down to business. How tiresome for you. For me, I prefer to be tupped from behind. I don't have to suffer their bad breath, and they get it over with nice and quick.'

The three of them burst into laughter while Emmy looks confused. 'But how are we to know what to do?' Emmy asks.

'Trust me, love,' Maria tells her, giving my knee a squeeze, 'he'll be more than happy to show you – or tell you – what he wants you to do. Think of it as learning to ride a horse. Just take a deep breath, climb on, and you can pick up the rest as you go along.'

I don't know how to ride a horse either, but I cling to those words as I sip my wine, letting the alcohol smooth away the tremors. I think of Mrs Macauley's ledger, of the figures beginning to decrease at last, rather than constantly growing larger. I think about undressing in front of a stranger, a man. But don't I do the same in front of Emmy each night? And if he has rancid breath, can I not hold my breath for a minute or two, or however long it takes for it to be done? I think of St Giles and my mother, may her soul rest. In London, death never feels too far away. I remember Jonathan and hope that he is still alive. As soon as Mrs Macauley lets me out of her sight I will go and find out his fate, I vow, but unless I do as I am told, I have no future myself.

The first knock at the door shakes me out of this spiral of dark thoughts and Mrs Macauley shoos us all out to the kitchen apart from Maria. 'Not a peep. Wait here until I come for you, Sukey.'

On the kitchen table there is the usual punch bowl, ready to be carried out, but this evening there is also a silver salver piled up with pretty macarons, something fancy for a special occasion. Camille's eyes brighten and she reaches for one, hissing as Cook slaps her hand away. 'Not for you, miss. Mrs M's counted 'em and if there's one missing I'll not be taking the punishment for it.'

Hattie hovers in the doorway. 'Hush up. I can hear 'em talking. Sir Horace is there, definitely. I'd recognise that wheezy old voice anywhere.' She pauses and cocks her head, her brow furrowed as she concentrates. 'Kellett, I reckon, that funny cove who was here the other night. And someone new. Strange accent. English but with something mixed in.'

'The man from across the sea,' I say. 'From the West Indies.'

He really does exist then, and he's here. He's come for me, just like Madame Vernier promised.

'You may as well lie with some rum-soaked old sailor,' Camille says, her accent sliding from Calais to Cardiff. 'They got this idea down on the docks, you know, that if a man catches the pox all he has to do is lie with a virgin and he'll be cured.'

It is as well that I don't have time to fret further for Mrs Macauley returns; taking me by the wrist, her grip is an iron shackle as she leads me into the parlour, like a prize cow being brought in for auction. 'Gentlemen, may I present to you, Miss Sarah Maynard.' I feel her index finger poke my lower back so that I stand tall. 'Our darling Sukey is as good as a daughter to me so I won't be letting her go for a penny less than she's worth. Do bear that in mind as you make your bids.'

Hattie had been correct in her identification of the three men present. Sir Horace sits alone in the good armchair and the other two take the sofa. Tobias Kellett and the man who I presume must be Madame Vernier's young gentleman. I thank my stars for he is better than I'd dared to hope. Not Camille's pox-addled sailor at all. He looks kind, I think. If only he lives up to Madame Vernier's promise of bidding high and wins out.

Sir Horace chuckles as he accepts a glass of punch from Maria. 'My dear Sukey, you look petrified. Do we scare you so easily? You know me a little, do you not? And I certainly hope that we might be even better acquainted before the night is done.'

'You should not tease the girl, Sir Horace. In her position would you not suffer as she does?' The young stranger speaks up for me and I manage a grateful smile which he returns.

Lounging back amongst the cushions, he looks no older than five and twenty, his skin darkened by the sun and wrinkled around the eyes and mouth enough to indicate that this is a man who smiles and laughs often. He reminds me of the young men from home, rather than those I have met in London. Men who spend time outdoors, who do a hard day's work and don't just lounge about all day drinking and gambling. Unlike his two companions, he wears no wig. His blond curly hair is tied back from his face and his eyes are a striking shade of hazel. He looks like an adventurer or perhaps a soldier. Someone who knows the world outside of London and who has learned already not to take himself too seriously. Oh God, please let him pay for me.

'Sukey, this is Mr Jonas Drake.' Mrs Macauley introduces us. 'You met Mr Kellett last night and Sir Horace is . . . Sir Horace.'

Kellett draws on a pipe as he sits, legs crossed, his face impassive as if we are boring him immensely. He blows out a cloud of smoke and plucks at a loose thread on his cuff. He does not look at me at all. I don't know why he makes me feel so uneasy, but I do know that I don't want to find out.

'A pretty little thing.' Sir Horace is full of bluster. 'So like her mother in looks. I only hope she has inherited her mother's various talents to go along with that pretty visage. I was very sorry when Eve left us.'

He knew my mother? I open my mouth to speak but Mrs Macauley gives my arm a pinch, a warning to keep quiet and behave.

'We all miss her greatly, even after all these years,' she replies, moving the conversation briskly on. 'More drinks, gentlemen, while we conduct our business?'

Maria has the champagne chilled and ready. She doesn't look at me as she serves but she gives my hand a quick squeeze as she passes, behind Mrs Macauley's back.

'Going back to the mother,' Mr Kellett says, and I hear Mrs Macauley make a dark sound in the back of her throat, too quiet for the others to hear. 'I have a question. For if Sir Horace knew this maid's mother, how often was he in the habit of visiting with her. For if he was tupping the mutton on the regular, might he not possibly have fathered the lamb?'

I try not to gasp at the idea. I cannot accept that this man could be my father. Better to have none than to imagine this.

Sir Horace feels as strongly as I, for a different reason. 'How dare you, Mr Kellett? Are you insinuating that I might attempt to commit incest?' His indignation pushes his hefty frame to the edge of the sofa where he teeters, lacking the additional strength or commitment to stand and challenge his attacker physically.

'I do not insinuate that you do it knowingly, sir, only that people will talk. You know the rumour mill of Covent Garden will set its wheels turning before you would have a chance to even climb the staircase with the girl.' Kellett drains his glass and holds it out while Maria darts forward to fill it.

'You mean that you will make sure of it. Ha! And what of it. At my age why should I give a damn what the gossips say?' Sir Horace is red in the face, his left hand desperately searching his person for an item, eventually revealed to be his handkerchief. His forehead is damp with sweat, and powder from his wig is making a pretty paste as it forms into clumps on his wrinkled brow.

'Sir Horace.' Mrs Macauley makes her decision. 'While I can absolutely assure anybody who asks that you are not Sukey's father, for I know it to be a fact that Eve only came to your notice after giving birth to her daughter, I do think that Mr Kellett has a point. Perhaps you should withdraw from the contest and reduce the risk of malicious gossip.'

'But . . . '

'And so,' she carries on, turning away from him, 'I shall hear the bids of Mr Kellett and Mr Drake now. Mr Drake has already begun us at fifty guineas. Mr Kellett?'

'Eighty,' he declares, his glance at Drake triumphant.

It seems such an impossibly large amount of money that my hopes fade away. Certainly, I don't believe that Sir Horace would have bettered it, even if he had been left in the race.

'Ninety then,' Mr Drake says calmly, and I hear Maria gasp.

'One hundred.' Kellett is nonchalant.

'Mr Kellett, you and I do not know each other but my father has often spoken of you.' Drake is unruffled and I lift my head. Perhaps all is not lost. 'He tells me that you drive a hard bargain, that you do not like to throw good money away on causes that you don't think deserving. I tell you now that I am determined to win. I am new to these shores, and I want to make my mark in whatever way possible, even if it is by paying a ridiculous sum for this lovely girl. Let me make my final bid of one hundred and fifty guineas and let that be the end of it.'

I beg Mrs Macauley silently to accept this offer before Kellett says another word, but when I dare to glance towards her, she seems dumbstruck. A woman who has just struck gold when all she was looking for was silver.

She clears her throat. 'We have a deal, Mr Drake. But do you have such an amount of money about your person? I cannot just accept your word in this instance, no matter how excellent a recommendation you come with.'

Mr Drake smiles and moves his foot, revealing a small leather bag that has been sitting on the floor unnoticed. 'I have some in gold and the rest in bank notes. Having just arrived in the country, it was the only way to get my hands on such a sum at short notice. I trust that is acceptable?'

Sir Horace is muttering to himself, though I cannot tell if it is Drake or Kellett he is most annoyed by. Kellett himself seems to be a fair loser and does not say a word. In fact, he looks almost pleased to have been saved such a large sum of money.

'An exhilarating auction, Mrs Macauley,' Kellett drawls. 'Congratulations, Mr Drake.' He clicks his fingers in Maria's direction. 'Girl, my blood is up with all this excitement. I'll take two guineas' worth of whatever you're offering. In fact,' he says, spying Hattie who is peering around the corner, nosy as ever, 'let me double that for the pair.'

Just like that it is over. My fate sealed, for this night at least. Camille parades in from the kitchen to find that only Sir Horace is left to her. Mr Drake follows Mrs Macauley out to her office to finalise the deal and I feel my spirits lift, just the tiniest amount. There is no turning back now. Anyone can learn to ride a horse. Even me.

7

The parlour is empty, the girls having taken Sir Horace and Tobias Kellett upstairs. I sit on the sofa and wait, looking up as I hear footsteps approach. Emmy is here with a brimming cup of punch.

'Cook says you're to drink all this down.' She hands it to me. 'There'll be more sent up to the room.'

'I don't know what I'm supposed to do.' It comes out as a whimper that I don't recognise, my voice as adrift as the rest of me.

'It can't be that difficult.' Emmy tips the cup towards my mouth so that I have to drink or risk spilling the punch on my dress. 'Look, the girls do this night in, night out. Lovely as she is, Hattie's a dolt and Camille can't speak a word of French. She can't even read or write English, and no one's ever seemed to care. You're worth ten of each of them. If they can do it, so can you.'

'But I don't want to be like them.' I know it's useless. She doesn't understand.

'What choice do you have? Come on, Sukey, see sense. If it makes you feel better, just imagine that each kiss is worth a coin. A mark on Mama's ledger. Just smile and say pretty things and do what he asks.'

I hear the creak of the stairs and drain the cup, giving it back to Emmy as Mrs Macauley appears alone.

'Mr Drake has been shown to the room.' She presses her lips together and I'm surprised to see that she too is nervous. Emmy leaves the parlour as her mother comes to sit beside me, taking my hands in hers, squeezing them tight. 'Sukey, let me say this now to make it absolutely clear. You will make Mr Drake happy. You will do whatever it is that he pleases. He seems a gentle fellow. I don't expect him to request anything unreasonable. The first time is always a trial, but it will be over before you know it.' She releases my hands and cups my face instead. For a moment I can see something in her eyes, something that might be close to affection. 'I must say that I wish my first time had been with a man like Mr Drake. If you are wise, you'll please him for your own sake. So that he comes back for you.' Then she is all business. A list of instructions that I try to store away before she gets up and waits for me to follow her.

I know the way to Camille's bedchamber, of course, but I suspect that she wants to make sure I arrive safely. We pass the first landing where I hear laughter coming from Hattie's room. Upstairs I can hear Sir Horace complaining to Camille from Maria's room, probably still in a rage over Tobias Kellett's earlier words. The only silent room is the one containing Mr Drake, Emmy exiting it as we arrive.

'He's very polite,' she whispers to me as she passes.

Mrs Macauley knocks and, when he answers, she opens the door and pushes me through, closing it firmly behind me. I almost expect to hear a key turn in the lock, but that would hardly give the right impression.

I have been inside Camille's bedchamber a hundred times

or more. To clean, to light the fire when she has an important gent expected, to collect her gowns for laundering. For the first time I am to entertain a man myself. The fire is already roaring, the jug of punch that Emmy delivered sitting on the side table. She has poured a cup for Mr Drake, and he sits in the armchair in front of the fire, looking up at me expectantly. He has pulled off his boots and lined them up neatly by the hearth. He looks comfortable, entirely at odds with my own feelings, my insides churning, my top lip damp with sweat.

'You look terrified,' he says, laughing at first before realising that I genuinely am. 'Come, Sukey. Come and sit by me. We can talk for a while if you like. If that's easier? And fetch yourself a drink.'

I do as he says, trying not to spill punch onto the floor as my hands shake. I can feel Drake's eyes burning a hole between my shoulder blades and I take a big gulp of the overly sweet liquor before turning back towards him. There is no second chair and so I sit on the floor by his feet and wait for him to tell me what I am supposed to do.

'Does it make it easier if I tell you that I haven't done this before either?' he says. I look up at him, surprised. 'I mean, the act itself, yes, of course. But I have never been to a place like this.'

'Really, sir?' Things must be different in the West Indies. Certainly, there is no behemothic city like London from what I have heard.

'Please, don't call me sir,' he begs, smiling. He has a lovely smile, though one of his teeth is cracked.

'Mr Drake then?'

'I usually just go by Drake,' he says, 'though my family call me Jonas. Won't you do the same?'

'Jonas.' I repeat it though it feels odd on my lips. Are we to be friends then? I am confused.

'You know, you remind me of someone I used to know in Barbados. She and I were the best of friends.' He stares down into his cup, and I see that it is empty. I scramble to my feet.

'Did something happen to her?' I pour more punch for him before retaking my seat.

'She died. These things happen out there, you see.' His expression is suddenly morose.

'I am sorry,' I tell him sincerely. 'Perhaps one day we too might be friends.'

'I hope so.' He gives himself a shake and stands up. 'Here, take the chair. I should not forget my manners so easily. I can sit on the bed. Let us talk for a while and get to know one another. There are hours left before dawn and I'm in no hurry, are you?'

I am certainly in no hurry to find out what comes next, so I move to the armchair, pulling it around to face his perch on the bed. 'What would you like to talk about?'

He shrugs. 'Whatever you like. That girl who brought up the punch, you and she must be friends. What would you talk about with her?'

I think about Emmy. There is so much that we say to each other that this man would find trivial or silly, though in London I feel us growing apart. Our positions have not changed much – Emmy has always been the preferred one, the rightful blood relative while I am the cuckoo in the nest – but I had never felt before that we wanted such different things out of life.

'We talk about the future,' I tell him. 'What our lives might be. What is likely to happen and what we dream of.'

'The future? And what would you wish your future to be?'

I cannot tell him the truth and now I wish I had said something different.

'I always thought that I would live my life in service,' I tell him. 'As a maid of some description. The house I grew up in, they looked after me, educated me, and in exchange I would clean and sometimes cook when I grew older. It was training, I was told, for when it was time to leave. I thought that I would end up in a big house somewhere.' I hear my tone turn wistful, as if I have ever longed for such a life. 'But in the end, I came to London.'

'Then see how quickly fortunes can change, for here you are. And you will never have to be hidden away or invisible like those servants in those big houses.' He talks as though I am fortunate, that my position here is something that any young girl might dream of. Does he really think me lucky to be here?

So surprised am I by this idea that I am fortunate, that he sees me as something more than a maid, that I allow him to charm me. He does not have much work to do in this regard. Another cup of punch and I listen to him talk, telling me tales of his voyage over the sea, how he spent days with his head in a chamber pot before gaining his sea legs, how blue the skies were over the Atlantic compared to the grey and white of London. He has had adventures, and I am lost in them, so much so that I forget to be scared. Until he finishes a story and pauses, taking my hands and pulling me up as he stands.

'And now we know one another. A little, at least.' He takes my face between his palms, rougher than I would expect from a man of his means. 'But this is not the only reason we are here, is it?'

'No, sir. Jonas.' I correct myself hurriedly. My throat is dry when I try to swallow. 'Jonas, you know that you will have to instruct me. For I have truly never done anything like this before. I have never even been alone in a room with a man before.'

His face is gentle as he bends to kiss my lips, and I catch the cinnamon on his breath from the punch. 'My darling Sukey, it will be my honour to instruct you.'

He turns me around and begins with the buttons on the back of my gown. His next kisses land on the nape of my neck and make me shiver, despite the heat of the fire before me. He has done this before, this disrobing of a girl – a woman – for he makes just as light work of my stays. Sitting once more on the edge of the bed, he lifts my left leg, removing the shoe. He holds my frozen gaze as his fingers trail slowly up my calf, and it is only my sense of self-preservation that prevents me from yanking myself from his grasp as those fingertips reach the bare skin above my stocking. There he lingers for a few seconds before taking grasp of the material and pulling the fabric off. This ritual he repeats on the right leg. Neither of us have spoken a word during it.

I brace myself and wait for the removal of my shift but perhaps he senses that this would be too much on the first night. Instead, he throws back the bedclothes and walks to the other side of the bed, beginning his own undressing as he walks. I crawl into bed quickly and pull the sheets around my neck. I have done nothing wrong so far, I reason. Soon this will be over and at least the next time – if there is to be a next time with him – I will know what to expect.

The bed rocks a little as Jonas joins me, the stingy width of the mattress pushing us close so that I can feel the heat of his body through my thin shift and his breath is a light breeze through my hair.

'I will be gentle,' he promises, 'although there may be a brief moment of pain. You needn't be scared. It is what every woman must go through.'

I have been told this so often that it has started to sound meaningless. At least after this, I will no longer have to nod and look grateful for the sage advice. Jonas rocks himself to land above me, his body a barrier to the light in the room but I am happy for the act to take place in darkness. I close my eyes at first but then cannot bear it. Better to have some weak vision than be at the mercy of surprise.

He is gentle as he pushes my shift up from my knees and instructs me to lift my hips, then my shoulders, that he might strip it from me altogether. The bedsheets have been peeled right back but the heat from his body is like a furnace. Even as his kisses travel south, I feel sweat prickling my hairline and in the pits of my arms. It is not so bad, I tell myself, it is not so bad. And then he moves my legs apart and I know that it is about to happen. There is no turning back now and, after this, I am marked forever. I cannot go back to my old, innocent life. I will always be a whore.

He kisses me hard on the mouth and whispers, 'I'm sorry.' I feel his body surge and then his mouth is smothering my cry as I understand that it is done, the initial stab of the pain mercifully brief before paling into a heavy ache that continues as he moves, unrelenting, his hands holding my shoulders down, until he suddenly cries out himself and my legs are wet and he rolls away.

I lie there and wait for him to speak. Was he pleased with what I did? Though I didn't do much . . . Should I fetch him another drink? I hear a gentle snore. He is asleep. What am I supposed to do now?

Mrs Macauley's instructions! I hope that I remember everything. Sliding from the bed, I find beneath the bed, beside the empty chamber pot, a bowl of vinegar-smelling water and a cloth that Emmy must have brought up earlier. I quietly wash my nether regions in the water, wincing as I push the cloth inside myself. I must rinse out every trace of Jonas Drake, Mrs Macauley had told me. Any part of him lodged inside me could bring about a baby. Her concoction, she claimed, was tried and tested, for not a single girl at Little Wild Street had had a baby in five years.

I push the bowl back and use the chamber pot quietly, praying that Jonas does not wake before I am done. The ache is now in my belly, and I want to lie down, but not on the damp mattress. In the end I find my shift, thrown to the foot of the bed, and fold it over the wetness, noting the dark stain in the midst of it.

Blood. A relief, for it is proof for anyone who needs it that Mrs Macauley has sold me as a genuine maid. I have done my duty and tomorrow I will find out what comes next.

8

Emmy comes and finds me the next morning, shaking me from a sound sleep to a bleary awakening. There is a piercing pain in my head and my mouth is dry as sawdust. I stare at her, memories slowly trickling back, then look over to see that Jonas has gone. I am alone in the bed and his boots are no longer by the fireside.

'He's downstairs with Mama,' Emmy tells me, her eyes shining as she clambers over me and lies where he lay, on top of the sheets. She sniffs at the pillow and pulls a face. 'How is that men smell so strange? Even the rich ones.' I have no answer for her. 'So do you feel different now?'

I stare up at the ceiling. 'Did he look happy? Jonas, I mean. Did you hear anything?'

'It's very annoying. Camille is in Hattie's room so I can't listen through the floorboards. She's in a foul mood today,' she says, and it is an awful moment before I realise that she is still talking about Camille and not her mother. 'She saw your handsome gent in the light of day and is even more angry that she was left with Sir Horace. The old goat got so drunk that he pissed the bed last night. Still, I don't know why she's so mad when it's Hattie's bed that took the soaking and God knows who will clean it up now that you are Mama's golden goose.'

I laugh a little but my head hurts too much. It is a wonder how Emmy's language has changed in these short months. If Mrs Ashley had heard her talk about a gentleman pissing the bed, she'd have been sent to her room with no supper. I sit up and my stomach churns. 'Goodness, Em. I feel ever so queasy.'

'Too much punch on an empty stomach,' she tells me. 'Mama said you might not feel so well this morning.' She climbs back over me and throws something at me, a silk robe. 'You're to put this on and go and see her as soon as Mr Drake has departed.'

The room is cold, and I shiver as I pull on the robe that Emmy brought, feeling anew that sting between my legs as I take my first steps. The girls often go down to breakfast like this, *déshabillé*, one of the few French words Camille actually knows. Now I am one of them.

Mrs Macauley's door is shut as we wind down the first flight of stairs. Jonas must still be with her. I can hear her voice through the wood, but it is too quiet to make out the words. They have been talking for some time. What is there to say? Unless he wasn't pleased. But he seemed as though he was. Or was he just being kind, to save my feelings?

'Come on!' Emmy hisses and grabs my wrist, yanking me from where I stand frozen to the spot on the landing. 'Don't let her catch you.'

In a daze I follow her to the kitchen where the others wait expectantly around the table, Camille with a curl in her lip. I make sure to sit as far away from her as possible.

'Well then, girl, or should I say lady?' Cook booms, and the inside of my head feels as though someone is swinging around a hammer.

'Lady?' Camille sneers. 'She's no better than the rest of us now. Let's see who's interested in a girl with no maidenhead to break and who still can't tell a prick from a potato.'

'Well, he's still with Mrs M.' Maria rests a hand on my shoulder and squeezes. 'Means you done well, love. Very well.'

'Really?' I reach for a hunk of bread. 'He's not asking for his money back then?'

'I wouldn't be so sure,' Camille mutters.

'No,' Maria says firmly. 'If that gent is still in with her, it means there's something to discuss. Like a permanent arrangement.' This last sentence she sings in Camille's direction, winding her up as easily as a clockwork mouse and letting her go.

'If that useless excuse for a bawd has ruined my chances with the first decent fella to walk in here in months, I'll pack my bags,' Camille threatens. 'I've been years here, wasting the prime of my life on the likes of Sir Horace. She promised me, you know. She promised that if I trusted her, she'd take me with her to St James's. A fine establishment, with dukes and lords falling over themselves to see me. And yet we're still bleeding here. Still stuck in this falling down house in the arsehole of London, sucking off drunk old men who spent all their money at the card table years ago and have nothing left but a poxy title and hair everywhere but on their head.'

'Sir Horace does have a very hairy back,' Hattie muses.

'And even he don't appreciate me,' Camille goes on. 'He'll go with any girl who's available and happy to put up with his slobbering and groping, and then he pisses the bed after he can't raise a cockstand.'

'You can go elsewhere whenever you please, Camille.' The icy tones of Mrs Macauley cut through Camille's whining, and we all shut up. 'I hear Dotty Gardner has a spare room these days.'

I watch Camille's face twist, her brain no doubt telling her mouth to keep shut, her mouth ignoring that wise counsel. 'I'm just saying that you made me certain promises, that's all. And now I don't even have a bedchamber to call my own. You gave it to *her*.' She jabs a finger in my direction, and I'm surprised to find that I feel a sudden satisfaction. Weeks I've spent, emptying her overflowing chamber pots and laundering her stinking, stained bedsheets for no thanks. Time the shoe was on the other foot.

'In case you have forgotten – and this goes for all of you – none of you have a claim to any of those bedchambers. They are *my* bedchambers, for I pay the rent and therefore I decide who goes where. Those rooms are for entertaining our gentlemen.' Mrs Macauley looks around to make sure we are all giving her our full attention. 'The best room for the best client, Camille. That's how it's always been. And for the time being, our best client is Mr Drake.' She takes a deep breath and draws herself up tall. 'I've made some decisions. Camille, you're in with Hattie for the time being. Sukey, you've done well. Drake's agreed to pay for your services for the next fortnight and we'll see where we are after that.'

She sweeps out and there is a collective gasp as we realise what she has done. The pecking order has gone topsy-turvy. Camille no longer the favourite, her complaining has moved her to the bottom of the pile, while I have catapulted suddenly to the top. Emmy jumps up to hug me and Hattie and Maria both voice their congratulations. I know Hattie doesn't care about sharing a room; she never minds a jot about anything trivial like that. It is Camille who worries me. Camille who sits there with her arms folded and her eyes narrowed to daggers. I have made an enemy.

The next two weeks, over Christmas and into the new year, pass in a blur. Each evening Jonas arrives and is shown up to the room that I now call my own, where I wait for him. My dread has dissipated somewhat, now that there are no surprises. He is always gentle, and I am grateful for that. My aim is always to please him, for while he pays for my company, I can avoid Sir Horace, Tobias Kellett, and the myriad lonely men who come by our house. I make sure to have the fire lit in advance, bidding him to sit so that I can pull off his boots as he warms his hands close to the flames. Emmy arrives with food and drink, for often he comes straight from working in his father's business where he is learning to follow in his footsteps, and we sit, and he eats and we talk.

Of course, it is mostly he who talks. I am not foolish enough to imagine that he considers me his equal. I listen and he appreciates what little I do have to say, when he pauses in his orations, and I know that it is time to prove that I have paid attention. This appreciation has already been shown in the gift he gave me on his Christmas Day visit. Perhaps it was to demonstrate his gratitude, for having a place to go on a day that is supposed to be so joyous. He exchanged the box with me for a glass of fine claret that Mrs Macauley had bought in specially, knowing that lonely men will always pay a little extra on Christmas. I sat before the fire like a child to open it, unsure at first what it was inside. Deep-blue silk patterned with an exquisite embroidery in red, white and gold. A garment of some sort.

'A kimono,' he told me. 'The Japanese women wear them, and they are the most beautiful and most refined in the world. A friend brought it back from the Orient and as soon as I saw it I thought of you.'

He helped me to undress, wrapping that soft silk around me before tying it at the waist. In front of the looking glass, with the flickering firelight behind me, I could have been a princess from some faraway land. Indeed, Jonas must have thought the same for he made me remove it immediately so that he might enjoy me on the bed. I clutched at his back as he thrust, pulling him closer to me so that he wouldn't notice my gaze over his shoulder, fixated on that work of art that I had so carefully hung on a wooden peg on the wall, the most beautiful thing I had ever seen.

For all Camille says, Jonas Drake is not just some common roughshod planter from the Caribbean. His family own an estate in Lincolnshire as well as their Barbados plantation and the house here in London. Jonas was born here, though he has no memory of the city from childhood; after some troubles on the plantation, his father decided to take the family out there to manage it himself, leaving a trusted cousin here to look after things. That cousin recently succumbed to a weak heart, and it was decided that Jonas, being the elder of two living brothers and now having one and twenty years, should become the family's representative in England. Jonas doesn't want to be another of those rich sons, running amuck through London town and destroying the family's hard-earned reputation as they debauch and drink their way through their allowances. He wants to bolster his family name, to become a respected man in his own right.

'A man of ambition,' Madame Vernier says when she comes to collect her finder's fee.

'A man who understands loyalty,' Mrs Macauley replies, though she looks less than a little happy about handing over so much money to a woman she obviously dislikes.

The end of the fortnight has finally come about, and Jonas kissed me goodbye this morning. There is family business to sort out in Lincolnshire, he told me, and he'll be away for a month or so. To my great relief, he has put down a retainer to make me his while he is away. I will be saved from the uncertainty of the nightly soirées a little longer.

'He will be willing to make a long-term commitment?' Mrs Macauley asks.

'I think it likely that he will offer to become Sukey's keeper,' Madame Vernier replies, smiling at me. 'He is so taken with you, my dear. I think that by the summer you shall be in your own apartment and free of financial worry.'

Mrs Macauley snaps open an ornate fan, wafting it before her face. 'What a turn-up. Sukey, you must ensure that Mr Drake makes his offer as soon as possible.'

'You really think that Jonas will want me all to himself?' It was every harlot's dream, to be kept, not to have to worry about money and only having one faithful man to keep happy. A marriage free of the disadvantages.

'Already he allows you to call him by his first name? This is a good bit of business, mark my words. And my percentage shall remain the same, don't worry about that.' Madame Vernier smiles beatifically.

'Percentage?' Mrs Macauley's face falls. 'Gisele, are you mad? I thank you for bringing Mr Drake to our door, but you've been more than fairly compensated.'

'The deal is not concluded though, Lucy, is it? Until the

ink is dry on the contract, you cannot be certain that another young girl won't catch his eye.' She smiles. 'There is a pretty little Negress over on Charlotte Street, I hear. From Barbados too, originally, so I'm sure she would love to join Mr Drake in reminiscing over their former home.'

'You want me to be grateful to you? Is that it?' Mrs Macauley is furious.

'I am,' I say quickly. 'I am grateful, Madame Vernier, ever so.'

'Excellent. Then you may pay Madame Vernier from your own pocket.' Mrs Macauley shoots me a look that brooks no argument. She makes a mark in her ever-present ledger. 'You still get twenty per cent so I calculate that you may clear your debt to me in little over a year if you can keep Mr Drake on a leash for that long.'

A year? But I do not despair. All I have to do is to continue along this path and for every day that passes, my debt will fall.

Mrs Macauley closes her ledger with a snap. 'Now, I think we are finished.' She looks pointedly at Gisele Vernier, and I wonder again what their history is.

'Actually, there is one more matter of business I wished to discuss. Your girl Camille. I would like to extend her an invitation. Fees to be negotiated, of course, but I think it could be good for both of you. Introduce her to a higher class of gentleman. Inch you closer to that elevated address you have always longed for.'

'You seem awfully eager to improve the circumstances of my girls all of a sudden, Gisele.' Mrs Macauley raises her eyebrow.

'Lucy, my darling, this is business. Financial sense, nothing more. I make money, as do you, and we show the younger generation how it should be done, no? You always talked about how important it was to you to leave a legacy.'

The torment is writ right across Mrs Macauley's powdered face. It's no secret that this house is not what she hoped for. Times have changed and for every improvement Lucille Macauley makes, she fails to make ground on those superior establishments. London moves too fast for her to keep up. Men of quality do not come here when their clubs and establishments are too far away. Things here will continue to decline.

Mrs Macauley reaches over and yanks the bell pull. 'I make no promises but if she agrees then I think an equal split is fair.'

'You'll receive twenty per cent. These are my terms now, Lucy. My invitation, my friends and my connections.'

Jakes sticks his head in the door just as I think that Mrs Macauley will lose her composure, her face reddening as she battles her every instinct. 'Fetch Camille,' she barks, and Jakes knows well enough to disappear rapidly.

She makes us wait. Punishment for being so shoddily cast down the pecking order. Finally, Camille drags herself in.

'Camille, Madame Vernier has a proposition for you.' Mrs Macauley presses her lips together and looks away, removing herself from the conversation.

'Madame. It would be an honour to hear what you have to say.' Camille bobs a curtsey, and I bite the inside of my cheek to stop from smiling. Really, she has no shame!

'My dear, how would you like to be a real life *Cendrillon*? If you will allow, I cannot promise a pumpkin, but I can be your fairy godmother. What do you say? Will you put aside your filthy apron and your rags and go to the ball?' Madame Vernier casts a sharp eye over Camille's clothing.

Camille shoots a pointed glance in my direction. No doubt she has cast me as one of the ugly stepsisters in her version of the fairy tale. 'Madame Vernier, I would consider myself blessed. If I am permitted, of course. Mrs Macauley does have very strict rules about—'

'My girl, three evenings ago you offered your arse to a boy for less than two guineas, with his friends permitted to watch the proceedings. You have shown very little regard to my rules.' Mrs Macauley snaps her fan open emphatically. 'Having said that, I will spare you for this one night on the proviso that you do not bring this house any further into disrepute.'

A thick silence falls upon the room, Camille's cheeks reddening as she contemplates how this revelation might affect her standing with Madame Vernier. That woman, amazingly, doesn't even blink.

'I am recruiting on behalf of a wealthy gentleman for his annual ball which is infamous for its debauchery as much as its secrecy and opulence. It is an honour to be invited, though let me be clear. You will be attending not as a guest but as the entertainment. He demands the best in looks, in cleanliness and in terms of willingness to play a part in the bacchanale.' Madame Vernier speaks matter-of-factly. 'You must be open to everything and everyone. These are gentlemen – and some ladies – who are used to getting what they want, and they do not like to be refused or kept waiting. I have watched you, Camille. I like your ambition, and I don't think that you would let anything stand in your way when it comes to elevating your position.'

Camille's conduct is seen as a boon then. I can see that she's unsure whether to be offended or flattered. But a ball is a ball, after all. An opportunity to wear fine clothes and be admired by powerful men is not to be sniffed at.

'Whatever shall I wear?' she wonders, pointedly.

'I will provide you with a gown and the accessories. There is a certain theme to the proceedings, and you must look the part. I shall pick you up from here at five o'clock sharp next Wednesday afternoon and there will be time for you to dress and prepare once we arrive at the location.'

The fee is agreed, a large sum that brings the shine back to Camille's eyes. It annoys me greatly that she has emerged so triumphantly out of her petulant games, but at least she may stop tormenting the rest of us with her dark moods. Madame Vernier takes her leave, and the three of us drop any pretence of amity that we upheld in her presence.

'I will need rest to make sure that I look my best for this ball,' Camille says, a sly smile about her lips. 'And Sukey's gent is out of town, is he not?'

'A fair point. Sukey, you can share with Emmy again since you won't be working for the next few weeks. And don't pull that face at me. When Mr Drake returns, so will your privileges. Camille, you'll be present in the parlour as usual, tonight and every night before the ball. I expect best behaviour from you while you reside beneath my roof and represent my good name. Understood?'

'Perfectly, Mrs Macauley.' I hate the smug look on her face. 'I hope you don't mind terribly, Sukey. I know how your pride has swelled since your good fortune.'

'It is ever so kind of you to think of me, Camille, but it does make perfect sense for me to share with Emmy while Jonas is away. I don't mind at all, especially since Madame Vernier says that he's keen to become my keeper. I'll soon have everything you or I could ever dream of.'

I take pleasure in each word, even though I know I may have

to eat them if Jonas doesn't live up to my expectations. Still, it is worth it to see the look on her face as she storms out of the room, the door slamming behind her.

'I have to say, Sukey, that being a bitch don't suit you. You're a good girl. That'll serve you better in the long run.' Mrs Macauley dismisses me, and I flee, a little ashamed.

Of course, I should have listened. But when you're young you think you know better. Until the moment it's too late, and you realise that you don't know anything at all.

✷ JANUARY 1766 ✷

Miss Camille de le Croix, Little Wild Street, Covent Garden

A minx of the highest order, her reputation is known widely and to many who have revelled in her charms. Bordering on two and twenty, despite her claims to a lower figure, she is far from a maiden, but she is most open-minded, and her years bring her certain skills that the younger wench does not possess. Accordingly, she does not come cheap. Expect to pay no less than three guineas for anything more than the most basic of demands.

9

With Camille reinstalled in her old lair, she restrains herself to aiming the odd barbed comment in my direction. Otherwise, she annoys anyone within earshot by talking about nothing else but the mysterious ball she is due to attend. There is no topic of conversation that she cannot talk over: the latest fashions, the state of Sir Horace the evening before, even the Piper after rumours abound the Garden that he has been spotted and thwarted in taking a girl from Haddock's bagnio. If you believe what you hear, he is almost seven feet tall, with a tricorn hat and a coat made of red velvet. Maria says the girl from Haddock's is a notorious attention seeker and not to listen to a word of it. Not that we have much opportunity when Camille is around.

'They won't be able to take their eyes off me,' she tells us at dinner, refusing to eat more than a morsel lest she ruin the tiny waist she plans to show off. 'The host himself will be desperate to know who I am.'

'A better tactic would be to see who is there and find out what you can. There will be other pretty girls there, not just you. You must be canny. Talk to the guests and flatter them. Ply a few of them with wine and make 'em talk. Find out which establishments they frequent and tell them why our house is better, or at least worth a go.' Mrs Macauley wipes up gravy from her plate with a heel of bread, plotting hard. 'Don't get ahead of yourself, girl. You need to work on your charm. Show a bit of humility for a change.'

'Humility?' Camille snorts at the idea.

Emmy nudges me. 'Maybe one day we can go to one of these balls together.'

'That would be nice,' I lie. Camille seems to expect that the ball will be elegant and the gentlemen courteous, like the balls that rich folk attend during the season. From what I've overheard from Maria and Hattie, the truth is that it will be closer in resemblance to Smithfield Market. Girls being herded past the rich and debauched, going to the highest bidder. There is no picking or choosing. Your status is barely a rung above the servants who run around ensuring that no glass runs dry and that any mess is cleaned up or hidden away. For a harlot, the reputation she has and must cling to is based on her willingness to please rather than her chasteness, the very opposite of a real lady.

'Before I forget, Sukey—' Mrs Macauley changes the subject, and I pay attention '—Gisele Vernier asked if she can speak with you the day after tomorrow.'

'Speak with me?' This is exciting, though mystifying. 'Why?'

'Damned if I know.' She licks gravy from her fingertips. In the kitchen she often sheds the refinement she displays elsewhere. 'She said there are some lessons you should learn, to help your cause with Mr Drake. Manners and etiquette and the like.'

'Etiquette?' Jonas has never seemed unhappy with how our meetings have gone.

Camille giggles. 'Our pet savage being taught how to behave? Who'd have thought it?'

'Don't you dare call me that!'

'Oh, come along. Isn't that why your Mr Drake wants you in the first place? I've met men like him before. They can only get excited if they feel they're taming some wild, exotic beast. Ever so odd if you ask me, but every man has his own—' She shrieks suddenly as Cook manages to spill cold gravy from her plate into her lap as she clears the table.

'Well, dearie, if you'd eaten the good food I put in front of you, there'd have been nothing there for me to accidentally spill,' Cook tells her, winking at me when she's sure that neither Camille nor Mrs Macauley can see her.

'Can we be civil, for goodness' sake?' Mrs Macauley pushes back her chair. 'Sukey, have an early night. I don't need any trouble downstairs and you're a distraction for our guests when you're not available to them. Besides, you want to be fresh of face when Madame Vernier sees you next. She's not one to be crossed, trust me. And Camille, hush your mouth. You may just learn at that ball about the odd tastes men can have. I'd hate for your words to come back and bite you.'

When Madame Vernier comes to call two days later, I'm as excited as a kitten with a sunbeam in her sights.

'For Christ's sake, girl, sit down and stop fidgeting!' Cook loses her patience as I try to distract myself beforehand, attempting to help her in the kitchen but clearly acting as more of a hindrance.

I sit by the fire and try to stop grinning, eventually even Cook's grumpy expression softening, my joy infectious.

'You can always come and help me empty the chamber pots if you're so keen to have something to do,' Emmy suggests, but she is just teasing, I think.

Emmy is perfectly normal with me, but I realise that we haven't spoken much since the night that Jonas first came to Little Wild Street. I do not mean that we don't talk, for we do. We just don't speak about much that matters. We make small talk and speak of things that have happened in the house, but we do not share our feelings and thoughts, those intimate details that have forged our friendship over the years. Something has changed and if Jonas is the reason, then I do not know what to do. I hardly have a choice over his patronage.

'I would help you,' I tell her now, regarding the chamber pots, 'only I can't get my gown dirty. Not when I am to see Madame Vernier.'

'Oh, Madame Vernier. I had quite forgotten about her,' she says, which is a lie. I have not shut up about Gisele Vernier for two days.

She is so fashionable, a higher quality version of Mrs Macauley and far more pleasant. I want to be like her. Able to go where she pleases and to speak with whomever she wants. Her clothes are expensive, and she doesn't look like a courtesan in fancy clothing the way that Camille does when she wears her nicest gowns. She looks like a real lady.

'She's been sniffing round here a lot recently, Gisele Vernier.' Cook looks thoughtful.

'D'you know her?' I'm eager for any snippet of knowledge about my new mentor.

'Yes, you could say that.' Cook's gaze is into the past. 'Long time ago now though. She ran around with your mother, Emmy, and with yours, Su. Quite the trio they was back then. I think they thought about setting up their own house at one time or another but then you two came along and that was the end of that.'

'I didn't know you knew my mother.' I look more closely at Cook. I've always thought her to be much older than Mrs Macauley but actually her face is no more lined than her mistress's. She is plumper and she wears old, greying dresses that are clean but hardly of the latest fashion. I suppose she fades into the background.

'Them three thought quite highly of themselves,' she says. 'Didn't have much time for the likes of me. Eve was nice enough, though. Always had a smile on her face and was never rude like the others could be.'

I stash away this precious information. I cannot remember my mother's face, but I like Cook's version of her, someone who was kind. Mrs Macauley has never wanted to talk about her, despite her claim that they were the best of friends, but perhaps Madame Vernier will be more forthcoming. I must have patience though, I caution myself. I don't want to irritate her.

There is a knock at the door, and I leap to my feet.

'Calm yourself.' Cook laughs. 'She's just a person, Sukey, no better than the rest of us. She's no one special.'

I nod and smile and don't tell her that she's wrong.

Madame Vernier is dressed in impeccable navy silk, a fur trimmed cape around her shoulders. In the dark hallway of Little Wild Street, she looks otherworldly. Out of place, like a queen visiting her lowly subjects.

'Come along, Sukey,' she says. 'Let us take a ride in my carriage.'

She has her own carriage, it seems, with soft leather seats that match her attire. A footman helps me to climb up first, and then we set off, heading away from Covent Garden.

'Where are we going?' I ask.

'Nowhere in particular but we cannot be overheard here. Before Mr Drake returns, I thought it might stand you in good stead to understand a little about the life you are embarking upon. He will have expectations of you, and it is vital for you to live up to them if you want to retain his affections.'

'Expectations?' My heart sinks. What else is there?

'It is perhaps the greatest trick in a harlot's life, to sell her maidenhead. To convince a gentleman to pay a ridiculous sum of money for a girl who has not the faintest idea what she is to do in the bedchamber. But immediately afterwards, he expects that she will know every trick in the book. That she will submit to his every whim and fancy and introduce him to a few of her own.' She pats my hand, sensing my panic and confusion. 'However, just as men have their coffee houses and their little clubs where they can sit around and gossip or – as they like to call it – talk business, so we women have our own methods for sharing intimate knowledge. We have to do it behind closed doors, but we have our ways, nevertheless. You may speak to me, Sukey, about anything you wish to know.'

'I do speak to the other girls,' I assure her. 'To Hattie and Maria, at least.'

'And that is better than nothing, but I do not want to leave you with Lucille Macauley's girls as your only measure of success. Don't you want more, Sukey? Covent Garden is fine for some but if you want to keep hold of Jonas Drake you must become something more.'

'I do want something more. I want to be like you,' I tell her. 'And Mrs Macauley, you know she isn't a mother to me at all. She would have sold me to Sir Horace if I hadn't run away. You saved me, ma'am, truly you did. I don't have anyone else who looks out for me the way that you do.'

'Not even little Emily? I thought the pair of you were so close.' She sounds surprised and I feel guilty.

'Emmy's afraid. Afraid that her ma will sell her off to Sir Horace in my place and – and I don't want to think bad of her, but I don't think she'd have cared so much if we were both in the same boat, as they say, but now that we're not . . . '

'She's scared that you'll leave her behind, that's all,' Madame Vernier tells me firmly. 'Be kind to her. It might be that Lucy sells her own daughter to an undeserving man. I know how desperate she is to move from that shambles of a house you call home. But it is up to you and me to protect Emmy. I knew your mother, Sukey. My heart broke when I heard what had happened to her, and now that I have met you, her daughter, I know I have the chance to make it up to Eve.'

She shocks me then, wiping away a stray tear from her own cheek before turning away, her gaze fixed out of the window. Perhaps I should be brave and ask her what exactly it was that happened to my mother, but I am too scared to come out with it directly.

'Why are our lives so precarious?' I wonder aloud, hardly expecting an answer, but Gisele Vernier takes me seriously.

'I tell you honestly: because we are women. And not only that, but we are women who make our living by lying on our backs and opening our legs for men who don't care about anything but their own short moment of pleasure.' Her grip on my hand tightens. 'You are a whore, Sukey. You should take pride in that, no matter what anyone else says. It is a profession as old as time and undervalued in spite of it. What you must do is learn to respect yourself. Be strong and rise above the dregs.'

I stare at her, at the tears that filled her eyes suddenly, blinked away in a moment. 'But how do I do that?'

'You are your mother's daughter,' she tells me. 'Eve wasn't a fool, and neither are you. She was dealt a bad hand, but you have a chance to do so much better. You have Mr Drake; you must not lose him. When he returns you must make sure that his infatuation with you continues. Men are simple creatures, and he is no different. Smile. Do what he asks of you, no matter how distasteful. Listen to him talk. Learn his favourite pastimes. Have his favourite wine on hand when he comes to visit you. Your aim, that which we spoke about in Lucy's office, is for you to end up in your own apartment, gladly paid for by Drake.' And then, as if she thinks I might need further convincing, she said: 'Away from Lucy Macauley, where you might really make something of yourself.'

'You think it possible?'

'I think it very possible for you, Sukey. But Lucy won't let you leave easily. You're her ticket to leaving that hovel she calls a house of pleasure.' Madame Vernier's laugh is derisive. 'All the fancy painted paper in the world cannot conceal the cracks in her walls. Why should you slave away to make her fortune?'

'I owe her money,' I say. The last figure scrawled beneath my name in her ledger, even taking Jonas's retainer into account, is still a sum I could only dream of. 'But in a year or two . . . ' Or less, perhaps, if I can convince Jonas to remove me from Little Wild Street. Maybe there is a way for Emmy to come too, not as a maid but as my friend. With Jonas's patronage and a little help from Madame Vernier, we can pay off my debts even sooner and begin to make our own fortune, the two of us. The sooner, the better.

Madame Vernier reads my mind. 'You can't afford to wait and so I have a plan. You will have your liberty sooner than you think, Sukey – only please, I beg you . . . let us keep this between ourselves. You must not tell a soul, not even Emily. She is her mother's daughter, and she will put family first if she has to choose. I'd hate for you to discover that the hard way.'

Her carriage draws up on Drury Lane and her driver hops down to let me out. I know that I should ask her more questions, about her future plans and how I fit into them, but all I can think about is my own future. One that has to be free of Mrs Macauley.

10

I wake early the next morning, Emmy snoring softly beside me. I hadn't heard her come up for I had been blessed to fall asleep as soon as I'd lain down in bed. Quiet as a mouse, I creep out from under the bedclothes into the icy January morning, my breath a white cloud. Shivering, I grab the kimono that Jonas gifted me for Christmas. It is so beautiful that I cannot help but wear it to show off, but it does not keep me warm. I flee down to the warmer kitchen where there is a fire ablaze, and I can hear Cook outside arguing with the baker's boy. He's giving her some cheek, a brave lad, for Cook isn't one to mess with. I pull up a chair and rub my hands together. Everyone else is still asleep and probably won't be up for hours.

It is the day of Camille's ball, and she will be intolerable. I sigh, realising that if all goes well for her then tomorrow, she will be even worse. I need Emmy to be my ally. Perhaps if I show her that I am able to think about someone other than myself. She's taken over many of my old housekeeping duties since my success with Jonas, but I am not Camille, I tell myself. I don't think myself above a bit of hard work.

Invigorated by my brilliant idea, I start by lighting the fire in Mrs Macauley's room, the curtains around her bed drawn tight as she snores through the morning. I carry water up to all of the bedrooms, taking no small amount of pleasure in throwing open the drapes in Camille's room and suffering her curses with a smile. I am sweeping the parlour floor when Emmy finally shows her face, yawning after her late night.

'You aren't supposed to be doing the housework anymore,' she accuses.

'I woke up early,' I say. 'And I thought that perhaps we might go out for a walk today. It's been so long since we left this house, it has started to feel quite like a prison.'

'You went out yesterday,' she reminds me.

'Yes, well, that was different. It wasn't for my own amusement.' It had honestly been a very pleasurable excursion, getting to know Madame Vernier better, but I hardly want to rub Emmy's nose in it. 'Remember all those long walks we used to take on Sunday afternoons? Let's explore! We've been in London since last autumn and still I barely know my way around.'

'I don't think Mama would like it. Not after the time you ran away. Besides, she's asked me to attend on Camille this afternoon before she leaves for the ball.' Halfway out of the door she turns: 'Are the bedpans emptied and cleaned?'

'Yes,' I tell her.

'Then I'll make a start on Mama's room.'

Her reaction stings. We have been friends for so long. How have things changed so quickly? When we lived with the Ashleys, nothing ever divided us. I had known my place, not being a blood relative and there only because of the money sent from London. I was so grateful to Mrs Macauley then, not knowing that I was incurring such debt. Emmy always spoke up for me when Mrs Ashley had scolded or slapped me. Now, everything is different, and I hate it. The thought of spending a day trapped indoors with Emmy who barely wants to speak to me, and Camille whose only interest lies in boasting, feeds my desire to brave the icy streets outside. But where can I go?

Jonathan. I feel yet another twinge of guilt as I realise that I've barely given the poor boy a second thought in the weeks since I made my failed escape. I can walk to Mincing Lane. I know where Dr Sharp resides. Surely, he will know by now what has become of Jonathan.

Mrs Macauley is at her desk by the time I've finished my tasks and eaten a strained meal in the kitchen with Emmy and the other girls, everyone in dour spirits. I grit my teeth and beg her for the opportunity to be allowed out alone.

'Where on earth do you need to go to on a day like this?' She makes a good point. Tiny flakes of snow are starting to fall past the window. It is barely two o'clock and yet dusk is already beginning its descent.

There is nothing to be gained in reminding her of the day I had run away. 'I wish to buy a new pair of gloves. Madame Vernier thinks mine not fine enough for the company I hope to be keeping.' This is not exactly a lie, for she had said something similar to me the day before. I have a shiny new guinea that Jonas gifted me, and that Mrs Macauley doesn't know about, so it will be easy enough to pass by a glovemakers on my way to or from Mincing Lane.

'How do I know that you will return?' She puts down her quill, her sharp eyes watching me closely. 'Should I really trust a runaway?'

'Yes,' I tell her. She will never understand but I can at least try to explain. 'I ran away because I was scared. I thought that nothing could be worse than what you had planned for me. I know better now. Here, I have friends, and I have Jonas. I would never risk losing the opportunity that he offers me. I know that there is nothing for me out there but poverty and danger.' It is as perfect an answer as I can muster, and I can see the indecision in her expression. 'I promise to be home before dark.'

Her sigh is heavy. 'You had better be. Camille's ball is this evening, and I have enough concerns with her without having to deal with you in addition. Tell Jakes to come and see me and then you may go.'

'Thank you, ma'am.' In my excitement I find myself bobbing her a curtsey and I swear that she is smiling a little as I flee her room.

Maria has a fur-lined cape that a beau gifted her last year, and she is kind enough to lend it to me. I have sturdy leather shoes from my days tramping the muddy lanes and fields of Surrey which will do far better than the flimsy slippers I wore on my last venture to Mincing Lane.

The cold takes my breath away as I step outside, freezing tiny crystals along the inside of my throat. If the day before fooled Londoners into thinking that spring will soon be upon us, today winter has returned in its full force, and I have not chosen the best day for a stroll. The city doesn't stop for any weather though and even Little Wild Street is busy. Before I turn to walk in the opposite direction I see the head of that man again, the one I had mistaken for Jonathan a few weeks earlier. I don't know how when this man is so tall and well built. He is walking towards me and winks when he sees me staring. I slip into the crowd before he comes any closer. How dare he wink! And then I remember that he has seen me on the doorstep of Mrs Macauley's house.

He knows what I am. Perhaps he thinks to charm a cheap half hour with me, but he is out of luck and I walk fast away from him.

Weaving my way towards Fleet Street, I hope that I remember the way correctly. The city looks so different than my last journey in this direction – not because of the daylight, dying though it is on such a dour day, but because of the people. The noise and the aliveness of them. The clatter of horses' hooves and the smell of the roasting chestnuts; accordion music playing on a street corner and the laughter of young boys as they run and play, my gloved hand checking the security of the purse tied around my wrist as they push past me.

I find Mincing Lane and almost pass the doctor's house without noticing since there is no queue at his door today. His surgery must have set hours that the locals are familiar with. Or perhaps he is out. I muster up the courage to ring the doorbell anyway.

'Yes?' It is the sour-faced housekeeper who answers. Mrs Day, I remember. Behind her I hear music playing. Someone is at home.

'Good afternoon.' I put on my best church reading voice. 'I was hoping to speak with Dr Sharp if he's available.'

'The doctor is out.' She goes to close the door on me, no mention of where he's gone or when he might be back.

'And his brother?' I blurt out. After all, it was he who ensured that Jonathan was taken into the surgery.

'Mr Granville Sharp?' The woman peers down at me suspiciously. 'What do you want with him?'

'He and the good doctor took care of a boy recently. They suggested that I return at a later date to find out how he was doing.' It doesn't seem as though the housekeeper recognises me. I suppose that is a good thing since I did not make a good first impression. I certainly look less of a street urchin now, with my borrowed cloak and my clean dress. 'His name was Jonathan. And I am Miss Sukey Maynard. Please, if Mr Sharp is at home, I would only take up a few moments of his time.'

'Stay there.' She closes the door and I wait patiently. After a few minutes she reappears. 'He will see you.'

This time it is a neat, cosy parlour that I am shown into. This room is the source of the music. There are sheets of it strewn across a narrow sofa, and a musical instrument, a horn of some sort, has been propped up on a cushion. Before the fire stands the man that I remember from that December day. Granville Sharp.

'Miss Maynard,' he greets me. 'Won't you sit?'

I take a seat on a battered velvet armchair, sinking down so much that it quite hurts my neck to look up at him. After a moment, he realises his error and throws the sheet music to one side, sitting down opposite me so that we can converse more easily.

'Sir, I'm ever so sorry to inconvenience you,' I start, 'and perhaps you'll wonder why it's taken me so long to pay a visit.'

'This is about the boy, Jonathan Strong,' he interrupts, and I see that he has only just remembered who exactly I am. 'Today you look rather less . . . ' He struggles and then gives up on finding the suitable words to describe my former chaotic and inappropriate appearance. 'You look well now.'

'Thank you, yes.' I smile and try not to look embarrassed.

'Jonathan is doing better,' he tells me. 'My brother told me that he was asking about you only the other day. It will lift his spirits immeasurably to know that he will one day be able to thank you in person.'

'I'm so happy to hear that he's well,' I say. 'And is he residing somewhere close by?'

Mr Sharp's face slides into uncertainty. 'Well, it's all a matter of perspective.' He steeples his fingers, his elbows resting on his knees. 'Jonathan has been quite ill, Miss Maynard. In fact, if you had not brought him here to us, he most likely would not be alive now. You saved his life.'

It should not be a shock. After all, I had thought him dead when I very first stumbled over him. But to be credited with saving a life is something quite unexpected.

'He will recover?'

Mr Sharp sighs. 'His eyes are badly affected, as is one of his legs. They are caring for him still at St Bartholomew's, but it is hoped that he will be able to leave there in a month or so. His surname is Strong and so his nature is proving to be also. He will always carry some trace of his wounds, but I think he should be able to have a decent life. A useful life.'

'A useful life is all any of us can hope for,' I murmur, thinking that Mr Sharp would appreciate this piety, whereas in reality I am horrified. How quickly life can change for any of us. One moment in perfect health, the next maimed irreparably. 'May I give you my address? I would like to contact Jonathan once he is further recovered.'

'Certainly.' There is a small writing desk in the corner of the room and Mr Sharp rises to fetch paper, scribbling my name and place of residence. God willing, he will never realise the sort of house I live in.

I go to take my leave, turning to ask one last question before

I exit the room. 'Sir, I do wonder . . . has Jonathan ever said *why* his master did such a thing to him? To try and – I don't suppose he meant to kill him but . . . '

Mr Sharp looks sad. 'I have not asked Jonathan why but know that there may not be a good reason. Not one that either you or I can understand. I am sorry that I do not have a better answer.'

It may not be the answer I was hoping for but strangely it does make sense. I do not leave the house light at heart, but I do feel comfort in the knowledge that Jonathan still lives.

11

Camille has us all buzzing around her like honeybees to a flower as she gets ready for the ball. By the time she sweeps out of the house into Madame Vernier's carriage, she looks fit for a royal ball, though I am not as sure as she is that any prince will be present.

'At least we'll get a quiet night,' Maria says as we wave her off.

'But we'll pay for it in spades tomorrow.' I shiver and close the door. 'God, I hope there's no one of importance there. Can you imagine? We'll never hear the end of it!'

'None of that talk, please, Sukey. The good fortune of one of us is the good fortune of all.' Mrs Macauley swoops out of nowhere to castigate my sour grapes. 'I didn't hear any of your sisters complain when you were crowing about Mr Drake not so long ago.'

'That's not true,' I grumble as we traipse back to the parlour.

'You can make yourself useful tonight by helping Emily mix the punch. I've invited a few select gentlemen to call on us this evening after dinner. We have another auction to prepare for, and at least tonight we won't have the distraction of Camille's antics.'

Another auction? I look quizzically at Emmy, who is doing

all she can not to look in my direction. 'Emmy?' Has she . . . ? But surely, I would have been the first to know if she has bled, just as she had been the first to know when I had.

'Emily is a young woman now, Sukey, just like you. And she has a fine future ahead of her.' Mrs Macauley's smile doesn't quite reach her eyes.

'When did it happen?' I ask Emmy as I wait at the kitchen table for her to fetch the punch bowl.

'Does it matter?' She puts down the silver bowl with a bang. She still hasn't looked me in the eye.

'Yes! I thought you would've told me. Your best friend. Your sister.' I feel my temper rise alongside the hurt. 'We used to tell one another everything.'

'I didn't think you'd care,' she says. 'Besides, it was only this morning. I was upstairs and you were down, and then you went out. You had other things on your mind.'

The rebuke is as breath-taking as a slap round the face. How can I rebut her accusation when I was the one who ran away and never thought once that Emmy might have wanted to come with me? It is only now when I look at her closely, that I see the shadows under her eyes, her cheekbones sharper than they were when we lived in a small market town, the air gentler on the lungs, the food fresher than any I'd seen in London. Is Emmy truly so enthusiastic about her fate, or is she simply trying to please the mother she still barely knows?

'I do care,' I say. 'I know that I haven't always shown it, but I promise you I do. I know I have at times been selfish but I'm sorry.'

'Yes, well.' She sniffs and pours sugar into the rum and water and lime juice in the bowl, giving it a stir with the wooden spoon. 'Things can't stay the same forever. If – when – Mr Drake comes back for you, Mama will give you anything you ask for. You're lucky, Su. I hope I may have a fraction of your fortune.'

'You will, Emmy. You will.' I try not to choke on the lie. Unless a miracle occurs, there is no second Jonas Drake to rescue her from her fate.

'We'll find out soon enough. Mama plans an auction in two days' time,' she replies, pushing past me out of the kitchen.

Mrs Macauley has dug out one of her own gowns for Emmy to wear to meet her prospective suitors, a slightly old-fashioned and over-embellished robe of dark-green velvet with a stomacher that sparkles with cheap stones. With her hair curled and powdered, Emmy looks a younger version of her mother, albeit with blonde rather than dark hair. I don't think it suits her but perhaps if she doesn't look as young as she is then Tobias Kellett won't be interested. Perhaps none of them will be and we'll have a little longer together, just the two of us. Just until Jonas comes back for me.

'Sukey, you can wait on our guests this evening. Hattie will help until she's wanted elsewhere.' Mrs Macauley marches us back downstairs as the first guest arrives.

Emmy stands beside the harpsichord as Maria picks out one of her regular tunes, a porcelain doll rather than a living, breathing woman. She doesn't look like my friend any longer. I glance in the mirror that hangs on the wall opposite the fireplace, blinking at my own reflection. My hair is pinned up in a way that it never had been in the country. I press a palm to my stomach, to the place just below where I had first felt the cramps that preceded my bleeding. My outer appearance might look the same but hidden changes have taken place, and it is silly to pretend otherwise. Emmy has accepted that; perhaps it is time for me to do the same.

It is noon the next day before anyone realises that Camille has still not returned home.

'Damned girl,' Mrs Macauley rages. 'How am I supposed to organise an auction tonight when I'm having to worry about that silly little strumpet?'

'You hear all sorts about those parties,' Maria says soothingly as Mrs Macauley throws herself into the armchair, fury radiating off her more powerfully than the heat from the fire. 'The gentlemen, they take special tonics that keep them going all night and into the next day.' Hattie giggles, stifling it as she catches Mrs Macauley's gimlet eye. 'That's why they need a steady supply of harlots, 'cause they wear 'em out and they pass 'em around until they can't walk straight. That's why I was happy to let little Miss High 'n' Mighty get dressed up in her finery and trot along there. She's probably exhausted and sleeping it off.'

'Sounds delightful,' I say, wincing, though I can't deny it gives me a tiny bit of pleasure to imagine Camille's face when she realised what exactly was expected of her. Hardly just dancing with eligible gentlemen as she fantasised about, as if she were a debutante attending her first ball of the season.

'Well, I hope it is worth her – oh!' Mrs Macauley sits up as there is a knock at the front door and we hear the thump of Jakes' feet as he clomps his way up the stone stairs that lead up from the kitchen. 'That had better be her. Who else could it be at this time of day?'

We wait with bated breath.

'Ma'am.' Jakes appears, a poor butler in his heavy leather boots and his ancient rat-tailed wig. 'Madame Vern-yay.'

'Lucy!' The woman rushes in, as immaculately dressed as always, putting the rest of us to shame. She glances around. 'Camille?'

'Not here.' Mrs Macauley gets to her feet. 'What's this about, Gisele? Have you lost my girl?'

'Not lost.' Madame Vernier bites her lip. 'Not lost, I think, but perhaps . . . misplaced.'

'*Misplaced?* What the hell does that mean? You'd better start talking, lady, else I swear you'll have my man to answer to, and he don't have anything against hurting a woman. He's not the chivalrous type.'

My own experiences with Jakes confirm this. Madame Vernier approaches the sofa, and I hurry to make room for her as she almost falls to sitting. 'Would you like a tot of rum?' I suggest.

'You look like you've had an awful shock,' Maria agrees.

'Hattie, go and fetch the bottle and some glasses,' Mrs Macauley orders, Hattie not looking best pleased to be missing out on the obvious gossip.

'Thank you, Lucy, I . . . let me start at the beginning. From last night.' Madame Vernier removes her gloves and settles in for her story.

They had arrived at the party early, having collected two other girls on the way. Camille had been her usual charmless self, marking herself as the belle of the ball, and indeed, Madame Vernier said, she was the prettiest there. Some gentlemen liked to be seen with an unknown girl on their arm, one who wasn't so obviously one of the paid guests, and Camille fitted the bill perfectly. Almost able to be mistaken for one of the ladies of the Quality who had been invited (and apparently there were several who liked to attend such soirées, with their husbands no less). Madame Vernier had warned all of the girls not to get carried away with the champagne and wine, that they may have a little to calm their nerves but that they should keep their wits about them.

'Some of the gentlemen, they lead more sheltered lives,' she explains. 'In the countryside and whatnot. They are suddenly presented with such a selection of girls, all pretty and all available, that they cannot help themselves. They lose all inhibition and forget that there are still rules to be followed.'

Camille, as usual, had known best. Madame Vernier had warned her once more as the great ballroom filled up and the dancing began, and indeed Camille's lessons had paid off. She'd managed to pass off a basic waltz with an army captain and taken another spin with a sugar baron from Antigua before removing from the ballroom on his arm.

'I assumed they had made an arrangement. There were bedrooms made up for the purpose.' Madame Vernier sighs. 'I should have made sure, but she is no novice, after all. I supposed that she could find her way to a bed and would know what to do in it.'

'I'd have done the same,' Mrs Macauley admits, nodding to Hattie to pass around the glasses of rum that she's poured. 'Did you see her after that?'

'There was a minor skirmish between two of the other girls which took me a little time to sort out. When I returned to the ballroom most of the guests had moved on to the gaming tables or gone upstairs. None of my girls were there and I was pleased. I assumed that Camille was in demand. It was only later, when the last of the carriages was leaving and the other girls had gathered back in the ballroom, that I realised that she was missing. I checked every bedroom. No sign of her.' She knocks back her rum. 'I asked around and discovered that one of the footmen had seen her leave on the arm of a masked gentleman.'

'She left the ball?' Mrs Macauley looks livid. 'What time was this?'

'The footman said it was just before midnight.' Madame Vernier is pale.

'And what time did you discover that she had gone missing?'

'Ah.' Madame Vernier looks away. 'It was still dark outside but . . . it must have been six o'clock this morning. That's when the duke ordered the last stragglers to leave.'

There was a long silence. 'Six o'clock?' Mrs Macauley asks finally.

It seems unbelievable that the sensible, sophisticated Madame Vernier could have made such a bad mistake. To lose a girl, to lose Camille – hardly the most subtle of all women – is impossible. Her face shows that she knows this, a clear reflection of her humiliation, and she can barely bring herself to look at any of us. She is a different woman from the one whose carriage I sat in just a few days ago. How can she have lost Camille?

'These balls, you don't know what it's like. It's so crowded, you go all evening without seeing the same person twice. You don't understand. I saw her go upstairs. Doing the job I'd paid her to do.'

'You paid her already?' Mrs Macauley looks aghast. 'Surely not?'

'Not I. But I showed the girls their wages before locking

it away in the carriage. They were to collect their money on leaving at the end of the night. I left my footman in charge. Camille told him that I had given permission for her to collect her earnings as she was about to go on to a private engagement with a gentleman. I admit, it isn't usual, but neither would it have been out of the question for me to agree to something like this.'

'And he didn't even think to make sure? To come in and hear it from the horse's mouth as it were?'

'He couldn't leave the carriage, not with the money sitting there.' Madame Vernier lets Hattie fill her glass once more, sipping at the contents this time. 'I'm sorry. This has never happened to me before. Usually, the girls are so grateful to have been chosen, they don't want to misbehave. They all hope that I'll choose them again. And I do, those of them who do well and who are requested. It is odd, is it not? I hadn't thought her a flighty girl. It is why I chose her.'

There is truth to what Madame Vernier says. Camille is lazy. For all that she talks about moving to a higher-class seraglio or taking her own rooms, life is easy for her at Little Wild Street. She chooses her own clients and charges them more than almost any girl in the Garden. She has someone to empty her chamber pot and take care of her laundry. A good life, compared to so many others. Camille is annoying and arrogant, and her pride deserves a fall, but she isn't a thief. I see Maria and Hattie exchange a look and know that they are thinking the same. The money that Madame Vernier offered wasn't enough to carve a new life for herself, even with Mrs Macauley's cut added in. Something must have happened to her.

'Thieving little cunt,' Mrs Macauley decides, her lip curling as she pronounced the 'c', and I hear Emmy gasp. It is the first time I've heard her mother lose her composure. 'When I get my hands on her . . . Who was this gent? D'you know him?'

'I confess, no. I asked anyone who had seen him, but he wore a mask, as did so many at the ball. Whatever his identity, he was trying to hide it. I only wonder — perhaps Camille discovered who he was. Perhaps . . . '

I catch Maria's eye. Surely it can't be. That Camille of all people has gone off with a real-life prince.

'Don't be ridiculous. Royalty wouldn't fall for Camille's lies. She'd have been had for a whoreish farm girl from the Welsh valleys before the sun was up.' Mrs Macauley's mind is made up. 'No, she's run off with your money is what she's done. She's done nothing but complain and make trouble these last few weeks and this is her farewell.' She gets to her feet wearily. 'She can go to hell if she thinks she's not replaceable. Emmy, you take Camille's room. It's time we held your auction. Tomorrow evening, as planned. Jakes!'

Her man appears in a matter of seconds, and she issues him with her instructions. Five gentlemen to be invited to bid upon Emmy at nine o'clock tomorrow evening. Starting bids to be no lower than twenty guineas. The promise of other available but less virginal girls for the losers.

'Excuse me, ma'am,' Maria interrupts. 'I never went to school, but I can do a simple sum, and I count four gents left over and only Hattie and me available since Sukey has her arrangement still in place.'

'And you cannot break that arrangement. Mr Drake will not pay for the girl when she might have picked up disease.' Madame Vernier has regained her composure, the rum dampening her guilt.

I can see from Mrs Macauley's face that she had hoped to get around this condition in the agreement and am once more grateful for Madame Vernier's intervention.

'You can double up, can't you? We know that Sir Horace will be one of the losers and for his few shillings he can't expect much more than a quick shake of his wig. No, since my Emmy will be the centre of attention, we can distract them easily. I'll have two rounds of bidding, two losers in each. Sukey can sing a little to earn her keep and we'll serve up plenty of punch and wine.'

Maria and Hattie look less than thrilled but I feel nothing but a huge sense of relief. Madame Vernier leaves us, Mrs Macauley goes upstairs, and we are left to speculate over what has become of Camille.

'It must be the Piper,' Hattie says, adamant in her belief. Of all of us, she knows the most about his so-called activities. She is Covent Garden born and bred and knows every missing girl, even if just by sight.

'At such an exclusive party?' I am less convinced. 'How would he secure an invitation?'

'He takes harlots and where else can you guarantee the best.' Hattie's logic is sound. 'Remember that no one knows who he is. There's no reason why he couldn't be a wealthy gentleman. He must take the girls away from Covent Garden. Where better than a big house in Mayfair or the like where nobody would think to look for them.'

It is sobering to think that one of us could be swooped upon so easily and I cannot help but fear for Camille, despite our many differences. We continue to discuss the possibilities and arrive at no conclusion as to whether the Piper is responsible. Our knowledge is limited where his shadowy figure is concerned. No one has ever seen him, not unless you believe he is truly a giant of a man. Hattie makes a good point. A gentleman of the quality would make the perfect Piper. Someone beyond suspicion. Someone who a girl like Camille might trust.

✳ FEBRUARY 1766 ✳

Beatrice Brooks, Pall Mall, St James's

A beauty so freshly arrived in London that there is not much to be said of her, but that her looks and deportment mark her out as the highest of her league. Fine-figured and well-spoken, it is said that a certain duke has her in his sights. Expect her to be in keeping before long.

12

The sense of déjà vu is overwhelming as we gather in the parlour for a second auction in as many months. Emmy has fixed a smile to her face, but its rictus quality gives away her fears.

'It will be all right,' I had said to her earlier, sitting on her bed – the bed that had been Camille's and, for a little while, also mine. Emmy hadn't dared to sit down once she'd been laced tightly into her gown, one of Camille's that had been altered to fit. An almost new gown, which should have been another clue that Camille hadn't just run off, though no one else agreed with me. She'd never have left so many pretty gowns behind, not unless she really had snared a prince. I said this, without thinking.

'You say that, but didn't you run away without thinking of the consequences?' Emmy snapped.

'And I was wrong to.' If I don't exactly feel lucky now, I do appreciate that things could be so much worse. I don't know what Jonathan did, but there is nothing that could justify what his master did to him. For all her faults, I know that Mrs Macauley would never hurt me that way. And if the Piper is real then I have also managed to evade his gaze. 'Or at least, I know now that there is nothing else for it, not unless you are happy to end up begging on the streets. We have no trade, no skills or family business. What else is there? Marriage? And to whom? A drunk like Sir Horace who is constantly down to his last few shillings?'

Her smile tightened. 'Oh, I know this, Sukey. I always did. It doesn't make it any easier though.'

'I know.' I hugged her, feeling her body stiffen then melt against mine. 'Love, I know. But Sir Horace cannot afford you, and the other gents, they sound much better.' The image of Tobias Kellett reared up in my mind, but I pushed him firmly aside.

'If I end up with Mr Kellett, I think I might faint,' Emmy murmured in my ear, her arms around my waist. It was the closest we'd been since the night of my own auction.

'You are stronger than you know,' I said, kissing her cheek. 'And whoever he is it'll likely be over in a few minutes. The pain is not so bad, no worse than a bad graze. The best advice I took was to have a cup or two to drink beforehand. I think you told me that. It makes it all better.'

'All better?' She laughed and rested her forehead against mine. 'And you trusted me, even though I couldn't possibly know? Maybe I should have run away with you. My sense of direction is better than yours and I would have taken us far away, to the streets where Jakes doesn't know his way like he does around the city.'

'I walked straight into his manor,' I admitted ruefully, though in fact I was now glad about the way events had unfolded. I was glad that I had run, for Jonathan's sake, but I was also glad to be back with Emmy and to have been matched with Jonas, though I was trying not to think too much about him. Two more days until our agreement was at an end, with still no guarantee that he would extend it. 'You mustn't be afraid, Emmy. What will be will be and whatever happens we have each other.'

I was talking to myself as much as to her.

It is inevitable. We all know it, our fears confirmed on his arrival. Tobias Kellett walks in looking every inch the wealthy merchant he is. A richly embroidered waistcoat, shoes so polished they are like mirrors. A bag of coins that he produces from an inside pocket and throws so casually onto the table before him as he takes his seat. Sir Horace starts his grumbling immediately and the other three gents, three young men, all of them sons of better men, who went to school together and think themselves worldly to brave the slums of Covent Garden, share glum looks. They have money, yes, but not the sort of money they'd be willing to fritter away on a pale slip of a girl like Emmy Macauley. Somehow, within the confines of Camille's fine gown, she looks smaller and younger than usual. A porcelain doll who might shatter if a strong gust of wind blows. She stares blankly ahead of her, resigned to her fate. The Emmy who tried to help me not so long ago, who had spoken words of common sense and made this profession of ours seem so every day, has disappeared at the worst possible moment.

I serve drinks as the first round of bidding commences, Sir Horace and one of the young men bowing out after not being able to produce more than the minimum twenty guineas apiece. Maria and Hattie tossed a coin of their own earlier and it is Maria who leads Sir Horace away, her face a perfectly composed picture of beatification.

'What about the mulatto?' one of the boys asks. 'I'd make do with her. I've never had a Black before. She must be worth less than ten guineas!'

I have Madame Vernier to thank for reminding my guardian so recently that I am beholden to another. 'She's in keeping to another, I'm afraid. At least until Monday.' Mrs Macauley does not look happy.

'Drake?' Tobias Kellett puts his pipe to his lips and regards me through narrowed eyes. 'Foolish boy. I haven't seen him recently though. I had heard he'd gone up to Lincolnshire to get married.'

I freeze where I stand, half bent over as I ladle punch into cups. Married? No. Kellett is lying. He must be. 'He is on business, sir. In Lincolnshire, as you say.'

'Business?' Kellett chuckles. 'I suppose that is one way of looking at it. His betrothed has the land that his father wanted to get his hands on so in that regard I would say it is an excellent business deal indeed. But I wouldn't hold much hope in seeing him again by Monday. He'll have a new house to get used to, a wife to bed and break in. She's a handsome woman they say. And she can trace her family tree back three centuries. Drake Senior is hoping that her father can help him into a seat in the Lords.'

It can't be true, can it? I don't mean the marriage itself; I am under no illusions there. Whatever my hopes for Jonas, I know a man like him couldn't marry a girl like me. Not only a harlot but a mulatto. But he would have told me. We have talked about such intimate matters. He told me about his childhood, about his family's house on the plantation, about how his so-called equals in London look down upon him for being too 'native'. He would have told me about something so important. But why would Kellett lie? He has no interest in me, no reason to go out of his way to upset me.

I pass around the cups and avert my gaze from Kellett's, knowing that my cheeks are burning and my eyes damp with tears. It's lucky that no one pays me any attention. Mrs Macauley is keen to get on with the auction and I know that the last thing Emmy needs is to see me being upset when she has the almost certain fate of being handed over to Tobias Kellett. When I'm able to, I flee to the kitchen with the excuse of mixing more punch.

Cook has her feet up before the fire, a mug of hot milk in hand, though there's probably at least one tot of rum in it. She glances at the empty punch bowl. 'Thirsty tonight, ain't they?'

I nod, unable to speak past the lump in my throat, and busy myself with the punch making, my tears adding to the brew.

'It's not so bad as all that, surely?' Cook is smiling when I look up. 'You girls, you lurch from one disaster to another and never realise how good you've got it.'

'Good? What's so good about it?' I demand. 'Having to stand there and smile and sing for those disgusting men? And the one gentleman I thought was decent has left me to go and get married. He won't be thinking of me anymore. Not when he has a pretty wife and a big house in the country. Come Monday, I'll be lining up with the rest of them in there, ready for some sweaty old man to hand over a couple of damp coins to put his hands all over me.'

Cook laughs so hard she almost chokes on the smoke from her pipe, slapping her knees in mirth. 'Oh girl, that tickles me that does. Tickles me no end.'

'It's not funny!' I retort.

'Yes. Yes, it is, you just don't know it yet.' She calms herself down, seeing how upset I am. 'You ain't got nothing to worry about. Oh love, where d'you think all the money came from for the fancy wallpaper on them walls, or that silver bowl you're pouring cheap rum into? Married men. A bawdy house without them would fail within weeks. It's the wives who drive them into the arms of a pretty little thing like you. You ain't goin' to nag them, you ain't goin' to refuse to spread your legs or blush when he asks you for something less usual. You'll pour him his punch and his wine, listen to his boring tales from the coffee house and speak when you're spoken to. All for a few gold coins. If your gentleman isn't running here as soon as he arrives back in London, then my name ain't Nan Carpenter.'

'I didn't know that was your name.' I smile and wipe the tears from my cheeks with the heels of my hands.

''Course you didn't.' She shakes her head as she gets to her feet. 'You girls, you're only interested in what's happening to you. You forget to raise your eyes and look around at what else is going on.'

Drawing me into a warm embrace, she smells of tobacco and bread, a combination that makes me feel safer than I have for weeks, a hug of true comfort.

I have not received many such embraces in my life. The Ashleys weren't great advocates of physical contact in any regard; I couldn't even remember the Reverend Ashley kissing his wife on the cheek, though they had been very close in their opinions on all things. I had grown up alongside Emmy, our childhood spent sharing a tiny cot in the smallest room in the Ashley's house, but even then, there had always been an anxious thought, the unspoken fear that one day we might be ripped apart. That Betsy Ashley would get fed up with feeding and clothing a mulatto brat who wasn't even her own blood and pack me off on an apprenticeship. That the day might arrive when Mrs Macauley would stop making her regular payments to cover my costs. That even though the Ashleys were people of God, that there was only so far that their charity could spread.

I realise now that as adamant as I have been about not calling this house home, there is no place on earth where I can find more people who care about me. I am luckier than I thought.

I am glad that when I return to the parlour, the deal is done. Kellett has already whisked Emmy upstairs and even Mrs Macauley looks a little out of sorts. She is worried for her daughter, but not enough to stop her from suffering. All I hope is that Kellett may not be as cruel as I fear. I toss and turn that night, alone in the garret room while Emmy does her duty. I give up on sleep long before dawn, staring uselessly up at the cracked ceiling as I bundle the bedclothes around me and listen out in vain for any sound, any indication that the house is beginning to wake.

I must have dozed off in the end for it is Emmy herself who nudges me awake, climbing silently over me, then wrestling for a blanket. I can smell sweat and something masculine lingering on her skin. I lie there for a moment, her body heat welcome, her breath warm on the back of my neck.

'How was it?' I ask.

I hear the catch in her throat. 'It . . . it was not . . . Not what I expected.'

I turn to face her in the darkness, the whites of her eyes sparkling. I put a hand gently to her cheek and brush tears away with my fingers. 'It's done now, that's all that matters.'

'Mother will be pleased about that at least.' Her laugh is

brittle, not like Emmy at all. 'And I don't think that Mr Kellett will be requesting an evening with me again. I don't think I was up to his expectations.'

'His expectations?' I sit up, indignant.

'He said that I was too skinny. That my gown must have been altered because my bosom had looked fuller when I was dressed, and that he wouldn't have spent so much money if he'd realised just how useless I would be.' She sniffs away more tears. 'He left as soon as it was done and told me he'd be asking for a reduced rate because I had been poor value and not what had been promised.'

'How dare he! All that was promised was given. He paid for innocence and that's what he got.' I think back to my time with Jonas and wonder if he too had felt duped over my lack of carnal knowledge. 'Stupid man.' There is more that I want to say but Emmy throws her arms around me and knocks the breath from my lungs. I let her sob, soaking my shoulder as she bawls.

'Thank you for being kind,' she says when finally she lets me go, a sheepish smile on her face. 'I know I have been stand-offish with you in recent days and I'm sorry. I hope that Mama thinks the same as you. I just wanted her to be proud of me.'

'He won't get his money back,' I tell her, no doubt in my mind about that, though the reason has nothing to do with Mrs Macauley being proud of her daughter or otherwise. The sum will already be balanced in the books, though Emmy doesn't have an entry in the debt ledger like the rest of us: the benefit of being heiress to this tiny dynasty. 'And look how fortunate you are! If Mr Kellett does not wish to pay for your company again then you are luckier than the rest of us who must cross our fingers and hope that he ceases to frequent this house.'

'He is not a nice man,' she confirms. 'There was something . . . I was glad that Jakes was just downstairs, let me say that for once.'

'I never thought we'd be grateful for Jakes.' I try to make light of it, but later as we dress, I see marks on her hips, from where Kellett had held her down.

I hope that now, since he claimed to have found the goods lacking, he will just quietly slink away, never to be seen or heard of again at Little Wild Street. Although unexpectedly, at breakfast, Mrs Macauley is full of smiles and praise for her daughter, with not a word about Kellett apart from the amount of gold coins he has left in her possession. Perhaps he didn't speak against Emmy after all. Maybe it was just part of his spiteful character, to terrify a young girl into submission. Whatever happened, I am glad to see Emmy's mood brighten, followed by my own not much later as there's a heavy knock at the door, Jakes swearing as he has to put down his mug of ale to answer it.

'It might be Camille,' Hattie says, both her and Maria looking to the doorway in hope.

'For her sake I hope it ain't,' Mrs Macauley growls. 'I don't want to hear that useless thief's name uttered again under my roof, d'you hear?'

Jakes reappears a few minutes later without Camille but with an envelope, handing it directly to Mrs Macauley before tucking back into his plate of bread and ham.

Mrs Macauley breaks the seal and retrieves a short letter, perusing its contents silently before looking in my direction. 'Good news, Sukey,' she says. 'Mr Drake sends his regards and informs me that he has arrived safely back in London. He'll be paying us a visit this evening.'

My heart thuds loudly and it's astonishing that no one else

seems to hear it. It isn't that I doubted Jonas so much as that everyone else had given so many reasons for him not to return to me that I had become half reconciled to my fate. Will he tell me the truth about where he'd been? Do I have any right to demand it? I know that I don't. Our relationship is financial and physical, not emotional.

'That's wonderful news, Sukey.' Emmy beams across the table at me, and my heart breaks for her. 'I'm so happy for you.'

'It is good news indeed,' Mrs Macauley agrees, though she watches me pensively, as though she had hoped for a different outcome. 'I shall speak with him first, of course. It's important we know whether he means to keep you or if this is just a whim of his.'

Emmy winks at me just as the sun comes out, the kitchen filling with its light as though it is blessing us all. I should be over the moon at my own good fortune, but I can't help dwelling on her fate. What will her mother do if she cannot please her next customer? Mrs Macauley protects her investments – her girls – but only as long as they can bring her happy customers and shiny coin. I think that even she will be kinder to her own daughter, and I hope that I am right.

13

Camille's room is once again mine and I am sent up there to wait while Jonas has his discussions with Mrs Macauley in the parlour. I had asked to be present, but she just laughed in my face. 'You're like a lovesick kitten,' she'd said. 'One look at your face and he'll name a low price for you. A man doesn't like to pay for something he could have for free.'

It isn't true, though. I'm not in love, not at all. I am relieved to have Jonas back and I like him well enough. He is pleasant to look at and courteous. Besides, I already know about his new wife. It isn't as though I have any silly ideas about him and our future together – I know there isn't one. Not in the traditional manner, at least. Whores don't marry the gents who pay for their time. Growing older together, perhaps having the perfect children who would grow up in a loving home where they could be anything they wanted, I know perfectly well that none of that is possible.

I drink some wine while I wait, poking the fire to stay warm. The weather outside is still bitter and the room is taking some time to warm up. To distract from my boredom, I decide to poke around in Camille's belongings. Mrs Macauley has already voiced her intention to box the whole lot up to either sell or, for those items without an obvious monetary value, for use as fuel on the kitchen fire. Accordingly, there seems no harm in satisfying my own curiosity.

I begin with her coveted gowns. Maria had told me that Camille asked her regular gents to only pay Mrs Macauley for basic services. Behind her closed bedchamber door, Camille would then fulfil whatever fantasy the customer had, from the mundane to the outlandish, the rest of her payment to be made up in gifts such as these, of which the bawd could not take her cut. Neither could she confiscate the gowns since Mr Such-and-Such and Sir Thingumabob would surely want to see their gifts being worn on their visits. It is a mystery to me how Camille lasted so long at the top of the tree when she had been so unwilling to play by the rules. Or why she has thrown it all away so easily.

I hold a fine scarlet gown up against my body, turning this way and that before the dressing table mirror. It would suit me very well and I determine to ask Mrs Macauley if I might have it. For a fee, of course, or perhaps I can follow Camille's example and ask Jonas to purchase it for me. Emmy could help me with the alterations, for I am a few inches shorter than Camille.

I move on to the drawers of the clothes press. Stockings of silk and wool, folded neatly, and something else: a wooden case. Hoping for jewels, I slide it out, carrying it over to the bed, one ear listening out for footsteps on the stairs.

The box is fastened with a simple clasp but inside, rather than jewels or the like, I find something that makes my jaw drop. A fat stash of banknotes. A fortune by most people's standards. Beneath it sits a pile of letters, fastened together with a blue silk ribbon. It is then that I hear Mrs Macauley's voice and just have time to shut the box and put it back in its hiding place, diving to the armchair beside the fire as the bedroom door opens and a smiling Jonas is there, Mrs Macauley at his heels.

'Jonas!' I scramble to my feet. 'Mr Drake, sir.' I bob a little curtsey as Mrs Macauley raises an eyebrow at my initial informal greeting. 'It is a pleasure to see you again.'

'The pleasure is all mine.' He bows and turns to Mrs Macauley. 'I would be most grateful if you could have some refreshments sent up. As I mentioned, I have barely had chance to eat in my haste to call upon dear Sukey.'

It is a struggle to keep the smirk from my lips as I see the look on her face. Not many men talk to Mrs Macauley as though she were a lowly servant. 'I'll send one of the girls up shortly.'

She disappears and Jonas settles himself before the fire. I take up my usual position, helping him to remove his boots and waiting for him to speak.

'Oh, I have missed this,' he says with a groan as I knead the cold from his feet. 'It is good to be back in London. Lincolnshire may improve once it emerges from winter, but for now I must say it has little to recommend it.'

I remember what Tobias Kellett said. About Jonas's real motives for leaving London. 'Your business there went well, sir?'

'It did, Sukey. It did. My father will be pleased with what I achieved.' He snorts a dry laugh. 'For once.'

'That is good news indeed, sir.' I wait for his correction, to desist with the 'sirs' and call him Jonas, but it has been twice now and no word from him. I feel an unwelcome niggle in my stomach as my worries return. 'Your conversation with Mrs Macauley went well?' I feel the tension return to his body and sit back on my heels. 'Sorry, sir, it is none of my business.'

He looks down at me, his face pale with fatigue. 'Of course it is, Sukey. Don't be a dolt. I am just . . . it has been a long few days and a tiring journey back to the city. Forgive me if I'm in strange humour. I must say that your Mrs Macauley is particularly tiresome today.'

'She can be,' I agree.

'Trying to make demands of me,' he complains. 'Well, I said to her, she needs to have patience. I have barely been in the country more than a few weeks. My head quite spins with everything that I have to do, everything that is expected of me.' He leans forward, hooking his arms beneath mine and pulling me up to sit on his lap. 'This place, with you, it is the only place where I feel I can be myself. You alone do not judge me. You alone do not care about my family history or have expectations of me. I have spent the long coach journey dreaming of this moment, here with you.' His hand fights fabric to make its way beneath my skirt. 'You are the only person in my life who makes no demands, Jenny. You let me be whoever I want to be.'

Jenny? I hold my breath and wait for him to correct himself but that does not happen. Is Jenny his new wife? I dare not make a liar of him by asking why he does not tell me the truth. Instead, I simply allow him to flatter me, to undress me, to give me orders that I carry out without question. What Jonas really thinks about as we writhe and sweat on the bed is beyond me. All I must consider is that I have him and must keep him. He is my security. The man who can save me from both my debts and from the riffraff who find their way to our parlour. If Madame Vernier is correct, then one day soon, I might leave Little Wild Street and move to a place where, with Jonas's support, I will be my own mistress. And isn't that even better than being a wife? He might like that I make no demands but soon I must find the courage to press him further. Without him, I will be left with nothing.

We lie in bed late the next morning, like ordinary lovers do. It is a changed experience from our first few nights together and I hope it bodes well for my future with him. His enthusiasm, if anything has grown during our separation, and I think briefly of his bride. That he won't talk of her can be taken in any number of ways. It is a risk, but I decide to bring up the subject. You cannot expect an answer without asking first a question.

'How do you like being back in the capital?' I start, hoping that he might just come out and admit the real reason for his absence.

'Oh, it is what it is.' He stares up at the canopy of the bed, frowning. 'Perhaps one day I'll become used to the noise. It's never silent here, have you noticed? Even in the dead of night, such an infernal racket!'

'It's the same where I'm from, so I understand what a shock it is,' I told him. 'I have never been north, but I suppose it to be not so different from Lincolnshire. Madame Vernier told me that you—'

'Gisele should not be gossiping,' he snaps, then takes my hand in apology for his bad humour. 'Sorry, my sweet. I just – it is complicated. My reasons for going there . . . ' I wait and wonder if he will finally tell me the truth. 'A cousin of ours was keeping the house for us but he fell victim to a fever last year. Partly that is why I came back to England. My father hates the voyage. He'd far rather sit overlooking his land in Barbados drinking rum on the veranda. He has quite renounced the civilised life of an Englishman.' He sighs and pulls me against his chest, his chin resting on my head. 'I thought that I should be a good son and volunteer myself for the task. And if I were to truly be a good . . . ' His heart beats fast against my cheek as he gathers his words. 'Sukey, would you think badly of me if I told you that I am not a bachelor? That is, I was when we met but no longer.'

'You are now married?' I whisper, trying to sound surprised. 'That is why you went away.'

'Yes.' He kisses my forehead. 'Yes, but I promise you it's – I think of it as a business transaction. She feels the same; I would not have married her otherwise. She gains her freedom, away from a father who is over-protective and miserly. Her dowry gives me the funds to repair our estate to its former glory. Don't mistake me, I hope she will bear me an heir. She has made every effort to perform that duty, and I pray that God will bless us, but she is reconciled with me living in London for long periods. My London house will be kept ready for her, whenever she needs it, but our arrangement I plan to honour.' I try to smile but it is too difficult, and I see him frown. 'Sukey, you do know that if I had any choice, it would be you by my side. In public, not just hidden away like this.'

'Then I consider myself doubly lucky,' I say, 'that you have chosen me to be your wife in all but name.'

'I do not deserve you, Sukey, truly I don't. My own little wild savage.' He kisses my hand, and I try hard not to mind about his choice of words. 'We will have so much fun, I promise you.'

After Jonas's departure, I wash and dress quickly, eager to catch up with Mrs Macauley and find out what she and Jonas spoke about. I have one hand on the doorknob, ready to leave the room, when I remember Camille's box and its mysterious contents and turn back. I count the bank notes first, fifteen of them in total, each valued at twenty pounds. They seem genuine enough to me, though I am hardly familiar with currency of such value. A treasure by any standards. Why would Camille run away and leave this behind? It doesn't make sense. Although I hardly want to consider it, the Piper springs into my mind once more as a valid reason for her disappearance.

I turn my attention to the letters. There are twenty-three in the bundle, the earliest dating back to the previous September. The handwriting is neat and uniform, the words full of overwrought sentiment and emotion. A waste of time since Camille can't read, but then I suppose she might appreciate the artistry of each page. They are love letters, from a lad who signs off his missives with the letter W. I read each of them — none is over two pages long — and while I glean no clues as to his identity, I do gain a new understanding of what a man might like in the bedchamber, for the author does not restrain himself from describing what he loves most about Camille and what he wishes from their next meetings. I quite blush to read some of the passages, even after carrying out similar activities the night before. But who is this mysterious W? Not a visitor to Little Wild Street, for his scenarios take place elsewhere, in a tiny, rented room or a snatched moment in his place of work, wherever that is. He refers to her 'slipping away from her prison' and promises that one day he will rescue her. Someone must have read these to Camille. But who around Covent Garden had such skills at handwriting, even amongst the few that could write? A paid scribe, I decide. There would be a few around, more than likely, if I ask someone who knows the area better than I.

I replace everything where I found it and go down to the kitchen where the rest of the household are lingering as usual, all except Mrs Macauley and Jakes. I'm starving, but I decide to begin my investigations promptly before anyone can leave. Hattie and Maria are my suspects. I know that both had some basic schooling and may have deciphered W's messages for Camille.

'Coffee, love?' Cook asks, plodding around the table with the pot in hand.

'Please.' I add sugar while I wait for Maria to finish her tale of the previous night's customers, one of whom is still passed out upstairs, awaiting a rude awakening from Jakes and a hefty bill for the wine.

'So, what did Jonas have to say?' Emmy asks me. Her question implies more curiosity than the flat tone of her voice. She is trying to be happy for me.

'Not much,' I tell her. 'I think he was glad to return to London. He said that Lincolnshire is not for him.'

'Oh, imagine if you can hook him good and proper. A keeper, Su! You've landed right on your feet there. He's a handsome chap as well, in't he?' Hattie grins. 'If only we all could be as lucky. You'd better keep your eye on him or else I'll be straight after him.'

She doesn't mean anything bad by it, I know, but still, I feel a nagging pull at my stomach. Fear, or something close to it. And guilt. Because I still have the nerve to think myself above Hattie and the others. I don't think I could do what they do, taking coins from whoever offers. I just couldn't. Without Jonas, I don't know what would become of me.

'I am very lucky,' I agree, then change the subject quickly. 'And I was wondering. I'd like to write a letter, to share news of my good fortune with someone who helped me once. Is there anyone around here who can do that for me? A scribe?'

Emmy looks at me confused. 'But you can write well, Sukey. You used to teach the younger children at the church school.'

'Yes, only my handwriting is almost illegible. The person I wish to write to, I want to make a good impression.' I try to send Emmy a message with my eyes, to shut her gob and let Maria or Hattie give me the answer I was looking for.

'The bookshop,' Maria says. 'On the corner of Drury Lane there's a little shop which looks like nothing much at all because the windows are so filthy but if you go inside, you'll see them all, books piled up and on shelves from the floor to the ceiling.'

'A bookshop?' I try to think where she means. 'And the owner, he scribes for people?'

'His son does a bit of writing himself,' Hattie tells me. 'Pamphlets for those who want to spread a message. Political stuff that he's been in trouble for before. And he writes the odd story. You know – tales about poor maids from the country and how they are ruined by the young city men. Full of stallions and love engines and heaving bosoms.'

'Filth,' Maria clarifies. 'Absolute filth he writes, I recommend it highly. But he's a friendly enough sort. He's been known to pop in here from time to time when he's sold a few of his little books. Caleb his name is. Corner of Drury Lane. He has a lovely hand, I have to say. In more ways than one.'

'And that's not all that's lovely about him, so I hear.' Hattie cackles. 'He always used to ask for Camille – I reckon that's how she repaid him for his services – but perhaps now one of the rest of us'll get a look in.'

Caleb at the bookshop. So, Maria and Hattie both know

him and he is a likely candidate for the actual writer, especially bearing in mind the explicit nature of the letters. But then who is W?

'I suppose that in Camille's absence there will be more than one disappointed customer,' I say, reaching for a hunk of bread and trying to look less than interested. 'Anyone that you've got your eye on, Hattie?'

'Me?' She pulls a face. 'As if I get to choose! I ain't fussy, Su, you know me. I do my job and take my payment. I'm happy with that. It's easy and I don't have washerwoman's hands like my old ma. What else do I need?'

'Hattie don't even have any debt,' Maria informs me. 'She paid up to Mrs M last year and still she's here.'

'Where else would I go?' Hattie retorts. 'It ain't like I got a lad waiting to marry me, not like Cam—' She stops suddenly. 'You know what I mean. There's nothing better out there. Anyway, I like it here. Food on the table, no husband to knock me about. This is an easy life.'

'What were you about to say about Camille?' It is Emmy who speaks, even quicker than I am to pick up on Hattie's slip. 'Did she have a beau? A real one, I mean, not one who paid. Was it this Caleb?'

Maria rolls her eyes as Hattie looks to her for help. 'Not Caleb. Will. The son of Mr Hobbs over on the Strand. It was just a dalliance if you ask me. The lad has no money to speak of, though he will inherit his father's business.'

Hobbs owns a haberdashery of middling reputation. He provides fabrics of a decent quality for a reasonable price, hence why he is popular with customers of our ilk, the courtesans and whores of means being unfailingly loyal to a man who doesn't scorn them or inflate his prices. Camille is, or was, a regular patron; she has an addiction to pretty gowns and talent with a needle. Perhaps she was also addicted to the haberdasher's handsome son. Perhaps he knows where she's gone.

'She wouldn't have done anything daft then. Like marry him?' I say it lightly, as if I'm not overly curious even though I'm dying to drag Emmy upstairs and show her the letters.

Hattie bites her lip. 'She said that if she married anyone it would be him. But then she wasn't the marrying kind, I don't suppose. She's no shopkeeper's wife, is she, our Camille?'

No. Camille de la Croix absolutely isn't a shopkeeper's wife. But what about Cerys, the real girl behind the fancy dresses and haughty persona? The life of a harlot is based upon fortune after all, and eventually even good luck can run out. The existence of Will Hobbs, his letters and the stash of bank notes suggests that Camille was planning to exit this life for a new one as a married woman as soon as she felt that her star had waned. Why then would she throw it all away for a man she had just met? Even if that man is the mysterious Piper, by all accounts she chose to go with him. Unless she had expected that she would be allowed to return. The longer she is gone, the more I fear that something truly awful has befallen Camille.

14

'Camille must have gone mad,' Emmy speaks my thoughts aloud as we wait in the salon that evening, I for Jonas who is due to arrive any moment, she for the chance to be shown off to whichever gentleman arrives to seek pleasure, her mother still hoping beyond hope that she can secure her daughter to a gentleman of standing. I have told her of everything that I found in Camille's room and she is as mystified as I.

'I know,' I reply, one eye on Hattie and Maria. The older girls have already made it clear that they are well rid of their rival. Not in a nasty way, of course, but I know that they won't be drawn into the mystery of Camille's disappearance. 'We should go and see this Will Hobbs. Would you come with me?'

'We should talk to him,' she agrees, 'but he won't know who the masked man is. We need to find someone who was at the ball.'

'Madame Vernier.' Obviously. But she told us what she knew, and she didn't know who the man was. She hadn't even seen him, I remember. She'd only been told about him. 'I wonder. There must have been a list of invited guests to the ball. They don't just let anyone attend.'

'Would Jonas know?' Emmy looks at me. 'You should ask him.'

'He was in Lincolnshire,' I remind her.

'Yes, but he is of that circle, isn't he? He knows Madame Vernier, after all. And Tobias Kellett.'

'That doesn't mean anything.' I feel myself grow defensive. It seems traitorous even mentioning Jonas's name in the same conversation as the nefarious Kellett. And as if he knows that we are discussing him, I hear his distinctive knock at the front door.

'Of course not! All I'm saying is that these people all know one another and one of them must know the man who took Camille. And maybe it is the Piper, for where better for him to hide in plain sight than a masked ball?'

It makes me shiver, the idea that this mythical man might actually be real and walking amongst us. Perhaps even visiting our own home. Bad enough when he was a spectre lurking on the dark London streets, but at least then you could stay indoors and be safe. If he were able to pass as a gentleman . . . why, then he could be anyone.

'I'll ask Jonas if he knows anything,' I promise. 'In the meantime, don't say a word to anyone. We'll speak to Will tomorrow.'

'And you should send a message to Madame Vernier. Tell her that you need her advice about Jonas. Ask her about the balls. Who goes to them, who decides the guest list, all of that.' Emmy squeezes my hand as Jonas appears in the doorway, his smile reaching from ear to ear. 'Good luck.'

Mrs Macauley is happy to let me accompany Emmy down to the Strand the next day in order to pick out some fabric.

'She is disappointed in me,' Emmy confesses as we walk briskly, the temperature a little higher than in recent days but the wind still bringing a shiver. 'She thinks that I should have bewitched a young gentleman by now. Just as you have.'

'I wouldn't say that I had bewitched Jonas,' I say, laughing to try to keep the bitterness from my voice. 'I think it is simply that we suit one another.'

He called me Jenny again last night, as he thrust between my legs and gasped another woman's name into my neck. She must be the wife. Why else would that name be suddenly on his lips where before it was only mine that he uttered? It is disquieting that he thinks of her when he is within me. But then if she is who he desires, why is he paying to come to me? A wife must provide whatever a husband requires, as I have been given to understand. Is there something wrong with her?

'After you left me last night I started to think,' Emmy says. 'What if it was the Piper who took Camille, and what if we know him?'

'Who could it be?' I don't tell her that I feared the same.

'Someone who would receive an invitation to the ball, but who is also a frequent visitor to Covent Garden. All of the girls are from here. Perhaps Camille knew him and that's why she went with him so easily. And Daisy. She vanished into thin air but what if she simply climbed into someone's carriage?'

The missing girls: Camille, Daisy, the coffee house girl, a couple of others who I didn't know and who were certainly, from what I had heard, not the sort of girl who would attract the attention of a gentleman with enough wealth to have his own carriage. I say as much to Emmy.

'But don't we know more than one person who moves amongst society as though its borders did not apply to them? Tobias Kellett. Sir Horace. Jonas Drake.'

I don't like that she is associating Jonas with the Piper. 'You speak of people who can well afford to pay for a harlot's time. Why steal girls away?' Anyway, everyone knew that Daisy Gardner had every reason in the world to run away from home.

'That I don't know,' she admits.

'Then let us stick to the facts. I cannot speak for what happened to Daisy, but we know that Camille had some sort of relationship with Will Hobbs. We will talk to him and find out if he has heard from her.' I pick up my pace, eager to get out of the cold and away from the direction of Emmy's questioning. 'There still may be a very simple answer for her disappearance.'

Hobbs Haberdashery is a magical place. I have only been once before, a week after Emmy and I had been brought to the capital, but I have dreamed of one day returning with money in my pocket. And indeed, I do have a small purse of coins with me. It seems a shame to waste the visit, but also, I hope that my custom might distract Mr Hobbs Senior from noticing my interest in his son.

'Afternoon, ladies,' says the shopkeeper, a smartly dressed man, his wig a perfectly genteel shade of grey. His waistcoat and cravat are tailored from an eye-catching yellow and navy striped silk, and he wears the finest silk stockings beneath navy breeches. 'Little Wild Street?'

'Well remembered, sir,' I say, giving a small curtsey. 'Our patron, Mrs Macauley, has decided that we should have new gowns for spring. I'm sure you can provide some suitable fabrics, Mr Hobbs.'

'Indeed, miss. Indeed. I have to say, it's been a while since I last saw one of Mrs Macauley's girls in this here establishment. I do hope all is well.'

'Well indeed, sir.' I retrieve my purse, jingling with the coins Jonas gifted to me the night before, as soon as I mentioned wanting a new wardrobe, something fit for our new home. I see the storekeeper's eyes glisten.

'This way, ma'am.'

I follow him to the rack of silks while, from the corner of my eye, I see Emmy collar a young man who is occupied in slicing lengths of linen with the sharpest pair of silver scissors I have ever seen.

'I need something suitable for strolling through the park,' I tell Hobbs.

'Any particular park?'

'Hyde Park. And St James's. I shall shortly be moving to another part of town you see so I cannot rely on what suits for Covent Garden.' I modify my voice to what I think a lady from Mayfair or thereabouts might sound like. If only I can persuade Jonas that this move is necessary.

'Ah.' He nods, understanding me more than I am comfortable with. 'Congratulations, ma'am. In that case, I would suggest this.' He shows me a breath-taking brocade that reminds me a little of Mrs Macauley's elaborate wallpaper. Ivory silk woven with blue and red flowers. 'Some lace for the sleeves and this lighter silk for the petticoat.' He stands back and surveys my body from top to tail, taking my measurements with his eyes. 'It will not be cheap though. This is the finest silk, woven in Spitalfields itself. No imitations.'

'How much?' I demand.

All of the money in my purse as it turns out. Emmy is still deep in discussions with Will and so I make the shopkeeper show me some other options before handing over all of my riches and watching him cut the silk, packaging it neatly for me to carry away. Knowing how easily Jonas handed over the coins makes it less of a wrench to part with it. There will be more where that came from and it will be worth it to see Jonas's face the first time we go walking, arm in arm.

'Will doesn't know much,' Emmy tells me as we walk out past a trio of ladies, real quality rather than our gaudy façade. 'But he's certain that something bad has happened to Camille. He hasn't heard a word and he's been to all the places she used to go to. The taverns and the tea rooms alike. He is distraught. I think he would have wept if his father hadn't been there.'

'Did he say anything about the money?' I ask, impatient.

'Yes. God help either of them if Mama finds out what they were up to.' Emmy shakes her head but looks impressed. 'To stop her from getting her cut, Camille was sending her gents straight to Will. They would pay for whatever they were told, not really paying much attention, and Will would package up something slightly cheaper, folding the leftover coins into the parcel for Camille. I am not sure who would be the more furious if they discovered such a trick: Mama or Mr Hobbs for losing out on his sales. Once they had a proper nest egg, they were going to marry, though they were never agreed on exactly how much they needed.'

Ah, Camille. Poor Will never had a chance, but she was filling her pockets with gold. I could well believe that she'd leave the boy behind without a second thought, but the money?

'What about the bank notes. I didn't find coins.'

'She must have exchanged the coins for the notes. I suppose they're easier to conceal. And there's too much. From what Will was telling me, he thought she'd have about thirty pounds saved by now.'

'Thirty?' My jaw dropped. So even Camille's lover didn't know the extent of what she'd been up to. 'Where the hell did she find the rest?'

'I don't know.' Emmy looks troubled. 'Do you think she stole it?'

'It's possible.' I hadn't realised how crafty Camille could be; evidently neither had Will. 'Or she might have made the money through some other means.'

'Such as?'

'I don't know.' The more we discover about Camille, the more questions I have.

It is worrying, but I find that having this common goal has cheered Emmy up no end, and I care far more about her than I do for Camille. We trudge along in companionable silence, and I feel the warm glow of friendship heat me from within, despite the winter day

'I've missed you,' I say as we turn onto Drury Lane.

'I've not been anywhere!' she says with a grin, but I can tell she knows what I meant. 'Here. There's Dotty Gardner. We should talk to her about her Daisy.'

I am still convinced that Daisy Gardner has run away but I want to maintain this camaraderie. This investigation means something to Emmy. 'I suppose there's no harm in it.'

I doubt that the older woman has ever been a beauty but when I first saw her, just a few months before, she had appeared moderately respectable. She wore dresses that were old but clean, and she had been proud of her business and her daughters. She had been a seamstress by trade and in the past, she might have touted for the business of making a gown out of the fine material I have just purchased. Like so many of us, she has turned to paying her rent by answering the door to gentlemen who have a few guineas spare for a tumble with her or her daughters. Their house isn't like ours, not a bawdy house primarily, but a family home.

Today Mrs Gardner sits on the front step of her house, her skirt trailing in a filthy puddle of God only knows what. Her face has sagged terribly, as if the pride in her family was what previously kept her youthful. Now, she has only one daughter left at home and she, they say, has caught the pox by trying to keep as many gents as possible walking through the door. It has taken only a season, one solitary quarter of a year, for a family of women who had walked these streets with their heads held high, to now being reduced to sitting in the gutter. Even on the busy street people make every effort to stay away from Mrs Gardner, a great swathe of the road left around her in case her misfortune is catching.

'Good afternoon, Mrs Gardner,' Emmy says, trotting gaily up to her target as if it were a glorious afternoon and we were paying a visit to a friend like ladies did.

Mrs Gardner looks up, her expression vacant at first. 'What d'you want?' She is drunk, her words slurring.

I look to Emmy, then rush in. 'We wondered if you'd had any news about Daisy. Your daughter.'

The old crone scowls up at me, her mouth twisting into a sneer. 'I know who me own daughter is, Negress. And what business is it of yours? Who are you anyway?' She struggles to stand up, her body soaked in rum, her clothes drenched in piss judging by the stench that rises up as Emmy lends a hand to get the woman to her feet. I fight the urge to gag, and God knows how Emmy keeps from vomiting, her face practically pressed into the foul fabric of Mrs Gardner's dress as she is hefted upwards.

Emmy takes a step backwards, panting from her exertions. 'I'm Emily, Lucille Macauley's daughter. And this is Sukey. We have met, once upon a time. Last year when we came to live here.'

Mrs Gardner clears her throat and spits into the street, narrowly missing me which I think is a disappointment, judging by the sour look she shoots in my direction. 'Tell that old bitch to keep her hands off my customers. Sneaking round here like thieves! Fuck off! My Daisy might have left me, but my gentlemen are loyal. They wouldn't stoop to the likes of you.' This last jibe she aims in my direction, I notice. 'They got standards.' She sways hard and just manages to catch hold of the door frame. 'My Rose is a good girl. You don't listen to what they say. Filthy gossips the lot of 'em. Filthy, filthy, rotten bastards.'

She dissolves into sobs so violent they shake her body, her dress hanging from her bones as though she is already halfway to becoming a skeleton. Emmy is the one who takes her by the arm, steering her gently inside the house and sending fierce gestures with her head for me to follow them.

If Mrs Gardner herself stinks of piss, then her house smells of something far worse. I can't see that any gentleman in his right mind would set foot in it, even if Rose Gardner were offering to spread her legs with no payment required. It is a small house, crooked and as precarious as its tenant. There are just two rooms downstairs, the back room used as the kitchen though it doesn't appear as though any food has been prepared recently. There is a moulding loaf of bread on the table with a knife beside it. A kettle hangs over the empty hearth. How can anyone stand to live here?

'If you want to help then get us a drink, girl.' Our hostess sinks herself into a chair by the non-existent fire and waves towards a clay jug on the table. Emmy fetches it and pours what smells like rum into a cup, a strange sight of civility in this house that has fallen apart.

'Where is Rose?' I ask. The house is silent, that deep quiet that speaks of neglect and isolation. 'She is still here, isn't she?'

'None of your business.' But the woman can't refrain from glancing upwards, just a tiny movement of her head but it sends a shiver down my spine that I won't understand until a few minutes later when, having left Emmy in the kitchen, I climb the rotten wooden stairs to the floor above.

It has only been a matter of weeks since Daisy Gardner disappeared and yet the destruction of her family home is advanced. Perhaps it had already been in progress, the speed at which Mrs Gardner – Alice, as the priest calls her when he comes to read her the last rites just a few hours later – has declined, being just the last throes of an illness that has festered within the walls of her home for years.

The rotten odour grows stronger as I reach the landing. I should turn back, knowing that nothing good awaits me, but I know that if I go back to the kitchen then Emmy will insist on going herself. The first room is empty, just a straw mattress on the floor marking out where Alice Gardner sleeps. The second room is a different matter.

The door is stiff, the wood swollen so that I have to use my shoulder to push against it and force it open, choking as I find the source of the foul odour. Rose Gardner is not going to save her mother. She is already dead, her body rotting where it lay. Even in this cold weather, the flies have found her and laid their eggs, wiggling offspring now feasting on a young woman who surely did not deserve her fate. The nightmarish vision of her face, covered with sores, the flesh falling away from the bones, will never leave me. Alice Gardner does know her daughter's fate, I realise she has just put that knowledge aside, as easily as some refuse to believe that the earth is not flat.

I gag, tears burning my eyes as I retreat quickly. I feel my stomach turn over and I cannot stop myself from vomiting onto the landing floorboards, gasping back air as I hear Emmy calling my name from below. I wipe my mouth with the back of a hand, holding out the other to warn Emmy as she arrives at the foot of the stairs. I must look a sight, for she steps back immediately, divining what I must have seen.

The whole street comes out to look when Alice runs out into the street screaming. She is hysterical, and then she collapses. It is Emmy who runs to fetch the priest, from the chapel round the corner, as the rest of us look on, ashamed. None of us cared enough to ensure that they had the help that they needed. No one had noticed that Rose had not been seen for days. We have all seen Alice Gardner's suffering and given it a wide berth. We are all guilty. People like us, on the lower rungs of the ladder, we are always standing on the edge of a precipice. Disaster is far easier to come by than fortune, but it is so much easier to ignore that truth. How can any of us live if we acknowledge the cheapness of our lives?

15

Of course, Mrs Macauley blames me for associating her establishment with the Gardners' sorry fate. My fault, even though it was both Emmy and I who sent a message for the magistrate and the priest to attend on Alice Gardner, and to advise them of the death of Rose. I could not care less though. All I can see when I close my eyes are those wriggling maggots, feeding on Rose Gardner's emaciated body. Emmy is quiet as Cook serves dinner and I know she feels the same as I do.

'Any time people gossip about that filthy woman they'll talk about the two of you,' she fumes as we eat around the kitchen table, at least the others do. My appetite is gone, my nose still full of the smell of rotting flesh. 'They'll look at my house and wonder if you caught the clap off that whore of a daughter. And talk they will, you mark my words.'

'They're dead, Mama. And you don't catch the pox from being in the same house as someone. You catch it from being desperate enough to not have a choice,' Emmy retorts and I let her speak for me. We can't both fit into the Coffin, and I don't want to be the one to force Lucy Macauley to make a choice. It's far less likely that she'll punish her own flesh and blood.

'What did she look like?' Hattie hisses in my ear. 'Could you still tell it was Rose? They do say that with the pox your skin comes off in great lumps and your nose sinks into your face. Was that what it was like?'

'Oi!' Cook bellows loudly, making us all jump. 'We'll have none o' that talk in my kitchen. Alice and Rose Gardner was good people. They deserve better than for people to be whispering and making up stories about 'em. Let 'em rest in peace, for God's sake.'

'Cook. Sit down.' Mrs Macauley presses her lips together so that they disappear from her face entirely. 'We both know that Alice had fallen on hard times, but it was her choice to let such sorry specimens of men frequent her house. There's a reason why I'm hard on you girls and it is this: the success of this house relies on us following my rules. You are safe here under my protection. Next time you feel like complaining about it,' here she eyeballs Hattie, 'or running away,' my turn, 'think on Alice Gardner and what she did to her own daughters.'

Cook looks as though she has more to say but knows there is little point. She makes do with bashing around the pots and pans as she washes them up in the sink. Huffing and puffing until Mrs Macauley sighs and leaves the room. I move my untouched food around my plate. Poor Alice. Poor Rose. When had either of them last eaten a proper meal? Or had the gin taken over so thoroughly that food had been the last thought in their heads?

'Should we tell Mama about what we've found out?' Emmy whispers as I pick at a piece of dry bread. 'What if Daisy was took by the same masked gentleman as Camille? The Piper.'

'Daisy wasn't stolen. You heard Alice. She said she left.' I chew on the tough crust, then throw it down onto my plate.

'Everyone thinks that Camille ran away,' Emmy reminds me, 'and we know that's not the case.'

'Well, we don't know it for certain.' I sigh. 'We only know that she had a good reason to stay here, but there could have been an even better reason to leave.' Every morsel of new information that we find confuses me more.

'The money though! So much of it. Only a fool wouldn't come back here for it. We should tell Mama.'

Of course, Emmy wants to give the money to her mother. I think about what Madame Vernier told me, reminding me that Emmy is a Macauley, and I am not. I do not doubt Emmy's loyalty to me but I also know that whether I wish it or not, Mrs Macauley will have those banknotes in her hand before the day is over. And so, it came to pass.

'That'll just about cover her debt,' she muses when we pass the money over, the three of us gathered at the desk in her office as Jakes glowers in the corner. Out comes the ledger. 'At least I shan't have to go to the bother of informing the magistrate.'

'But, Mama, don't you see? Camille didn't run away at all. She wouldn't have earned enough from one night to risk losing this.'

Emmy's eagerness is met by a blank stare. 'My darling, you have a lot to learn about the types of men who frequent these balls. Rich men, with wealth beyond belief. Trust me, Emily, if this mysterious gentleman promised her private apartments in Mayfair with her own servants and a generous allowance, she'd have bitten his hand off. It's every harlot's dream. Three hundred pounds is nothing in comparison.'

We leave the room dejected, Emmy furious. 'You said not one word,' she says to me. 'I felt a little fool in there.'

'It was your idea to take the money and the letters to her,' I remind her. 'I was against it.'

'You are against anything that doesn't concern you directly. All you care about now is yourself. Stupid Jonas Drake and that shrivel-faced Madame Vernier, they're the only people you listen to.'

'That's not true.' I can see Jakes lurking, listening in and no doubt planning to run in and tell Mrs Macauley on us as soon as he has the chance. I think quickly. 'There is one place we haven't been.'

'Where?'

'The scribe. The lad at the bookshop. He knew Camille and he probably wrote those letters that Will sent to her.' I wasn't hopeful that a shop boy could help us but it was something to do. Something to take Emmy's mind off her present troubles. 'It's late now but we can go in the morning.'

'Of course!' Her face lights up. 'Oh, Sukey, what dolts we are. We should have gone there on our way home from visiting Hobbs.'

We may well have had we not been distracted by the tragedy of Mrs Gardner. I do not remind Emmy of this though.

Fowler's Finest Books is indeed only a few doors away from the Gardner house, a nondescript establishment with windows so filthy that I have to squint to see the books on display behind the glass. Not attractive to the casual customer but if what I've heard is correct, this is a bookshop for those who know what they are looking for.

I see Emmy hesitate and so I push open the door, a small bell chiming out to announce our arrival. Inside, the shop is as dim as its murky windows might suggest. A couple of lamps fixed to the walls flicker, well away from the stacks of books that line the walls. Haphazard is the word that comes to mind. There are shelves, yes, bowed under the weight of the many tomes that are piled up any which way. The floor too is stacked with books so that it is almost like navigating a maze to make our way through. At the very back of the shop there is a desk behind which sits a young man. I gasp as I see him and he looks up, removing a pair of spectacles from his face. It is the same man I have seen. The Negro I first mistook for Jonathan.

'Hello. Can I help you?' he asks, getting to his feet. His accent is steeped in London. 'You're two of Macauley's girls.'

Emmy shoves past me. 'Are you Caleb? We think you know a friend of ours. Camille de la Croix.'

He rolls his eyes. 'What's the daft strumpet done now?'

'You are Caleb then?' My tongue starts working again.

'Yes.' He comes over to us, peering at me with interest. 'What's all this about?'

'Did you know that she's gone missing?' Emmy is almost accusatory in her tone, and I see him take a step back. 'That the Piper may have taken her?'

'Camille? Are you sure she didn't just find someone else to pay her bills for a while?'

'I think that's what someone wanted us to think. Except that she left everything behind. All of her expensive gowns. And three hundred pounds. Do you know of any gentleman who would pay her more than that and make it worth her while to forfeit such an amount?' I watch his face carefully but all I see is surprise.

'Three hundred?'

'In banknotes.'

He leans against the edge of his desk. 'You think she's gone the same way as Daisy Gardner?'

'Yes!' Emmy becomes excited. 'You believe in the Piper too?'

He chuckles. 'Hell, no! There is no Piper. Not in the way that people talk of him. But do I think someone's taking the most promising harlots of Covent Garden and enticing them away? Yes, I do.'

'The most promising harlots?' I'm confused. 'Daisy Gardner?'

'Don't take my word for it. It's all in here.' Caleb reaches over to the bookcase closest to him and pulls down a thin tome, handing it to Emmy.

'*Harris's List of Covent Garden Ladies*,' she reads aloud. 'What is this?'

'A guide. For those gentlemen who enjoy the company of women and want to know who is worth their time and money.' Caleb grins at the look of horror on our faces. 'It's our bestseller. And 'cause I'm generous, I'll let you have that for free. It'll come in handy, I dare say. He usually publishes a new edition around Christmastime. *Joyeux Noel* and all that. You want to make sure that he writes something complimentary about you, else Mrs Macauley'll not be best pleased.'

I feel my face flame with rage. 'How dare you, sir. We came here in good faith, seeking assistance, and you insult us like this?'

'Insult?' He has the decency to stop laughing. 'Why would I insult you? This is Covent Garden. This business would fail if it weren't for the harlots and those who frequent them.'

I remember what Hattie and Maria said about him. He writes filth. Stories that imagine those activities that are usually hidden away behind closed doors. 'You think yourself superior, by writing about such things. You don't care what happens to girls like Camille and Daisy.'

''Course I care. I know all those girls, better than you do, Miss Sukey Maynard.' He nods towards Emmy. 'And Mrs M's own daughter. See, I know everyone and everything around here. I talk to people and they tell me what's going on and who's up to what. I don't think myself superior. *I* don't pretend that I'm too good for the people around here.' He is looking at me, his gaze piercing, and I know that he doesn't think much of me, but not for the reasons that most people have.

I grab Emmy's hand. 'Let's go. This boy can't help us.'

I am still shaking with anger as we arrive back home and Emmy wrenches her hand from mine, staring at me with concern. I notice she still has that guide to the local whores under her arm. I reach to take it from her, but she moves away from me, heading towards the staircase.

'Where are you going?' I ask. I can tell that she is annoyed at me.

'To read this. There might be a clue. Other missing girls.' She begins her ascent.

'Well, let me help you. I know you think I was being unreasonable, but that idiot boy doesn't know anything. He was just trying to tease us.'

'Yes, well, he knows people, Sukey. He knows Camille and he knew Daisy. He'd know about any other missing girls and, if he's right, they'll be in this book.' She holds it aloft, the key to the great mystery according to Caleb.

'Very well. Read the book, from cover to cover, and you'll see that there's no solution there.'

'Then what do you suggest we do next?'

'I don't know. Come on, Emmy. Come to Camille's room and let us have one last look in case there is something we haven't seen.'

We divide up the room into two halves, each taking our time to go through Camille's drawers, the cupboard, the space beneath the bed that is simply full of dust and a disturbing number of mouse droppings.

'Nothing.' Emmy collapses onto the bed, pulling a face as she presses the pillow to her nose. 'Why do men stink so? Is it their perfume? Why do they bathe in such stuff?'

I laugh as I join her, taking a sniff. Rose water and perspiration. I lie down beside her. 'I hope that you find a gent like Jonas so that you don't have to spend every night in the parlour.'

'I don't,' she says. 'I did at first but now I've decided that I'd rather be like Hattie.'

Like Hattie? I have always felt sorry for her, the least pretty of all of us, with a thick waist and hands like bricks, but she is more good-natured than anyone I've ever known. She takes the gents who only have half a shilling, those who are drunk or not fussy, and she smiles as she leads them upstairs. She, like Maria, has her regulars, those who will only see her and are happy to sit in the parlour for hours until she's available, if need be, but none of them are men of good standing. A tailor. A carpenter. An innkeeper from the Strand. These are the sorts of men who come to see Hattie. I can't understand why Emmy would want the same. Certainly, her mother will not allow it.

'Why would you want that?' I ask.

'Because I've realised that these men are all the same. They wear different clothes, and some have more expensive wigs, but really when it comes to it, they all want the same from us. A gent sees me and thinks one thing. He doesn't care what my name is. He doesn't want to talk to me or find out anything about me. I can't give him an heir, even if I bear his child, and he certainly won't pay for its upkeep. If he gives me the pox I have to suffer quietly. If I give it to him, he can get me locked up.'

'Jonas cares about me,' I tell her. 'We talk about all sorts of things, it's not all just about him. He asks me questions and he tells me things about his life. We have grown close over the time we've spent together. I trust him not to hurt me and I trust that he will look after me.'

'You could talk to him on our behalf.'

'Talk to him about what?' I prop myself up on my hand. 'Emmy, he doesn't know anything about Camille. Don't you think I would ask him if I thought for a moment that he did?'

'But what's the harm in just asking?' She is so damned stubborn that sometimes I want to shake her. She might want to be like Hattie, but I don't. Jonas is all I have to save me. But she is like a terrier with a rat in its mouth. 'I want to go to one of those balls and see for myself. Jonas knows Madame Vernier and so perhaps he knows the gentleman whose ball it was. Ask him. All he can do is refuse to answer.'

'And even if Jonas knows who hosted the ball, even though he wasn't even in London at the time and probably wasn't invited . . . what then?'

'Tell him you're worried. That you just want to be sure that your friend is safe. If he likes you as much as you say he does, then he won't like to see you upset.' She grins at her own cleverness. 'Flatter him; isn't that what Maria says always works a treat? And if not, cry and make him feel guilty.'

'But why bring Jonas into it at all? We can just ask Madame Vernier next time she pays us a visit. She was distraught when she was here last but maybe she has found out something since.'

'Madame Vernier might never come here again. Not after Mama was so angry with her about Camille. Please, Sukey . . . ask Jonas. Must I beg?' She kneels up on the bed and presses her hands together as if in prayer. 'You know that if our positions were reversed, I would do the same for you.'

I sigh and think of Alice and Rose Gardner. Something is amiss in Covent Garden. I feel the chill of it in my bones. Perhaps Emmy is right. What harm could asking a few questions lead to? At the worst Jonas will tell me that he cannot help and at least I'll have tried.

'Very well,' I say finally. 'I'll ask if he knows anything but just this once.'

Emmy falls on me, embracing me tightly. 'Thank you, thank you, thank you.'

I fear she will end up disappointed. Jonas has barely been in England for any time at all, of which a fortnight he spent in Lincolnshire getting married. I feel my mouth twist as I think again of his bride – Jenny. But he doesn't love her. He'd told me that without me asking a single thing. One quick question now to set our minds at ease. He can't get upset over that.

16

I keep my bargain with Emmy. Like always, that evening, Jonas and I sit and talk by the fire while sharing a bottle of wine. I know that I have half an hour or so before he turns his thoughts to more amorous occupations and think myself clever to start off with a more general question, about his thoughts on London society compared to that in Barbados. I know that he misses his home overseas. Like me, London isn't yet home.

'I heard there was a magnificent ball just a week or so ago,' I say, sipping my wine and trying to keep my tone light. 'Madame Vernier told me that everyone of importance was in attendance. I suppose that if you'd been in London, you would have gone?'

He looks irritated. 'Those sorts of parties aren't the way I like to spend my time. But,' he concedes, 'I suppose I would have gone, purely to mingle. There are many of my father's old acquaintances in the city and I haven't had the chance to meet with them all thus far. Perhaps next time there is such an event I can escort you?'

'Me?' I am surprised and elated. 'Would you not be expected to go with your—' I stop myself before I can utter the word. Wife. Such a short and inoffensive word, and yet I knew he won't thank me for reminding him of her.

'The sort of party you talk of isn't for everyone. Sophy – I could never expect her to attend such an event.' He stares into the fire, and I try not to react. Her name is Sophy? Then who on earth is Jenny? 'There are two sides of me. Two versions of Jonas Drake. One is for you, and one is for her. Does that make sense? They are not so very different from one another, but there is a separation that must be maintained. These parties that are organised for pure pleasure, where the likes of Gisele Vernier draw up the guest list and where girls are paid to be present, are not for my married life. They are not for wives.'

'Those parties are for men to escape from their lives,' I suggest. 'To find a place where you can be yourself, away from the responsibilities of a household and from your position?'

'Exactly!' He smiles finally. 'I knew you would understand. I feel that you know me, Sukey, more than anyone else in this Godforsaken city. More than—' I will him to say her name, but he stops himself in time. 'In fact, I did hear that Tobias Kellett is throwing such a party a week on Friday. I had thought to decline the invitation but perhaps you will come with me?'

'I would love to,' I say, quickly adding, 'but may I ask one favour? May I bring Emmy with me?'

'Emmy?' He looks confused.

'Mrs Macauley's daughter.' I watch the confusion depart his face, replaced by wariness. 'I know how important it is that you make time to talk to gentlemen of business, like yourself. I won't know a soul there but if Emmy were by my side, you wouldn't have to concern yourself with my welfare all evening.'

'Of course, then.' He beams. 'The more the merrier.'

So easy! All I had to do was pretend that I understood him, to show him that I knew how it had to be. His wife can have his respect and his name. I have his time and my share of the money he has agreed to pay Mrs Macauley for my company. As long as I follow those rules, I will have his protection. For now, that seems more than enough.

Tobias Kellett lives on King Street, in a great mansion that makes me fear him even more. Three storeys of pure grandeur, more of a palace than a house where one surly merchant lives alone. Carriages line up ahead of us, waiting their turn to drop off the esteemed guests at the door, bright light beaming out onto the wide carriage sweep.

'Anyone can lease a house,' Mrs Macauley sniffs, but I can see how impressed she looks, and I see her glance at her daughter. If she could arrange a permanent match between Emmy and Kellett, we might all be leaving Little Wild Street behind sooner than she'd previously hoped.

'What does he do, Mr Kellett?' I ask.

'It might be wiser to ask what Mr Kellett does *not* do.' Jonas speaks through gritted teeth. He's been in a foul mood since picking us up in his carriage, and I do not know why. 'He sells goods. Sugar and a lot more besides.'

'And that is how he knows your father?' It makes sense. If the Drakes own a sugar plantation, then Tobias Kellett must be the man to sell the goods they ship to England from the West Indies.

'Yes.' Jonas thumps on the roof with his cane. 'We shall be here all night. Let's get out and walk.'

Silently we three women obey, though I think mutinously that he'd never have made his wife walk along the dirty pavement in all her finery. Emmy and I have once again raided Camille's gown collection, and I hope fervently that we will blend in with the other ladies. Mrs Macauley certainly thinks that we pass muster, but I am not so convinced. I have seen how Madame Vernier dresses; I saw the dress that Camille wore to that infamous last ball, and we do not quite match up. Still, I have Jonas by my side, ill temper or not.

Jonas shows a card to the footmen who guard the front door, their leers in the direction of us women letting me know that they know exactly why we have been invited. Jonas's face flushes as he sees the way they look, at me and then back to him, and he hurries ahead into the house. I am about to go after him when I hear Mrs Macauley gasp and turn back to see why. The next carriage has disgorged its residents, a tall man dressed as fine as if he were the King of England himself, his wig powdered and regal. Beside him stands an equally impressive woman.

Mrs Macauley throws up her arms. 'Mr Ross, is that you underneath all that paint? Lucy. Lucy Macauley? You probably don't remember me, but I played Phyllis when you were Bevil Junior. *The Conscious Lovers* at Drury Lane.' She pauses to take a breath; her cheeks flushed red. 'Such a long time ago now but—'

'Time?' He interrupts her with a wave of his hand. 'My dear woman, of course I remember you. Little Lucy! Fanny dearest,' he says, turning to his wife, 'see how I am still beloved.' To us he says, 'My wife feels that I should do more to keep my old friends and acquaintances, instead of constantly seeking out the new.'

'I am married to a magpie in human form,' she confides to us. 'A wonderful man in so many ways, and yet he cannot help himself. Anything shiny and untouched.' She raises an eyebrow as Mr Ross's gaze lingers on Emmy. 'Come, husband, I will catch my death if we stand out here much longer.'

Ross looks disappointed to be forced away from his captive

audience but bows deeply to Mrs Macauley before letting his wife drag him into the house, the mellow strains of violin music beginning to wend their way towards us from the brightly lit interior. We follow them inside and I realise that I have already lost Jonas but Mrs Macauley draws Emmy and me close.

'You know who that is?' she says, her gaze still fixed on Mr Ross. 'David Ross the actor. And his wife, the infamous Fanny Murray.'

'Who?' Emmy is too busy looking around us, at the marble of the great statue, a Greek goddess who dominates the hallway, at the rich red carpet that lines the staircase leading upstairs, though more footmen guard the ascent.

'Who?' Mrs Macauley is appalled. 'Girl, how you can call yourself kin of mine is one of life's great mysteries. She is everything that you should aspire to be. You find the right sponsor and you can rise up, out of the gutter, and marry a gentleman of fine standing such as Mr Ross. She was no better than us before she seduced him.'

I find myself far more captivated by the idea of Mrs Ross than her husband. She is proof in front of my eyes that a whore can aim for more in life. Though, I remind myself, Jonas, wherever he currently is, is already married. That avenue is closed to us, at least for now.

'An actor?' Emmy pulls a face. 'And why can I not rise up with my own help? Or with Sukey's help?'

I open my mouth to speak but Mrs Macauley's glare freezes my tongue.

'Sukey may think she's fallen on her feet but it's early days with Mr Drake. Far too early to be certain of his future intentions. Now come.' Mrs Macauley grabs her daughter's arm, walking her in the direction of the music as Jonas reappears. 'Let us mingle.'

We follow the current, the corridor full of bodies dressed in the latest fashions, the women's dresses low cut, the men's jackets designed to show off their form. The passage disgorges us into a large oblong room, the noise growing to such a level that it is like being in the middle of Covent Garden on a busy midweek morning. Men are guffawing at one another's jokes as the ladies beat away the heat with their fans and look around, always on the watch for someone more important, someone more interesting.

I find Jonas by one of the refreshment tables, guzzling down champagne as though his life depends on it. He is nervous. He did not mean to abandon me, he just required a little Dutch courage.

'I thought I had lost you.' I let him pass me a glass and drink deeply myself.

'Do you dance?' Jonas asks me, his lips pressed to my ear to be heard.

I think back to our Dorking days, to country dances and farm boys who never picked me to partner them. 'No, but I would like to watch.'

We desert Emmy and Mrs Macauley, who is making a beeline for Tobias Kellett on the far side of the room, and pass through into another large room, this one occupied by a string quartet, the source of the music we had heard from the hallway.

Four couples stand in the centre of the room, preparing to dance. The quartet begin to play, and a minuet begins, one couple in particular immediately attracting my attention with their skill and poise. Like so many of the couples present, the gentleman is older, his face distinguished but lined by his experience. His partner is young, but her steps are carefully placed, her gaze concentrated though her body moves easily.

On the other side of the dancing couple, I see Madame Vernier. She stands alone, a glass of champagne in her hand. As she notices me, she raises it to me and nods, a half-smile on her face. She looks completely at home amongst this company, as if she was born to it, even though she can't have been.

'Could you teach me to dance like that?' I ask Jonas as the music slows and the couple make their final movements, preparing to be replaced by a fresh pair.

'You wish to dance a minuet, and for me to teach it to you?' he teases. 'Dearest Sukey, you don't know what you're asking, for I have not the patience for such a task. You should ask your mentor. Presumably she has the right connections to sort you a teacher if you so wish.'

My eyes follow where he points; the young woman who has just left the dance floor is now conversing with Madame Vernier, her eager partner at her side. As I watch, the man speaks to Madame Vernier, and I see him pass her something small that she secretes away in a pocket in a trice. Could this girl be a whore? She must be one of Madame Vernier's girls, fulfilling the role that Camille played immediately prior to her disappearance. She looks so pure, so much like a lady, and she even moves like one.

As the girl turns to walk away on the arm of her beau, our eyes meet, and I realise that I recognise her. The light has caught the sharpness of the cheekbones that on her mother I had thought due to lack of sustenance. Her dark hair is a match to her sister's, and I blink away the sudden image of Rose Gardner's face, sunken and pale in death. But surely, I am mistaken. This can't possibly be Daisy Gardner. Can it?

I am staring. The girl – Daisy? – notices, tugging on her beau's sleeve and letting him drag her away through the crowd. Madame Vernier has already disappeared, and I can feel Jonas grow restless beside me.

'Another drink,' he says. 'Let's hope Kellett is serving better wine than your Mrs Macauley buys in.'

I let him lead me in search of refreshment, looking out for Emmy. She met Daisy Gardner once, before the girl vanished. She will know if the dancer really is the missing girl or if it's just my imagination playing games. She can tell me if I am going mad.

17

Half of the evening has passed before I see another face I recognise. For all that there are harlots aplenty at the party, it is a civilised affair downstairs. Jonas seems to know everyone, despite his relatively recent arrival in England, and they seem obsessed by my presence. *Where on earth did you find such a creature?* As irritating as it is for me, I smile each time, but I see the furrow in Jonas's brow growing ever deeper as they peer at me and laugh.

'Perhaps you would rather spend time with your friend,' he suggests eventually. 'I must speak business with a few of these good gentlemen and I fear that your presence is distracting.'

'I can occupy myself for a while,' I tell him, and he vanishes into the crowd without a backward glance.

The heat of the room, along with the unwanted feeling that I have failed Jonas in some way, has me seeking an escape. At the back of the room, French windows have been left to stand open in the hope that the early spring breeze will cool the interior. That is not the case, but I am allowed easy access to the courtyard garden outside.

A central fountain spews water into the air, the jet emerging from the mouth of a young naked man, his impressive form carved from stone. Shrubs and carefully placed trees provide hiding places; I can see no one in the garden and yet I know I'm not alone. Soft murmurs and muted giggles betray the couples who have come outside to find their thrills rather than battle with the footmen to gain access to the upper-storey bedrooms. Under cover of darkness, they seek their pleasures, which means that the marble bench beside the fountain is left unoccupied, and it is here that I sit, glad to stretch out my feet and wiggle my pinched toes in the silk slippers Jonas gifted to me.

'*Cherie*, I hoped you would come.'

I turn to see Madame Vernier sweep towards me. I think of Emmy: she would want to know if that girl is Daisy Gardner. She wouldn't be afraid to ask Madame Vernier for the truth.

'I saw you earlier,' I say, 'but we were too far away to say hello.'

'Jonas is quite the conversationalist. His father will be proud of the connections he's making in London.' She sits beside me on the bench. 'Your match is a very fortuitous one. Thank goodness Lucille listened to me for once.'

'You seem to know quite a few people here yourself,' I say, willing myself to be bold. 'You and your girls must be very popular at parties such as this one.'

She looks a little sheepish. 'I suppose Lucille is still furious with me. Honestly, Sukey, if I had had any idea what a liability Camille was, I would never have suggested her for one of these parties. I only hope that the gentleman who offered her the world really does possess the means to honour his promises. You do hear such tales of woe, of girls who turn up months later with a child in their belly or the mark of the pox. So many end up in the gutter, or dead.' She shivers, the temperature dropping quickly as it is wont to do at this time of year. 'If I hear of her, I will send word immediately. Tell Lucille that.'

'I will,' I promise. 'So, you haven't heard anything? Or know who this mysterious gentleman was that she left with?'

'No. I have asked and asked but no one but that one footman saw her leave.'

'So many missing girls,' I muse, 'and yet I thought I saw one of them this evening.' I can't look at her in case I give myself away.

'What missing girls?' she asks.

'Daisy Gardner is one of them. She vanished from Covent Garden just before the new year. Her mother and sister both died recently, and I suppose no one has told her. I don't even know if they had a proper burial.'

'This is London. The city is no place for innocents,' Madame Vernier reminds me.

'Indeed.' I dare a glance, but her expression never wavers. 'Though I swear I saw her this evening, at this very party. You know her, I saw you speak with her. She danced a minuet and then she and her gentleman came to you.'

'A minuet?' She thinks for a moment. 'You must mean Beatrice. Isn't she striking?' She smiles, a little bashfully. 'She is the first of my new set of girls. My new sorority. You can keep a secret Sukey? For I would hate for Lucille to catch wind of my scheme before it is properly underway.'

'Scheme?'

'A seraglio if you like. I mean to train a new style of courtesan right here in London. Teach them the art of our profession.' She pauses to make sure that I am giving her my full attention. 'The life of your ordinary harlot is a miserable one, Sukey, don't you think? There is no respect available to us. Men take what they want, and we are to feel grateful for the measly coins they throw to us. The women, the bawds like Lucille and like Mother Jenkins whose house we learned our trade in many years ago, Lucille and I and your mother, they are no better. The bawd takes all the money and hands out a pittance to her girls. She claims rent and the cost of bedding and wine, but she charges it all back to the very girls who support her and keep the roof over her own head.'

'And you wish to do things differently?' I ask.

'I have rented a house in Pall Mall and soon you will hear of nothing else. My plan is that it will be a school of sorts. My girls will learn French and they will learn to dance. When they are educated, they will be so talented they can infiltrate any ballroom in the country, and no one will be able to point them out as a common whore. Marriage will become a possibility. Security and wealth, all those things that have eluded the common jezebel.'

'It sounds wonderful,' I say honestly. 'If it were not for Jonas, I would be begging you to let me join you!'

She brushes my cheek with her hand. 'My darling, I'm very proud of your accomplishments. But I am just beginning. Beatrice, as you saw, has been taking dance lessons every day for the last month. She is my first experiment and already she has secured the attentions of a duke.'

'You must be so proud, to have raised her up so far in such a short space of time,' I say. 'Where on earth did you find such a clever girl?'

'You've heard of the old bawd's trick of meeting the coach as it arrives in the city? All manner of young, innocent girls fall off with barely a penny to their name and great hopes of securing work once they arrive. Very occasionally there is a pearl in amongst the grit.' She stands then, brushing down her skirt carefully. 'You mentioned missing girls, Sukey. How many others are there missing? Do people talk?'

'No one else seems to care very much,' I reply.

She nods. 'Then do not fret.' She turns to leave as Jonas appears. 'Ah, Mr Drake. I was just saying how lovely your escort looks this evening.'

'She does indeed.' He holds out his hand to me. 'Come, Sukey, Mr Kellett has given his permission to pass by his guard dogs.'

It takes me a moment to realise that he means for us to go upstairs, to spend the rest of the evening in one of the fine bedrooms up there, reserved for Tobias Kellett's most privileged guests. It is my duty, I realise, my purpose for being at the party in the first place, but it is frustrating. I want to seek out Emmy, to tell her what I have seen and heard. To put her mind at ease.

'I should find Mrs Macauley first,' I say. 'She might worry about me having disappeared.' I think about mentioning Camille, but I don't think Jonas knows who she is.

'She will soon realise you are with me,' he says, grabbing my hand and leading me back inside the house at a rapid pace. Is he trying to rush me upstairs without any of his new friends seeing me?

I want to argue but the words dry up on the tip of my tongue. It isn't the end of the world if I have to wait a little to talk to Emmy. What is the urgency that I felt in the pit of my stomach? I was mistaken; that girl cannot be Daisy Gardner. She just happens to look a little like her. Everything Madame Vernier told me makes sense. Her new venture sounds exciting, a far better proposition for a young girl than the traditional bawdy house that Mrs Macauley presides over. I even understand why she wishes to keep it secret while she finds her girls, skimming the cream from the common, watered-down milk of the London street girls. There is just something that niggles at me, though I can't put my finger on what that is. An invisible splinter catching at my skin.

Jonas's pace is rapid now that his blood is up. In a trice we are through the reception rooms, my feet almost tripping as he drags me through the crowd. I am happier once we emerge in the hallway, almost empty now that all of the guests have arrived.

I follow Jonas up the stairs, the noise from the reception rooms fading as we ascend. The corridor at the top is almost serene, candelabras placed on tables at regular intervals so that we could easily see our way. The spell is only broken by the faint sounds of copulation, the thick wood of the doors only doing so much to deaden the sound.

'It would have to be the furthest room,' Jonas grumbles, his free hand already plucking at his waistcoat buttons as though he simply cannot bear to wait another second to be on me.

I want to ask him what is wrong. I've never seen him like this, almost frantic. I have always been grateful for his calm and gentle manner, but the man dragging me along the corridor is not the Jonas Drake I have known over the previous three months. In his haste, I trip on the thick rug, and almost fall, Jonas finally stopping in order to right me.

'Watch what you're doing!' he scolds, and I stare at him, affronted.

I want to say something, but I don't. And besides, both our attentions are taken as a door behind us opens, the dancing couple emerging further down the corridor, towards the staircase. He looks dishevelled now, not having bothered to redress himself properly, a large wine stain ruining his shirt. She still looks beautiful but the red flush on her face removes the innocence of earlier. He walks off alone, his business with her completed, and she takes a moment to check her reflection in the hallway mirror.

'Daisy,' I call. She turns and stares at me, her eyes wide. Before I can say another word, she whirls around and flees. If not for Jonas's tight grip on me, I would have followed her. Can it really be Daisy Gardner after all?

'Sukey!' Jonas clicks his fingers in my face. 'I didn't bring you here so that you could gossip with your harlot friends.'

I let Jonas lead me into the green bedroom, the walls papered in a bilious shade that I am sure Mrs Macauley would have favoured. My actions are by rote as we begin, my fingers working the buttons on Jonas's breeches, stroking that part of him that swells beneath the fabric as I think over what I have just seen. It was Daisy; must have been her. Her shock, her immediate reaction upon hearing her true name. Her rapid escape. Had Madame Vernier reinvented the girl from the poor family, saving her from the pox, or did Daisy herself choose to make a new start? Unless I can talk to her, how will I ever know?

18

For the first time, I find Jonas changed from the caring man I thought I knew. His ardour feels different, more impersonal. There are no soft words or kind caresses, and his impatience is unparalleled. The room is wasted on us when he barely allows me to unfasten his breeches before he is pulling up my skirts, thrusting into me like the drunks do to the street girls in the alleyways around Covent Garden. I cling to the bedpost and weather the short-lived storm, wondering what I have done wrong. He takes but a few moments to spend himself, another brief moment to wash in the bowl provided, before leaving me there alone in semi-darkness, the fire burning as low as I am now starting to fear that his passion for me has become.

It is after three o'clock in the morning when we leave Kellett's party, but only two of us climb into Jonas's carriage. He has chosen to walk to his own home, the St James's house he shares with his wife, being so close on foot, he says, that it hardly seems sensible for him to escort us back to Covent Garden. Our goodbye is a brief brush of his lips against my cheek and I know that he was not happy with me, though I cannot think what I might have done wrong.

Mrs Macauley informs me curtly that Emmy is otherwise

engaged and will be sent home later that day. I assume that Tobias Kellett has changed his mind about her, but for some reason Mrs Macauley looks subdued. Perhaps he drove a hard bargain. Her mood seems most often affected by her financial fortune and I wonder what she would say if I lost Jonas's support. I will have to double my efforts on his next visit and pray that he is simply in bad humour, that it was one of his new London acquaintances who has affected his spirits, and that he has not measured me beside the other harlots who were present and found me wanting.

Emmy arrives back at Little Wild Street just before midday, so late that Mrs Macauley has almost worn a hole in the rug before the fire in the parlour. It isn't like her to show her feelings in front of the rest of us, but then I suppose that, after Camille, her concerns are justified. Besides, what mother doesn't worry about her daughter failing to return after a night of dancing, even when she knows perfectly well what company she is keeping?

'Here she is!' Mrs Macauley pushes Emmy before her into the parlour, triumphant in voice. I see that there is a small velvet bag in her hand. Payment no doubt, and plenty of it judging by its fatness, like a pig at market.

'Come and sit down, Emmy,' I say, pushing Hattie out of the way. 'How was it?'

She sits, her hands clasped in her lap. On her wrist is a silver charm bracelet that I haven't seen before. Her face is pale, dark shadows beneath her red-rimmed eyes, though I tell myself that is likely just lack of sleep. 'It went well.' Her tone lacks any emotion.

'And they want to see you again?' Mrs Macauley presses. They?

'I think so.' Emmy's smile is weak, like watered-down gruel. 'Laura says they will send word.'

'Laura? Lord above, I am glad I never get invited to no fancy balls. It's bad enough dealing with the men. Least with them I know how to hurry 'em up.' Hattie sighs and shakes her head. 'Women, they make you earn your money.'

'Not helpful, Hattie, thank you.' I elbow her in the ribs. 'Who was it? Mr Kellett?'

'You know he doesn't like me,' she reminds me, her eyes welling up.

'Not that it's any of your business, Sukey, but Mr Kellett has many influential connections. Lady Laura and her husband are known to spend a fortune on harlots, but they are meticulously picky. If they find a girl they like then they pay well to keep hold of her.' Mrs Macauley is almost rubbing her hands together in glee.

'Until they wear her out.' Hattie says it quietly, but we all hear. I don't know who these people are, but I can tell from the worried glance exchanged between Hattie and Maria that they harbour suspicions.

'At least they paid you well,' I say, trying and failing to catch Emmy's eye. 'And you don't have to go back. Not if you don't want to.'

'What do you know about it?' She turns on me suddenly, her eyes welling up. 'You're so lucky. You have Jonas who is nice to you and charms Mama. One day he'll take you away and you'll never think twice about the rest of us stuck here.'

A heavy silence falls over the room. I don't know what to say.

The truth is that, although I have my concerns about Jonas, she is partly right. If he offered to take me away, I would not think twice. I would leave Emmy behind to save my own skin. I feel sick at my own selfishness.

'This is a topsy-turvy life,' Maria says eventually. 'There is nothing certain and so you learn to get along with things. Tomorrow Jonas may send word that he is moving back to the West Indies. A new young gent might walk in and be taken by you, Emmy. You honestly never know. The only certainty we have is that we have little say in the matter. We just have to take the money when we can and be grateful when they're nice to us. And trust me, under this roof they mostly are decent, thanks to Mrs M and Jakes.'

'I do my best by you lot,' Mrs Macauley agrees. 'Not that I get a lot of thanks for it. At least one of you is grateful to me.' She gives me a narrow-eyed look and I feel my blood rise.

'But you won't make me go back, will you, Mama?' Emmy says. 'I don't . . . I mean, I can do better here. I prefer it here. Those people, I didn't like them. Not one bit, Mama!'

Mrs Macauley's lips press together. 'Emily. You are just starting out and so I shall forget this little outburst. I realise you know no better, but listen up, girl. This is how you make a success of yourself. Finding friends in higher places than we can reach from Covent Garden. You will do as I say and be glad that you can earn a good living from so little effort. Why, do you not feel grateful for the opportunities that I have granted you? Do you not thank the Lord that I came and rescued you from a dour existence with my sister and her Bible-loving husband?'

I see Emmy flinch and know that I will have to speak up for her. She never will speak up against her mother. 'Some of us never asked to come here,' I tell Mrs Macauley. 'You didn't give me any choice in the matter, and, yes, I do hope that Jonas takes me away from here. I don't want to be here.' Once I have begun, I find the confession impossible to halt. 'You know this; you know why I ran away, and I wouldn't have come back if Jakes hadn't found me. There are decent people out there. People working honest jobs. I was happy for that to be my fate. Instead, I'm stuck here paying off a debt and the only reason I have any chance to do so is thanks to Madame Vernier. No thanks to you, so no, I am not grateful to you. Not for anything.'

A heavy silence falls over the room and Mrs Macauley's lips twist into a bitter smile. 'You should count yourself lucky, Sukey Maynard. If it weren't for Mr Drake and his deep pockets, I'd be inclined to wash my hands of you and have you sent off to the Marshalsea for your debts.'

I wait for Emmy finally to say something, to find the courage to come to my defence, but her gaze is fixed to the floor. She looks entirely defeated, nothing left of the cheerful girl who had been so pleased when her mother had summoned her to London, who had been so enthusiastic to do as her mother bid her, even when she had known what that entailed. The reality of our new life is destroying her. If even Emmy cannot survive this new life of ours, what hope do I have?

'You couldn't do that,' I argue. 'Besides, if I told the justice what goes on here, you'd be in more trouble yourself, and perhaps I should do just that. Save us all from your threats and ledger book.'

'Hush now, Sukey!' Maria hisses at me, and I am taken aback by the change in her usual gentle manner. 'Would you destroy all of us so easily? Some of us need this place. If I end up out on the street, you'll be damning me to the same fate as your mother.'

Emmy grips my hand, and I know I should still my mouth, yet I can't help it. 'Why so little faith, Maria? You might find another trade, or at least a better place to ply this one.' I keep back what I know about Madame Vernier. I'm not sure that Maria is the kind of girl she is looking for. Too wise and too set in her ways to be moulded. 'I didn't choose this life.'

Hattie moves away from me. 'I know you think you're too good for the likes of us, but you ain't. You've just had a bit of luck. You've never had to survive out there alone. You'd not be complaining the way you do if you knew what a real hard life was.'

'It's not like that,' I plead.

'Yes. It is.' Emmy turns on me, her rage taking my breath away. 'You're just another Camille. Thinking you're better than the rest of us. Telling me to be grateful that some old bag and her husband want to pay me to lie in bed with them and follow orders. I had to thank them for this silver bracelet when I wanted to throw it in their faces!' Her face is red, and her words tumble out in a breathless torrent. 'In fact, you're worse than Camille. At least she was honest. You acted like you were scared, running away, and leaving me like you did. You don't care about me, or anyone else. Soon as you snared your rich gentleman you stopped giving a damn about us. You couldn't even be bothered to ask a few questions about Camille and find out what really happened to her. All you care about is your precious Mr Drake.'

Emmy might have carried on her rant but Mrs Macauley steps forward and slaps her so hard across the face that every one of us winces. 'Calm yourself, girl. You're a Macauley. We're made of sterner stuff than this.'

'I can't . . .' Emmy stands so quickly that she appears unsteady, her eyes not quite focusing as she struggles with her words. I reach out a hand to her and she knocks it away.

'Get some sleep. I'll bring up some hot water so you can bathe.' Mrs Macauley puts her hands to her daughter's shoulders and kisses her reddened cheek, Emmy flinching. 'Forgive me, I really am so very proud of you. The worst is over now.' She smooths a hand over Emmy's hair and releases her.

'I'll come and help you,' I say, ready to follow her upstairs, desperate to talk. To apologise. To find a way to fix what I have done.

'No.' She almost shouts the word. 'No,' she repeats, quietly this time. 'I want to be alone, Sukey.' She flees the room as though she cannot bear to be close to me.

'Leave her be. She just needs some sleep.' Mrs Macauley jingles her bag of coins. 'She'll be grateful once she sees just how happy the Armitages were with her. I tell you, I've a mind to send out word that we are looking for new premises. What do you say, girls? Would Golden Square do you? Or should we head further west? St James's could be ours! You won't be looking so sour when you're bouncing on the lap of a lord, Hattie, I promise you that.' She is completely unaffected by what has just happened, even as I am shattered. I know that I have been a fool, but Hattie doesn't look convinced by Mrs Macauley's joviality and even Maria doesn't smile.

The Armitages' money may make Mrs Macauley content for a time, but what little camaraderie existed beneath the roof of the Little Wild house has been lost. It started with Camille's disappearance, and has been continued by my rash words, but Emmy's predicament has made clear the ambition of Lucille Macauley. She doesn't give a damn about any of us if we can't make money for her. And that includes her own flesh and blood.

A black cloud has descended upon the house. Even Cook seems out of sorts, kicking out at the cat for getting underfoot when usually a gentle scolding and a head scratch would have sufficed.

'Won't you talk to me,' I beg Emmy after three days of silence. It is Sunday, the only day of the week when even Mrs Macauley agrees we should shut up shop, and we would usually be enjoying a late breakfast only it is hard when the atmosphere is so rancid. 'Please, Emmy. Look. It's such a lovely day. Do you really want to sit indoors with your mother?'

'What else should I be doing?' she asks, her voice flat. 'Besides, she wants to fit me for a new gown. There's another party next week and she's trying to convince Tobias Kellett to secure invitations for me and Maria.'

I had noticed the parcel of silk that had arrived the day before but was too nervous to ask Emmy about it. 'She can do that this evening. Come, Emmy, let us take a walk in the sunshine. We can go wherever you'd like.'

'Don't fret about me so, Sukey. With a little luck, soon you will be living somewhere else, and I won't be your responsibility any longer,' she says, getting up from the table.

I follow her, desperate to make her talk to me, but as we reach the hallway, I see a young lad standing there.

Jakes scowls at me. 'This lad reckons he's got a message for you. Miss Maynard, he calls you.' His lip curls as he says my name.

'A message?' I push past Emmy. 'From whom?'

'A shilling would be nice,' the boy says, cheekily. 'I come all the way from Mincing Lane to deliver you a note from Dr Sharp.'

'A shilling?' I laugh and give him a farthing, which is more than he deserves, and take the letter, barely more than a scrap of paper. He runs off to cause mayhem somewhere else. Emmy's curiosity is getting the better of her, but I choose to ignore her and wait until she has stomped her way upstairs. Dr Sharp is another reminder of my rejection of her mother, and, now I know just how much my desertion has upset Emmy, I don't want to rub it in her face.

'Back again already,' Cook says as I scuttle back into the kitchen, away from prying eyes. Cook doesn't count; she is the very definition of a confidante. I know that all the girls talk to her about their woes, and she never shares a single word with the rest of us. She has cleared away the breakfast things already and is now preparing to brew a pot of tea.

'Emmy hates me, and I can't bear to keep apologising to her,' I reply, stealing a lemon biscuit from the plate she has laid out beside the tea tray. 'Are we expecting company? Or is Mrs M just feeling a little fancy today.'

'Her French highness, Gisele Vernier, has sent word that she would like to pay us a visit. On a Sunday of all days!' Cook raises her eyes to the heavens. 'No one knows when neither, so I'm to sit here like I've got nothing better to do, waiting to send up the tray when she deigns to bless us with her company.'

I pull a sympathetic face and sit down, laughing as I reach for another biscuit, and she slaps my hand away. Cook's biscuits are the best. Even the fancy French swirls that Jonas sometimes brings for me aren't a patch on them. I've watched her make them and it looks easy enough, but she swears there is a secret that she'll never reveal.

Emmy sidles in and sits down beside me. 'What was in that message then?'

'Talking to me now, are you?' She pulls a face but I can see she's trying not to smile. I decide to let bygones be bygones. 'I haven't read it yet. Did I tell you about Dr Sharp?' I know that I have but I hope to coax an interest from her. 'I suppose this note is news about Jonathan, the boy I found.' Perhaps reminding her of the one good deed I've done will help thaw her.

The note from Dr Sharp is short, just a few lines scrawled in a precise hand:

Sukey,

Jonathan has been judged well enough to leave the hospital. My brother has secured him work as an errand boy with Mr Brown of Fenchurch-street, an Apothecarist. He is much recovered and owes a debt of gratitude to you. It is my opinion that without your involvement, he may not be with us today and I have told him as much. Jonathan has expressed a desire to thank you in person. Granville shared your address with me. I was unsure if you would be amenable to Jonathan turning up on your doorstep and so I thought it wisest to message you and you may contact him at Mr Brown's if you wish.

Yours,
Dr W Sharp

For once I have done something right. Something that isn't purely for my own benefit. Jonathan is alive and well. It is a nice feeling, to know that after all these weeks I might see him again. But then what if he is disappointed to find out what I am?

'You saved a life,' Emmy tells me, reading it over my shoulder. I see the way she looks at me, softer than before. 'I know that you mean well, Su. Jonathan is living proof that you're a good person. You must go and see him.'

'I will,' I promise her. 'Will you come with me?' I would feel so much better with her by my side.

'Of course.' She picks at a splinter on the table. 'And about before, what I said . . . It's just that I thought this would be easier. That I was born to it and when the time came it would feel natural, like it seems to for Hattie and Maria. You even, though you were so scared about it. Everything's going right for you, Sukey, and I am happy for you. Honestly, I am. Only everything for me is horrible.' She starts to cry then, and I feel awful. 'I don't want to go to the party next week, and every time I see Mr Kellett, I feel sick. But who else is there? Sir Horace? Someone to pay a few coins for me, as if I were Rose Gardner. What if I end up like her?'

'You won't. Whatever I said about your mama, I know she runs a clean house. She looks after her girls.' After all, it is easier to keep her girls safe and working than to have the risk of her house being known to harbour the pox. Thinking of Rose Gardner reminds me of what I saw the other night. With Emmy not speaking to me, I haven't had the chance to tell her before now. 'Madame Vernier is on her way here,' I said. 'And I never had a chance to tell you what I saw at Kellett's house.' I pause to make sure she is paying the proper level of attention. 'I saw Daisy Gardner there. She's changed her name, but I swear, hand on heart, it was her. And she's working for Gisele Vernier.'

19

We lie, Emmy and I, on Camille's bed, our stockinged feet entwined. The arguments of the past few days and weeks are forgotten at last, and Mrs Macauley is safely ensconced in her office with Madame Vernier whose eventual arrival was heralded by much harrumphing from Cook. I had taken it upon myself to measure Emmy for the new gown and been shocked to see the fresh bruises upon her arms, on her thighs.

'Mrs Armitage,' is all she says.

'I am sorry,' I reply, close to tears. How had I not realised quite how bad things were? Emmy is so mild mannered, so averse to temper tantrums, and yet I haven't seen that her uncharacteristic behaviour had an understandable cause. I have been a bad friend. Again.

'I suppose in a way I should be grateful,' she says. 'Ma was so bitterly disappointed when Kellett didn't offer to keep me. She so wants me to be a success. Like Fanny Murray – look at her now. Respectably married.'

'Only to an actor,' I remind her. Hardly a respectable position as far as the higher echelons of society are concerned, though it is a loftier profession than many.

'But a wife she is, nonetheless. He must really love her.' She sighs. What chance do we have for the same? 'What is it like with Jonas? Does it get tiresome, having to always be ready in case he turns up? Doing whatever he asks of you?'

At first it had been a novelty, getting dressed up each evening and being able to swan around the parlour in the knowledge that when I heard the knocks at the door, I could look forward to seeing who entered with interest rather than trepidation. But Jonas has only paid me one visit since the party and left after barely an hour during which he had been ill-tempered and left bruises on my arms. He hadn't even bothered to make an excuse for his changed behaviour. Why would he when he didn't owe me any?

'He has never hurt me. Not intentionally at least.' Jonas's roughness is nothing compared to what Emmy has been through.

'Won't you find out if Jonas has any friends in need of a whore with limited experience but free of disease?' she says lightly. 'I can speak a little French and read and write. Useful attributes, I think, that certainly put me above the ranks of streetwalker.'

'Any of his friends would be lucky to have you,' I say. I think about Madame Vernier's new style of brothel. Isn't that exactly the sort of place where Emmy would fit in, and have her choice of decent gentlemen? But Mrs Macauley would rather die than send her only daughter off to make money for her rival. A rival who, at that, had misplaced the last girl to be placed in her care. 'As long as we're together, Emmy, I don't doubt that we'll succeed. Somehow.'

'One day you will have all of London at your feet and I will be by your side. Ma, Jonas Drake, Tobias Kellett, none of them can stop us,' she joins in, and we both laugh.

I'm glad to see her spirits rise. 'You and your ma will be in

St James's soon enough. Imagine it! The huge rooms and high ceilings. Windows that let in the light!'

'That would be nice.' She sighs and moves closer, until our bodies are pressed together, and I feel her arm move around my waist. 'I thought that when we came back to London it was the start of a new life. Aunt Betsy was kind enough, but I never felt that it was home.'

I stifle a smile. If Emmy hadn't felt at home with the Ashleys, how did she think I had felt? The pious Betsy Ashley had never hesitated to remind me of what a sacrifice she was making to let me sleep under her roof.

'Let us stop moping. It's such a nice day.' She sits up. 'Why don't we pay your Jonathan a visit?'

'Now?' I stare at her.

'Yes! Come on, let's go out. The sun is out and it's only mid-afternoon. How far is Fenchurch Street? Less than an hour's walk, surely.'

'Then why not?'

It is pleasant out, the good weather holding and the streets busy but not as chaotic as on any other day of the week. In our Sunday best, Emmy and I walk arm in arm, as though we have not a care in the world. Back to how things had used to be. I feel happy for once, the sun beaming a deep warmth into my bones. So carefree do I feel that I do not see the person loitering outside the church of St Clement Danes until he has already seen us, skipping his way between carriages on the Strand to appear before us.

'Afternoon, ladies,' he greets us as if we have long been friends.

'Good afternoon,' Emmy replies gaily. 'Fancy seeing you here, Caleb.'

Fancy indeed, as if we don't all live within a few streets of here. 'I didn't think of you as a fervent churchgoer,' I tell him, aware that my tone is sour. There is something about this man that affects me, makes me feel awkward, and I don't like that.

'Church?' He looks back over his shoulder to St Clement Danes. 'Yes. Well, He brings people to Him in mysterious ways. Isn't that what they say? Something like that.' Caleb grins and winks and I want to push him into the gutter for his cheek. 'What brings you two out on such a glorious day?'

'We're going to visit a slave boy,' Emmy announces before I can stop her.

Caleb's face falls. 'You what?'

'Ignore her, she's confused. He's a former slave. He was injured some months ago by his old master and we simply want to make sure that he is recovered.' I would rather not have told Caleb anything. I see him looking at me now, thoughtfully, and I wish he would go away.

'I wouldn't mind meeting this lad,' he says to me.

'Why?'

'Because.' Caleb sighs as if I am the irritating person in this conversation and not him. 'Look, my mother was a slave. That's how she came to be here, in London. She was sent here from Jamaica to be a ladies' maid when her mistress married some lord or other. There are people who can help your friend, if he needs it. People who understand his position.'

'Oh, then you can come with us!' Emmy leaps in before I can come up with an excuse. 'Sukey saved his life, you know. He would have died if she had not found him. She hasn't seen him since that day, but we heard that he wants to thank her in person. He's working for an apothecary on Fenchurch Street.'

'Then I would be happy to escort you there to receive his gratitude,' Caleb says, winking at me again. 'You can never be too careful, two young ladies out alone.'

I bite back a retort and give in to what is going to happen anyway now that Emmy has told him our destination. We start to walk, and Emmy starts questioning him on the book he gave her, the pamphlet listing all of the local harlots. I don't know why Caleb annoys me so. Perhaps it is his refusal to take anything seriously. The way he spoke of Camille and was so dismissive of Emmy's theory about the Piper. I know that I am being unreasonable but there is something about the authority that he claims that needles me. His knowledge of Covent Garden that so greatly surpasses mine; his familiarity with Camille. Which reminds me of something . . .

'Caleb, you said something the other day. That you thought someone was taking all of the good harlots out of Covent Garden.'

'Did I?' He strides on and Emmy and I have to trot to keep up, annoying me further. 'Well, it makes more sense than some Piper fellow, don't you reckon?'

'So you think that Camille has been enticed away? Perhaps to work somewhere better?'

'Camille?' He ponders for a moment. 'I don't know. You said she left a lot of money behind and that don't seem like Camille. I can see her disappearing in the middle of the night with the money sewn into her gown but to leave it all behind? No. That's too much to give up for anyone, let alone her.'

'You know her well, then?' I've never seen him at Little

Wild Street but both Maria and Hattie know him, and they'd mentioned him paying to see Camille.

'Well enough.' He clips the words short, not wanting to say more. I suppose there is one obvious reason for him knowing her, and I don't know why but I don't want to dwell on that too long.

'You'll let us know if you hear from her? Or anything about the missing girls?' Emmy chimes in and he agrees easily enough.

Emmy seems to enjoy Caleb's company, so I allow them to make small talk as I ponder on what little Caleb has managed to tell us about Camille. No one who knows her believes that she would willingly leave her money and her valuable belongings behind. But Caleb, on our first meeting, had also been quite convinced that the missing girls had chosen to leave Covent Garden, that they had found better opportunities. I think about Madame Vernier's new venture, and about Daisy Gardner who I am almost convinced has become the enigmatic Beatrice. It is quite possible that the fate of the two girls is linked.

At Caleb's pace, we arrive at Fenchurch Street in no time and now I am nervous. It does not help that Caleb is with us, especially now that Emmy has inflated my purpose in coming here. What if Jonathan has no memory of me? He was barely conscious during our first encounter. It irritates me no end but I find myself wanting to impress Caleb, or at least not to look a fool in front of him. I hope we can find the right place. How many apothecaries can there be on Fenchurch Street? I dig out the note. Mr Brown is the apothecary in question. My eyes search the shop signs, my heart sinking as I realise that they are all shut up for the day of rest. How foolish to come on a Sunday, but then when else could we have escaped without having to answer a hundred questions from Mrs Macauley?

'There!' Emmy points up ahead. 'Is that him?'

A lad is emerging from a doorway up ahead and I am struck by a flash of recognition. Yes, it is Jonathan, I am sure of it. His skin colour is a clear marker, of course, but, more than that, it is obvious that this is a young man who has suffered injury. He walks far more easily than he had on the night I found him, but his limp is pronounced. A patch covers one eye, but he no longer looks in such a sorry state. He is dressed in neat, clean clothes and he has filled out. Proper food and care have brought meat to his bones and an easy expression to his face. He turns to walk in our direction, his gaze passing over us, his mouth falling open slightly as he sees our strange trio.

'Jonathan?' I manage to squeak out his name as we meet.

His wide-eyed stare moves from Caleb to me. 'Is it you?' he asks, amazement in his voice.

'Yes. Sukey.' I hold my hand out and he darts forward to seize it in both of his, rough from labour but strong now as they had been so weak, his good eye filling up. 'Forgive me for coming upon you unannounced. Dr Sharp wrote to me. I wanted . . . he told me that you are much recovered, and I wished to make sure with my own eyes.' I remember my manners. 'And this is my friend Emmy. And this is Caleb.' I hear Caleb snort at my refusal to include him as a friend.

'You saved me.' His tears fall now. 'Thank you. Thank you, a million times over. I cannot . . . ' His smile is so bright that it breaks my heart. 'I hoped to see you, to thank you like this in person. Thanks to God that this happy day has come.'

'Yes, thanks to God,' I echo, then added: 'And to Dr Sharp, of course. I suppose it was he who helped you all these months.'

'Oh yes,' he agrees.

'And you are quite recovered? And working, earning a decent wage?' I wince to hear myself, sounding quite like the pious Reverend Ashley. *Earning a decent wage.* Coming from me, she who trades sin as currency.

Still, Jonathan does not know any better. 'I am.' He draws himself up proudly, though he's barely taller than I am, and Caleb, who has been mercifully silent so far, towers above him. 'Mr Brown is a kindly master. He gives me lodging as well as a salary. It is but a room or I would invite you inside.' He looks worried now, concerned that he has committed some social faux pas.

'Oh no, you mustn't worry,' I say quickly. 'I can see you have somewhere to be. I won't keep you.'

'Oh no,' he says quickly. 'It is just that I must walk every day to help my leg. Doctor Sharp says that it will never be what it was, but that there is much room for improvement.'

'Your previous master did this to you.' Caleb speaks for the first time and his voice is surprisingly gentle. 'He thinks you dead?'

Jonathan nods. 'It is a blessing for now I am free from Mr Lisle.'

'He won't find you?' Caleb looks serious. 'I know other slaves in London. People you can talk to, who know how to stay free.'

'Oh no.' Jonathan sounds nervous now, glancing around to see if anyone is watching our strange group. Three Negroes and a pretty young blonde girl are noticeable. 'I have Doctor Sharp and his brother. They said that they will help me if need be.'

'I am sure of that. But if you ever want to meet people like yourself – like us – you can come to Covent Garden and seek me out. Caleb Fowler. Of Fowler's Finest Books on Drury Lane.'

'Thank you, sir.' Jonathan bows and I can tell that he is a little overwhelmed at being confronted so unexpectedly.

'I promise you, you would be most welcome at our gatherings,' Caleb continues, 'and it would be a place where you might meet with Sukey as well. We are a group of both men and women. Both former slaves and free.'

Jonathan meets my gaze. 'In that case, perhaps I will try to come along. Next time I am in Covent Garden I shall pay your shop a visit.'

I manage to drag Caleb away before he can continue his evangelising regarding his mysterious group of Negroes which he did not feel in any way inclined to mention to me on our first meeting. Still, he has barely invited me to join them, instead merely offering me as a temptation to Jonathan. Am I not worthy enough? I am not a former slave; I do not know what other horrors may have befallen Jonathan. But I also know that Caleb is in the same position as I am. Both of us are the children of slaves, born free in this so-called great city. How dare he judge me?

✳ MARCH 1766 ✳

Delphine Du Lac, Pall Mall, St James's

An elegant woman who is happy to drop her refinement for the right gentleman. Certainly, no virgin, she is nevertheless spoken of well since her arrival in St James's. She is said to be from foreign parts, though whether Huguenot or Saxon, she has fluency in the language of love.

20

To Emmy's relief, there is no word from the Armitages but one week later, she is again ignored in the salon. Mrs Macauley insists on dressing her to look like a young country maid, certain that her clientele will pay for innocence. She forgets that everyone who calls at Little Wild Street knows very well that Emmy is her daughter and that she has no maidenhead left to give. And so, with Hattie and Maria unable to afford not to angle themselves at the more affluent of our regular gents, Emmy is left alone, silent in the corner, until eventually a drunk merchant stumbles in, fresh from a successful day's trading. He grumbles but stumps up the coins that Mrs Macauley demands for her daughter. Emmy has to act as a crutch to hold him upright and I hope that, for her sake, he is so far gone that he won't manage to ask too much of her.

'Where is Mr Drake?' Mrs Macauley asks me when we were alone. She stands by the fireplace while I sit on the sofa, sipping the cheap wine she serves on quiet nights like this.

I know she is losing patience with both me and him. The instant his payments lapse I will be in the same situation as Emmy, hoping for a quiet drunkard with enough money in his pocket.

'I suppose he is busy,' I say airily, trying not to show my concern as I make up a version of what I hope might be the truth. 'Madame Vernier says that he is making financial arrangements to secure his position in London and then he will be able to finalise plans to become my keeper on a more permanent basis.'

She laughs. 'Well, let's see if that happens. He is certainly taking his time. When you've been in this game as long as I have, you know that nothing is set in stone until the money has exchanged hands. Gold is all that you can count on, Sukey. You'd do well to remember that.'

'Is that why you send Emmy off with anyone who pays. I thought you wanted more for her than that?'

'Has that wine gone to your head, girl?' She sounds amused rather than angry at my criticism of her. 'Emily is my daughter, yes, and it's my duty as her mother to prepare her for every eventuality. God knows if I had been as precious as you are about who I let between my legs at your age, I'd've been dead long ago. When we get to St James's, Emily will have experience that will serve her well, while you have to hope and pray that Mr Drake sticks by you. It will be a nasty shock for you, my dear, when he throws you aside.'

'He will not.' Even I can hear the uncertainty in my voice.

Mrs Macauley just smiles. 'I hope to be proven wrong.'

There is a knock at the front door and my heart leaps in my chest as I send up a silent prayer, one that is unexpectedly to be answered when Jakes appears. 'Mr Drake,' he growls. 'Said he'd go straight up to the room and for you to send Sukey with the wine.'

I jump up, triumphant. 'I will fetch the nicer wine. Jonas won't drink this evil stuff.'

As I move towards the door, Mrs Macauley shoots out a hand, pulling me back until I face her. 'Don't get too giddy, girl. You have no contract with this man, and he owes you nothing. When the ink is dried on his signature, then you can start to have faith in him. Not before. Trust me. For your own sake.'

The problem is that she has never given me a reason to trust her before. I'm certainly not going to start right here and now.

'Will I see you this evening?' I ask Jonas as he dresses the next morning. It is still dark outside, but at least he has stayed the night. I tried my best to accommodate his needs, but his impatience persists as does his reluctance to acknowledge when he hurts me. He remains distant; I suppose he has a wife to get back to now. He must save his good humour for her these days.

He makes a study of the buttons on his shirt, keeping his head turned away from me. 'Not tonight, Sukey. I have a dinner engagement on the other side of the city.'

'The day after then?' I know I'm being too insistent, but I can't help myself. Every time I look at him I hear Mrs Macauley's warning. Without a contract, I have nothing. I am no longer so certain that any contract will be forthcoming and that makes me fearful, even as I wince at the spreading ache between my legs that he seems determined to leave me with after each recent encounter.

'I will send word.' A brief kiss is deposited on my lips and then he is gone.

Perhaps he is struggling to balance the financial commitments of his new marital status with those of his leisure time. A new household is probably quite expensive to set up. Once that is done, it will be my turn. I sit up and regard my reflection in the mirror above the small dressing table in Camille's room. I think that I look well. My skin is clear and my hair thick, though I will have to comb out the tangles. I must be patient and soon he will revert to his old self.

There is a knock on the door and Emmy charges in, not waiting for me to answer. 'What the hell do you think you're playing at Sukey?'

She yanks the bedclothes away and I almost fall out of the bed in shock. 'What on earth are you talking about? I haven't done anything.'

'That's not what Mama says.' She stands at the foot of the bed, eyes blazing. 'You told her that I was unhappy. That she is a bad mother for selling me off to all and sundry.'

'I didn't say that. Not exactly.' I waver, knowing that I had indeed said that. 'But she should take better care of you. It was only a couple of months ago that you were going to be her golden child. The girl who sold her maidenhead for a fortune and became the queen of Covent Garden.'

'So, you think I'm a disappointment then.'

'No! Not to me.' The words are coming out all wrong. 'I just want her to take better care of you. To treat you like a daughter rather than any of the rest of us. To stop trading you to men like Kellett. To people who hurt you.'

'Really?' Her laugh is bitter. 'Well, whatever it was that you hoped might happen, it's done the very opposite. She had promised me that I wouldn't have to see the Armitages again, only now they've sent word that they want me for a party they're having on Saturday evening. They're offering a lot of money, more than even Jonas pays for a week with you.' Tears are rolling down her cheeks. 'She told me that you were right, and she knows that I'm worth more than this place. And to prove it to me, she's accepted on my behalf. I have to go to the party, Sukey, because of you!'

'That isn't fair,' I defend myself. 'I am sorry, but you know I never meant for this. Emmy, how could I have known?! I only wanted to help you.'

'Then stop. Your help is of no use to me.' She slams the door behind her as she leaves.

Hattie and Maria are also a little cold with me. I try to remind them that I am nothing like Camille by helping Hattie to mend a hole in her gloves, by writing a letter on Maria's behalf to her brother who is working off his conviction for theft on a plantation in Virginia. They thank me but afterwards I realise that my actions have only served to compound my foolish words. I am a better writer than Maria because of my education, something that she has never had. I am not a seamstress, but I can sew a neater stitch than Hattie after years with Mrs Ashley who was not averse to slapping my legs if I did not meet her strict standards when it came to hemming the church linens. I spoke out as if I am superior to them, and I am continuing to behave in that same manner.

'Is there nothing I can do?' I ask Cook in desperation, the pair of us chopping vegetables for that evening's stew. She alone is treating me no differently than before. I suspect it is only because she can't be bothered to get involved in the petty politics of the brothel, but I'm not about to look a gift horse in the mouth.

'Have patience, dearie,' she tells me. 'It takes real effort to hold a grudge against someone. Eventually it will feel easier for them to forgive you and let things go back to normal.'

As far as Hattie and Maria are concerned, I think she is right. But with Saturday's soirée at the Armitages' growing ever closer, I know that my friendship with Emmy is balanced on a precipice. For if the evening goes badly, she will surely blame me for it. I can't say that I would think any differently if our places were switched.

'If only there were a way to stop Emmy having to attend the party,' I say.

Cook wipes her hands on her apron. 'If you're that desperate there is one person you could talk to.'

'Who?'

Her sigh is laboured. 'I hate to say it but the only person who gets Lucy's back up – proper, I mean – is Gizzy Vernier. And say what you like about that woman, she knows the right people. She's a clever woman. Devious, you might say.'

She is right. Mrs Macauley does seem to despise Madame Vernier, but at the same time she listens to her. Both women know the perils of being too proud in our profession. If Madame Vernier could find Emmy someone like my Jonas, or at least an alternative to the Armitages, then it would be worth the risk of invoking Mrs M's wrath.

I chop the rest of the carrots as quickly as I can and race out to find paper and ink. Thanks to my prior assistance, I know that Maria has stashed a small supply of writing materials in one of the parlour cabinets. Scrawling a quick missive, I dash out into the street with a few coins in hand. It doesn't take long to find a young boy willing to take the note to Pall Mall. I don't know the exact address, but these lads are resourceful. I am sure that Madame Vernier's name along with the description of it being a house of women will help him find the right place.

21

Indeed, Madame Vernier does come to my aid, within a matter of hours. She obviously recognises the need for discretion, her reply coming via the kitchen door where only Cook, my ally, might intercept it. Her note is just a few lines, an invitation to visit her the next day at her Pall Mall house at two o'clock, the full address of which is provided. *Bring Emily*, she urges, *for I may have a solution to her dilemma.*

A solution! I see it as a chance to save not only Emmy but our friendship. If I can fix what I have broken, then won't she forgive me?

'Be careful what you wish for,' mutters Cook as I say as much aloud.

'Weren't you the one who told me to contact Madame Vernier?' I laugh.

'I was, only now I've had a chance to think on it, I'm not so sure it was a good idea.' She sits down heavily at the kitchen table. 'If Lucy finds out that you've taken her only daughter to see her greatest rival then I don't like to think what she'd do to you.'

She is overreacting, surely. 'But she's let Madame Vernier help her several times. With me and Jonas. With Camille.'

'Exactly. Camille.' Cook leaps on my poor example. 'There's

something fishy about all that. I don't know what it could be, but that girl wasn't flighty. She was blinded by her own beauty, but she knew it wouldn't last. That's why she was so vicious to the girls. She knew she had to make her money now while she could. She'd not have upped and left the way she did without a very good reason.'

'I haven't heard you say anything about it,' I accuse. 'Why didn't you speak up when Mrs M said that Camille must have stolen the money and run off?'

'Because no one in this bleedin' house listens to me. I'm just the old ugly whore who couldn't get a cully to pay for her anymore and ended up in the kitchen. All anyone cares about is if their grub's on the table when they expect it. Added to that, was any of you even the slightest bit sad to see that girl go?' She doesn't even seem angry, only resigned.

'I'm sorry.' I can't defend myself against her accusations when they are completely true.

'It's not just you. No one spoke up for her, and I understand why. She never learned that you were allowed to make friends, not just enemies. She thought that the only way to succeed was to trample the other girls, when they were never trying to fight her in the first place.' She sighs. 'She reminds me of Gisele Vernier in her younger days, if I'm honest. That's what really worries me. Look, she may well be able to help Emmy. I don't doubt that there's no one else who could. That's why I suggested it. But don't be a fool. Don't go trusting her blindly. Not until you know exactly what happened to Camille.'

Her last words are still stuck in my head the next day as Emmy and I head out on foot towards the more fashionable area of St James's where Madame Vernier's house is to be found.

Pall Mall is a genteel and quiet street, and I am very glad that we have dressed for the location. Madame Vernier would not be pleased if we turned up looking like the Covent Garden hussies that we are. It is another city, another world altogether. The hectic chaos of our usual environs is completely absent. Here, ladies stroll past, wearing dresses that obviously cost their wearers far more than my most treasured gown. The shops have polished doorknobs, and their windows are gleaming clean. Across the road I spy a bookshop, as removed from that of Caleb's father as it is possible to get. I doubt that they sell books advertising the whores of the city. Instead, there is a gilt painted sign, a window display of smart looking volumes, and no hint of impropriety.

'I don't know what you think she can do.' Emmy has sulked all the way, but she still came on the journey. Even the slightest chance of escaping the Armitages has brought the light back to her eyes.

'Isn't it worth finding out? I can't think of anyone else who might help us.'

She hasn't exactly been civil with me over the past day, but she is talking to me, in a manner of speaking. When we reach the address that Madame Vernier gave me, she lifts her hand but it is trembling so much that she can barely manage to raise the brass hammer of the door knocker. I lean across and knock more smartly before taking that cold hand in mine, squeezing tightly and hoping to bring her some reassurance.

The maid who answers looks no older than twelve years old, her skin an almost identical shade to my own, her eyes wide as though she is not used to greeting guests. 'I can help you?' she stammers.

'We're here to see Madame Vernier,' I tell her. 'Miss Maynard and Miss Macauley. She is expecting us.'

'Mathilde!' I hear Madame Vernier's voice along the passage within. 'Show them in, you foolish girl.'

Mathilde blushes deeply and steps back, allowing us to enter the house. I can see immediately why Madame Vernier is so proud of her new enterprise. Mrs Macauley would die if she saw how her old rival has risen above her. The entrance hall is airy and light, a large chandelier hanging from its high ceiling. The tiled floor is highly polished and the biggest vase I've ever seen dominates a mahogany side table, pink camellias in full bloom. I hear footsteps and head towards them, meeting Gisele Vernier in the doorway to a large sitting room.

'Excellent timekeeping, Sukey.' She nods her approval, and I can't help but smile. 'Matty, be a dear and fetch up the tea set. Cook should have it ready.'

The girl disappears and Emmy and I take our seats on a sofa next to the fire while Madame Vernier sits opposite in a large armchair. In this room, with large paintings on every wall, an expensive-looking Turkish rug on the floor and more vases full of flowers on almost every available surface, the Frenchwoman looks every bit the lady of St James's. Looking around me, it is difficult to believe that the rich furnishings have been paid for by nothing less than the trading of bodies, that through selling herself, Madame Vernier has been able to pay for not only these expensive chandeliers but the silk gown that she wears and the diamonds that hang from her ears.

'What a lovely house,' I say. 'How long have you been here?'

She waves away my compliment. 'Just a month or so. Believe me, if you'd been here a week ago you would not be admiring this room. In fact, the upper floors are still in progress. I have two bedchambers ready, for business, of course, but even my own is still looking little better than a cell.'

I sense Emmy's heightening anguish. 'You said that you might be able to help us. With Emmy's problem.'

'Ah yes,' she says. 'The Armitage party.' She pauses at the clinking of china as little Mathilde struggles in with a heavy tea tray. 'Here, girl.' She gestures to the side table, sighing heavily as she gets up to help her. 'Practise, Mathilde. You must learn to do these tasks without being shown or I will find another use for you.' The girl is dismissed, and I wondered where Madame Vernier had found her. There are not many of our complexion in London, though I suppose that a high number are in service, hidden behind the walls of houses like this one. Caleb's image springs into my thoughts and I push it away immediately.

'Is there any way that you can prevent Emmy from having to attend the party?' I ask as Madame Vernier unlocks her tea caddy.

'Why certainly,' she says, turning to smile in Emmy's direction. 'Although it won't be an easy decision for you to make, Emily.'

'It's not difficult at all,' Emmy says quickly. 'I would do anything not to go.'

'Yes, but . . . ' Madame Vernier sighs and comes to sit, letting the tea infuse in its pot. 'If you were to tell your mother that you refuse to attend the party, what do you think might happen?'

Emmy looks down at her hands as they rest in her lap. 'She would throw me into the Coffin. She might even wash her hands of me since I can't manage to attract a single gent to our door. I'm of no use to her apart from the money she can make from me.'

It is the first time I've heard Emmy admit it. The loyalty to her mother has been tested too strongly and the strain of Emmy's predicament has resulted in this fraying of the bonds between them. I want to smile but don't dare.

'You are quite correct, Emily. And that is why this decision is a tricky one. You cannot just refuse to attend the party. You need an alternative solution. That is what I offer you, but it will mean leaving Little Wild Street, perhaps for good.' She reaches out to the table beside her and rings a small bell. 'I have someone you should meet.'

Emmy and I stare at each other. Emmy, to leave Little Wild Street? This isn't what I'd hoped for, not so soon. We are so distracted that we don't even notice the woman who enters the room to answer the bell. Not until she speaks.

'Well, look what the cat dragged in.'

'Camille?' Emmy's face is white, her shock as deep as mine.

'The one and only. Though these days I go by Delphine. Delphine Du Lac. Can't have Mrs M finding out that I've been here all along.' How can I have forgotten how infuriating she is? Camille takes the armchair beside Madame Vernier, clear ground left between them and us.

Alive and well, then, and smug with it. From the glittering emerald and diamond pendant hanging from her neck, I can now understand why she'd been happy to leave her money behind at Little Wild Street. She has found a way to make far more than she ever would in Covent Garden. Her dress is silk, the latest fashion, and her powdered face is impeccable. She looks like a lady, not just a whore dressed up and trying to pass as one. She takes my breath away. And that is before I consider what Madame Vernier's part in this transformation has been.

'You lied.' I can't stop the words from exploding out. 'You knew where Camille was all along.' I will not call her Delphine.

Madame Vernier's lips press together in annoyance. 'Yes, I told you what I thought you would believe. But only in order to save poor Delphine. In certain circumstances, to save a life, might it not be seen as a good thing? Even your Reverend Ashley might agree with me on that, Sukey.'

'How do you know about Reverend Ashley?' I ask, confused.

She looks to the heavens. 'Girls, there is so much you don't know. So much that your mother, Emmy, has neglected to tell you. Or your sainted aunt Betsy who, when I knew her, was working from Haddock's bagnio and making a reasonable living from the desires of men, all until that man of God decided to save her soul.' She shrugs her shoulders. 'Well, who am I to judge people on their choices.'

Camille laughs and I notice that even that has been improved so that it tinkles rather than grates. 'Shall I pour the tea, Gisele? And then we might hurry things along a little. I have an errand to run.' Even her accent has changed, no longer the strange impersonation of a Frenchwoman, but translated into a precise and pleasant English.

Madame Vernier nods her assent. 'Look at how Delphine has improved herself. Her gown, her jewellery, her manner. What I am offering you, as your solution Emily, is this. To become my next protégée.' She turns to me. 'And Sukey, please accept my apology for lying to you on two occasions. The girl Daisy is indeed living here, as Beatrice. I saved her from the awful fate that befell her sister and mother and brought her here. She has exceeded all my expectations, but I think, Emily, you could be my greatest success.'

Camille hands me a cup of tea and I try not to look as shattered as I feel. I want to save Emmy, of course I do, but I never expected to lose her. If she comes here, to this house, her problems will be over. She might be happy here. But I will be left behind, without her. Facing her mother's wrath and not even able to visit Emmy, for I am sure that Mrs Macauley will forbid it if her daughter humiliates her so.

This is too much, all at once. Every mystery solved in an instant. All the result of Gisele Vernier's machinations. It should have been obvious. The missing girls around the time of her arrival in Covent Garden, the plans she shared with me quite openly. This new version of Camille, too. Before, she'd not have passed me the salt at the dinner table; now she is serving me tea and asking if I require more sugar.

'I'll have another bedchamber prepared and you needn't worry. I don't run my house like Little Wild Street.' Madame Vernier laughs, and Camille joins in. 'I don't have lewd parties every night. Instead, once a week on a Friday evening I have a dinner. Invited guests only and certainly no more than ten of us at the table. I make introductions for my girls, to men who have means to support a certain lifestyle.' She looks to me. 'I might invite Jonas to bring you this week if you would like, Sukey. My guests are certainly men he should get to know if he wants to rise up in the London ranks.'

I don't know what to say but manage a small nod. Perhaps this could be a good thing. Emmy would be safe here, wearing beautiful dresses and only having to tend to the finest of gentlemen. Jonas will be grateful to me for the invitation to Madame Vernier's select circle, and he might finally commit to being my keeper.

'You must do it, Emmy.' I turn to her. 'Your mother will not treat you kindly if you refuse to go to the party. This way you'll be safe, and I won't tell her where you are, not if you don't want me to.'

She looks torn. 'I – I don't know, Sukey. It's all so sudden. And I only just found her again. My mother, I mean. If I betray her like this, she'll never forgive me.'

'Goodness, who cares!' Camille jumps in and I wish to the heavens that Madame Vernier had not invited her to join us. 'She doesn't treat you like a daughter. As far as she's concerned, you're just a source of income, same as the rest of us were at Little Wild Street. The only difference is that she wanted to have a legacy. Not just end up some old crone like all those other bawds. You've already disappointed her. What else can you offer her?'

'You have not disappointed her, Emily.' Madame Vernier shoots Camille a sharp stare. 'Poor Lucy just does not have the access to the right sort of people. She wanted to match you with a lord or a duke but how when she knows none? It is not your fault, my girl. I can show you as much.'

Emmy remains silent, staring down into her untouched cup. I can't tell what she is thinking. To me it seems there is no decision to be made. She must know that what Camille says, blunt though it is, is more than true.

Madame Vernier shows her wisdom. 'You need time to think. I understand. You feel that it will be a betrayal of your mother, Emily, but I urge you to realise that it is she who has already betrayed you. I can give you until tomorrow. If I don't hear from you by the evening, then I shall sadly assume that you have chosen to suffer the attentions of the Armitages.'

Emmy has time to think, and I have time to convince her that this is the right decision. For both of us.

22

Camille escorts us out of the house, saying that she needs to visit the local apothecary. Once we are out of earshot of Madame Vernier, she grabs my upper arm, twisting it until I cry out.

'What on earth is wrong with you?' I demand.

'I want my money. I know you'll have found it by now, you sneaky little wench. And keep walking, this is a nice part of town. Don't draw attention.'

'You're too late,' I tell her, not unhappily. I wrench out of her grasp but do as she said and walk on. 'Mrs Macauley cleared out all your belongings. She found the money and used it to pay off your debts.'

She utters the first syllable of a curse before remembering where she was. 'That dirty thief!'

I'm not going to tell her that it was I who handed over the money, or that I visited her former beau, the haberdasher. Presumably she's forgotten all about that old life now that she has a duke or a lord of whatever, along with plenty of jewels.

'Can I tell Hattie and Maria about you?' I ask. 'They've both been so worried about you, and I'm sure they won't tell Mrs M.'

'Maria already knows,' she tells me. 'She was supposed to find the money and keep it safe for me. She must have been too late.'

'What?' I am flabbergasted. Maria isn't a dissembler, and she hasn't behaved oddly at any time since Camille left. 'Did you tell her not to tell us?'

'No.' Now it is Camille's turn to look confused. 'No, I went along with Vernier's plan because she promised me a lot more money – no more ledgers or debts. She said that I could come and see if I liked it here. That if I didn't, and wanted to go back, then I could say that I'd been taken against my will and hope that Mrs M believed it. Trust me, though,' she says with a laugh, 'I only needed a day to know that I wouldn't need that lie. I'm never going back to Little Wild Street.'

'Is it so much nicer here?' I ask, trying to gauge Emmy's reaction to what Camille is telling us, but Emmy's eyes are fixed firmly on the ground.

'She doesn't suffer fools gladly, but if you're sensible and know how to play the game, it is another world. A world where someone finally sees my value. I cannot tell you how much that means.' Camille looks around. 'I do actually need to visit the apothecary.'

'Wait.' I stop her. 'I swear, Maria doesn't know you're here. Why do you think she does?'

'I sent a message,' she says, her brow furrowing. 'Vernier helped me to write it. It's all part of my training, you see. Learning to read and write properly in case the gentlemen want to send and receive messages. They love it apparently. Makes them all excited and it's a lot less work than the other things that get them hot and bothered.'

'And she definitely sent it?'

'Yes. Why wouldn't she?' She is annoyed now, looking around as if someone might spot her talking to the riffraff. 'Look, Maria probably just thought she was being discreet and didn't want to get Mrs M in a fit. Ask her when you get home. You'll see.'

She disappears into the shop and leaves me with my confusion.

'I swear down, I never got no note from her.' Maria has a different story to Camille's and I struggle to believe that she would lie. She looks truly shocked. 'I'd have told you! Maybe not Mrs M, I'm not a fool.'

'I suppose the Piper never took her then,' Hattie muses. 'But then what about Daisy Gardner?'

We are in the parlour, waiting for the evening's business to roll in. Mrs Macauley is in her office as she often is during these quiet moments before chaos ensued, calculating based on the previous night's tally whether she needs to drive harder bargains than usual or whether she can relax and see what unfolds in the hours before dawn.

'I may have seen Daisy Gardner,' I admit.

'What? Where!' Hattie forgets herself in her excitement.

'Hush, for God's sake!' Maria hisses. 'You want Mrs M to hear you?' She turns to me. 'Sukey, you'd better tell us everything you know right now.'

'I know who the Piper is,' I tell her. 'You'll never guess.'

'Who?' Hattie is beside herself.

'Madame Vernier.' Emmy jumps in before I can make my dramatic announcement, her tone flat. She has been quiet since we returned, and I fear that her dilemma has grown rather than being solved.

'You what?' Maria looks confused.

'Gisele Vernier is the Piper herself and I only wish she'd play her tune for us.' I am careful not to give any impression that either myself or Emmy have any intentions of joining the Frenchwoman's household. 'She got herself a big fancy house in Pall Mall and both Camille and Daisy are working there. Them other girls as well, I suppose. Camille was all dressed up in silk and jewels. She said she's earning more money than she ever thought possible, and their clientele are members of the ton.'

'I don't know what to say,' Maria says, and she looks so upset that I almost wish I hadn't told her. 'I suppose it's a relief to know there's not some man out there spiriting away girls, but I'm not sure I'd want to work for such a shady character as that Frenchwoman.'

'I do! I've a good mind to walk myself to St James's myself this very moment and beg for an audience with your madame,' Hattie says with a laugh. 'If she can turn a Gardner into a goddess then imagine what she could do for any of us!'

'You can't trust her,' Maria warns. 'She's sat in this very room and lied to our faces. If Camille's letter went missing, what else might she be hiding from her own girls? Does Daisy even know about her mother? She's not a selfish girl. I can't see why she'd abandon her family like that.'

'Maybe because her mother was a pox-ridden gin-addled monster? She beat those girls, you know, when they were small. Rose told me that once when she was in her cups herself. She had them taking in gents before they'd even bled, just charged extra and drank herself into a stupor so she couldn't hear them crying.' Hattie shakes her head. 'I can't blame Daisy for leaving and never coming back.'

'Nor me,' I say, horrified. As much as I sometimes despise Mrs Macauley, at least she allowed us a childhood.

'Still, would she have left her sister to rot an' all?' Maria knows better. 'No, trust me, that Vernier woman is up to no good. She saw a desperate one in Daisy. And as for Camille, *if* she did write a letter, she'll have fallen for a bit of sweet talk. She'd follow anyone who tells her she's pretty and gives her a nice dress.'

I can see Emmy's face as she listens to Maria's damning verdict on Madame Vernier, and it worries me. She is wavering still, even though the spectre of Mrs Armitage hangs over her.

'It is a lovely house,' I say quickly. 'And Daisy – why, she looked like a proper lady when I saw her at the party. I almost didn't recognise her on the arm of a real duke! Imagine if we all went to Pall Mall.'

Hattie cackles. 'Don't let Mrs M hear you. She'll hand you over to Sir Horace for tuppence every night for a week to teach you a lesson.'

'Sir Horace!' Maria laughs then. 'You'd be lucky. More like Tobias Kellett and I'll tell you now that you're the luckiest of us here for not having to spend a night with that ghoul of a man.'

We are disturbed by a heavy knock at the front door and we all groan. It is still early for custom and none of us are in the mood to entertain. Hattie runs off to fetch the punch and the rest of us stand, ready to greet our first gentleman of the evening.

'Just a note, ladies, no need to get excited.' Jakes holds out a folded paper to me.

'Who's it from?' Emmy asks.

The girls crowd me, but I don't recognise the handwriting. It is neat and carefully written. There is the name of a tavern, the Shakespeare's Head, and a time. Ten o'clock. In an hour's time. I know of the tavern, though I've never set foot inside. The only signature is the curl of a C. Camille? I don't think so. Even if someone wrote the note for her, she would be far more likely to send for Maria or Hattie. There is only one other person I know whose name begins with that letter and, I hate to admit it, I am curious to know what they might want.

I try to conceal my surprise as I look at Jakes. 'How much to let me slip out, just for half an hour.'

He chews on his pipe. 'How much is it worth to you?'

'Can you not just give a straight answer?' I think for a moment. What can I afford, and what might he accept? What is this strange rendezvous worth? 'A shilling,' I decide.

'Make it two and we got a deal. And I'm a kind fella so you can pay me tomorrow after you've earned it. Though I won't lie to Mrs M if she misses you.' He shakes my hand and walks away whistling.

I study the note again. What does Caleb want?

It is a quiet evening, and Jakes opens the door for me to run out just before ten o'clock. It had been a sunny day with hints of spring, but the clear skies have let any warmth fly away and the cobbles are slippery as I hurry my way into the piazza. Most of the customers at the Shakespeare's Head seem to have been there for a while, judging by their conduct, and I have to keep my wits about me, several times having to evade hands that grope as I pass. I weave my way through the tightly packed tables until I find him, almost hidden in a nook at the back.

'You came.' Caleb sounds almost surprised.

'Yes, though I thought twice about it. What do you want?' I let my annoyance show.

'To talk. I didn't want you to have any distractions and, take no offence, but I can't afford to buy your time at your mistress's rate at the moment.' He steers me towards a table before I can refuse. 'I'll buy you a drink. I think you'll want to hear what I have to say.'

I doubt it but after all, this meeting is costing me two shillings. I should at least hear him out. He orders two ales and I don't bother to complain that I'm not partial to the stuff.

'So, I heard something,' he tells me. 'About Camille and them other girls. I thought you'd like to know since you were so worried about them.'

I hold my hand up to stop him. 'We found Camille. I saw her earlier today, with my own two eyes and she's well. Angry with the world, but well.'

'Her natural state then,' he says, and I cannot help but smile along with him. 'Well, I'm glad to hear that. But it's about more than Camille.'

'Go on.'

'So, she wasn't the only girl to go missing. There was the Gardner girl. There was another girl between them. And last year three girls disappeared and ain't been seen since. All of 'em were on last year's *Harris's List*. All three of them had recommendations.'

Harris's List. The book that Emmy had taken on our visit to the bookshop. The gentleman's bible, listing every harlot of note in London, good or bad.

'You think that someone's picking out the decent harlots and enticing them away?' I have to laugh. He thinks he knows it all, but he doesn't know about Madame Vernier. Though it sounds as though he's on her trail. 'Perhaps the Piper's simply a man with an insatiable appetite for whoring who needs his own harem.'

He rolls his eyes. 'This isn't about some man wanting to

stick his maypole where the sun don't shine. It's about money. Someone is taking away the younger girls, those with a good reputation, who look well in a fine gown and won't give anyone the pox. They can use the girls to make money. Bawds have been doing as much as long as London's existed. We've only noticed this time because the girls are from the same few streets.'

'A bawd?' Shall I just tell him what I know? 'Camille is working for a woman named Madame Vernier, but she's in a very discreet place in St James's. Daisy is there too.'

'Vernier? The Frenchwoman?'

'You know her?' I'm surprised. As much as Caleb has claimed to know everything that goes on in Covent Garden, I cannot see her giving him the time of day.

'I know Tobias Kellett,' he explains. 'Now that is a man I'd not piss on if he were on fire.' He takes a gulp of ale. 'He's a customer of my father's. She came into the shop with him once. He spends a good amount of money on indecent books. Pa gets them in special for him and, I tell you, his tastes are quite something.'

I decide not to ask for specifics. Even the little I know of Kellett turns my stomach. 'Yes, Madame Vernier is an acquaintance of his. Do you think he's behind this?' Kellett has money but neither Daisy nor Camille would have gone anywhere with him. Perhaps Gisele Vernier is simply the face of his enterprise. What would that mean for Emmy if she were to take up Vernier's offer. I need to find out what's going on before that can happen.

'It don't make sense, none of this. Why all the secrecy? There must be something we're missing.' He is deep in thought.

'I can talk to Hattie and Maria again.' I pause before asking my next question. 'Why did you want to talk to me? I didn't think you liked me very much.'

Even in the dim lighting and with his dark skin, I swear his cheeks redden. 'Says you who until this evening has barely spoken a civil word to me?'

'Exactly.' I make my point.

'Because of Jonathan.' He stutters a little. 'He trusts you and if you would help someone you've only just met then I suppose that you'd do even more to help those you know.'

I smile, enjoying his discomfort, and this small amount of praise, but I have been gone too long. If Mrs Macauley finds out that I left the house during our busiest period she will be furious and, if Emmy is to safely escape, I must remain on her good side.

'I have to go,' I say, getting up to leave. 'I'll come by the shop tomorrow.'

He bids me goodnight and I see him go to join a table of young men in the corner as I reach the tavern door. Caleb is part of Covent Garden. He belongs here in a way that I do not. I try not to feel jealous as I make my way back to Little Wild Street. Annoying as he can so often be, Caleb is cleverer than I thought. Perhaps I have judged him too harshly, for if we work together, I am sure that we can solve the mystery of the Piper. I cannot let Emmy get swallowed into that Pall Mall house without knowing that she'll be safe.

23

'I cannot think of anything less appealing,' Jonas tells me later that night when I broach the subject of dining with Madame Vernier and her esteemed guests that Friday. 'And my wife will expect me home to dine. Not that I have to explain myself to you.'

'I only mention it in case you were not already aware of it,' I say quickly, lowering my eyes. I may have been too bold. 'I heard that there would be important gentlemen there. Madame Vernier is said to have excellent connections, and I thought perhaps they might be of use to you.'

We are lying in bed, and I know that this moment is when he might be most vulnerable. When he is spent, and his guard is down. He still hasn't said anything about making our arrangement more permanent and, without wanting to be desperate about it, I am sure that Madame Vernier's dinner will lead him gently towards making that offer. Once he sees that I can acquit myself admirably in polite company, how can he not?

'Oh God!' He lies back and crosses his arms over his forehead. 'Of course, you're right. I hate this damned city. This constant need to be talking to the right people and being seen in the right places. I cannot bear it.'

'It's only until you're established,' I assure him as if I know of such matters other than what I have overheard in the parlour of an evening. 'It may be hard work at first but after that people will come to you rather than you having to make such an effort. And of course, in such a house, it would hardly be suitable for your wife to attend.'

He smiles and leans over to kiss me, his hand grabbing at my breast. 'It is just such an inconvenience, not to mention that I prefer to pay for your time in satisfying my needs, rather than to sit beside me as I am forced to make small talk.' He rolls over, his back to me, and I soon hear his breathing settle into soft snores.

I hadn't wanted to press him but now I have no clear answer. Will he go, and with me? His reluctance to pay for my time is a dark omen, but I try to put it out of my mind. He has simply had a bad day and chose to take it out on me. That is my place. To make him feel better, however that can be done.

'Have you decided?' I find Emmy as soon as I wake, huddled under the blankets in the room that used to be ours. Jonas has slipped out while I slept, with no word about the dinner party. She looks more miserable than I have seen her for some time, remarkable in itself.

'How can I betray my own mother?' she asks me.

I sit beside her. 'I don't know, love. And I cannot even tell you that Madame Vernier will be better for you.' I tell her about my meeting with Caleb, not having had a chance to the night before. 'But even if she is enticing girls away, look at what she has done for Camille. For Daisy. It is not an easy decision, but you have to choose. Will it be the Armitages and the certainty of that, or will it be Madame Vernier's house to find out what exactly her scheme is?'

Her reply is to pull the bedclothes over her head, and I cannot blame her. I am glad not to have to choose between those two forks in her road. I leave her to her thoughts and go down to the kitchen.

'Good morning, Hattie. Maria.' I sit down and reach for the coffee pot, but it is empty. 'Is there any more, Cook?'

She looks harried. 'No, unless you fetch it yourself. Her highness upstairs has me run ragged. She's decided all of a sudden that we're to host a party here tonight.'

'A party?' I look at Maria, who just shrugs.

'Yes, a party.' Mrs Macauley surprises us all, appearing suddenly. She doesn't often impose upon us at breakfast time. 'It seems that everyone is throwing them these days and so we can't be left behind.'

'Everyone who?' Hattie asks, but I know very well. Word has travelled from Pall Mall of Madame Vernier's plans. Mrs Macauley is staring straight at me.

'Sukey, since you seem to have finished breakfast, perhaps you would join me upstairs.' She turns on her heel and I know better than to make her wait.

We reach her room, and she indicates for me to sit. 'What did you wish to discuss?' I ask, sitting on my hands to prevent them from trembling. Has Emmy gone to her already, told her everything?

'Mr Drake came to me this morning before he left,' she says, and my heart ceases racing. 'He wishes for you to escort him to a dinner party on Friday evening. At the house of Giselle Vernier.' She looks at me expectantly.

'A dinner party?' I try to look stupid, not so difficult in that moment. 'How exciting.'

'Exciting? Perhaps. An opportunity, definitely.' She leans back in her chair. 'Can I trust you, Sukey? That is what I need to know.'

'Of course.' I can't help but smile. Here is the proof that Jonas does care about me. He had been so adamant about hating the idea of the dinner party that he could only have changed his mind in order to please me. 'I shall be on my best behaviour.'

'Yes, you shall. And you shall report to me on everything that conniving bitch says. I want to know who is there and what is spoken about. If Giselle Vernier sneezes funny I want you to make a note of it.' Mrs Macauley bites her lip. 'I'm trusting you as a representative of my establishment. My last emissary absconded, and I had a lot more faith in Camille than I do in you. Will you prove me wrong?'

A spy? I think about Emmy. This could help her. If she does choose Madame Vernier, I can tell Mrs Macauley whatever I want her to hear so that she won't realise immediately what Emmy has done. I can give Emmy time to decide if Madame Vernier really is the right choice and, with a little luck and help from Vernier, I'll be out of Little Wild Street and safely away with Jonas before Mrs Macauley discovers my deceit.

'I will gladly tell you what I observe,' I say.

'Good girl. Oh, and Mr Drake requested that you wear the ruby silk for the party. He will not visit before then, but I have assured him that you shall still be his, exclusively. For now.' She regards me pensively. 'Has he mentioned anything about making your situation more permanent?'

'Not yet, ma'am.'

'On Friday you should make it a priority to press him for a decision.' She selects a letter from a pile by her left hand, slitting the seal with a wickedly sharp letter opener. 'It has been almost three months now. Time for him to make a formal commitment or we should seek an alternative arrangement. I can speak to Mr Kellett about securing you an invitation to the Armitage party on Saturday. I've heard that they often like to have a selection of girls to choose from.'

'No, ma'am, don't concern yourself with that,' I say quickly. Imagine helping Emmy to escape only to become her replacement . . . 'From what Jonas said to me last night, I think it will be soon. He just needs to settle his new household and then he'll be in a position to negotiate our arrangement.' Pure lies, of course, but I am still hopeful. Why else would he have agreed to the dinner?

'I am a patient woman but remind him that this is a business that I'm running. With Camille gone, I need every girl in my care to pay her way. That includes you.' She gives her attention to the letter in her hand for a moment, her mouth turning up in a grimace. 'Mr Drake does not pay enough to guarantee your exclusive attention indefinitely. He has one week.' She rips the paper in two. 'Tell him so and let me know his response on Saturday morning while I still have time to send you with Emily to the Armitage party.'

She dismisses me with a wave of her hand, and I feel sick as I close her door behind me. From conspiring to rescue Emmy, I have suddenly fallen into the mire myself. Will Jonas react favourably to this sudden pressure, or will he decide to make do with his new wife instead? Still, I remind myself, Madame Vernier may help me if the worst comes to the worst. Ever since arriving in London I've dreamed that one day Emmy and I might live together, away from Mrs Macauley. Perhaps that might happen sooner rather than later.

I go to tell Emmy the good news. The bad news I keep to myself; she doesn't need to worry about me. The hour is getting on and she will have to explain herself to her mother if she lays in bed much longer. I worry that she might confess her dilemma and that would never do.

'I don't understand what that has to do with me,' she says as I explain the task that her mother has charged me with.

'If you leave, our plan is to make it look as though you've been stolen. Taken by the Piper. Your mama doesn't know the truth about Camille and Daisy. She won't suspect where you've gone and when I inform her about goings on at the dinner party, I will talk about everything and everyone but you. That way, if you need to return for any reason, we can weave a different story, one that will allow your mother to accept you back.'

She sits up. 'Do you think that would work. Wouldn't Madame Vernier tell her the truth?'

That I don't know. 'She lied for Camille. Why not for you? And later, if you decide to stay, it won't matter if Mrs M finds out. You'll be beyond her reach and that of the Armitages.' A reminder of why we are contemplating such deception.

She untangles herself. 'I should get up before Mama thinks I'm ailing.'

I hide my smile. She is going to make the right decision, I am certain. Now all I have to do is ensure that she arrives safely at Madame Vernier's house without her mother finding out.

24

In the end, Emmy makes her decision alone, without me knowing. I do not hear her leave but I know that she has when I go up to Camille's room and see that on the bed she has left the silver bracelet given to her by Mrs Armitage. A sign that her choice has been made. It stings a little, but I know she's done it to save me. If she had disappeared while on an errand with me, I would have fallen under suspicion. This way, nobody notices that she is missing until we are gathered in the parlour for that evening's soirée. Emmy has been gone for hours already.

'Did anyone see her go out?' Mrs Macauley paces up and down the room. 'Sukey?'

'I was helping Cook in the kitchen all afternoon,' I say, which was the truth. Once I'd hidden away the bracelet, I endeavoured to remove myself from suspicion by making sure that I spent every moment between Emmy's disappearance and its discovery in the company of at least one other member of the household.

'Jakes!' she bellows and he comes running, shame faced and small for all his size. He had popped out to the tavern during the afternoon, and it was during that period that Emmy left. 'Get out there and find my daughter.'

'But who will watch the door?'

'I will manage.' She shocks us all by pulling a sharp silver dagger from one of the cabinet drawers. 'It may have been a while, but I still know how to handle one of these things. Not that it will come to that.'

'Bleedin' 'ell,' Hattie mutters, beside me.

The party is cancelled. Mrs Macauley writes a note to that effect and fixes it to the front door with a nail. Word must get around quickly, for no one even knocks at the door in the hopes that we are still open for regular business. Hattie drinks all of the punch and Maria stares into the flames of the fire for hours. Mrs Macauley continues to pace, and to curse. As for me, I sit there quietly, praying that no one asks me where I think Emmy might have gone. Jakes returns in the early hours of the morning.

'No sign,' he tells his mistress, and I see how scared he is to tell her so. 'I been everywhere I can think of. Only person who might have sighted her, they said they saw a girl dressed up in finery climbing into a carriage up on the Strand this afternoon.'

Mrs Macauley stares at him. 'In finery?' She takes off at pace, running up the stairs, the rest of us following close on her heels.

I know the dress. The emerald gown that she wore on our first night in the parlour. Emmy had always left it in the press in Camille's room and now it is gone. Mrs Macauley whirls upon me.

'How could you not notice it missing?'

She is terrifying in her anguish. 'I – I don't know. I didn't look.'

'She had no money, how could she . . . ?' Mrs Macauley freezes. 'She couldn't . . . no!'

Off she goes once more with us on her tail, down one flight to her own room. It is common knowledge amongst the women of the house that although she keeps most of her money in a heavy iron safe, secured under a slab of stone in the kitchen floor that Jakes hefts up once a week, she keeps the daily takings in a locked desk drawer. A drawer that is no longer locked and no longer holds a single coin. When I looked at the woman's face, I almost felt sorry for her, so distraught was she. So betrayed. I never knew that Emmy had it in her to do such a thing, even I who have spent days convincing her to leave.

'She robbed me.' She sinks into her chair, staring into nothingness ahead of her. 'My own daughter.'

'But how? You keep the key on your person at all times?' Jakes is confused. He looks unsure as to whether this part of Emmy's escape is also his fault.

'I . . . There was a spare that I kept. I showed her one day, thinking she might soon earn the right to hold it. I never supposed . . . ' Mrs Macauley shakes herself. 'Well then, that's it.'

'Mrs M?' Hattie is confused.

'Get back downstairs. The night isn't over yet and you will all need to earn back the money Emmy has stolen.' She stands tall, vengeful, and looks each of us in the eye in turn, her gaze lingering longest on me. 'One of you knew she was going to do this. At least one of you helped her. I don't know who, but you can all work to pay me back.'

'Mrs M!' Maria has had enough. 'This is no one's fault but Emmy's. Why should I pay for her thievery? She'll turn up sooner or later.'

Mrs Macauley laughs, a granite-edged wheeze that makes me shudder to think what she would do to me if she knew that I had anything to do with Emmy's disappearance. 'So you don't think the Piper has taken her this time? Or was that just Camille, another wicked thief.'

'Punishing us for Emmy's mistake isn't fair,' Maria insists. 'I've always been a hard worker, you know that. I don't have any debt to you other than my bed and board.'

'Well, things change,' Mrs Macauley informs her.

'Yes. P'raps they do,' Maria replies, 'for I have defended you all these years. I know there are bawds who treat their girls far less well than you do, and you have always been fair until now. I'll tell you this now: I will not pay for what your daughter did. I will leave before you take that money from me.'

Hattie and I stare at one another, stunned. I feel foolish, for I did not predict this. Even allowing for the shock of Emmy's thievery, Maria is the most steadfast of us. The most pragmatic. I hold my breath and pray that Mrs Macauley will be sensible. That Maria will withdraw her threat.

'You cannot leave,' Mrs Macauley tells Maria. 'Or I shall call on a Justice of the Peace and tell him that you have robbed me.'

It is Maria's turn to laugh. 'The only Justice of the Peace you'd risk calling here is Percival. The same Justice Percival who used to come here weekly to see Camille. You think she didn't tell him all about you? Your ledgers and your manipulation? And think about when you last saw him. Not since Camille left, so you can see he has no loyalty to this establishment and none to you. Call on him at your peril, Lucille Macauley, for I suspect it may be you he arrests, not me.'

Sweeping out without a backwards glance, Maria has easily won the battle and Mrs Macauley sinks back into her chair, her head dropping into her hands.

'Out!' Jakes shoves Hattie and me, physically removing us from the room and slamming the door behind us as I hear what sounds like sobs coming from a woman who I had thought incapable of tears. In the distance I can hear Maria in her room, loudly gathering her belongings.

'What now?' Hattie whispers.

I feel shaky, my feet uncertain as I walk across the floorboards to the stairs. 'I don't know.'

There is a saying to be careful what you wish for, and I have never felt it so keenly. I never thought that Emmy's leaving would destroy the whole house. After Camille's departure, everything had gone on as it always had done. At least, that's what I had thought. Perhaps her desertion had cracked the foundation of our modest house and now Emmy's subsequent flight is bringing it down around our ears. I cling to the banister as we make our way to the parlour, and fear that I have been too clever for my own good.

The parlour is cold, the fire almost out. While Hattie stokes it, I go to inform Cook of what happened. She is heating milk and yawning, at the end of a long day.

'God help us,' she murmurs when I tell her about Maria's leaving. 'There'll be nothing left of us before long.'

We can't even say a proper goodbye to Maria, not with Jakes checking her bag and escorting her from the premises. 'You know where to find me,' she calls to Hattie over her shoulder, and then she is gone. Jakes slams the door and shoots the bolts.

'Mistress says get to bed,' he growls, and Hattie and I don't stay to argue.

'Where will Maria have gone?' I whisper as we stand on the landing. I don't think that Mrs Macauley can hear us from where we are, but I don't want to risk incurring her wrath after everything else that has happened.

'We both used to work at a tavern, 'bout five minutes from

here,' Hattie tells me. 'Mrs M spotted us there and offered us better terms to work here. To be fair to the old bawd, I don't have no regrets.' She laughs drily. 'I've always had low expectations. You can't get disappointed that way.'

'Will Maria be all right?' I worry. It is late and even though Maria owes nothing to Mrs Macauley, I doubt she has savings. Where will she sleep?

Hattie reaches forward and pulls me into a tight embrace. 'Don't worry your pretty little head over our Maria. You're still a novice here but we're born an' bred. I'll go and find her tomorrow, but she knows a lot of people round here. She'll be fine.'

I take her word for it. What else can I do? I don't sleep though. With both Maria and Emmy gone, there is just Hattie left to tend to the gents in the parlour. Mrs Macauley's ambitious plans to move our little household to a more salubrious location are all but destroyed. She will be either defeated or desperate and I fear the latter.

Without Jonas, and his money, my only use is in becoming like Hattie. Taking to bed any man who pays the going rate. The Friday dinner party is my last chance to impress upon Jonas the urgency of him putting our relationship in writing. A signed contract will save me. Anything less and I am just another Covent Garden whore living on the memory of a broken promise.

25

The house is silent when I finally give up on sleep. Dawn has broken and I feel none of the triumph I thought I would after saving Emmy from her mother. Perhaps it is the way it all happened. That she did not even say goodbye. I told her to go; I can hardly be upset that she did as I asked. Yet I feel betrayed.

Cook is also out of sorts. 'All good things must come to an end,' she tells me, full of ominous portent. 'I did tell Lucy to take better care of her own flesh and blood.'

'Yet she didn't listen.' I spoon porridge into my mouth listlessly.

'Well, she never has done.' Cook kneads bread with her heavy hands. 'I tell you, how was she expecting a girl who grew up in a church family, out in the countryside, to have the temperament of one who lived her whole life on these streets.'

'She thought that Emmy would turn out like her.' Which, when I think about it, makes perfect sense. Family businesses, our own royal family, rely on the son emulating those who have gone before him. Just because we are women, does the same principle not apply?

'She thinks that since she's survived the worst, anyone can do the same.' Cook slaps the dough into a bowl and places it by the fire to rise. 'Not many have suffered worse than old Lucy and even fewer have survived but she has to realise that not everyone is capable of such things.'

'What things has she suffered?' I ask.

'Ah, see that's not my place to say. She finds out I've been opening my gob and my life's not worth living, not at the moment. There's nothing more dangerous than an injured animal.' With that, she picks up her basket and gets ready to head out to the market.

At a suitable hour, I walk to Drury Lane to keep my appointment with Caleb. With all the chaos of the evening, I didn't have a chance to talk to either Hattie or Maria but I do have a plan of sorts. I'll see Emmy at the dinner party and can ask her to find out about Kellett. Madame Vernier will know what sorts of pies he has his fingers in.

I walk into the shop but there is no sign of Caleb. A man sits behind the desk, his head in a book, but he is as far from Caleb as you could imagine. A small, skinny, pink-skinned fellow with a balding head and crooked spectacles.

'Can I help you, young miss?' he asks with a smile. 'Mr Henry Fowler at your service.'

'I was looking for Caleb,' I tell him, taking a step back.

'Ah, he's just popped out on an errand,' he tells me. 'He'll be back in no time. In fact, speak of the devil.'

I turn to see Caleb coming in the door. He winks at me and walks past to the desk. 'All sorted, Pa. The last edition was a good seller apparently.' He takes what looks like a small purse from his pocket and hands it over to the man – did he really call him Pa? 'I'm to get on and finish the next as soon as possible.'

'Thanks, son.' Mr Fowler nods in my direction. 'Why don't you take your young lady upstairs and I'll keep an eye on the shop.'

I can hardly believe my eyes when I see Mr Fowler wink at his son. My goodness, does he imagine this to be a courtship of sorts? Though what sort of gentleman of good standing would encourage his son to be alone with an unmarried girl like me? Still, if anyone knows better it is Caleb and so I follow him up a rickety staircase at the back of the shop and along a passageway into a room that seems to serve as both kitchen and bedroom, a curtain drawn across to separate the two living quarters.

'Coffee?' I nod and Caleb holds the kettle to his ear, listening to judge how much water is within before hanging it above the fire that is burning low. He throws on some more fuel and fetches the coffee pot. 'Take a seat.'

'Your father,' I begin, before running into the problem of how to phrase the question that I really want to ask.

'Could almost be my twin, we look so alike,' he says with a grin, all bashfulness disappeared. 'No, good old Henry is better than most fathers, though we're not blood. He was married to my mother. I was already three years old by the time they met.'

There is no woman's touch to these living quarters, clean though they may be. I sit at the small table. 'He has always treated you as his own?'

'Never anything less.' He busies himself with the pulverising of coffee beans, the rich aroma filling the room. 'She died in childbirth when I was five. Took my baby brother with her, or the other way around, who knows. Henry never blinked. Just told me that he was lucky to have at least one heir and that everything he had would be mine one day. Which is everything you see here and nothing more, but it's more than a lot have.'

'You are lucky,' I agree. 'My own mother died when I was a child, so we have that in common. No one knows who my father was. I suppose in our line of work it's never certain.'

He looks up and I know he hears the bitter note in my voice. 'Finding people who care is the only thing that any of us can try and do. My own father doesn't know I'm alive, though it's no fault of his. My mother was brought from Jamaica when the daughter of the family married and moved to London to be with her husband. She realised that she was with child on the ship, halfway across the Atlantic. Her mistress wasn't a cruel woman, but a slave is a slave. She met Henry in church, and they fell in love. He helped her to get baptised and then they married. He went to her mistress and told her that in the eyes of God, his claim on my mother was superior to hers and, lo and behold, my mother was freed.'

'Is that true?' I ask, amazed. 'About marriage freeing her?' I have never heard of such a thing but then, marriage is so often the only path for women that it is a credible suggestion.

Caleb snorts. 'Not really, but Pa is the king of clever words. He can make the tallest story sound like the truth. It's an old wives' tale that a slave who has found God cannot be enslaved any longer. London isn't the West Indies. From what I've heard, over there the so-called men of God won't let a slave into their churches. Here, they are welcomed in. Anything to save a poor soul, as they say. Baptism is seen as the key to freedom, though it ain't laid out in the law books as such. Still, it don't stop the poor beggars from trying. Just ask your friend Jonathan.'

'Jonathan?' He catches me by surprise. 'What do you mean?'

He looks a little ashamed. 'I saw him the other day. I was out and about, and he was running an errand for his new master, the apothecary. We got to chatting and I invited him to join the fellowship that I'm a member of.'

'Fellowship?' I try not to laugh. Fancy words are not only his father's purview it seems.

'Yes, fellowship.' He defends his choice of term. 'Just as you lot have your sisterhood, we are fellows. Though we do allow women an' all. We meet up and share stories and make merry. Nothing odd about that.'

'I do not have a sisterhood. I don't know what you mean.'

'Maybe you don't call it that, but you women have your little ways of sharing knowledge, 'specially you harlots. Keeping up with the gossip and such. The fallen sisterhood, they call it. Just a more subtle way of referring to those of you in that line of work, as you say.'

'The fallen sisterhood,' I repeat. My own experiences have taught me that a so-called sister is as likely to stab another in the back as to help her out, but perhaps this is what Hattie was talking about when she said that Maria knew people who would help her out. Her 'sisters'. Just as I considered Emmy to be my own sister.

'He's doing well, Jonathan,' Caleb tells me. 'He reckons he's getting stronger by the day, though he'll never be the same. Lame in one leg and blind in one eye. Still, when he says that he's happier now than he's ever been, I believe the lad. He's an optimist, though he has no business being one.'

I laugh, for what Caleb says is nothing but the truth. After the sorry state that he was in, I cannot understand how Jonathan isn't stewing in bitterness and hatred. We make do, I suppose, thinking about my own situation. It is the humanity in us, to live with the hand that we are dealt. Just as I accepted my role as maid when I lived with the Ashleys, I am as good as resigned now to my profession, the oldest of them all.

Prompted, I tell Caleb the story of how I found Jonathan as he pours water over the coffee grounds and lets the brew sit. He is hardly Emmy, but I find that I haven't enjoyed conversation so much in a long time. There is no necessity for constant flattery, the way there is when I talk to Jonas. I do not need to soften my words the way that I have to with Emmy. Caleb speaks as he sees and there is something freeing in that. I forget to find him irritating and begin to enjoy telling my tale.

'You done something good,' he tells me at the end of my story. 'Shame you got caught by that old bastard Jakes, but you saved a life in the meantime. 'Sides, there's a very good chance that if he'd not found you, you'd be dead.'

'I'm not a complete fool,' I tell him, indignant. 'I might have managed quite well on my own.'

He laughs almost loud enough to shake the windowpanes. 'If you say so, Miss Maynard, if you say so.'

'Do you really think me so incapable?'

His face turns serious. 'No, not incapable. But you're new to this city. You're new to understanding what it means to be a Negro on these streets. Even now, you might not like living at Mrs M's, but you're safe there. You earn a fair wage. My mother never got paid a penny in her life. Even after she married Pa, she worked here in the shop and every penny that was handed over by customers was his. He'd have handed it all over to her if she'd asked but . . . ' He rubs his eye and I wonder if that was a tear that he didn't want me to see. 'Jonathan's the same. He was *owned* by that man who tried to kill him. All legal and above board.

There ain't no warrant out for his arrest 'cause really, did he do anything wrong, according to the law?'

'Yes.' I say it loudly, then think twice. 'Surely.'

'Truth is, there's just as much chance that by drawing that man's attention to the fact that Jonathan is still alive, you'd just hand him straight back over. To the man who owns him, still. And the fact that you don't understand that is why this city is so dangerous for you. There's bad people and then there's very bad people and you ain't never met any of the second lot. I have. And there are folk at the fellowship who've known them only too well an' all.'

He is saying it kindly, I know that, but it still stings that he thinks me so naive. Perhaps he is right, and I have led a sheltered life all this time, in a small town, away from the cruelty of the city. Caleb has never been a slave himself, but he has lived a life with the shadow of that trade laying over him. That Jonathan trusts him so quickly tells me that they have an affinity with one another. They share a familiarity with something that I cannot understand, at least not with such brutal proximity.

We drink coffee and talk more, and Caleb tells me that there'll be another meeting of the fellowship on Sunday that I might come along to, and that Jonathan will be there. I agree immediately. Talking to Caleb has made me feel self-indulgent, so buried in my own affairs, but it has also been a comfort. I am less alone with him, in a way that even Emmy cannot make me feel. Maybe the fellowship is what I've been searching for. A place of belonging and friendship, away from the fallen sisters and away from the men who want to buy us and have their way with us. Away from Jonas.

If Jonathan can see the light after being in the darkest of situations, then there is hope for all of us.

26

The house doesn't open for business that evening, or the next. The official reason is that the household is suffering from an undisclosed but temporary illness. Mrs Macauley is locked away in her room, not speaking to anyone but Jakes. Neither Hattie nor I are permitted to step foot outside and I am glad that I managed to see Caleb when I did. My main concern is the meeting that Sunday. I am desperate to see Jonathan and, though I am loath to admit it, Caleb too. Before that, of course, I still have the Friday evening dinner. I know that Mrs Macauley won't forbid me from going to that. She still needs Jonas's money after all, especially after what she has missed out on this week.

Hattie helps me to dress for the dinner, in the red silk as directed. She spends an hour curling my hair; she has nothing else to do with our door firmly closed to punters. With only one girl available it would have looked even worse I suppose, though notes have arrived from concerned regulars, not least Sir Horace who has sent three missives and a bottle of port which he claims would assist in our recovery when heated and mixed with honey.

At seven o'clock, Jakes escorts me to the end of the street where Jonas is waiting in his carriage. I haven't had cause to travel anywhere with him since the ball some weeks earlier, and it is still quite a novelty to sit beside him as we head towards Pall Mall. He keeps the blinds down but otherwise we might be husband and wife, on our way to dine with friends.

'I heard a rumour about Mrs Macauley's house,' he tells me as we slowly progress along the Strand.

The illness. Not having heard from him, I'd assumed word hasn't made it to Jonas yet. I wonder if Mrs Macauley has made a catastrophic decision in closing her doors in such a dramatic way. 'I am well,' I assure him. 'Hattie just ate something that she shouldn't, and Mrs Macauley took precautions. She keeps a very clean house.'

'Ah.' He seems happy with my explanation. 'I had thought to cancel our dinner engagement, but Madame Vernier seemed quite insistent on us being there, for some reason.'

For Emmy, I suppose. How have her two days been, away from everyone she knows? 'I believe Madame Vernier feels invested in our arrangement,' I say instead, then take a risk. 'She is convinced that we have a great future together. If only it weren't for Mrs Macauley's ambition.' I sigh dramatically. 'I fear that she may have other plans.'

'What does your bawd have to do with us, other than collecting my hard-earned money?' he queries. 'Surely she should mind her own business as long as you are paid for.'

'I agree entirely, as does Madame Vernier, but Mrs Macauley is looking to move to St James's herself. If another gent were to swoop in and offer more money for my company, she would take it in an instant. Seeing as how we don't have anything formal in place. Nothing in writing. Nothing to stop her.'

He groans. 'This is what I hate about this city. The obsession with money and status is obscene. Contracts and business dealings. Should I purchase you as I might a horse? Possess ownership papers to prove that you are mine and belong to no other man? How ridiculous!'

Not so very different from the recording of a marriage in the parish register, binding a couple by the law of the land. I do not say this, of course. I do not say anything. For weeks Madame Vernier has spoken about my arrangement with Jonas as if it were a foregone conclusion. That he will happily agree to be my keeper. Yet still I wait and he refuses to put me out of my misery.

'Then if she asks me, I will be clear that she is not to trouble you again,' I tell him, fighting to keep my voice steady. 'I shall tell her that you have no interest in becoming my keeper and she will leave you alone.'

He stares at me, then sighs in irritation. 'Well, there's no need to be like that, Sukey. I simply do not enjoy being pressured into things, that is all. Be patient, that's all I ask. And yes, do tell her to stop troubling me. I shall go to her when the time is right and not before.'

Is that a positive answer or not? I am loath to press him again when he is clearly so agitated on the subject. Besides, we are close to Pall Mall, and I want us to arrive looking the picture of happiness. A couple to be envied. I want to make Camille jealous.

Light blazes out of every window in the house as our carriage pulls up outside, and I wonder how much it costs Madame Vernier to keep the house running. Between the window tax and the cost of candles, she must have some obscenely wealthy clients. A butler opens the front door to us and then announces us in the drawing room upstairs. We are the first proper guests, just Madame Vernier and Tobias Kellett present ahead of us.

'Evening, Drake.' Kellett pops the cork from a bottle of champagne. 'How do you like this place then?' Perhaps he is behind all of this. His money, at least.

Jonas still looks annoyed but gives the room a perfunctory glance. 'It is very nice. And this is your new enterprise, Madame Vernier?'

'Kindly assisted by Mr Kellett.' She graciously accepts a saucer of champagne from her accomplice. 'We are just beginning but I must say that our girls have proved themselves exceedingly capable so far.'

Her girls. Where are they? Where is Emmy? Leaving her mother was no small decision. Besides, now that I know for certain that Kellett is involved here, perhaps she has seen or heard something that will shed light on these remaining missing girls. 'Is Emmy here?'

Kellett raises an eyebrow; presumably I am not supposed to speak. Madame Vernier interjects before he can say something: 'She will not be joining us this evening. It's too soon and she has barely started her lessons. You may run up and speak to her quickly though, Sukey.' She rings the bell and the same young maid who I had met on my previous visit arrives within a matter of moments, out of breath.

'Mathilde, please show Miss Maynard to the bedchamber where Miss Macauley is residing,' she instructs. 'You're to wait with them both and then bring Miss Maynard back down to the dining room on the hour.'

The girl bobs a curtsey and turns to me, silently bidding me to follow. She leads me up the staircase to the second floor. The corridor we walk down is wide, the walls almost entirely covered with large oil paintings that look expensive. Even here, with not a soul in sight, the candles are lit. It all seems such a waste to me and I wonder if anyone would notice if I liberate a couple of the wax candles to replace the less pleasant smelling tallow that we rely on at Little Wild Street. Mathilde looks over her shoulder to see why I'm dawdling, and I hurry to catch up.

Strangely, she does not knock at the door we come to. Instead, she reaches into her apron pocket and withdraws a key which she uses to unlock it. I follow her into the room and find Emmy there, sitting on an armchair beside the fire doing embroidery. She is dressed in a fine gown, as if she were expecting to dine after all.

'Sukey!' She drops her work to the floor as she jumps up and embraces me. 'Oh, I'm so glad to see you! I've been so bored here, though Madame Vernier assures me that will all change soon enough.'

'Your voice,' I say, pulling back slightly in wonder. She is already using the same modulated tones as Camille. 'Is this what they teach in your lessons.'

She blushes. 'Amongst other things, yes. We must learn to speak like real ladies. I am not allowed to speak like myself, at any time. Not just in accent but in the words that we choose. I have to read the latest novels so that I am able to join in topical conversations.' She waves towards a pile of books on the table beside a large four poster bed. 'But the worst is the dancing lessons. Sukey, my only lesson so far was an utter disaster. Camille almost lost control of her bladder, she was laughing so hard at my attempts.'

I remember seeing Daisy Gardner dance at the ball. As though she'd been doing it all her life. Soon Emmy will be able to do that. I feel a pang of something that I am ashamed to admit is jealousy.

I sit on the edge of the bed and Emmy joins me. Mathilde stands at the door, as if guarding us, which I suppose she is. 'They keep you locked in?'

Emmy half-smiles. 'It is for security,' she tells me. 'I have to follow the rules of the house, and that includes staying in this room except for when I have my lessons. Mr Kellett comes to my room every morning to tutor me in elocution and posture. Mathilde brings my meals, and I am allowed out for dance lessons. Those are with a Frenchman, Monsieur Ravelet.'

'It sounds as though you're busy.' I glance towards Mathilde, but she was not watching us. Rather, she stood still, like a statue, staring straight ahead. I want to ask Emmy about what she has seen, tell her what Caleb and I have been discussing, but I don't know if I can trust this girl. I can't get Emmy into trouble when she has just arrived here. 'You are happy though, with your choice?'

'Yes.' I am rewarded with a proper smile this time. 'Sukey, I am so glad you persuaded me to come here. Madame Vernier has been lovely, and she makes me feel special. Even Mr Kellett does not seem so disappointed in me now. He praised me this morning and said that my new surroundings were making all the difference.'

I am amazed. Happy, but surprised that in only a few days, Emmy has changed so much.

'He even . . . ' She lowers her voice, one eye on Mathilde who hasn't blinked once. 'He bedded me this afternoon and declared me much improved.'

'That's wonderful.' I say it because it's what her expression demands, but how disappointing to have made so much effort to help her escape Kellett and his ilk, only for her to land in his own house, presumably having to bed him without being paid. I force a smile and think about what I can ask her in front of her tiny gaoler. 'And Daisy? Have you spoken with her?'

'Beatrice,' Emmy scolds. 'That's her name now. I have hardly seen her, for she's in great demand. She has a duke and a lord battling for her time. Can you believe it?'

I shake my head. 'Did you ask her about her mother? Her sister? She does know?'

Emmy looks a little ashamed. 'I cannot be sure. We are never alone together and if I were to upset her, Madame Vernier would be furious. I mentioned it to Camille, and she told me never to mention it under any circumstances.'

I understand Emmy's predicament, but it seems an awful secret to keep. One day Daisy – Beatrice – will find out the truth and it could be devastating for her.

I am startled by a muted metallic bang, reverberating through the house. Neither the young maid nor Emmy bat an eyelid.

'It's a gong. To announce dinner,' Emmy tells me. 'You must go. Madame Vernier despises tardiness.' She smiles though and she looks so much happier than I have seen her in a long time.

'Does she have her own version of the Coffin,' I joke.

That smile disappears. 'Not quite, though apparently there is a cellar to the house that does the same duty. Camille told me it's cold and full of spiders and rats. It doesn't sound as bad as the Coffin though. She didn't sound scared when she told me about it.'

The maid jangles her keys, and I bid Emmy goodbye, promising to visit again soon. Retracing my steps I wonder why I have such a feeling of foreboding as I leave her. The house seems perfect. A world away from the cramped rooms Mrs Macauley occupies in

Covent Garden. Perhaps I should ask Madame Vernier directly if she would take me. She has never mentioned the possibility and now that I am here, I wonder why.

I catch sight of myself in the large hall mirror. Perhaps I do not have Camille's sparkling blue eyes or Emmy's golden hair, but I lured in Jonas easily enough. It must be for him that she leaves me in Covent Garden. When he first arrived in London, he would have felt more comfortable there. But now that he is taking too long to decide on the next step for our partnership, I need to make some decisions of my own. If Jonas were to abandon me then I would have nothing. I need to make sure that I have my eggs in more than one basket.

27

An interesting collection of guests have been invited to the dinner party. Madame Vernier and Tobias Kellett occupy each end of the table. I sit to her left with Jonas opposite me. Beside me is Beatrice's Lord Cartwright, a surprisingly elderly man in comparison to the rather more vital-looking duke who had taken pleasure in her company at Kellett's party. Thankfully, Cartwright does not try to make conversation with me. In fact, I fancy that he moves his chair a little away from me as we are seated. He fixes his gaze firmly to Beatrice's bosom across the table, or talks across Camille, to his left, at Kellett. Camille's beau is a very ordinary-looking young man, heir to some fortune or other. His name is Matthew, and his countenance is as everyday as his name suggests.

There is a feast on the table. Kellett must have invested heavily in this new venture for Mrs Macauley could never have afforded a fraction of the riches that appear on the heavily laden table. A mock turtle soup is announced, which I am relieved to discover is just a sort of meaty broth. Kellett carves up a leg of lamb, and there is roast chicken besides, alongside potatoes and boiled vegetables. Mathilde struggles to pour wine from the heavy bottles so Madame Vernier orders a sulky Camille to help the girl maintain full glasses in front of each of the gentlemen and herself; for the rest of us we make do with a small glass apiece which is probably just as well.

Conversation is held between the men. Politics and talk about people I have never heard of. While Madame Vernier occasionally offers up a comment, I notice that she only does so when invited to by Kellett. Camille and Beatrice hold their silence, and I am grateful to do the same, having no opinion to offer on those topics.

After a dessert of blackberry jelly and pear tart, Madame Vernier rises to her feet. 'Girls, let us move to the parlour while the men talk business.'

I follow the others, noticing as we pass through the grand hallway that there is now a man standing by the door, well-dressed but clearly the St James's version of Jakes.

Camille sees me looking. 'Mr Palmer. Apparently, he's from a very well-to-do family originally but was cut off after a scandal.' This last word she said with a huge amount of glee. 'Most recently he made his money from boxing. He was good enough that Kellett hired him to protect him when he travels.'

'And now you girls have the privilege of his protection here under this glorious roof.' Madame Vernier's smile is wide as we take our seats, Camille and I on one sofa and the other two women opposite.

'Do we?' Camille seems a little more inebriated than the rest of us. 'I rather thought that he was protecting your investments. Isn't that why we cannot leave this house without permission?'

'You went out just the other day,' Madame Vernier replies, unbothered. 'Unaccompanied. So don't pretend you're a prisoner here. No more than when you were under Lucille Macauley's roof, I fancy. Or would you prefer me to return you to Covent Garden?'

It is a lightly thrown threat but there is steel to her tone that turns Beatrice's face pale. I think about Emmy upstairs under lock and key. But she is happy. She told me so and she had looked perfectly content.

'I wasn't complaining. Just making an observation,' Camille says, then changes the subject: 'Are they going to be long do you know? My gent is quite dull, and I'd rather get this over with if at all possible.'

I can tell from the set of Madame Vernier's face that Camille has already tested her patience on more than one occasion. Still, it isn't as though she didn't have plenty of warning before she'd filched her away from Mrs Macauley's stable.

'Sukey. Have you learned anything more about Jonas's plans for you?' she asks, ignoring Camille.

I wish she hadn't asked. I would love nothing better than to wipe the sly smile from Camille's face but the only news I have is hardly celebratory. 'Not yet. Though I think our attendance this evening bodes well, don't you?'

Madame Vernier smiles. 'Well, we had to make up the numbers somehow and Tobias was desperate to introduce Jonas to Mr Forrester.'

Mr Forrester. That is Matthew, Camille's dull cove. 'Is Mr Forrester important then?'

'Yes,' she says. 'He has a lot of money and not much imagination.'

'But why would Jonas be interested in that?'

Camille sighs heavily. 'Is it not obvious? Your Jonas needs money and Mr Forrester has more of it than he can keep count of.'

'Jonas has plenty of money,' I retort. 'It is only a matter of months since he paid a veritable fortune for me.'

'Hush!' Madame Vernier holds a finger to her lips. 'It is not our place to discuss the business of our men. You two must learn to keep your thoughts to yourselves.'

I smart a little at this mild rebuke and we all fall silent. Beatrice has said nothing much all evening. She just sits there with her hands resting in her lap. As far as I know, she has no idea that her family are gone. If Madame Vernier weren't there, I might be bold and risk telling her. Doesn't she deserve to know? I would want to, in her place. If Emmy had died, that is, for I have no parent left for me to grieve over and she is as close as I have to family.

A bell rings above the door, like one that would summon a maid, and I realise as the others stand that, of course, we are the servants this evening. The gentlemen have discussed their business and are now ready to partake of more pleasurable activities. I follow the others upstairs, hearing the loud, confident voice of Tobias Kellett drifting out from the drawing room door which has been left ajar.

'Ladies!' He beckons us in, the only one of the men on his feet. 'Hurry, hurry now.'

He shoots out a hand and grabs me by the wrist, stopping Camille with his other arm, outstretched. Beatrice is allowed through to where her duke is patting his knee, taking her place there. Madame Vernier stands beside the fireplace, an odd expression on her face as she looks around the room. She looks anticipatory, as though she has been waiting for this moment. As though something is about to happen.

The room reeks of tobacco and liquor. An empty decanter and glasses litter the low table that sits between the men, comfortable and lazy on their armchairs. Jonas has always been different to the other men I've come across at Little Wild Street, never as inebriated, but now he too is slumped in his chair, his eyes unable to meet my clear gaze. The other man, Matthew Forrester, is watching me. As, I realise with a nasty start, is Tobias Kellett who still has hold of my wrist.

'We've been chatting amongst ourselves,' he tells me, 'and it has been decided that young Jonas here needs to learn to be a real London gentleman. No more of his West Indian ways.' He turns his attention to Jonas. 'We are a civilised breed here, Mr Drake. If you wish to do business here, to mix amongst us, you must do a better job of fooling us that you are the same as us.'

'This is ridiculous,' Jonas mutters darkly. 'I'm as civilised as any other man here. Do I not have a house in a fashionable area? Do I not have a wife who many so-called London gentlemen were keen to woo last season?'

'Oh, certainly during the daylight hours you do a marvellous job. But you must understand, Mr Drake, that when you are known to consort with whores of the lowest kind, you cannot be taken seriously.' Kellett lifts his hand, my own arm elevating along with it. He means me. The lowest kind.

'She looks perfectly fine to me,' Mr Forrester says mildly. He is the only gentleman in the room who maintains a sober composure, sitting quite sedately with his legs crossed. 'Surely what takes a man's fancy is a matter of personal taste.'

'Come now,' Kellett jests. 'Would you bed a savage like this?'

I try to pull away, but he tightens his grip so that I'm not sure if the tears that fill my eyes are caused by pain or the sharp humiliation of his words. Even Camille looks shocked at what is happening.

'Madame Vernier?' My words are almost a whisper.

She doesn't take her eyes off me. 'Hush, Sukey. Let the men speak.' Her face is impassive, as if she doesn't know me or care what is happening.

'Jonas?' I turn to him, but he still refuses to meet my gaze.

'What do you suggest?' he asks Kellett. 'If my taste is so objectionable.'

Kellett pushes Camille hard so that Jonas has to react quickly to catch her before she falls onto him. 'Delphine is our newest girl. Refined, speaks like a true lady. Even your wife would not be embarrassed if it were known that you kept such a mistress as this one, for she could pass very easily as one of her own friends.'

'I have seen her before.' Jonas jumps up to allow Camille to take the chair while he stands beside it awkwardly. 'She was one of Macauley's motley waifs.'

'*Was.*' Madame Vernier is triumphant, and I feel my stomach turn as I see what she is about to do. I can feel my eyes start to sting with unshed tears, but I am determined that she will not see me cry. And neither will he. 'Look at the change in her. In just a few short weeks we have made her fit for consumption. Listen to me, Jonas, for how long have we known one another?'

'Too long,' he mutters, and I wonder now how he really knew her before, back in the West Indies. I have always assumed her to be a family friend, but perhaps her activities across the ocean were not so different to now.

'Trust me. Have I not looked out for you in the past? Did I not warn you when your father was ready to cut you off? Without my guidance just think where you would be. Not here in the fine drawing room of a wealthy London merchant.' Here she indicates Tobias Kellett. 'If you expect to do business with gentlemen like Mr Forrester then you must lift yourself up to his level. No more savages.' It is then that she looks at me, her eyes cold, as though she has not acted as my benefactor all these months. As though she has not taken me under her wing, or so I have thought.

'I'd rather you kept me out of this discussion,' Forrester says, then turns to Jonas. 'Are you taking the blonde?'

Jonas looks down at Camille, then up at Madame Vernier who gives him a sharp nod. 'Yes. I shall.'

'Jonas?' I give in to this simple plea, though I know that it is futile. He doesn't even have the decency to look me in the eye or say to my face that he is casting me aside.

'Then I suppose I have no choice but to take the mulatto.' Forrester gets to his feet, and I almost fall to my knees, my legs suddenly losing all strength.

'Actually, sir,' Madame Vernier dashes forward, 'we have another girl upstairs for you. I know you prefer your girls to be more . . . as they come, shall we say. But still, Sukey is . . . '

The girl upstairs must be Emmy, my poor friend who I brought to this place in good faith. I cannot understand what is happening. Madame Vernier has been my mentor for months. She paired me with Jonas in the first place, and now she is claiming that I'm not good enough for him? Why? My breathing is rapid as I try to maintain some façade of calm, but she is ripping apart all of my plans and throwing them on the fire. All of my hopes. Jonas is my only chance at surviving Little Wild Street. If he is willing to follow Gisele Vernier's advice so unquestioningly, to throw me aside so easily, I cannot cling on to those foolish dreams any longer. I am done for.

Forrester holds out his hand to me. 'This girl shall do. I have no need for you to tell me otherwise, Mrs Vernier. I'm not a man to take orders from the likes of you.'

I know her well enough now to see how angry she is, but he is rich and influential and has more backbone than Jonas. 'Very well. Mathilde, please take Mr Forrester to the Jade room.'

With every ounce of will in my body I try to force him to meet my gaze, but Jonas turns away from me as Forrester leads me out. I have been such a little fool. All that time, believing his excuses when all along he is just another acolyte of Tobias Kellett. Cook warned me, several times. Even Mrs Macauley, in her own manner, let me know that Gisele Vernier was not to be trusted. I've let vanity and pride smother my usual common sense. I am nothing to these people but a lesson to be learned, then cast aside once used up.

We follow the little maid, Mathilde, along the corridor to a sumptuously decorated bedchamber where she leaves us. A fire is already blazing, and a decanter of tawny liquid has been left on a table by the fireplace. Forrester pours a large glass and hands it to me. 'Sherry,' he says. 'Drink it down.'

I do as he bids me, starting with a small sip but ending with gulps that burn gently down my throat as the tears stream down my face. Forrester watches me impassively, unbuttoning his jacket and loosening his cravat as he does so. He is unlike Jonas. There is no conversation, only instruction. He removes his own clothes methodically before taking it upon himself to remove mine. If I could not see the undeniable proof of his arousal I would wonder if he is even interested in bedding me. It is like the first time again; I suppose that in a way it is. He is the only man apart from Jonas to see me this way, naked and afraid. I know that I am lucky. He isn't rough and his tastes are straightforward. He tells me what he wants of me, and I obey. It could be so much worse.

As he grunts softly above me, I let my tears dry. My mother died in a terrible place, abandoned by all who had known her. That won't happen to me, I won't let it. I will never be Jonas's mistress. I know that now. But this man didn't think twice about accepting me. There will be others like him. I let each thrust strengthen my resolve. There is no shame in this; the shame is on those who think that they have broken me. That I will let this be the ending of me. Madame Vernier thinks she has beaten me, but I won't let her.

28

'I shall tell Madame Vernier that you met my expectations,' Forrester tells me, dressing quickly, dawn having broken over the city.

'Thank you, sir,' I say, sitting up in bed, pulling the sheets around me. My head is still spinning from her betrayal. Why had she watched over me for all those months? Does Tobias Kellett hold some power over her? 'I apologise for my behaviour,' I add. 'I don't . . . I never cry. It was just a shock. I have only ever been with Mr Drake, you see.' No more Jonas. Not now.

He looks at me. 'You're very young. And unfortunate. I dare say you will struggle through life. You thought that Mr Drake would change your fortune?' I nod. 'Well, now you know better. We are all born in our place and very few of us can change that, for better or for worse. Accepting that fact will make the struggle a little less painful.' He drops a coin into my hand. A guinea. 'A little extra. I suppose they keep a good amount of what I paid for you when it is you who do the work. That I do not agree with, especially after that rather cruel treatment they subjected you to last night.'

'Thank you, sir.' I squeeze it tight in my fist, more grateful that he noticed what was being done to me, though the guinea is nothing to sniff at now that Jonas has cut me loose.

He picks up his jacket and strides towards the door. 'Good day.' And he is gone.

The house is still and silent as I creep back along the corridor. If I could only remember which room Emmy is kept in, I'd seek it out, but I can't. Besides, I would need the key.

I don't know where Jonas is either. I am in two minds over whether seeing him again would be a good or a bad thing. I would like an explanation, but I understand that he does not owe me one. I was only ever a temporary possession. Acquired to satisfy a need, then traded away just as another man might trade a horse.

Madame Vernier's man – Palmer – still guards the front door. He watches me as I make my way down the stairs. I can't read his expression.

'Madame Vernier wants to see you,' he tells me. 'She's in the parlour.'

I don't want to speak with her, but I sense from the way he stands, his back to the door, that this is not a choice. I take a deep breath and enter the room where she is drinking coffee by the fire, looking remarkably fresh after being up all night.

'Ah, good morning.' She throws a small purse to me as I sit, and I just manage to catch it. My earnings. 'Coffee?'

I nod, glad of a distraction, something to hold in my hands so that my nerves don't force me to fidget. I take the cup and saucer, made of bone china. She still trusts me with her best crockery then, if not with Jonas.

'You must be wondering why we were so cruel to you last night,' she says, taking a sip from her own cup. 'I can explain. I wasn't able to before, but now that everything is going to plan, I don't see why you cannot know.'

'Know what?' I have a feeling that I am not going to enjoy this explanation but it's better than not knowing.

'When your mother was still alive, we lived – me and her and old Lucy Macauley – in a bawdy house together. We were all ambitious, but Lucy and Eve fell on bad fortune. Both ended up with child. Lucy had family to help her out, but Eve had no one. Just you, once you were born, and she did love you. So much so that she would do anything to earn money and keep you fed. Even if that meant stealing custom from her two friends.'

From her expression I can see that whatever my mother did all those years ago, it still rankles with her. Odd, when she has spoken so fondly of her friend before. 'I'm sure that if my mother were alive, she would make it up to you. We all do desperate things from time to time.'

She laughs. 'That we do. And if nothing else, she taught me an important lesson, Sukey. She reminded me that I can only rely on myself. I learned that I could be as devious as anybody else, and I learned that even your closest friends are capable of betrayal.'

'My mother betrayed you?' I don't believe it. Mrs Macauley has never said a bad word about her and Madame Vernier never mentioned it before.

'For one reason or another I had to leave London. I ended up in the West Indies, married to an uncouth lout who worked as a lawyer. His best client was Jonas Drake's father, that's how I came to know that family. My husband was a drunk, and violent with it. Hardly the life I had hoped for and so I looked to the one I had left behind. Jonas's mother was a sickly young thing. The doctor said that another child would kill her, and her husband did love her enough that he baulked at taking the risk. That didn't mean that he didn't have needs, needs that I could provide and that my husband encouraged once he saw how much I could earn in his client's bed. I became Mr Drake's trusted confidante, especially when his younger son began to exhibit a worrying predilection for slave women. One in particular. His father turned a blind eye for a little while, but the girl was particularly fertile and it wasn't long before there were a couple of bastard infants like yourself running around the compound. Jonas claimed that he was in love with her.'

'Her name was Jenny?' I know the answer even before Vernier nods.

'The senior Mr Drake had to weigh up the benefits of the free labour with the constant presence of his son's weaknesses, right in front of him. I knew I was coming to London. My husband finally had the good grace to drink himself to death and so I wrote to Tobias, an old patron of mine. It was he who had introduced me to my husband in the first place, when I needed to get out of London many years ago. Before I left, I offered my advice to Jonas's father and he took it. The girl was gone by then, dead from her third labour in as many years, and Jonas was sent here. This is his last chance to make something of himself, to keep his father happy and money in his pocket.'

My throat is dry as sand. I take a sip of coffee; bitter and almost cold, it makes me gag. 'And what part have I in this tale?'

'You played your role well,' she tells me, condescendingly. 'I needed Jonas to feel safe while I introduced him to the right people. It is his father's wish for him to make something of himself and I knew that Tobias could assist me. We have long been allies. In fact, he has spent all these years patronising Lucy's establishment in order to keep me abreast of her movements. Not that she has done much in my absence. Still in the same locale and still struggling to maintain a semblance of a reputation. Hardly worth bothering with.'

The way she talks, it sounds as though she has been plotting for a long time, ever since she left London in the first place. But why? It doesn't make sense.

'You needed me to help Jonas feel comfortable in London?' She nods. 'Because he missed Jenny.' A thought clicks into place. 'And Emmy. You wanted Emmy and I was the only person who could convince her to come here. She would never have trusted you otherwise, not when her mother clearly didn't.' I was never important to her, never more than a convenient pawn.

'Oh, Sukey! You look so sad. Do as I did and learn from this hard lesson. Nobody does anything in this city without an ulterior motive. Including you.'

I have heard more than I can bear. 'You may be right about a lot of things, but that you are wrong about. There are good people. People who live to help others and don't expect anything in return.'

She snorts. 'And where are these saintly people? Can you even give me one example?'

I get to my feet, determined not to let her see what she has done to me. 'Doctor William Sharp. A brilliant man who doesn't just use his skill as a surgeon to help those who pay. I have seen his good deeds in action. Just a few months ago he saved the life of a poor slave whose master had beaten him half to death. I have seen that former slave recently and he is doing well. He is alive because of Doctor Sharp. I only pity you that you have never trusted in anyone for long enough that they show you their goodness.'

'Then go to him now,' she tells me. 'Tell him who and what

you are and see how he recoils from you. You will see just how good he is when his door slams in your face.'

She is so certain in her damning of me, and I know that she is right. I concealed my profession from the Sharps precisely due to that reason. Unable to bear her company any longer, I carefully place my cup and saucer down, refusing to show her any further weakness in my spirit. Damn her if she thinks I'll let her take further pleasure in her cruelty.

'I shall see myself out,' I say, and manage to walk steadily out of the room, past Mr Palmer in the hallway who opens the front door for me. In the street I overcome my wiser instincts and open the purse that Madame Vernier gave to me. Five guineas and a folded note.

The note is from Jonas. A curt few lines explaining that he feels it wise to sever our relationship, such as it is, as he has decided to change his patronage to Madame Vernier's establishment. He thanks me for my time and my company and wishes me well.

He is nothing more than a coward. I rip the paper into shreds, letting them fall into the gutter where they mingle with the manure. Maybe Camille, with all of her experience, her pretty hair and her new voice, is more worthy of his attention. I try to feel anger towards her, but I cannot. There are only two people to blame for my current predicament: Madame Vernier and myself.

The house on Little Wild Street is cold and dark when I arrive. No one has bothered to lock the front door, and Jakes is absent from his post. In the parlour, the fire is still ashes, and there is no sign that any revelries occurred the night before.

In the kitchen I find Cook, stirring porridge in a cauldron over the fire.

'Where is everyone?' I ask.

She looks up. 'In bed, Sukey, it's far too early for anyone else to be out of bed, even though we were closed again last night.'

'She still refuses even Sir Horace?'

'Well, there is only Hattie left,' she reminds me. 'Old Horace may have standards as low as his belly hangs but even he likes to think he has a choice of girls. Lucy took Jakes to the Golden Cross to see if she could find any new girls to replace Maria and Emmy.'

The Golden Cross is a coaching inn. Young girls – and if they can pass as maids all the better – are swooped upon as soon as they descend from the coaches that come from the provinces.

I sit down heavily at the kitchen table, my feet aching. The pretty shoes that go with my gown have not been constructed for walking. 'I've been a fool, Cook.'

'Which of us haven't been at one time or another,' comes her reply.

'No, but I have been the worst kind of fool. I have let my vanity get the better of me.' I sigh. I should have seen the truth sooner. In Jonas's refusal to commit, in the way that Madame Vernier singled me out for praise and yet never invited me to join her seraglio. She saw in me a girl who has never been admired before and she knew that I was naive enough to fall into temptation.

'Gizzy Vernier?' Cook looks over her shoulder. 'Yes, I wondered how long it would take that one to cause mayhem in this house.'

'You're not surprised.'

'I think if you prod your memory, you'll remember that I warned against that woman once or twice.' She lifts the pot onto the table. 'Porridge?' She dishes up two bowls and pushes one towards me. I am suddenly ravenous, craving the warm saltiness of the oats.

'What else can you tell me about her?' I ask, blowing on a hot spoonful.

'I know she's a sly one.' Cook looks wary. 'I don't know what else you want me to say.'

'Please,' I beg. 'I need to know. She said some things. About my mother, I just . . . I know she's lying. I know she wanted to upset me, but I need to know the truth. Even if it isn't something I want to hear.'

Cook looks down at her hands but eventually she does answer. 'Lucy told me never to tell you about our past but if Gizzy's up to her old tricks then maybe you're better off forewarned.'

'Tell me,' I demand, though I feel a cool chill fall upon me.

She lowers her voice, though there is no one else there to hear. 'Back when you and Emmy was just tiny babies, the four of us – Lucy, Gizzy, your ma and me – we were all still working together for Mother Jenkins just a couple of streets over. Lucy and Eve had taken it upon themselves to share the raising of you two. I think Gizzy felt left out, if I'm honest, and that she didn't like.'

'What about you?'

She shrugs. 'I'd never been one of them. I wasn't pretty enough or in demand but that was all right. I had a sweetheart at the time. We were to be married and although he didn't have a lot of money, there was enough that I could leave the whoring behind and be a wife instead. Raise a family.'

'Did he know your profession?' I know that she has never married, and I always assumed she hadn't been interested.

''Course not. Not then, though later on, yes, and he left me behind. Another gift from Gizzy. Did I mention earlier that she's a vindictive shrew of a woman?' Cook grins though I can see regret in her eyes. 'She punished all of us in one way or another, but Eve it was who bore the brunt of her anger.'

Whenever Madame Vernier has mentioned my mother, I've thought she was speaking with great fondness. I heard what I wanted to.

'Even though those three were close as anything, Gizzy was a little like Camille. She thought herself better than everyone else, even her friends. She was much in demand and whenever a gentleman came along who looked like a good prospect, Mother Jenkins pushed Gizzy in front of him. She reasoned that a whore with a babe in arms was of no interest to a man of good quality. Lucy and Eve had squandered their chance of a keeper. Only there was one chap who disagreed. He was no one of great importance but he had a minor title and a reasonable allowance. Gizzy did her usual act for him, but he wasn't interested. Turned out he'd spotted Eve on the street and followed her in.'

'And that's why she's so angry at me now? Because my mother stole one rake from her?' That can't be it, surely.

'It was the start of it,' Cook confirms. 'He was never Gizzy's to start with but Eve started to have problems. Her things went missing. Her best gown was found burnt on the fire when no one was looking. And then—' She stops. 'See, this is the bit I don't want to tell you. Because it's awful and you'll never forget it once I say it aloud.'

I can tell how bad it was from the tremble in her voice. 'My mother died not long after this, is that not right?'

She looks down into her bowl. 'Gizzy Vernier didn't kill your mother. Not directly. She was too clever for that. She did the next best thing. She started a rumour.'

'A rumour?'

'She whispered it in the taverns, to the men. I know it was her, 'cause I heard it from someone I trusted and I asked around and had it confirmed. It was too late by then. She told 'em that if they thought they might have the pox then the cure was to lie with a Negro woman. Proven. She paid a beggar to put on decent clothes and say that he'd had the cure himself, from the Negress at Mother Jenkins. The only rule was that they could not mention the pox, for fear of ruining whatever charm or spell Eve was supposed to cast over them as part of the cure.' She looks up at me and laughs. 'I can never think about that without marvelling at how ridiculous it sounds. But so many of them believed it. Desperate people do ridiculous things. Eve was never so popular, and she never suspected a thing, not until after she'd caught it.'

I have long wondered how it was that my mother and I ended up in the St Giles slum. Now I know. Cook confirms what I can easily guess happened next. Mother Jenkins couldn't keep a poxed whore under her roof. She paid my mother what she was owed, which wasn't much, and threw her out onto the street. Cook had told Mrs Macauley as soon as she'd realised what had happened. It was Lucy Macauley who told everyone she could think of about what Gisele Vernier had done. While she might have foreseen the women turning against her, Vernier had forgotten that she had made false promises to cursed men. She had broken several unspoken rules, and plenty would have been happy to see her dead for what she'd done. Her wicked scheme had worked but it was also what drove her out of Covent Garden and into a whirlwind marriage to a man heading to the West Indies.

'She came back for revenge.' I taste bitterness in the back of my throat, the ashes of the relationship I had thought I had with the woman. When she had known all along that I was orphaned because of her. And still she sees herself as the victim. I think about the night before, about what she said to me just an hour or so ago, and I want to scream. 'That's why she wanted Emmy. Mrs Macauley doesn't know.'

'Doesn't know what?'

We look up to see Mrs Macauley herself, standing in the doorway and I am lost for words. She knowingly brought my mother's killer into this house and watched her befriend me, knowing that my life could have been different. But I have in my turn taken her daughter away. Why couldn't they have told me the truth earlier?

Cook rescues me. 'Take a seat, Lucy. You're goin' to need a drink for this. Maybe more than one.'

Lucy Macauley is but a shadow of her former self. It is as though, in losing Emmy, she has lost herself. She lets Cook sit her down and pour gin into three glasses, time of day be damned. 'Sukey is going to tell you everything, Lucy, and you are to listen and not interrupt. None of this is her fault.'

Mrs Macauley regards me suspiciously. 'Why do I doubt that?'

I take a sip of my gin, letting the burn trickle down. 'I'll admit I've done wrong, but this all started with you.'

'Stop.' Cook is firm. 'The fault lies mainly with Gizzy Vernier, but also with you, Lucy. You've been a fool for letting that scheming jezebel set foot in this house.'

'Gizzy?' Mrs Macauley's face hardens. 'She's responsible for Emmy's disappearance?'

'Yes,' I say, 'and I'm sorry that I lied. I knew that Emmy was going to leave. She was terrified about having to see Mrs

Armitage again. She was in such a state, and Madame Vernier promised her that she would protect her.'

Mrs Macauley knocks back her gin in one. I expected my admission to set off an explosion and yet she seems barely moved. 'I should have known,' she mutters. 'You're right. What a fool.'

'I told Sukey what Gisele did to Eve.' Cook moves the gin bottle away. 'Why did you let her come into this house in the first place?'

To her credit, Mrs Macauley looks me in the eye. 'For the money. We were never going to escape the Garden without it. I lied to Camille about that. Gizzy brought Jonas and his fortune. Suddenly Tobias Kellett was spending more money here than he has in years. We went to his party. Sukey, he's never let any of my girls into his house before. We were so young when . . . when your mother died.' She does look away then, her shame too great. 'Gizzy promised me that she wasn't that person anymore and I chose to believe her because I thought we'd all be better off, you included. I was wrong and you should hate me. I'll accept it if you want to leave. No repercussions. No one need ever know you worked under my roof.'

She is offering me everything I have wanted since I first arrived. I look at Cook, but she seems as unsettled by this behaviour as I am. 'Lucy, she doesn't just have Emmy. She took Camille an' all. She lied to your face so that she had time to lead your daughter away. Her and Tobias Kellett, which'll explain why he hasn't shown his overfed, fancy dressed arse here for a while.'

Mrs Macauley reaches for the gin bottle. 'So, Camille and Emmy have gone to my greatest rival. What else?' She pours a full glass. 'Well, come on! There must be more. More disaster brought to my cursed door.'

I drink down my own gin. 'She has tempted Jonas to her house. He no longer wants to pay for my company.'

She looks at me and for once her smile is kind. 'I'm sad to hear that, Sukey. Sad because I know you foolishly hung your hopes on a man who could barely make a decision for himself. Do not let this experience scar you, Sukey. Keep your head held high, for his desertion is no reflection on you.'

I am lost for words. Never has she spoken to me so kindly or with any ounce of compassion. I want to be angry at her for withholding the details of my mother's death, but I find I cannot be. She brought Madame Vernier into our lives and chose not to warn us, but now I know the woman who killed my mother. Leaving Little Wild Street would be easy. I could sell the trinkets that Jonas gave me and find myself a job in service, I am sure. However, and perhaps the gin is influencing my thinking, if I can maintain this new alliance with Mrs Macauley, then vengeance might still be mine. If there is anyone in the world who hates Madame Vernier and now wants to destroy her as badly as I do, then Lucille Macauley is that woman. Together we might just succeed.

29

On Sunday afternoon Mrs Macauley tells us to prepare for the following evening when we will be reopening our doors. To hear as much is almost a relief, though I know that I will be expected to entertain and entice for the first time, now that I've told her of my intention to stay. I need a distraction, desperately. With nothing else to do, it has been too easy to think about nothing but revenge. Going through each memory of my time with Madame Vernier and wondering where I might have deduced her true nature. Thinking of my mother and how it must have felt to discover that a former friend had pronounced a death sentence upon her head.

The meeting of Caleb's fellowship of former slaves is held in one of the rooms upstairs in the Shakespeare's Head. I expect that there will be only a handful of people but to my surprise there are already fifteen or so when I arrive just before three o'clock. Tables have been pushed back so that there is space to mingle, and I spy Caleb deep in conversation with two men on the far side of the room.

'Sukey?'

I turn to see Jonathan, a shy smile on his face. He looks well dressed and has a new eye patch, sewn in the same material as his coat. 'Goodness, Jonathan. It is good to see you looking so well. I take it that Mr Brown is treating you well?'

'Yes. I have been blessed.'

As he moves into the room, I notice his limp and the slight awkwardness of his overall gait and steer us both towards two chairs.

'Sit, Jonathan, I shall get us drinks. Ale?'

'Let me,' he tells me, waving away my attempts to help him. 'Sukey, really, I am on my feet all day at work. It is the best way to overcome the injury. I sit too long and then I find I cannot move so well.' He makes his lopsided way to grab a waiter, and I sit myself down.

'You came.' Caleb has found me.

'I said I would.'

'I know. I just . . . ' He stops.

'Not like you to be lost for words,' I tease.

'No. I'm usually very good at using all of the words, all of the time. It's only that I do not wish to offend.' He pulls a chair forward so that he can look at me as we speak.

'Offend me? How intriguing?' And it is, a little. After our last conversation I know that I can trust him. He does not take the trouble to hide the truth from me, and, after recent events, that is a quality I cannot help but value. 'Tell me more.'

'It's just that when we first met I thought "She's a right one". I could tell, you see, that you didn't want to be one of us.'

'"Us"?'

'You know what I mean. Us that live in the Garden and round about. You came here thinking that we were the scum of the Earth, near enough, and you couldn't believe that you were stuck down here with us.' He gives my hand a friendly squeeze as I try to remind myself that he had warned me. He had told me that I'd be offended and he was correct, to a degree.

'I didn't think you were scum.' I hear my own words and do not believe them. 'It was just . . . I grew up—'

'In the countryside with a good old reverend who would tell you you're going straight to hell if he ever found out what you've been up to since you landed in London.'

'Perhaps I have mentioned it.' I can't help but laugh. How tiresome I have been. 'I've learned a lot over these few months. Perhaps mostly in the last few days.' If only he knew . . . 'From tomorrow I will be just another harlot in the Garden, lifting her skirts for anyone who pays. I shall learn to get on with things, just like everyone else does, and I'll be glad to have a roof over my head and food on my plate.'

His brow furrows. 'What happened to that fancy rake of yours?'

'Gone.' I press my lips together as they start to tremble. I cannot lose control. Not here in front of Caleb; not anywhere.

He looks uncomfortable. 'Sorry to hear that. The man is obviously a fool. I can't believe he found another girl in the Garden better than you.'

Flattery? I try to hide my surprise. 'Not in the Garden but of it. Camille. The Frenchwoman arranged it all and I – I was an idiot. She convinced Jonas that he can do better.'

'Wait, wait, wait, wait.' He holds up a hand to stop me talking while he thinks. 'This is the Frenchwoman we were talking about the other day? Camille hated her! But that's where she's ended up?'

Camille hated Madame Vernier? 'How do you know what Camille thought of her?'

'Well, you know. We used to talk a lot, me and her.'

He squirms on his chair, and I feel my cheeks flame as I remember that he is just another man willing to pay a woman to open her legs.

'It ain't what you think,' he tells me quickly, though now I am looking around for Jonathan. Goodness knows where he went to get those drinks. 'It weren't like what you're imagining, anyway. We just used to talk, me and her. Nothing more.'

'You paid to talk to Camille?' Does he think I am even more of a fool than I am? 'I could barely stand to listen to her talk, and I didn't have to spend a penny for the privilege.'

'No, well. She was handy, see. For my work. My writing. When I needed new ideas. Or just a bit of gossip to slip in here or there. She saw all sorts of coves. Rich, middling, old and young. As long as they paid what she wanted, she didn't care. No other harlot round here has such an eclectic collection of . . . gentlemen.'

'Eclectic?' I can hardly believe what I'm hearing. 'So you talked to her about your little stories? And used what she told you?'

'Exactly! I've got to publish a new story every week. Sometimes I have a rich period. Full of ideas and often the customers tell me what they want. When I got stuck I went to Camille and she'd help me out. That girl was a revelation. Said yes to anything, long as she got paid and she told me things that made my jaw drop, but I never lay with her. Not once.'

'Why? If she was so knowledgeable, were you not tempted?' I'm not sure if I believe him, though for some reason I want to, more than anything.

'At first. But the way she spoke about 'em. I don't know . . . I didn't want to join that bloody great list of men she looked down upon. Because she did. They thought they were better than her, that they were conquering her, making her do humiliating things, acts that their wives would faint at the very idea of, but she never saw it that way. She thought it was their great failing, that they had to pay for her time, to ask for her permission to be allowed to do those things. Too cocky by half, but I sort of admired her for it.'

What he says rings true. Camille was nothing if steadfast in her conviction that she was someone to be admired, no matter her profession. She hadn't set her cap at Jonas, but she would see it as her due if he offered to be her keeper. She would see it as my failing that I hadn't managed to hold on to him. Which brought me back to Gisele Vernier.

'The Frenchwoman. You said Camille mentioned her to you.'

'Vernier, right?' I confirm with a nod. 'This was last year. Summer? No, a bit later on. I had a customer request a story featuring Guy Fawkes.' He smiles at the memory. 'Instead of blowing up the Houses of Parliament, he gets his . . . ' He catches sight of my raised eyebrow. 'Anyway, so it must have been end of October. She said this woman was paying her for information. She was going through the *Harris's List* like it was some sort of Bible, asking which girls Camille knew, where they might be when they weren't on the lookout for a customer, that sort of thing. Camille said she never trusted her, but the money was good. And the woman had said she wasn't to tell anyone about it, especially Lucy Macauley.'

'But she told you,' I point out.

'You know what Camille's like. Only reason she never told Macauley is that she liked keeping a secret from her.'

'I'm so sorry!' Jonathan arrives clutching two tankards.

'Everyone wants to talk to me today.' He hands one tankard to me, the other to Caleb.

'Where's yours?' I ask.

'Oh no.' He waves Caleb away as he tries to offer his. 'I don't like ale. It gives me a headache and since my head aches often as it is, I am happy to go without.'

I feel bad. I should have gone to fetch my own drink, although then I would have missed out on this most interesting information. I wish Caleb had mentioned it before but then this had all happened months ago. Long before I knew of any connection between her and Vernier.

Caleb introduces me to a woman named Martha who is a cook at a local chophouse. She smiles and finds us both chairs close to the front of the room as Caleb takes Jonathan to meet a circle of men in the corner.

'Caleb is such a nice young man,' she tells me with a smile, and I realise she thinks that there is some romantic intention between us.

Before I can correct her, the meeting proper begins, with around thirty people gathered. I have never before been in a room where I am not alone, not the only Black person. In fact, I am amongst the lighter-skinned people there. I recall what Caleb said, about how I had thought myself above people from the Garden, and I wonder if that's exactly what he meant. Do I have much in common with these people? If I tell Martha what I do for a living, what will she think? I am sure she works far longer hours than I, for a smaller wage, but it's good and decent work. Good and decent work, and yet now I do not think that I would trade places with her.

A man addresses the gathering first, Patrick, who has an

accent close to Jonathan's, lilting but strong. He welcomes me, knowing my name although I have never spoken to him before. He picks out a few others, including Jonathan, thanking them for travelling and wishing them well in their new situations. I realise that the others too are recently freed, or escaped, slaves. Somehow, they have found this group, along with their freedom, and I feel a little like an imposter. Their story is not mine, though perhaps if my mother had lived it would have been. Another thing stolen from me by Madame Vernier.

After Patrick, Martha gets up and speaks. She has news from an abolitionist in New York with whom she has been exchanging letters and information. Individuals stand to ask for help finding work, sharing their skills and competencies. So many here are poor. Later I see Caleb buying ale for those who I know are out of work. He is not the man I thought he was, in fact he is far better than most. Yet again I have seen how judging people at first sight can make a fool of me. I look around and see how I have wasted so many weeks feeling sorry for myself when I have been given so much.

'You are surprised by how many good people there are in this world.' Jonathan is by my side, and I wonder how he can remain so optimistic after everything that has happened.

'I am a cynic,' I agree, laughing. 'I am used to people saying the right things and doing the opposite.' I am thinking of the Ashleys, how they would sneer and look down upon me now, upon all these people, and yet they are not the good Christians they had convinced me they were.

'Can I walk you home?' he offers as he sees me take up my cape for the short journey. I am glad for this will be our only chance to speak away from the crowd. I look to say goodbye to

Caleb, but he is now deep in conversation with Martha, and I can see him any time at the bookshop.

'You will be able to find your way back to the Browns?' I make sure as we emerge onto the piazza.

'If there is any job that would give me a better knowledge of the London streets, I cannot think of it,' he says with a laugh. 'I've been lost more often than not but in the last few days I've found more that is familiar than strange.'

'And you will be safe now?' I remember the state of him when I first found him. It is a miracle that just a few months later he is well and walking.

'My old master thinks me dead,' he assures me. 'If he had thought otherwise then he had weeks to track me down while I was lying in bed in St Bartholomew's hospital.'

'Do you know . . . ?' I want to know more, but without causing him to relive that awful night. 'Why did he do that to you? He could have just thrown you out and let you be free if he no longer needed your services.'

He is silent a moment before he answers. 'I heard that in England they cannot enslave you if you have been baptised. A child of God can only ever be free. It is a saying, I suppose. I was not sure it was true, but I tested it anyway. On that day I had enquired at the church closest to my master's accommodation. The act had not been carried out yet but nevertheless someone must have seen me and told him, for he knew it all by that night. He let me serve him dinner as usual, and had me polish all his boots, put his wardrobe in order and then he called me to the kitchen.'

'And then he just attacked you?' I am dumbfounded. In some small way I could understand a sudden burst of rage. That red hot violence that can drown the senses. But what Jonathan was telling me was that the assault on him, his attempted murder, was premeditated. His master had hours to decide what he was going to do, including the preparation of mundane tasks that he preferred his slave to do before the moment of his planned death.

'I thank God that I only remember the first blow.' Jonathan tries to smile, to take the horror out of his words, but he fails. 'He had a pistol in his hand, and I thought he was going to shoot me. Perhaps that was his initial intention, but he had time to realise that the shot would be heard.'

'He would be hung for murder.' He should have been anyway. Surely, despite Caleb's thoughts on the matter, we can still tell someone. One of the justices must listen, surely. With Doctor Sharp's testimony, there would be no doubt of Jonathan's being attacked.

'It is not classed as murder to do away with your own property in Barbados,' Jonathan informs me. 'Here, I am less sure. I cannot even say if he left me in the place where you found me, or if somehow I made my own way there. I don't remember anything else, for the next clear memory I have is of you, as I was lying there in Doctor Sharp's house.'

The walk is not long enough; already we are reaching Drury Lane. 'I'm happy that you're here to tell the tale, awful as it is,' I tell him. His optimistic outlook puts my own worries into perspective. I must try to learn from his example and make the best of the hand I've been dealt.

'That makes two of us.' This time he laughs freely. 'Sukey, I will never be able to repay you for the kindness you showed to me that day. I would not be alive now without your help. I hope you know I am grateful.'

'Of course! And there is nothing to be repaid, for I was only there because I was fleeing my own circumstances.' I hesitate to tell him more. I wish I were a seamstress or a scullery maid, anything more reputable than my actual profession.

Jonathan turns to me. 'Sukey, I, better than anyone, know that we're not always given a choice in this life. I am free now, a freedom that came at a cost, but I would not change anything about what happened. Now I have friends and an employer who pays me a fair wage. Now I can take a walk with you, I can pay a visit to Caleb and meet with folk who look like me, who want everyone who looks like us to be free. It may be that you cannot change your circumstances, not in this very moment, but as long as you keep hoping, one day that may change.'

'You should speak at the next Sunday meeting,' I tell him, only half joking, for he has given me pause for thought on my own situation. There hasn't been much to hope for of late, but I know better than anyone how quickly that can change. I just need to keep a look out and remember that even where there is darkness, the light is never far away.

✷ APRIL 1766 ✷

Emily Macauley, Pall Mall, St James's

What can be said of this young wench, newly transported to this more salubrious neighbourhood from her mother's house in Covent Garden? She is a pretty thing, but although her maidenhead is lost, her skills are yet to be fully developed. In her favour, it is said that she has some experience on both sides of the birch which may excite some.

30

The weeks pass and April arrives in London bringing sunshine and warmer weather. Inside the house on Little Wild Street not all is doom and gloom, although much still is. The main origin of light comes from an outside source: Grace. Hattie brings her from a local tavern, a pretty red-haired girl of two and twenty. Tired of dealing with drunkards for mere pennies, she leapt at the chance to join us at Little Wild Street. She is quick of wit but kind with it, and I feel some of my melancholy lift once she has been with us for a few days.

I join the nightly roulette of the parlour. Sir Horace, of course, continues to join us regularly. I am glad that Grace becomes his new favourite, and he must have seen good fortune pass his way for he never seems short of small gifts for her. Chocolates from Belgium, silver trinkets from the market, ribbons for her hair. I accept my fate and try to follow the example shown to me by the other girls. Laughing at the men's jokes, even though they are rarely funny; initiating conversation with the nervous younger ones; closing my eyes and bearing it when the man who pays for my time is less than desirable. I have become like any other whore.

I try not to think of Jonas but sometimes I cannot help it. Those wasted weeks dreaming about our future together, foolish as I now know those dreams to be. Now Camille is living that life instead. She would likely say that she deserves it more than I, that she has served her time, and she would be right. Now it is my turn to earn my place. All I can do is try to be stoic about my new status, and in truth it isn't half as bad as I had imagined.

'I think of it as a kindness,' Grace tells us over dinner one evening as I complain about my previous night's gent, a portly man who had perspired greatly, sweat dripping copiously upon my skin as he thrust. Of course, it is always these sorts of men who make the act last longest.

'A kindness?' I spear a piece of meat from my stew.

'Don't you feel sorry for them?' she asks. 'Most of them are lonely or sad. They come here so that we might make them feel better, even if just for an hour or so. It's what I tell myself. It makes it easier if I think of it as charity.'

Mrs Macauley snorts but doesn't say anything. She has still not returned to her old self but that is a blessing as far as I am concerned. Grateful that I did not take up her offer to leave, she has opened her box of memories for me. From time to time, she lets me take a bottle of port up to her office and we talk about my mother, the things she remembers from when they were young, both before I was born and just after. Before the worst happened. I am getting to know the woman whose last deed in life was ensuring my survival. At first Mrs Macauley is wary, her guilt at not telling me the truth writ across her face. I assure her that there is only one woman to blame for my mother's death, and that is not her.

Of Emmy there has been not a peep, nor a word heard. I'm not surprised, having seen how she was kept imprisoned in that room. Madame Vernier would have known that I would tell her old rival of her daughter's whereabouts. She may even have expected Mrs Macauley to turn up at her front door with a pitchfork. That she hasn't made any attempt to fetch back her daughter worries me, but at least if Emmy is happier there, I don't have to feel so guilty about my part in her decision to leave her mother's side. I'll see her again soon, I know. Once she has settled in and Madame Vernier is secure in letting her out of confinement.

In her absence I make merry with Grace and Hattie at home, and I find that my friendships with both Caleb and Jonathan have become as important to me as anything else. Jonathan is becoming more confident each time I see him, and I have learned that it is just Caleb's nature to play the jester. This is my new life, and I am beginning to feel content. Until the third Wednesday in April, when events turn everything topsy-turvy once more.

I am awoken by a banging at the front door, but I don't make any effort to rise from my bed. My head hurts and I am exhausted. It has only been an hour or two since I finally persuaded my last gent to leave, the third of what was a long night. I ache all over.

The banging continues and I hear Mrs Macauley shout out for someone to answer the door. Jakes has left, gone to his own bed as the sun rose. Still being in the room that was Camille's, I am the closest.

Pulling my silk robe around me, I make my way downstairs as noisily as I can. Since I have been disturbed, I reason that so should everybody else be. As I draw closer to the door, I can hear a soft voice behind the banging. Distressed. Suddenly worried, I lift the key from its hook by the door and heave the thing open. I am not prepared for the sight that meets me.

A girl flings herself at me, in floods of tears. It is Daisy Gardner, dressed for Covent Garden rather than as the Beatrice creature I have more recently become acquainted with.

'Will you let us in?' she begs.

She is not alone. Camille is slumped in a heap on the ground, her hair a matted tangle of hay. Her face is pale, her lips white. Beyond her stands a boy, his eyes like saucepan lids, staring down at her dishevelled body.

'What is wrong with her?' I ask, helping Daisy to lift her up. 'Is that lad with you?'

She looks at me quizzically and when I glance up again, he is gone. Just one of Mrs Macauley's sparrows, no doubt. 'Get her inside. I'll tell you everything,' she promises.

Camille is a dead weight but between us we manage to carry her through to the parlour. For a brief moment, Daisy lets go of her in order to remove her own cloak, which she spreads over the sofa before we lay Camille down. I only understand why when she is supine, and I see that Camille's dress is not supposed to be red. It is a dowdy brown thing that a servant might wear, and it is stained with more blood than I have seen in my life, seeping out of the fabric onto my own hands.

'Daisy?' I stare at her, horrified.

Mrs Macauley chooses that moment to appear. 'Could you make any more noise?' she hisses before seeing the tableau before her. 'Jesus Christ,' she whispers. 'Does she live?' She rushes to Camille's side, pressing her hand to that white face. Camille stirs a little and Mrs Macauley gives a sigh of relief. 'What happened?' she demands as she kneels by her former charge's side.

Daisy takes a step backwards, as if fearing Mrs Macauley's ire. 'I told her not to do it.'

'Do what?'

'She tried pennyroyal first but that didn't work. It just made her ill and Madame Vernier punished her for having to call out the doctor.' Daisy hesitates and I try to make sense of what she is saying.

'Tell me she did not go to Mother Barlow?' It is a plea from Mrs Macauley, and I see tears in her eyes as she lifts Camille's skirt and shift, blood covering her hands in mere seconds.

'I told her not to, but she was missing from the house last night. I guessed where she might be, but Madame Vernier was furious, and I had an appointment with a gentleman in Mayfair. When I was able to slip away, I went to St Giles and found her out in the street.'

'Who is Mother Barlow?' I interrupt.

Mrs Macauley looks Daisy in the eye and points towards the kitchen door. 'Fetch hot water. If Cook is awake, tell her I need old linens. Something to stem this blood if I can.' After Daisy has run off, she turns to me. 'Mother Barlow is a witch of a woman. She claims to help those who need to get rid of a baby before it is born. She preys on the desperate, for she kills as many as she saves. There are surgeons more skilled, but it is hard to convince them to help when they could face the gallows for it.'

'But Camille will live?' I cannot imagine this peacock of a woman not existing any longer. She has played the game far longer than I, I remind myself. She won't have taken such a risk without considering the outcome. She will recover.

But Mrs Macauley does not answer me. Cook comes bustling through with Daisy trailing in her wake and I am pushed aside as the older woman surveys the damage done, pressing thick fingers to Camille's lily-white neck.

'Is there time to send for the doctor?' Mrs Macauley asks Cook, deferring to her common sense and wisdom.

My breath stops as I see Cook shake her head. 'She is beyond pain now, though she will have suffered, I fear.'

'No! She is not . . . ' I lean over and take hold of Camille's hand. It may be just my imagination, but I fancy that I feel her skin cooling beneath my fingertips. 'Oh God!'

'Her heart has only just stopped. How long before you found her?' Cook aims her question at Daisy.

'I do not know exactly.' Daisy looks as helpless as I feel. 'I last saw her at breakfast yesterday. I suppose it was at least six or seven hours between me realising she was missing and being able to run out and look for her.'

'And you never thought to raise the alarm?' Mrs Macauley is quick to her feet, taking Daisy by the arms and shaking her. 'You did not think to tell anyone what you suspected?'

'I did!' Daisy is sobbing. 'I did. I told Madame Vernier as soon as the thought crossed my mind, but she would do nothing. She said it would be a lesson learned for all of us if Camille was butchered.'

Cook sits on the sofa by Camille's feet, her head in her hands. 'That ice-hearted harridan. Well, she's done it. She's killed one of her own girls.'

Mrs Macauley lets out a guttural sob before gathering her wits back to her. She turns to Daisy. 'Vernier doesn't know that you are here?' Daisy shakes her head. 'Good. Tell her nothing. She doesn't deserve the satisfaction, and I will not let her use Camille as a lesson for my own daughter. I would rather that you teach her instead. Tell Emmy what has happened here. Tell her she can come back to me, any time she wants. I didn't cast her out and I shall not hold a grudge. I can promise her that. Will you tell her?'

'I will.' Daisy wipes her face with the heels of her palms. 'You are a good mother, Mrs Macauley. If only every girl had one like you.'

'Your own mother lived a hard life,' Mrs Macauley tells her. 'You should not hold her actions against her entirely.'

Daisy looks unconvinced, which does not surprise me. 'I suppose I should go and see her. I wonder if she has worried about me at all since I left or if she has just been disappointed to lose my earnings.'

My God, she still doesn't know. Mrs Macauley and Cook just look at one another and so I am the one who speaks. 'Emmy hasn't said anything to you?' I don't know how to say the rest.

'Madame Vernier doesn't like us to talk. Whenever we're together, she's present. She sends us out to see our gentlemen when possible, so that people don't comment on the numbers coming to the house each night. And when we do host them at the house, she is very selective, pairing us before we even set foot downstairs.'

How, on top of this new tragedy, are we to tell her that her mother and sister are already turning to dust in the ground? In the end, Cook draws her quietly into the kitchen where she can sit her beside the fire and feed her brandy for the shock.

In the meantime, Mrs Macauley and I remove Camille's blood-soaked clothing, peeling it from her cooling skin, and wash her body. I find one of her nicest gowns from upstairs, one of the few that we haven't altered already, and we dress her as she would have wished. She would be furious to know that this simple mistake was what ended her life, but I think she would have been happy to know that she is going to her grave the beauty she always was. Our rivalry is at a permanent end.

Hattie emerges from upstairs as I finish arranging Camille's hair, and the sobbing begins again. She runs upstairs to fetch one of her favourite trinkets, a silver heart hung on a black ribbon that Camille had twice offered to buy from her, with Hattie happily refusing each time.

'She said she'd get it off me in the end,' Hattie says, her face awash with tears, and we cling to one another as we watch over our old friend, no longer our enemy. This is what Caleb meant by the sisterhood. It makes sense to me now, this feeling of kinship rooted in our shared experiences but also the fear that this could have been any of us.

In the end Mrs Macauley cannot stand it any longer and sends Hattie away, to assist Daisy in hailing a hackney back to Pall Mall and then on to find Maria who deserves to know. I don't know what Daisy is going to tell Madame Vernier; I can tell that she doesn't know yet either.

'I'll tell Emmy everything,' Daisy promises from the doorstep, her face tracked with dried tears. 'I'll tell her to come home.'

'Will Vernier let her leave?' I lower my voice in case Mrs Macauley is listening.

'That I don't know. But there is a window in the cellar that Camille went in and out of once without anyone catching her. I'll help her if need be.'

I trust her. I can see that her faith in Madame Vernier has been severely shaken, not only by Camille's death but in the concealing of her mother's demise.

'I promise you now,' Mrs Macauley tells her, 'that there will be a place for you here too. Our house may not be as fine as hers and I cannot give you a duke, but I look after my girls. I've never had one die on me, not in the ten years I've been running this place.'

Daisy nods and begins to cry again. 'Thank you.'

They disappear down the street and Mrs Macauley drags her weary body upstairs. She has a funeral to arrange and to pay for, and I know now that she is not all bad. Yes, she loves her ledger and her coins, but behind the hard façade has all this time been hidden a more vulnerable woman. If my mother had lived, might she have been just the same? Perhaps we might have lived all together, my mother and Mrs Macauley, Emmy and me, and run our own house of fallen sisters. What a life that might have been!

I hope that Emmy will listen to Daisy. I hope that she remembers that we love her. I hope that she will forget everything I said to turn her against her mother and realise that she could be safe at Little Wild Street, far safer than at Pall Mall. In the end, though, I understand exactly what Mrs Macauley feels. We have each made a grave mistake and it is possible that the price we have to pay is losing Emmy forever.

31

The only surprise visitor we have in the week following Camille's death is Mr Matthew Forrester. He arrives with no fanfare, and I wonder how he found me.

'You are already acquainted with Miss Maynard?' Mrs Macauley's eyebrows shoot up. 'Well, then I'm sure you know her skill in the bedroom is as unique as her appearance is in this part of London.'

Forrester cocks his head to the side, and I hope he isn't about to disagree with her appraisal of my talents. 'Indeed. Well, I shall pay for her time. Will this suffice?' He names an amount that is not extravagant but is at the upper end of what Mrs Macauley demands for the use of any of her girls. He must have been paying a lot more to Madame Vernier and has decided that he can get better value for his money here. I have been judged to be adequate at the very least.

We go upstairs and I am embarrassed to see how he looks around the place. Compared to the Pall Mall house, we are living in a hovel. Even Mrs Macauley's fancy wallpaper is peeling in patches where damp oozes through.

'I realise this isn't the sort of place you are used to, sir,' I tell him as I show him into my bedchamber.

'No,' he agrees. 'But it serves a purpose.'

'Why are you here? I thought you'd have preferred Madame Vernier's establishment. It's far more elegant.'

'Ah.' He removes his jacket and begins the process of shedding his clothes with little fanfare, just as he had the time before. Straight to the matter at hand. 'You see, I was curious to see what Tobias Kellett was offering. His parties are legendary and, as you will have noticed, I possess the same carnal needs as any man. In a perfect world, I would have nothing to do with Kellett and would keep my private affairs separate from my business affairs. However, as the eldest son, I have to follow in my father's footsteps. He came from almost nothing to raise a great fortune which I am learning attracts all manner of despicable personalities. Kellett is one of those. The man is a monstrosity but, although charm is not my forte, I must make some effort with him because there are certain business deals which profit from our association.'

Camille had called Matthew Forrester dull, but I think there is more to him than meets the eye. Just the knowledge that he despises Tobias Kellett as much as I do is enough to make me feel disposed to liking him. I walk almost eagerly into his embrace this time and our coupling is enjoyable enough. Afterwards, he dresses and leaves another guinea in my hand.

'I don't suppose you see much of Mr Drake these days?' he asks as he pulls on his coat and checks his reflection in the mirror.

'Not since the night we met,' I assure him.

'Good. He is an oaf.' He pauses as he opens the bedchamber door. 'I may call again in future.'

It is hardly an offer to become my keeper, but his words cheer me up no end. A regular client is to be treasured and Mrs

Macauley is pleased when I report what Mr Forrester told me about Kellett.

'Good job, girl,' she says, a smile on her lips for the first time in a long while. 'And this just proves that Gizzy Vernier cannot have everything she plans for.'

I wonder what Kellett and Madame Vernier will think when they find out. Madame Vernier had meant to humiliate me, I am certain. If what Cook told me is true, then I am lucky that was all she did to me. There may never be a way to bring her to justice for my mother's death, but I can do my utmost to be a thorn in her side. She'll be furious to know that her tricks have resulted in me stealing away one of her precious wealthy clients. I hope that I can see her face when she finds out.

I might be in Mrs Macauley's good books at last, but she is a businesswoman at heart and now that she has rediscovered her vigour, she has her sights firmly set on money-making. She finds another girl at the Golden Cross, just off the coach from Suffolk, and puts her to work immediately. We are back to bedchamber games, with all of us taking whichever bed is free each night.

By the following Sunday I am glad to have a place to go. The cramped rooms of Little Wild Street are beginning to feel oppressive. Hattie and Grace are nice enough, but we do not have much in common, and the new girl seems distrustful of all of us, though by all accounts she is not shy around the gentlemen.

Instead of waiting to see me at the Shakespeare, Caleb is waiting across the street as I exit. He is wearing a black armband. I haven't seen him since Camille's death, but I did send a message. He was not allowed to the funeral. It was just the five of us present: Mrs Macauley, Cook, me, Hattie and Maria, nothing about the event traditional or in keeping with custom. The burial took place at dusk, the reverend doing Mrs Macauley a favour in allowing Camille to be buried on hallowed ground when, as a whore who had killed her unborn child, she most certainly was not considered worthy. I did not ask why a man of God had ended up owing Mrs Macauley.

'We saw her off well,' I tell him, and he nods, sober in his composure for once.

'I know she had left the Garden already, but it seems odd to think I won't see her again,' he says, echoing how I have been feeling this week.

'I intend to let everyone know who is responsible,' I tell him. 'Let no more girls go missing who end up in Madame Vernier's cruel house.'

'Talking of missing, have you seen Jonathan?'

'No. I didn't expect to see him until the meeting today.'

'I was supposed to meet him two days ago in the tavern.' Caleb looks worried. 'He didn't turn up.'

'Perhaps he wasn't able to leave work.' I know that Jonathan takes his position very seriously. Whatever Mr Brown asks of him, he does. He is so grateful for all that has been given to him.

'See, that's the thing. I went to see Brown this morning after church. He said that Jonathan left suddenly on Wednesday afternoon. He was delivering to a customer and never returned, though the package was received as expected. He hasn't heard from him since.'

I stare at him. That doesn't sound like Jonathan. He loves his job, and he likes the Browns. 'Why didn't you tell me this earlier?' I demand.

'I only just found out myself,' he pointed out. 'Besides, what with Camille, I thought you had enough to worry about.'

I suppose he has a point. 'What about the Sharps? Would he have told them his plans?' He spoke so highly of the doctor and his brother.

'I doubt it. Far as I know, he hasn't spoken with them since leaving St Bart's.' He stops walking as we draw up before the Shakespeare's Head. 'With luck, he'll be here today, and we can ask him to his face. If not . . . '

'You think something bad has happened?' His seriousness is worrying me.

'I don't know. A slave, in London. I warned him to be careful. There is no clarity on the situation.' He shakes his head. 'Let us talk later. This may all be for naught.'

But Jonathan does not come to the meeting. His absence is commented on by others, and no one seems to know where he is. My concern grows as time passes and after only an hour or so I tell Caleb that I will go home. I need to send word to the Sharps in case they have seen him.

'I'll walk you home,' he says. 'No one here knows nothing but I know the name of Jonathan's old master and the name of the street he was living on. Tomorrow I'll ask around, see if there's any chance he's the one who took him back.'

'Jonathan wouldn't go back.' I know that for certain.

'Yes, but like I said before, he might not have had a choice. The law is the law.'

'What does that mean?' I snap.

'What it means in this case is that no one's tested it, not on English soil, not to my knowledge. If we were in Barbados, then it'd be cut and dried. Jonathan would be punished for running away and handed back to his master. Here, it's all a little more . . . ' He waves his hand in the air as we make our way out into the piazza. 'The slaveowners have a lot of wealth and influence, you know. A judge could find his career scuppered if he rules in favour of humanity rather than commerce.'

I think I understand what he's saying. There is no clear rule about slavery on English soil. Jonathan is both still a slave but also free. Until the moment someone declares it one way or the other, and no one is valiant enough to take that decisive step. To say that it is the most heinous crime imaginable, for one person to claim ownership over another.

We have just turned on to Drury Lane when Caleb suddenly pushes me into a doorway without warning. I manage to put out my arms to prevent myself from falling, whirling round in time to see him grab a young lad by the collar.

'Gerrof me! Gerrof me, you savage!' The boy is kicking and screaming but he is no match for Caleb.

'Why are you following us?' he demands.

The lad is around ten years of age. Dirty, blond-haired and sneering. 'I ain't.'

'You are and you're not good at it. I saw you earlier this afternoon, on Little Wild Street, and when I turned around a few moments ago I saw you hide from me. Why hide if you're just about your own business?'

'I recognise him,' I realise. 'He's been loitering near my house.' He's the boy I saw in the street the day of Camille's death. 'Were you following *me*?' I come to a quick decision. There is no way to guarantee the loyalty of any of these boys. They only understand one thing. 'I'll pay you a guinea to tell me everything.'

'A guinea?' Caleb almost lets the lad go in his astonishment.

'You ain't got a guinea,' the boy proclaims.

I produce my small purse where I still have the two guineas

that Matthew Forrester gave to me. I don't trust the new girl yet and there is nowhere to keep my money at the house. I pluck out one of the coins and show it to the boy. 'Here. But you have to tell the truth, or I swear we'll find you and you'll be sorry. Who told you to follow us?'

He stops wriggling and locks his eyes on the shiny coin in my hand. 'It were a foreign lady. A frog-eater. She pays me sixpence a day to keep an eye on your house and I'm to follow you if you leave.'

'You're to follow me?' He nods. 'Only me?' And again.

The Frenchwoman. What the hell more can she want from me?

32

The boy had been sent to follow me from the Pall Mall house all those weeks ago. His task was simple: find out who I visited and report back. Madame Vernier had been paying him his sixpence per day just for that. She'd become excited after he'd told her about Jonathan – trailing in our wake as we had left the Sunday meeting the week before – and paid him an extra shilling for using his initiative in following him back to Fenchurch Street. In fact, she'd been so pleased with this new information that she had told him that his duties were finished. He'd only come back to see if he could find any more information that she might pay for. His greed caught him out.

'Let him go,' I tell Caleb. He looks at me as though I am mad. 'Unless . . . boy, would you like to earn yourself another guinea?' He nods vigorously. 'Because if you can find out what happened to our friend, that is what your information will be worth. You know where I live.'

Caleb reluctantly lets him go and the boy runs off. 'What would a bawd want with Jonathan?'

An excellent question, one that I do not have an answer for until I think back over the last conversation I had with her. My heart sinks to recall that I had told her about a slave boy, almost killed by his master and now free. I had been so eager to prove her wrong that I said far too much. Jonathan had been brought from the very island on which she had been living for all those years. 'You said you know the name of Caleb's master. What is it?'

'Lisle. I know he lives up in Clerkenwell. A bit close for comfort, but Jonathan reckoned he was planning to return to Barbados once his business in London was done with.'

I hope he can't read the guilt on my face. 'Madame Vernier, she was living in Barbados for a good while. She knows many men like Lisle, and I think she'd betray her own kin if it helped her out in any way. If she realised who Jonathan was, I don't doubt she would trade information for coin.' I try to think. Would she keep Jonathan at the Pall Mall house? No, she wouldn't conduct such dirty business in an establishment she hopes to be seen as prestigious. 'You said that you know Tobias Kellett.'

Caleb snorts. 'Yes. A piece of work if ever I saw one.'

'Gisele Vernier's bordello is run from a Pall Mall house, with his financial support. He knows a lot of people both here and in the West Indies. It's likely that he knows this Lisle.' They both are devils, and like attracts like.

'You think they knew about what Lisle did and so when you mentioned Jonathan, they put two and two together. And now Lisle has him back?'

'Maybe.' God, I want it not to be true but if it is . . . 'I can't put it past her.'

'Then if she is the worst of people, perhaps we should go to the best of people for help.' Caleb starts to walk, and I trot after him. 'I'll take you home first and then go and speak to the Sharps. A man like Doctor Sharp has influence. His own power in a way.'

I desperately want to go with him, but I need to be at Little Wild Street in case the boy comes back. We agree to meet at the Shakespeare's Head the following evening to share what news we have. Perhaps there is nothing to fear. A young lad like Jonathan, free for the first time, he might simply have seen a better opportunity. Perhaps he's done something foolish like imbibe too much gin or lost his uniform at the gambling table. Deep down I know that none of these are possible. Jonathan had been overjoyed with his new position. He likes the Browns, he enjoys his Sunday social meetings, and his health doesn't lend itself to drinking or those more debauched activities. Something has happened to him, and I know that it is nothing good.

'The Sharps heard nothing,' Caleb tells me as we sit in the tavern over pots of ale. 'They didn't even know that he'd disappeared. And then I managed to find the Lisle house.'

'You have been busy.' I am impressed.

'Much good it's done me, for I have nothing to show for it. The house was shut up, Lisle gone. The maid at the house next door said he left last week. He was renting the place while the owners were in the countryside, and they're due to return to London any day.'

My heart sinks. If Jonathan had left under his own volition, then the Sharps were the only other people he might have contacted. And if Lisle did take him, we have no way of knowing where to. He might already have taken Jonathan out of the city. 'Our little spy hasn't returned, and I'm not sure he ever will,' I say.

'You think he has loyalty to this woman?'

'No.' The lad had spoken too easily once he saw the first

guinea. His only loyalty is to himself. 'But he doesn't have her trust. Why would she tell him anything? My only other idea is to see if we can get into that house.'

Caleb stares at me as though I am a mad woman. 'Straight into the lion's den? And you think what? That they just have Jonathan in there?'

'No. But there are two girls there who I trust. They'll know if a man named Lisle has visited the house and that might give us a clue.'

I can see he is warming to the idea. 'And you think they'll just let you in? Is it not dangerous?'

'They won't let me in the front door.' If Madame Vernier were to spot me, there'd be trouble, but I'm not scared of her. 'But someone told me that there's a way to sneak in. They have a bully on the door but not until quite late in the evening, when the gentlemen begin to arrive. If I get caught then I'll have shown my hand but it's not dangerous.'

We concoct a plan that is far from genius, but I think there is a chance for it to work. Caleb's writing is well known enough that he might be able to gain entry as a businessman with a proposal for Madame Vernier to consider. An alternative to *Harris's List* which is still months away from its annual publication. For a small cut, Caleb will offer to praise her girls, under their newly adopted monikers, making clear their quality.

'It's not a terrible idea,' he muses as we discuss the sort of things he might write, giving him fuel to feed to Madame Vernier. 'A summer edition to coincide with the height of the Season. I could make a fortune.'

'Let's find Jonathan first and then you can write your little directory,' I tell him.

I hope that the young maid, Mathilde, will be drawn away to tend to Caleb and her mistress. That would allow me to sneak into the house through the cellar window that Daisy mentioned. Presumably there is a cook that I will have to avoid, but I have my second guinea in case a bribe is necessary. Once upstairs I will just have to try each door and hope that one of them leads me to either Emmy or Daisy. My plan if caught is to claim that Mrs Macauley sent me to fetch Emmy back to her. And I'll also scream as loud as I can in the hope that Emmy would hear me and come running – if she is not still held under lock and key.

There is no time to waste. Jonathan has been gone for days already. The next afternoon we make our way to Pall Mall. 'Be careful,' Caleb warns me, and I can see that he is worried.

'I shall be fine,' I assure him, though his concern warms my heart a little.

I run down the steps to the cellar of the Pall Mall house while Caleb knocks at the door. As luck would have it, I don't even have to bother with the window, for the door has been left ajar and I slip inside. Through an archway ahead I hear voices, the coarse tones of an older woman who has little patience as she scolds someone. That must be the kitchen. I see beyond the open door that there are stairs leading up. Taking a deep breath, I run lightly past the door, hoping not to be seen. Pausing at the bottom of the flight, I hear nothing. I have made it past my first obstacle. Now to head upstairs.

Emerging silently behind the entrance hall, I can hear Caleb talking.

'I will need to check with my mistress,' Mathilde says.

'Very well. I shall wait here for her answer.'

I smile to hear his confident tone. He may get no further

once Madame Vernier becomes involved, but at least Mathilde is out of my way. I hover in the shadows as she crosses and knocks on the parlour door before entering. Quickly, I make my way out into the hall and run up the stairs.

This is where my plan becomes less clear and more dependent on sheer luck. I don't know how many girls currently reside in the house. Any one of them, not knowing me, might raise the alarm. I try to remember my previous visit. I had been sent to a bedroom on the first floor with Mr Forrester. These are the more luxuriously decorated rooms. Emmy had been on the second floor in a plainer bedchamber. However, by now she may have been moved, her training complete.

I walk up and down the corridor, my footsteps swallowed up by the thick rug that lines it, pressing my ear to each door. Not a sound anywhere. What do these girls do all day? Downstairs I hear the front door close and Caleb's voice echo in the hall. He has made it past the first barrier. I take a chance and open the furthest door to my left. That room is bare, no girl nor furnishing. The one next to it I think is the room I was in with Forrester. Yes, I recognise the blue velvet curtains, but there is no occupant in sight.

Beginning to despair, I hear a voice from upstairs. A girl. I move closer to the staircase, taking the first step, then a second as I try to determine if it is someone I know. Could it be Emmy? There is a quality to the voice that I recognise but her vowels have been adjusted. I throw caution to the wind and run up to the second floor. Peering around the corner, a smile springs to my face as I see that it is indeed her. Not only that but her companion is Daisy.

'Sukey!' Emmy cries out, her eyes wide. 'What are you doing here? How?'

'Hush!' I embrace her tightly. 'I came through the cellar. Is there somewhere we might talk?' I remember Daisy. 'You too. I need to know if you've seen or heard anything.'

She shows me into her room, closing the door behind us. 'Why are you here, Sukey? I won't go back. Mama doesn't deserve me.'

'I'm not here on your mother's behalf, love,' I say. 'I'm here because you aren't safe. Daisy did tell you what happened to Camille?'

'Camille made a bad choice,' she tells me, and the words do not sound like Emmy's. It is a repetition of an excuse. A denial. 'I know you want to blame Madame Vernier, but she didn't send Camille to that woman.'

'And do you think that Camille had a choice?' I see from her face that she is not moved. Logically, she is not wrong. Camille's fate could have befallen her in almost any bawdy house in London. I think of telling her about my mother but I am also here for another reason, for someone other than myself. 'It's more than just that, Em. Something has happened to Jonathan and your new bawd is behind it.'

'Jonathan?' She looks confused. 'But how would Madame Vernier even know him? They hardly mix in the same circles.'

'No. But she does mix in the same circles as his old master. The one who tried to kill him.' I allow her to think on that for a moment. 'We know that he vanished — was taken — from the place he was living a few days ago. I stupidly said something about him to Madame Vernier last time I was here. A boy was following me around, reporting back on where I went and who I was with. We caught him and he confessed that it was her who was paying him to do so. Recapturing a lost slave, well, I imagine it would earn her favour if not fortune.'

'She wouldn't do that,' Emmy says firmly. 'Her focus is entirely on us girls. On helping us to make something of ourselves. Besides, this isn't the West Indies, Sukey. Slaves are treated well here. Like servants.'

'Did you not hear me tell you what that man did to Jonathan? You've seen Jonathan as he is now. Seen how he limps and how he only has one good eye.' I am dumbfounded. Is she so caught up in this new life that she cannot see the trickery and deception that lies beneath it all?

'I heard something,' Daisy interrupts before Emmy could reply to me. 'It didn't make sense to me at the time but perhaps now it does.'

'Go on.' My patience is barely a thread.

'There was a gentleman who called last week for dinner,' she tells me. 'I hadn't seen him before. She called him Lee or Loyall, something like that.'

'Lisle?' I ask.

'Could have been. I wasn't paying him much attention, I'm sorry, but I remember that when he arrived, they embraced as old friends, and they talked about Barbados. That's where they have slaves, do they not? Is that where your friend was from?'

'Did they mention him? His name is Jonathan. Jonathan Strong.' To my surprise I begin to weep, sinking down onto the bed. 'This is all my fault. If only I hadn't been so stupid. I knew she'd been there, on the same island that Jonathan was from. I should have known that the two wickedest people I have ever come across would know one another.'

Emmy's face softens and she comes and sits beside me, pulling me to her shoulder. 'I was also at the dinner. I wasn't matched with the man, but I sat beside him for a while in the drawing room afterwards. He was very much in his cups. Not the usual quality that we get here but I got the impression that he and Kellett were old friends.'

'She uses those occasions to test her newer girls,' Daisy says. 'Do you remember, Em, the girl who wasn't good enough?' Emmy's laugh is bitter, and I spy an opportunity.

'Please, Em, won't you believe me when I say again that you cannot trust either of them, Vernier or Kellett? You could come home with me now,' I plead. 'Your mother misses you as much as I.'

'I can't,' she whispers, a tear falling from her cheek. 'If they catch me, my life won't be worth living. That girl, Kellett tried to break her and so she tried to run away. Only Mr Palmer caught up with her, like Jakes did with you. On the night that man was here, Kellett said that if anyone was willing to tame her, they could go down the cellar and do whatever they liked for only a shilling. The man, Lisle, said that he wasn't used to having to pay and that the problem in London was that slavery wasn't widespread enough. He said he had just that day found a buyer for his own runaway. He was just awaiting the sailing of the ship. They laughed about sending a ship of harlots over to the West Indies and wondered how much money they would earn for it.'

My body feels frozen. I am too late. 'A buyer? And this was last week?' He is gone then. They have swept him up off the street and sold him back into slavery. He will never survive it.

'Maybe not.' Daisy crouches before me, her face full of optimism. 'He mentioned a gaol. I don't know which one, but he was boasting about how simple it was to arrange, that he'd not even had to get his own hands dirty.'

What a despicable man. My mouth twists in hate. 'What happened next?'

The light fades from Daisy's face. 'Then he paid his shilling and went down to the cellar.'

33

They know nothing more. I dry my tears and drink the water that Emmy brings me. The news is so dispiriting that I am rendered weak with the wretched knowledge that Jonathan's fate is down to me. How can I tell Caleb this terrible news? Even if we find the gaol that Daisy has mentioned, we are probably too late.

'You must go, Sukey,' Emmy urges, taking my empty water glass.

'Will you not come with me? How can you bear to stay here knowing what these people are capable of?'

Emmy won't look at me. 'I cannot go back. I cannot fail yet again. Here I have gentlemen asking for me. And is Madame Vernier so much worse than Ma? A few weeks ago you wouldn't have said so.'

'I have learned my lesson,' I assure her. 'Your mother is a complicated woman but I do not believe she would allow real harm to come to her girls if she could prevent it. After what you've seen and heard, can you tell me that you believe the same of Gisele Vernier?'

Daisy is at the door. 'Come now, Sukey. I'll go downstairs and distract Mathilde so you can go out through the cellar.'

'I don't want to go without you,' I beg Emmy. 'Your mother

is desperate without you. She closed our doors after you left, for days. She misses you as much as I.'

She won't even look at me. When I reach out a hand to hers, she moves away, and I know that I have not been able to convince her. She knows everything and yet still she would rather stay here, in this beautiful house that feels more cursed every minute I linger. In the end I have to follow Daisy and leave my sister behind. Emmy knows where to find me if she needs me. I have to trust that she will not leave it too late.

'How often do ships sail for the West Indies?' I ask Caleb. He is waiting across the street for me, relief washing over his face as he sees me, replaced with desperation as I stammer out the news.

'I could not guess. I can ask Jim next Sunday at the meeting. He travels over from Limehouse to attend. He's been working down at the docks for years.' He sees the look on my face. 'I know Sunday is a long time to wait but without more information there's not much I can ask him, is there? We don't know the name of the ship or the captain. Besides which, Jim can't read nor write. Even if I send him a message, he won't waste money on a scribe if he'll see me in a few days' time.'

'Then how many gaols are there in London? Perhaps if we find the one he is – or was – kept at . . . ' Despair threatens to overwhelm me. 'We are too late. I know it. It's been too many days.'

He begins to walk towards home turning back when he realises that I'm not following. 'You're giving up so soon?'

'What do you suggest we do?'

He sighs. 'What about going back to Doctor Sharp? He is a man who meets people from all walks of life, from the gutter to the great, isn't he? Now that we have more information, he might know someone who could help. Besides, I was a stranger to him. He believed me when I told him I was a friend of Jonathan, but he'd be more likely to confide in someone he is more familiar with, if Jonathan had mentioned something to him, or if Brown has contacted him.'

I feel a flicker of hope, the plan giving me something to hold onto. He is right. Between us we had saved Jonathan before. There is no reason why we cannot do so again. 'I'll go right away,' I tell him.

It takes me over an hour to walk to Mincing Lane, but I am loath to waste what little money I have on a carriage. I think about how to present myself when I arrive but have forgotten about the dragon-like Mrs Day who, of course, answers the door to my knock.

'The gentlemen are both out,' she says, getting ready to close the door in my face.

'Please! Can I wait? Or can you tell me when they're likely to return?' I push my hand against the wood, leaning my weight against it. 'It is a most urgent matter.'

'You said that last time.'

'And I did not lie that time either,' I remind her. 'I promise you, it is vital that I speak to Doctor or Mr Sharp before the end of the day.'

She pushes back at the door but a moment later, the pressure eases. Someone is behind her, and she has turned to look back.

'Doctor Sharp!' I cry out. 'It's Sukey Maynard. I have urgent news for you.'

Mrs Day relents, shoots me a glare filled with vitriol, and

disappears down the corridor. She is replaced by a younger woman with a kind face. I leap back, suddenly unsure of myself.

'I am Mrs Sharp. William's wife,' she tells me. 'You're the girl who saved young Jonathan are you not?'

I nod, struck dumb. I hadn't even realised that Doctor Sharp was married, though of course it makes sense.

'Come in. William will be home at some point I hope and, if not, then Granville is holding a rehearsal this evening and he will not miss it.' She opens the door wide, and I duck inside the house. 'Some tea? Mrs Day was just brewing a pot. There'll be more than enough for two.'

She takes me into the same room I had been in on my last visit. There are two music stands in the middle of the room this time and several large cases that I suppose must hold musical instruments. She clears a pile of papers from an armchair and gestures for me to sit. As I do so, I hear the sound of someone coming in through the front door.

Mrs Day bangs into the parlour with a tray. 'Tea, ma'am.' She scowls at me and thumps her cargo down on the table. 'And Mr Sharp is home.'

'We're in the parlour, Greeny,' Mrs Sharp calls out.

'We?' He pops his head around the door. 'Ah. Good afternoon, Sukey, or is it now evening?' He manages not to look overly surprised to see me. 'It has been some months since we last met.'

I suppose that Mrs Sharp is to be trusted, so I feel free to tell them both everything I know about Jonathan and what might have happened to him.

'A gaol,' Mr Sharp muses. 'We don't know which one. Or if he is still there.' He stands up after a moment and begins to pace.

I glance in Mrs Sharp's direction, and she shakes her head, letting me know to leave him be.

'Why didn't Brown tell us?' he wonders.

'I don't think he realised,' I say. Jonathan has always spoken well of the man. I imagine he will be horrified to find out the truth.

'There is a Justice of the Peace who lives on this street. He might know where we can begin the search.' Mr Sharp retakes his seat. 'Let us pray that he is not already on a ship and at sea.'

Mrs Day barges in then. 'Supper is ready.' She shares another of her compendium of disgruntled scowls with me. 'Will I be setting another place?'

'Oh, no.' I get to my feet. 'I have already taken up too much of your time and I will be missed at home.'

'I will send word as soon as I can,' Mr Sharp promises, and so I let Mrs Day propel me along the corridor and out of the house.

Mrs Macauley seems strangely unconcerned about my tardiness in arriving home. Our own supper is being put on the table as I step inside, and she is opening a bottle of her best wine as I take my seat.

'Are we celebrating?' Hattie asks.

Mrs Macauley smiles, and it is the happiest I'd seen her, perhaps ever. 'We certainly are. For girls, we are finally moving from this hovel and into new accommodation.'

'What? How? When?' Grace guzzles down half of her glass of wine in one.

Mrs Macauley stands at the head of the table to address us. 'For years some of you have wondered why I entertain Sir Horace when he so rarely has money to spend.' She is correct in her claim. 'Well, for several reasons. Years ago, when he was wealthy, he was my keeper for a year or so. When he fell on hard times, I was too fond of him to cast him aside. Besides, every harlot worth her salt knows that men's fortunes often ebb and flow. Especially when they're so enamoured with the faro table, as Sir Horace is. You make allowances during famine and hope to reap the reward during the feast times. And, thanks to some good luck at that same faro table, my patience has received remuneration. Sir Horace paid me a visit as soon as he sobered up from his celebrating and paid me all that he owed for the last five years. One hundred and forty guineas which, together with my savings, will allow us to move to a larger house in Soho, with bedchambers for all. Sir Horace knows the landlord and we can move there next week.'

I smile and try to say the right things as they celebrate around me, and I drink my wine, but all I can think about is Jonathan. He might be lying on the floor of a ship's hold that very moment and Hattie is chattering on about having curtains at her windows and a bedroom with a floor that doesn't allow you to see into the room below.

'Bleeding 'ell, Sukey,' Grace scolds, noticing my failure to join in, 'will nothing in this place make you happy?'

'I'm sorry,' I say. 'It's just that I saw Emmy today and it feels strange for us to finally be moving to Soho when she isn't here to celebrate with us.' Only partly a lie, for I cannot help but imagine her joy at seeing her mother finally achieve her great ambition.

'Where?' Mrs Macauley sits down, her face suddenly serious. 'Is she coming home?'

'I don't think so.' I don't tell them my real reason for going to

Pall Mall. 'She knows about Camille, but she's doing well there. She seems . . . ' I don't want to say happy, and it is not quite the truth. 'I think that once she feels able to make you proud, she will return. I just can't say when that will be.'

'Well—' Mrs Macauley refills her wine glass '—she knows where to find us. For the next week at least.' She attempts to smile but I see how the news has affected her. I find myself commending her silently for her stoicism. If she marches to Pall Mall and causes a commotion, she might lose Emmy for good. This way, in allowing the decision to be her daughter's, there is a chance that Emmy will realise on her own just what a conniving bitch Madame Vernier is.

The following day brings news, some better and some worse A letter arrives from Granville Sharp. Jonathan has been found and he is still in London! Our worst fears have come true, though: it was Mr Lisle who discovered him. He has also seen no issue in selling on the lad he would have killed, and it is only days until Jonathan is due to depart on a ship bound for the West Indies. Mr Sharp writes of his intention to try to visit him and set his mind at ease, for he has an appointment to speak with the Lord Mayor. That alone impresses me enough to put my mind at ease, just a little. I send word to the bookshop and Caleb comes to Little Wild Street that night. Mrs Macauley's new softer nature continues for, while the parlour is quiet, she lets me speak with him in the kitchen as long as I am quick about it.

Caleb looks uncomfortable as he sits, even though the kitchen is like any other, no hint that it belongs in a whorehouse. I fetch him a glass of punch which he gulps greedily.

'Mr Sharp says that Jonathan is kept in the Poultry Compter,'

I tell him. 'They lied when he first enquired and said that he was not there, but Jonathan managed to get a message to Mincing Lane.'

'He has learned something, for the Jon I first met was meek as a mouse.'

'The good news,' I continue, 'is that Mr Sharp is confident of speaking to the Lord Mayor and having the sale nullified. He thinks that the mayor will see sense.'

'Then it may be that Sharp's not as wise as I thought him to be.' Caleb looks unconvinced. 'Sukey, you know there may be nothing we can do? It's good we've found Jon before they load him onto that ship, but it might be of no use. There are grey areas but no man to date has stood up in favour of the slaves, only of the powerful men who own them. The only chance is if the Lord Mayor accepts that the baptism is enough to set him free.'

'But you said that it isn't.' I wish he hadn't come. What little hope I had is rapidly dissipating thanks to him.

'Yes, but nobody really knows,' he admits. 'Some have got free just because their masters believed that it did. And others have been sent immediately back to the West Indies. If Sharp can somehow convince the Lord Mayor that a good Christian man would honour the intention . . . But a man of the law is so unlikely to do so. The Lord Mayor will have wealthy associates, probably who own their own slaves and will pressure him to act in their favour.'

'Don't say that!' I burst into tears, tiredness and the days of worrying over both Emmy and Jonathan finally overcoming me.

In an instant Caleb is by my side, pulling me to him. I fall into his embrace gratefully and sob my heart out. He is the only person who might understand how I am feeling, now that Emmy has gone.

'I might be wrong,' he tells me. 'I hope I am. And I will bring everyone I know to the Mansion House on the day that Sharp goes before the Lord Mayor. We will do everything we can to save him; do not fret on that account.'

'But it's my fault.' I sit up, wiping my face with my palms. 'If I hadn't opened my big gob to that evil woman . . . '

'How were you to know? You never told Lisle about Jonathan, she did. She'll answer to someone for her crimes one day. I swear that to you.' Caleb wipes away a missed tear.

'Answer to who? God?' I have to laugh. How unsatisfying.

'I'm sure God will have something to say to her, but I don't intend to wait so long,' he tells me, and I feel the thrill of his words in the pit of my stomach.

34

The next morning, Caleb sends a note, asking me to come to the bookshop at midday. I rise from my bed just in time to make the appointment, finding that Granville Sharp is waiting there for me.

'Sir, it is good to see you again,' I tell him. 'I cannot thank you enough for helping Jonathan.'

'I rather think it is the least I can do,' he says with a sigh, 'for I should have prepared him for this eventuality. I should have found him work where he would be more hidden away. Running errands all over the city led him into harm's way and it is my duty to help him now.'

I open my mouth to tell him that it is not his fault at all but rather mine, but behind his back, Caleb catches my eye, shaking his head. Telling Sharp about Madame Vernier will only lead to far more questions, and even if Sharp is fully aware that I am nothing but a Covent Garden harlot, it is far better to maintain this false veneer of respectability.

'We can speak with the Lord Mayor tomorrow,' Sharp goes on, 'but I must warn you that Lisle has been made aware of the fact and his man will do everything he can to remind those present that Jonathan is legally his.'

'His man?' Caleb sneers. 'He cannot even find the courage to come and face Jon himself?'

'That I do not know, but it is not unusual. Especially in the circumstances. As far as Lisle is concerned, he has sold Jonathan. The new owner will be there, I have been told, and his ship only waits for the tide.'

Sharp has only been passing by on his way to run some other errand related to his work, and so leaves us after just a few more words of warning that we must be on our best behaviour if we want to support our friend at the Mansion House. I see Caleb bristle, but I understand it. We want to show the world that we are not savages, that we are good Christians as much as any white man or woman is. That to enslave a man like Jonathan is heinously wrong. We shouldn't have to prove it, but the very fact of Jonathan's freedom being in question tells me that it is necessary.

'I'll be there,' I promise.

'You're certain? It's likely to be a very . . . masculine sort of place.' Caleb looks concerned and I cannot help but laugh.

'Masculine? It would be a poor reflection of my profession if I could not handle myself around a few men,' I assure him.

'I'd listen to Sukey if I were you, son.' Mr Fowler comes down the staircase into the shop, sharing a wink and a grin with me. He may not be Caleb's father in anything but name, but I can see his influence on the younger Fowler.

'Shush you.' Caleb laughs. 'Anyway, if you insist, then let me accompany you. I was planning to leave here at ten o'clock tomorrow morning, if that's not too early for you.'

It was, a little, but I could sacrifice my sleep for such a good cause. 'Not at all.' I should go but I don't want to go home yet.

To stew and ponder on Jonathan's fate while the other girls exchange trivialities and care not that a good man's future hangs in the balance. 'While I'm here, I should like to browse your book selection. I believe you are the novelist *du jour* in these parts.'

'If you say so.' Caleb's brow wrinkles in confusion.

'My profit sheet certainly says so,' his father chirps up from the back of the shop where he is making space for new books straight from a crate on the floor. 'And, Caleb, remember the new novel. Gartside said he can print a hundred copies if you get it to him by four o'clock.'

'Your new novel?' I remember then what it is that he writes, how he used to pay Camille for information on what men want, what they ask for, and my cheeks burn. 'I suppose it will be the next *Fanny Hill*.'

He looks at the floor and I swear that he too is embarrassed. 'I would write something else, but we need the money and that is what sells.'

'No shame in it,' his father reminds him. 'Always amazes me how prudish people are when half the Garden is making money from the pursuits of love. Or lust, at least.'

He makes a very good point. 'Which is your favourite?' I ask.

'Favourite what?' Caleb looks confused for a moment before it dawns on him. 'Of *my* books?'

'I recommend this one.' His father comes over, plucking a thin pamphlet from a shelf as he passes. '*Delphine Dumont: A Memoir*. A fine example of the genre and our most popular publication to date.'

I take it from him, noting that the author's name printed on the front is C. F. Loveday. 'You do not publish under your own name?'

'I don't much feel like going to gaol for corrupting the king's subjects.'

He makes a good point and, just from turning a few pages of the pamphlet, I feel the heat rise in my cheeks once more. I wonder if the fictional Delphine is a nod to Camille, and indeed the first scene my eyes have fallen upon is recognisable from a story I have heard her tell in the parlour. She must have borrowed the name of her own alter ego when she moved to Pall Mall. It is still strange to think that she will never again entertain – and infuriate – us all in her unique manner.

Caleb clears his throat. 'It is the first in a series. The latest is what I need to get finished today, for there is demand. Folk are waiting for it.' I hear the pride in his voice.

'Then I shall let you get on,' I say with a smile. 'I look forward to following Delphine's exploits. How much?'

'No charge for you, Miss Maynard,' Mr Fowler calls. 'Just a promise to spread the word if you enjoy it.'

I agree readily and leave before either Caleb or I can burst into flames over the high discomfort of the situation. If nothing else, it will take my mind off Jonathan.

I arrive home to find Maria in the parlour, drinking coffee with Hattie and Grace. The new girl, Jane, is presumably still upstairs in bed. She has not had much to do with us yet, but she doesn't seem daunted by her work, and has done whatever Mrs Macauley bids her to. Maria leaps up to draw me tight and I know that of all of us she will grieve the hardest for Camille.

'You're back?' I ask Maria, hopefully.

'Not yet, but soon,' she confirms. 'Mrs M has asked me to move to Soho with you, and I thought, well, why not?'

'You've forgiven her?'

'She has stopped making her unreasonable demands. And it's not easy outside of a reputable house, Su, trust me.' Her mouth is set in a firm line, and I wonder just how bad things are if Mrs Macauley is the better option.

'I hated working the taverns,' Grace agrees. 'You think you work for yourself, but everyone wants a little slice of your pay. If a waiter points in your direction, if you want to use a room, even if you just want that some blackguard doesn't curse your name or tell foul lies about you.' She shakes her head. 'I'm well out of that.'

I sit down beside Grace who whips *Delphine* from my hand immediately. 'Oh, this is a good one. My old beau used to read it to me, and we'd re-enact our favourite parts.'

Maria laughs. 'She used to work here, did Delphine. You'll have heard us talk of Camille. Well, that book is her legacy.' She has a twinkle in her eye, and I know what she is thinking. 'You've been to see Caleb, then, Sukey?'

'He's helping me with something,' I say. 'Nothing more.'

'Of course, love, of course.' She winks. 'But I wouldn't dismiss him so quickly. It's not easy to find love in our line of work. Not many men are willing to share their woman with one other man, let alone several a night. Least Caleb understands what we do. He makes his living in an adjacent line of work, after all.'

'I'm hardly seeking a husband,' I tell her.

'One day you might, that's all I'm saying. And you could do worse than Caleb Fowler.'

'Do I know Caleb Fowler?' Grace looks deep in thought. 'If his pen is any indication then he surely knows how to use his pr—'

'No!' I jump up. 'Caleb and I are simply helping a mutual friend. I don't . . . he's not . . . There is nothing more to it.'

'Methinks the lady doth protest too much.' Hattie lets out a cackle. 'Let us have our fun, Sukey. Things are looking up. We'll soon be in Soho with a bedchamber each in a house that doesn't feel as though it will blow over every time there's a gust of wind. Come and have some coffee with us. I've even got a little something special to celebrate Maria's return.' She holds up a bottle of what looks like rum.

'I need to speak to Mrs Macauley,' I say, and flee upstairs, unintentionally running into the very woman herself as I reach the first landing.

'Good timing,' she says. 'A word?'

I follow her into her room and sit down. While I'm here I should ask permission ahead of tomorrow. 'You don't mind if I go out tomorrow? I'll be back in plenty of time.'

'Yes, yes, fine.' She waves my request away as though she has never kept me here under lock and key. 'Can you do something for me?'

With my thoughts on Jonathan and my need to be at the Mansion House the next day, I can do nothing except nod.

'Excellent. I want you to take Jane under your wing.'

'The new girl? Is she not settling in?' It surprises me. She seems an old hand at the job, and as much as she barely speaks to the rest of us, she is coquettish enough for the gentlemen who visit.

'I require harmony in my house if Emily is ever to return, and I fear that if Jane continues to keep herself isolated then there will be future trouble.' She sees the pamphlet in my hand. 'Perhaps you could share that with her. Talk to her, share past experiences. Find out who she is. By the time we move to Soho she must be one of us, for that is when I will go and fetch back my daughter.'

This was good news indeed, for I had started to fear that Mrs Macauley had given up on Emmy. We would be in Soho in a matter of days though and I could wait that long if it meant having my sister back. It was certainly worth making a small effort to befriend Jane.

'One thing, though, Sukey.' I look back over my shoulder as I reach the door. 'Don't stray too close to that Caleb boy. He's a distraction and you still have a fair amount of debt to pay back.'

More fool me for thinking she has changed.

Jane is in the room above, the one that once upon a time was Hattie's. I go immediately, fearing that Mrs Macauley will have her ears pricked and knowing how easily sound travels between those two rooms.

I knock on the door but there is no answer. Pressing my ear to the door I hear nothing. Perhaps she has slipped out without anyone noticing. Jakes isn't at his post yet and the girls in the parlour are in high spirits; it would be easy for them to miss the sound of the front door. I'm in two minds over what to do, but this isn't Jane's private quarters. Hattie has more claim to it than her and she'll be expected to vacate it in a matter of hours.

I open the door to find that Jane has in fact not gone out. She is standing before the looking glass on the wall, admiring herself and lost in reverie. That is, until I cough, and she jumps, turning to look guiltily in my direction, her hand flying up to cover the jewellery around her neck that she was admiring in the mirror.

'Haven't you ever heard of knocking?' she demands of me.

'I did knock. Mrs Macauley sent me to see if you needed anything. Or in case you wanted someone to talk to,' I say, my eyes glued to her right hand, clearly hiding something.

'I don't need anything from you, and if you were the last person on God's earth, I would not want to talk to you.' She marches upon me, and I step back, out of the room. 'Get out, you dirty savage!'

I do as she asks without hesitation, letting her slam the door in my face. I know what I have seen, for she was not quick enough to conceal it. Around her neck hangs a pendant of emeralds and diamonds, quite distinctive in its octagonal shape. I have seen it before. She did not wear it on the day that she died, but I had seen it on both the day I had first visited Pall Mall and at the subsequent humiliating dinner. The necklace belonged to Camille. Which begged the question: how on earth did Jane, a common Covent Garden doxy, get her dirty hands on it?

35

I say nothing about the pendant to anyone. Apart from Emmy, who isn't here, I'm the only person who saw Camille wearing it. I have no proof that it isn't just an extravagant gift from a pleased gent of Jane's. Instead, I watch her that night in the parlour. Forrester has sent word that he is due and so I am allowed to act as bystander until he arrives, and I am attentive in my viewing.

Mrs Macauley found her at the Golden Cross inn, her usual fishing spot. Sometimes you found the innocents, those who wouldn't see through the blatant lies that tripped off the tongue of these conniving older women. Other times, you found those who had worked the provincial streets and taverns and wanted a change or had been told that the rakes of London spurted with gold. Jane had fallen into this second category; she'd taken to the parlour like a duck to water. No arguing, no quibbling about Mrs Macauley's cut. The perfect harlot. Perhaps too perfect.

I watch her on Sir Horace's lap, feeding him chocolate-covered raisins from a bowl. He is our guest of honour every evening now that he has saved Mrs Macauley's dream, and Jane has taken it upon herself to become his favourite. No one else cares much but now I am suspicious. Jane arrived at Little Wild Street after Camille's death, so her link to Camille could be through Madame

Vernier. The pendant, wherever it is now since Jane has never worn it publicly, would have been left at Pall Mall along with her other belongings, no doubt taken by Vernier. That leaves two options: either Jane stole the pendant from Gisele Vernier, or it was given to her by that wicked woman. A gift bears the suggestion of payment for something. I see her rub her palm across Sir Horace's crotch, the imbecilic gurn of pleasure on his face. In this moment he will do anything that she asks. I fear that this is the very reason for her coming here.

Forrester arrives to take me away from that miserable tableau and I am so happy to see him that I chatter away as we go upstairs, telling him all about our new premises and how impressed he will be to come to a nice house. As usual he is quiet, saying only what is necessary. Until he spots the novel by the bed.

'You have read this?' He picks it up, full of thought.

'You know, I hear the newest instalment of Delphine's adventures is being printed this very evening. I could easily procure you a copy if you wish.'

'Yes, that . . . ' He clears his throat. 'Yes, please, Sukey. I do find her tales mildly diverting.' I watch him as he turns the pages, trying not to smile. Perhaps I have found Forrester's darker side. He looks up, annoyed. 'You're still dressed?'

'Apologies.' I begin to undress.

'Leave your shift. And stockings.' He is head deep in the novel now. 'Then on to the bed. Or perhaps . . . ' He takes a deep breath. 'Sukey, are you familiar with the scene where Delphine meets the music tutor?'

The music tutor. A former frequenter of our house. He first came to visit us with his wealthy student who had been learning to play the harpsichord in order to impress young ladies, only to realise that they would rather marry him for his inheritance. He had visited Camille weekly until his benefactor decided to go off on a grand tour of Europe. Unable to afford harlots on his own meagre wage, he had tried to embrace his desires closer to home, been caught in flagrante with one of his female pupils and arrested for indecency. No one has heard of him since, but I do remember everything that Camille said about him.

I walk to the corner of the room where his cane is still kept. 'Yes, Mr Forrester,' I say, 'I am very familiar. And perhaps it is actually you who should be undressing.'

Forrester leaves me three guineas and departs whistling, a new man. I should sleep soundly but I cannot. Every time I turn in the bed another matter rises up to trouble me: how to rescue Jonathan; whether Emmy is safe; what my mother would think about all of this, and whether she'd approve of my desire for vengeance.

'But don't you think there's something very suspicious about it all?' I say to Caleb as we walk towards the Mansion House. I have told him about Jane, and my suspicions.

'Definitely,' he says, 'only . . . Can we think of Jonathan, for today? I know that your friend is important to you, but she can wait one more day.'

'But Madame Vernier is responsible for all of this,' I insist. 'This concerns Jonathan too. For what if he is freed? Where will he go then where they will not find him? The Browns, the Sharps, they are all known to these thieves.'

'He'll come home with me,' Caleb says. 'My old man was a publisher as well as a bookseller in his younger days. He gave it up when I was little. Nearly got caught a couple of times publishing books that were . . . frowned upon, shall we say? But his old hidey holes are still around the shop. Anyone comes round looking for Jonathan and we can have him hidden away in a trice.'

'He was publishing novels, like yours?'

Caleb laughs. 'No, he was more into politics, if you like. In favour of the common man. Speaking of which . . . '

We are coming to the Mansion House now and there is quite a crowd outside. I recognise several from the Sunday meetings. How many have given up a day's wages to show their support to Jonathan? It is heartwarming as much as it is heartbreaking.

'Stick close to me,' Caleb warns as people begin to file inside, turning left into the Justice Room, the place where Jonathan's fate will be decided. It is mostly men, as I had been warned. I attract a few strange looks but reward them with a smile.

Proceedings begin and I hop up on my tiptoes to see where Jonathan stands with Granville Sharp at the front. What is Jonathan thinking as he hears all this commotion around him? There is an endless line of other cases to be heard first, and I worry as I see the Lord Mayor in his ornate chair, yawning. What if he decides to end proceedings early? He might deem Jonathan's situation to be outside of his remit. After all, if not for Mr Sharp, then Jonathan would already have been taken to the ship that currently waits to sail to Barbados. Caleb points out the man who is the ship's captain; he is glaring at Sharp for wasting his time, but he seems otherwise at ease. He looks confident of leaving this room with Jonathan in his care. I had thought him a coward but now I am glad that Mr Lisle has not made an appearance. I'm glad that Jonathan doesn't have to face the man who would have killed him.

As other cases are dealt with, Caleb and I manage to make our way closer to Jonathan. I see his eyes cast down as he waits, and I think he must feel as sick as I do. He looks thinner after his days in gaol, his skin ashy. It seems impossible that anyone could hear his story and decide to send him back to hell, yet I know that it would be foolish to rely on human kindness in this case.

Mr Sharp shuffles his notes as they are called forward. Caleb whispers to me that his defence relies on the charge that Sharp has brought before the Lord Mayor, Sir Robert Kite: that Jonathan has been confined in prison without a warrant. Regardless of Jonathan's status as a runaway, he has committed no crime as such. The hazy legalities over slavery on British shores may count in his favour as much as against. Kite has already decided that his claim has merit, for that is why they are present before him now and it gives me hope. Beside the captain is a lawyer who announces that he is acting on behalf of Jonathan's new owner, a Mr Kerr.

Kerr's lawyer speaks first, reminding the Lord Mayor that the lad before him has been the property of Mr Lisle for several years. That, in fact, in allowing Lisle to act as his master for so long, Strong has been complicit in his treatment as a slave. Jonathan is nothing more than missing property, recovered after several months. He accuses Granville Sharp of theft, for it was his duty to return Jonathan to his master on understanding that he was a slave.

I watch Jonathan, his head bowing lower as we listen to the eloquent argument. I know the despair that he must be feeling, for any Englishman, accepting of the existence of a legal slave trade, might agree with this opinion.

Sharp restates his assertion that in a civilised society, it cannot be acceptable for people to be snatched up off the street as Lisle's men did to Jonathan. He does not speak a word about slavery or Jonathan's past. It matters not that Lisle attempted to murder Jonathan because that is not the charge brought. Jonathan's freedom hangs simply on the manner in which he was taken.

Kite is ready to make his decision. He peers over his spectacles at Jonathan who, as Sharp nudges him, looks up and meets the Lord Mayor's canny gaze. 'As I see it, this lad has not stolen anything, since a person cannot steal themself. You have not presented me with evidence that he has committed any crime and yet you took him off the street and had him imprisoned. I do not see that this abduction was lawful and therefore he is at liberty to go away from this place. That is my ruling.'

I daren't believe what my ears are hearing. 'Caleb, what does he mean?'

'I think . . . I think we won!' His face is alight and he grabs me in a hug, lifting me off my feet. 'He's free, Su. Mr Sharp did it.'

I can hardly believe it. As my feet regain the floor I see Sharp smiling, turning back to shake hands with a man behind him. He doesn't see the captain leap forward to grab his arm. 'Sir, he may be innocent of any crime, but I seize this boy as the property of Mr Kerr.'

Jonathan's legs give way, and he falls to the floor, the captain's hand still gripping tightly to his arm. The room is in uproar and Sharp looks devastated. Caleb is trying to push his way through to the front, grabbing my hand to drag me behind him, but the throng are not keen to let us through. I cannot see a thing, but I hear Sharp's words roar out: 'Sir, I charge you for an assault on this lad.'

I poke my head out to see from beneath Caleb's arm as everyone falls silent, looking to the Lord Mayor who is clearly wishing that he were somewhere else.

'Well, you heard the man,' Sir Robert says eventually, addressing the captain. 'Would you commit an assault now on this lad?'

The captain releases Jonathan so quickly that he almost falls to the floor. He looks to his lawyer, but the man just raises his shoulders, as confused by what has happened as everyone it seems. Only the Lord Mayor looks unperturbed, rising from his chair and declaring a recess.

'Is he saved?' Caleb asks me, his face streaming with tears.

I see Granville Sharp propelling Jonathan through the crowd towards the door. He catches sight of me and nods his head, sharing a victory smile.

'Yes,' I reply. 'He is saved.'

We fight our way out and find them outside.

'Mr Sharp, thank you,' I congratulate him. 'How did you manage it? I thought all was lost.'

Mr Sharp fiddles with his hat and his cheeks flush. 'I admit, I did not do it alone. It was the city coroner who told me to charge the captain with assault. As he explained it to me, once Jonathan's freedom was given, any attempt to forcibly take him could be classed as such, just as it would be if the captain had tried to seize me, or any other man in the room.'

'And Jonathan is free?' Caleb shakes his head in happy disbelief.

'Yes, though I cannot promise that they will not try again.' Sharp looks at Jonathan, his expression serious. 'The law is too precarious and until a man with more power than Kite is willing to stand up for all of humanity, you will have to tread carefully.'

'What must I do then?' he asks Mr Sharp, the grin fading from his face.

'You cannot return to Brown's. I cannot promise that those men will not come for you again, Jonathan. Do you have anywhere else you might go?'

'He'll be coming home with me,' Caleb assures Mr Sharp. 'Those men won't dare to show their face in Covent Garden. Won't you come for a drink with us, sir, to celebrate?'

He politely declines. 'I must return to my post. I have missed half a day of work already.' He turns to go but looks back. 'Jonathan, I will continue to read up on the law as concerns your position here. I am certain that good sense and common decency will prevail and that I can use our legislation to enforce it. If you ever see any of those men again, please send word and I will come.'

'To Mr Granville Sharp! To Jonathan Strong!' Caleb hoists his tankard high, and we join him in toasting Jonathan and his saviour.

We have been in The Shakespeare's Head for hours already and the sun is getting ready to set. I will be in trouble when I get home, for Mrs Macauley despises a drunken harlot. Jonathan himself is barely conscious, having decided on this occasion to indulge in a few drinks, but is happy in his cups. As the afternoon has turned into evening, we have been joined by more and more of our friends from the Sunday meetings. I feel the effects of the ale as Caleb grabs hold of my hand and begins to whirl me around the small space where tables have been cleared away for dancing. Musicians play and I have never felt so free from cares. I have never been to such a joyous gathering before.

The fiddler begins to play, a tune that I don't know but that seems familiar to everyone else. I feel the drum beat echo through my chest and can't keep the smile from my face.

'Another dance?' Caleb holds out his hand.

I let him take my arm. 'Won't the other girls want a turn?'

'What other girls?' He winks and laughs.

We are just playing at a flirtation, I know, but I am having fun. Most of my life since arriving in London has been engaged in providing fun and pleasure to others, no matter my own feelings on the matter. In this company I am allowed to enjoy myself with no concern for others apart from the natural wish that anyone has for their friends. It is a fine thing. And Caleb is a fine young man.

My goodness, I am quite drunk! I let Caleb spin me around and I wonder what to do if he kisses me. What will I do if he does not? I must be sensible, I tell myself. I am one of the fallen sisterhood. I have a debt to repay that ties me to Mrs Macauley for at least some time to come. I have nothing to offer a husband. Not fidelity, not child, for how would we know for certain who the father was? Perhaps if he would wait for me . . .

'I'll walk you home,' he tells me, for he too is aware of the time, and of the consequences if he is found to have kept me away.

He kisses me as we part outside Little Wild Street in time for me to begin work, and it feels like my very first kiss. For it is the first time that I have not only done so for free, but the first time that I have felt such a swell of emotion overcome me. Like my entire body is abuzz. I know that it cannot last, that Caleb, despite knowing what he does, can never abide my profession for long. That it is the heady mix of booze and unbridled joy that has allowed him to put aside those considerations for those short minutes, but somehow that doesn't matter.

✶ MAY 1766 ✶

Sarah Maynard, Queen Street, Soho

A young lady with dark complexion, said to be from Barbados. Certainly, her first venture into her current profession was with a gentleman from that part of the world. She is a comely lass with some spirit, though may be considered a little over ambitious in what she charges. She is not in keeping but is not always able to be free with her favours due to the attendance of one particular London gent.

36

The new house is on Soho Square itself – a house as far removed from our old residence on Little Wild Street as to be considered another league entirely. There are five floors, including the cellar and its impressive kitchen which Cook is over the moon with. While not as grand as Madame Vernier's Pall Mall house, the upstairs bedrooms are spacious and numerous enough to avoid arguments between Hattie and Grace – there are six and it does not go unnoticed that there is one left over for Emmy, should she return. Mrs Macauley takes two rooms on the first floor for a bedroom and office. The floor as one enters the house is comprised of two rooms. The larger parlour where we will entertain is at the back of the house, where noise can be kept from ebbing out into the street. At the front, a smaller room is furnished with a faro table for those gentlemen who enjoy throwing their money away on more than just women.

'I only wish my Emmy were here to see it,' Mrs Macauley sighs, growing melancholy after her fourth glass of celebratory champagne.

'She'll come back soon,' Cook promises. 'No one can bear Gisele Vernier for long.'

I have tried to put that woman from my mind but hearing

her name makes my anger bubble up once more. I am still determined to make her pay for my mother's death, but I haven't seen her in weeks. Making the move to Soho has been a welcome distraction and I enjoyed the packing up of clothing, of furniture, and seeing Mrs Macauley in a new light.

As for Jonathan, he has settled in well at the Fowlers' shop which is just as well since he has only been able to leave under the watchful eye of Caleb, escorting him to the Sunday meetings while keeping him occupied in the shop at all other times. Due to his almost constant presence, I have barely spoken to Caleb directly, but he gifted me a signed copy of his new *Delphine* and we have managed to share the occasional kiss away from the eyes of Jonathan and his father. I have not told him that I am using his writings to enhance my standing with Mr Forrester, who last week left me a fine pair of satin gloves on his departure.

Sir Horace is our guest of honour on our first night in the house. Mrs Macauley has hired out two girls from Haddock's bagnio to ensure that the bedrooms are kept full, and they are certainly skilled at flattery and seduction, even with the plainest of men. There is much that I might learn from them.

Jane still keeps herself away from the rest of us. Though I manage to sneak a rummage through her meagre belongings on an evening when she was occupied with Sir Horace and I was upstairs waiting for Forrester, there is not much to say about them. The pendant yes, but I had already spied that. Her constant attentions towards Sir Horace have attracted Mrs Macauley's notice which puts my mind at ease a little, and I see her push Jane away in favour of one of the Haddock's girls as she makes her move towards him.

'We cannot show favouritism here, Jane,' she says with her

most dangerous smile. 'Not unless he is willing to commit his patronage to paper and coin.'

Forrester is not due that evening and so I throw myself into the melee and snare a young eager boy of nineteen, from a wealthy family who would no doubt be horrified to know where their future heir is spending his evening. He pays five guineas and is blessedly so quick that I am hardly missed from the parlour, where Sir Horace is still holding court.

'And so I said to him – my dear, you must shut your ears a moment – I told him that his wife was cuckolding him with his own valet and everyone knew that she did so. But he was most unbothered because he in turn was buggering the stable boy on a nightly basis!' Our benefactor is in his element, regaling the room with all his oldest stories, bouncing Grace upon his knee as she giggles and makes sure that his glass is never empty. I enjoy watching Jane's bitter face as she deals with a more rambunctious young man who keeps grabbing at her bosom in a most annoying way.

I wander into the faro room but the atmosphere there is entirely focused on the table, presided over by Cook who has been transfigured into a voluptuous madam. Mrs Macauley has lent her a wig and make-up, and her gown is tight at the waist and low in the neck, so that I see several of the men struggling to concentrate on their cards instead of her assets. Her height and the width of her lower arms should be enticement enough that none of them will cause her problem, though just in case, trusty Jakes guards the front door as usual, a stone's throw away if he is needed.

All of the girls but Grace and I have moved upstairs with their lucky gents when a newcomer is admitted. It is Caleb, looking confused.

I rush up to him. 'Is everything well? Please tell me that Jonathan is safe.'

'Yes, Su, he's fine. I've been summoned by your mistress.'

'Mr Fowler.' Mrs Macauley appears. 'It is good of you to have come. Won't you come up to my office. You too, Sukey. This concerns the pair of you.'

Giving each other wary looks, we repair to her office where she pours good burgundy into crystal glasses. She has cut no corners in this new house of hers. Caleb drinks half of his down in one and I see Mrs Macauley try to conceal her grimace.

'What's all this about?' I ask.

'Revenge,' she tells me with a smile. 'I told you that I would fetch Emily once we had arrived in Soho and that time is now. This evening has gone splendidly and my girl will see that I can offer her just as much as Gizzy Vernier can.'

I don't tell her that it was not the décor of Little Wild Street that drove Emmy away; she does know that. 'But how will we show her when she doesn't want to come?' We cannot work the same trick twice; Madame Vernier has already seen Caleb once.

'Daisy Gardner wrote to me.' Mrs Macauley brandishes a letter. 'It's barely legible but I suppose one good thing about Gizzy's school for harlots is that her girls are getting some education at the very least. She thinks that Emily is beginning to see through Vernier's façade, that she is ready to consider a reconciliation.'

'And why am I here?' Caleb lets her refill his glass.

'I want Gizzy to know what happens to women who steal girls away and treat them so appallingly. I intend to march in there the day after tomorrow, after her bully has left for the day. Daisy says that he'll be gone by ten o'clock. However, in case there's any resistance, I would like to have some security. Three or four men should be sufficient to dissuade any unhappy circumstances. Perhaps from your little Sunday gathering?'

Of course she knows about that. Her little sparrows will have reported back on where I go and who I meet.

Caleb grimaces. 'You would like three or four men with dark skin to descend upon Pall Mall in broad daylight and expect that not a single passerby will call for the justices to come and arrest us?'

Mrs Macauley shifts uncomfortably in her chair. 'I suppose you make a valid point. Maybe if it was just you. Sukey and I, perhaps Hattie, we can hold our own to a certain extent . . . '

'No.' Caleb sighs heavily. 'My pa'll love this. A little adventure for him. A couple of his old comrades as well. I can speak to them first thing.'

'Splendid! And, of course, they will be recompensed for their time and efforts.' Mrs Macauley is thrilled, as am I to an extent. In two days' time, Emmy will be home, whether she wants to be or not. I hope that Daisy is correct, and she will come willingly. Dragging her out of Madame Vernier's house will only create more problems, I fear. 'I'll tell the girls in the morning. I'm sure they'll want to help.'

They will, for Camille. But there is someone else on whose behalf I want to exact my revenge. My mother, who had trusted Vernier and had no idea of her depravity, the lengths she would go to or the people she would corrupt in order to get her own way.

Which reminds me . . . 'I'm sure that you're right, only there is something I should tell you about Jane,' I begin.

Mrs Macauley wakes relatively early the next day, banging on all the doors, waking up grumpy and sleep-deprived harlots.

'What's all this about?' Hattie demands as we are on our way downstairs. Mrs Macauley is close behind us, like a collie rounding up sheep.

'I have something to talk to you about. Something important,' she says. I see Jane's eyes dart back upstairs. She suspects she might have been discovered and she is thinking of her pendant.

Mrs Macauley stands at the head of the kitchen table as we take our places. 'Girls, after the success of last night I have this morning been sent a letter of great import. Our little seraglio is already known to one of the most important and most influential gentlemen in all of London and he intends to pay us a visit tomorrow morning.'

'Who?' Jane asks immediately, and I try not to grin for I see her swallowing the hook along with the bait.

'Ah, my dear Jane, you shall find out in due course. However, he has asked me to keep my silence for now. If word were to get out then he would not be pleased, for he is so well known and every bawd in London town would kill for his custom.'

'When's he coming?' Maria asks.

'He says that he will be here at eleven o'clock tomorrow. Earlier, girls, than we are used to, but I believe he wants to see the house in the cold light of day. Candlelight and shadows might conceal much but we have nothing to hide. From now until then we are in rehearsal. You must all be dressed in your finest. Wear your jewellery. Powdered hair and make-up. Look as though you could walk into a ball at any of the great houses and pass for one of the ton.' Mrs Macauley claps her hands together. 'Go!'

We all dash upstairs, and I go to my bedchamber window to peer out. I only wait for ten minutes before I see Jane sneaking out, heading towards the corner where often lads wait to run messages. Our plan is working, and she is sending her message to Madame Vernier as we need her to. For how could that woman resist coming here to make sure that her great enemy does not triumph. And if she is in Soho then she cannot be in Pall Mall causing trouble or preventing me from rescuing Emmy.

37

Mrs Macauley and I borrow Sir Horace's carriage the next day at half past ten, having told the other girls the night before that we will go to fetch our special guest. By the time anyone – by whom I mean Jane – realises that we are taking rather a long time, we hope to be on our way back with Emmy. We arrive at a meeting place on St James's Square where Caleb, his father, and three of Mr Fowler's acquaintances are waiting.

'You gentlemen understand your roles?' Mrs Macauley asks and is rewarded by five nods. It has been decided that Mrs Macauley will wait inside the carriage just in case our plan has failed and Madame Vernier hasn't gone to Soho. Persuading Emmy to come with us will be challenge enough without a scene between the two older bawds.

In such a neighbourhood, it does not do to be too loud or dramatic. The men make their way with little fuss, Mr Fowler and two others knocking at the front door while the others go down to the kitchen door. Little Mathilde says not a word as they push past her into the house and I follow them inside.

'Go and gather your belongings,' I tell her, 'for your mistress will not be returning.'

She looks fearful. 'Where will I go?'

'You have parents?' Even though I might have assumed as much, my heart almost breaks as she shakes her head, her eyes filling with tears. 'Then you will come with me,' I tell her. 'Don't fret. You will be taken care of.'

I tell her to meet me in the hall once she has her things. There is no sign of Madame Vernier and the men are guarding the front door while I run upstairs quietly, heading to the room where I hope Emmy will be.

I find her asleep alone, the curtains drawn, the room heady with a miasma of sex, tobacco and wine. I let the sun in, dragging back the heavy drapes and pulling back the bedclothes as she begins to stir.

'What the – Sukey?' She sits up, her mouth agape. 'What are you—' Her eyes shoot to the door, full of fear. 'She'll catch you. Sukey, if she finds you here—'

'She won't.' I pull open drawers and find a jewellery box, full of trinkets and more expensive necklaces and bracelets. I throw it to her. 'Get dressed, Em, I'll help you, but we need to leave now, while Madame Vernier is away.'

'I can't leave,' she tells me, swinging her legs over the side of the bed. 'I'm not leaving, Su, and you can't make me.'

'Your mama and five men downstairs might have something different to say about that.' I resort to pushing her off the bed so that I can remove the sheet. It will make a rudimentary knapsack, good enough to carry her belongings to the carriage.

'Ma is here?' She moves to stop me as I pile gown on top of gown and empty the jewellery box on top. 'Is she very angry with me?'

'Oh, Emmy.' I stop and see that she has started to cry. 'She is not angry at all. Only desperate to have you back. And you should see it, Em, the new house. It is far finer than Little Wild Street. Not a patch on this place, of course. There are no such thing as miracles, after all. But you'll have your own room.'

'The house isn't what bothers me.' She is sobbing now. 'I just don't want to be a disappointment anymore. I cannot bear it.'

'Then come with me,' I tell her, drawing her to me. 'Your ma will be so happy to see you, and she's ready to listen to you now. She knows she did wrong. She loves you, Em.'

'Why are you being so nice about her?' She narrows her eyes at me. 'You hate my mother.'

'Your leaving helped me to understand her. Seeing how distraught she was, it has made me realise that she really has had our best interests at heart; she just hasn't always known how to show it.' I am exaggerating Mrs Macauley's altruism here, but I need Emmy to believe it.

She nods. 'All right then, Su. I'll come. But we must take Daisy too.' She hugs me tight and whispers in my ear. 'I have missed you so much.'

My own eyes now filling with tears, I leave her to finish gathering her belongings and go out into the corridor. When I find her, Daisy is already up and getting herself dressed. She gives me a nod and I know she has been waiting for this moment.

'Is there anyone else?' I ask her.

'Two more girls upstairs but leave them. They're loyal to Vernier.'

I have just given her instructions to make her own way to Soho when I hear shouts from downstairs and I run to see what is going on. One of Mr Fowler's friends is standing guard at the front door and he points to the door that leads down to the kitchen. I can hear a commotion down there and I remember what Daisy told me, about the girl in the cellar, and I need to take a few fortifying breaths before I go down there.

Madame Vernier has damned herself. For I arrive in time to see Caleb escorting not one but three girls from a cellar room. The shouts were for a hammer to take off the padlock that had prevented their escape. They wear rags rather than the finery of the girls upstairs, and none of them are much older than I am. I see bruises and marks on their skin, and I dread to think what has been done to them.

'What monster has done this?' Mr Fowler asks me, though we both know. He charges his comrades to take the girls to seek medical attention. Who knows what will happen to them after that. London is cruellest to those who have already lost so much.

The scene is horrific and I am glad to escape back upstairs. I find little Mathilde sitting quietly in the parlour and take her by the hand. She has a knapsack, all of her worldly belongings contained easily within it. 'You are free now,' I tell her as the men shepherd us all towards the waiting carriage. She looks up at me as though she doesn't know what that means.

We leave Emmy to guard Mathilde in the carriage, hidden away as Mrs Macauley and I escort Mr Fowler into our house. It was a tight squeeze with so many of us but necessary in order to maintain the deception. Fowler wears a smart and expensive jacket that had been left in the parlour at Little Wild Street and never reclaimed and has borrowed a wig from a wealthy lover of Caleb's fiction who has been promised the first read of the next *Delphine* in return. With a little powder, applied by Mrs Macauley as we bumped along the city streets, we hope he will pass muster as a wealthy new client for long enough to fool Madame Vernier. We passed her carriage, tucked away on another street around the corner. She must have been growing impatient, but she nevertheless has waited.

Once inside we sit Fowler down as Mrs Macauley calls for her girls, who have been dutifully waiting in the kitchen. 'I think you'll be very pleased with what I have to offer, Your Grace,' she trills loudly, a grin breaking out on her face as there is a knock at the door. 'Jane! Answer the door, won't you?'

Her scheme runs like clockwork. Madame Vernier has indeed arrived, with the intention of swanning in and denting Mrs Macauley's hopes of securing a duke for her house. We let Jane lead her into the house before Caleb and Jakes arrive to bar their retreat once they realise the deception. They take the women into the kitchen while I try to swiftly explain to Hattie and Maria what the hell is going on. Mrs Macauley goes to fetch her daughter and little Mathilde, and to check that the commotion inside has not alerted any attention on the street.

'I got up early for this?' Hattie yawns, not giving a damn about the politics or history of the two bawds. 'Well, if there's no duke wanting to tup me then I'll go back to bed.'

Sometimes I really do envy Hattie her simple life, free of complications.

'Sukey, I need your assistance.' I leave Mathilde in Maria's care for a moment and follow Mrs Macauley out, closing the parlour door firmly behind us. 'In the kitchen.'

The kitchen is busy. The two prisoners sit there, Madame Vernier and Jane, her spy. They are not restrained. Between Caleb and Cook, they stand no chance of escape.

'What are you doing, Lucy?' Madame Vernier injects as much

disdain into her voice as she can manage, no mean feat under the circumstances.

'I'm exacting justice in the only way I know how,' she replies. 'For my daughter and for Camille. And for those poor girls in your cellar. You know, if you'd been caught by the law then you would likely hang for what you've done, Gizzy.'

Madame Vernier laughs but I can see that she is shaken beneath that bravado. 'So, you will denounce me then, and watch me swing? And the same for Jane?'

'I ain't done nothing!' Jane protests. 'I only did what she told me 'cause she threatened me. Said if I didn't tell her what was going on here then she'd report me for stealing.'

'Liar!' Madame Vernier hisses at her treacherous accomplice. 'You took every coin and trinket I offered you, thankless spying bitch.'

'Let the girl go,' Mrs Macauley decides. 'She is harmless, and she has nowhere to go. That is punishment enough for a duplicitous wench like her.' She waits a breath. 'Let them both go in fact.'

'Let them . . .' I can hardly believe what I am hearing. 'But, Mrs Macauley! This bawd has been responsible for so much suffering. Those poor girls in the cellar. My own mother!'

'Do you want revenge? Do you want her to suffer?' Her words give me pause. 'Because I do. More than anything. And if she faces trial then we know what will happen. Tobias Kellett and her other wealthy benefactors will abandon her. She will be made an example of. Proof that all bawds are vile crones and that our girls – our charges – are fools, there to be taken advantage of. She will be punished, yes, and her life will end. But how does that add to her suffering? There will be an outcry against houses like this one and it is I, and women like me who operate in good faith, who will suffer. When she is dead, how can she repent? How can she come to regret what she has done? Better that she live knowing that I – that we – have bested her.'

I think about my mother, the woman who I was robbed of knowing, and I feel a white-hot rage surge through me. I want Gisele Vernier to pay. I want her to suffer, knowing that her past actions are what have led her to misery. And I know that Mrs Macauley is right. Death is too good for her. I want her to wake up every day repenting what she has done.

'Mr Fowler?' Mrs Macauley holds out her hand and Caleb reaches into his jacket pocket, removing a folded piece of paper and passing it to her. 'I took the liberty of having this confession written up, Gisele. This is my insurance. You shall walk free, but on one condition. You are to leave London this very day, never to return. Forget your fancy seraglio. By now there is a warning painted on its door to let the world know what it is. Your clients will abandon you. There is nothing left for you in this city. By signing this paper, you admit to your crimes, and it shall be used against you if you break the terms of our deal. Do you understand?'

'You really think I'll give in so easily?' Vernier's tongue drips with venom. 'Perhaps I'd rather take my chances with my loyal customers. An act of vandalism cannot bring me down so easily. Tobias will take care of things.'

'The choice is yours. But I've known Tobias Kellett for as long as you have, and I've never seen him commit one chivalrous act. He will not allow you to damage his reputation.'

Madame Vernier stares at her adversary and eventually laughs, though she is very obviously shaken. 'Very well then. I will sign your so-called confession. Perhaps it's time I returned to France. Paris is so much more fashionable than London.'

Madame Vernier takes the quill from Caleb and signs her name. I cannot read what is written but there is plenty there. I doubt Mrs Macauley will have left a single suspected indiscretion from the list.

'I'll take these two down to Charing Cross,' Caleb tells us. 'They can sort themselves out from there.'

The two disgraced women get to their feet. Jane looks devastated but Madame Vernier stands tall, shoulders back.

'Have you ever felt guilty?' I ask her suddenly. 'For what you did to my mother.'

She looks me in the eye. 'I suppose I regret that it worked so well, my little scheme. I thought it would teach her a lesson, nothing more. I'm not evil, Sukey. What I did to Eve – what I did to *you* – it felt necessary at the time, for my own success. You can call me cold-hearted, mercenary, self-interested. I'll accept those charges. But I never meant for Eve to die. I swear it.' She turns to Mrs Macauley. 'May we meet again.' And then Caleb is pushing her from the room, dragging Jane behind him.

We wait in silence for the sound of the front door closing on them and then Mrs Macauley picks up her precious signed confession. 'I thought it would be more satisfying.'

I know what she means, for this feels anticlimactic. Her confession about my mother has not helped. Even the thought of her being driven from London in shame does not make me feel happy. I have to take my satisfaction in those things that really matter. Gisele Vernier, regardless of her final words, cannot harm us now. Emmy is home and I have my sister back.

38

Emmy is upstairs in her bedchamber. She has been quiet since her return two days ago, barely leaving this room. Mrs Macauley has seemed wary of her daughter, suggesting that we leave her be until she is ready to emerge fully and join her sisters.

'You seem unhappy,' I say as she looks out of the window. 'Did I do wrong in coming to get you?'

'Wrong?' She smiles wryly. 'No. Do I look so ungrateful?'

I hesitate. 'I thought that it might make you happy. This new house, it is so much nicer. And your mama is overjoyed that you are returned to us.'

She moves to sit on the edge of the bed. 'I do not deserve it. I have been a terrible daughter and a worse friend to you.' She begins to cry. 'Sukey, how did this happen?'

I sit beside her, unsure what she means. 'You are not to blame. Madame Vernier had her own dastardly plans that none of us knew about until it was too late. If anything, the fault is mine, for I encouraged you to go to her.'

'You were just trying to protect me.' She smiles through the tears. 'You are always there to rescue me. My best friend. My sister.'

I hug her and feel guilty again. For as much as I had thought the Pall Mall house a safe place for her to go to, if I am honest with myself, I had also wanted to impress Madame Vernier. It was my ambition that allowed us to fall into the trap. I hope that my subsequent actions have made up for my past failures as a friend.

As night falls and the house fills with music and laughter, Emmy and I talk for hours. Mrs Macauley leaves us alone; perhaps she realises that her daughter must have some time to recover. I tell her everything that happened to Jonathan, about Jonas failing to protect me and about Caleb being more than I could have hoped for, although I don't see that we have a future. I tell her about what Madame Vernier did to my mother, and we both cry, for what our lives might have been if we had each grown up with a mother instead of the Ashleys, although as Emmy points out, we would have turned out as harlots regardless.

She tells me about the lord who seems besotted with her, old enough to be her father but rich as the king, and how pleased her mama will be if she can bring him here to Soho. She is ready to get back to work, to talk to her mother and to put the past behind her. It is like the olden days, before London, when we were mere children without a single idea of how the world works. Now, not even a full year later, here we are. We have survived so much and yet still we fall asleep in the same bed, knowing that if there is one person in the world who loves us, it is the girl sleeping beside us.

The next day the bookshop is busy when I arrive. The newest *Delphine* is flying from the shelves. I buy one of the last copies as a gift for Mr Forrester, and I see the joy and pride on Caleb's face as he exchanges his book for the money that will keep a roof over his and his father's head. And Jonathan's, I remember, for he is sitting quietly in a corner, parcelling up books to be sent out to customers. He sees me and smiles but makes no effort to come over. He is set on his work, and for now he has not much else. He needs time to settle into this new life, one that I think he can be happy in but that has removed some of his hard-won freedoms. When will he again feel safe to roam the streets of London as he once had? Maybe never, not unless Mr Sharp can find some assistance in the hazy areas of law that this land keeps in order to maintain its civility while exporting its cruelty to foreign lands.

'Come up,' Caleb tells me once the hubbub has died down. 'Pa!' Mr Fowler waves a hand of acknowledgement, deep in conversation with a customer.

I decline his offer of coffee. 'I said that I would come but I cannot stay long. You wanted to talk?'

'Yes.' He looks nervous. 'Sit down?' We both sit at the table, facing one another, and I can feel the nervous drum of his fingertips against the top of it. 'I was just thinking that, after everything . . . mysteries solved, Jonathan safe . . . we should perhaps speak of our future.'

The future. Our future. I had suspected as much the day before and had cowardly delayed this conversation. Now, I must find the right words to say. 'I do think that we have a future,' I say, 'but it is just that – something that cannot happen now, in the present. It is not for now. Forgive me, I've been carried away because how could I not? You can be quite charming, you know, when you want to be.' He laughs but I know that I am not telling him what he wants to hear. 'I'm not free to be anything other than your friend, Caleb. I know that you might say that it is possible. That I can work in the evenings and spend my days with you, but that's not fair. Not to either of us.'

'But don't you see?' he interrupts. 'I can buy your freedom. How much do you owe old Lucy? From what *Delphine* brings in, from the next edition, which is almost half written already, I can pay whatever you owe.'

Just a few months ago I would have flung my arms around him and said *yes, please.* But now I know that I would only be happy temporarily. That I would always feel indebted to Caleb. I am not scared anymore.

'No. I have done some calculations, and I think I can pay Mrs Macauley what I owe her within the year. After that, I will need savings, for once I leave her place, I may be some weeks without earning, and I know I'll never have a wage that brings me anywhere near as much.' My grand idea is for a school of some sorts, but I do not know quite how yet, and I need to be clear with Caleb. I need him to understand and believe that my mind cannot be changed.

'How long?' he asks.

'Two years,' I tell him. 'A short enough time, for I'm far too young to be wed, and if that's not your intention then I see little point in you helping me.' He laughs at this, and I am glad. 'I will still see you often, for I'm sure you'll need help with your books. For ideas and suggestions. We have our Sunday meetings and there will be nobody else for me. No man will occupy my heart, though I won't ask you to pledge similar. I—'

'I can wait,' he says. 'I can put aside savings. Find us a proper house to rent, for when we're married.'

I can't help but smile when he says that word: *married.* Because of all the possible futures I had expected as a child, this was never one of them. And there is no guarantee it will happen, I know that. I can look back over the past six months and see how I have changed. How will I be when four times that number of months have gone by? I kiss Caleb one last time, until our two years are up, and I vow to keep my resolve even though I wish this didn't have to be so.

But Jonathan has taught me the importance of hope, and the importance of making our own choices. As I leave, I say goodbye to him and his face lights up and I see that he will soon be better. I too will soon be better, and when I remember that dark December night when we met, both so desperate and lost, I see that we are both far stronger than anyone else knows.

Acknowledgements

It's widely acknowledged that writing a novel never gets easier, but this particular book really did its utmost to prove this fact. It took many drafts for it to resemble the vision that I had when I first started to write the story of Sukey and her encounter with Jonathan Strong. In fact, I wrote the first pages back in 2017 when I was still studying for my MA in Creative Writing at Birkbeck, University of London. To that end, I have to thank those in the writing workshop, led by Julia Bell, who gave feedback and encouragement. I have clung to your wise words over the years as I tried to wrangle this story into place!

Huge thanks are due to my brilliant editor, Manpreet Grewal, who gave great feedback, wasn't afraid to tell me when things weren't working but also never lost confidence in me (unless she just has an excellent poker face – either way, I got there in the end!). Thank you to everyone at HQ who has been involved in this book and my previous.

Every author needs a champion in their corner and mine is the incredible Nelle Andrew, literary agent extraordinaire. She thinks of everything before I do, cuts through the bullshit and has my back at all times.

Writing is a solitary business but so many people have been

on hand to read chapters, give general support or just be someone on hand to listen. Thank you to all my friends and especially to Harriet Tyce, Lou Kramskoy, Ruth Ivo, Luan Goldie, Nadine Matheson, Kia Abdullah, Helen Monks Takhar and the D20 authors.

A few of the characters in this fictional story are based on real life people. Jonathan's story has been changed to fit the timeline and narrative of the novel but several of the events in this book really happened including the involvement of William and Granville Sharp in his recovery and later in helping him escape slavery. I considered writing an author's note, but I first came across his story in David Olusoga's book *Black and British: A Forgotten History* and I would urge anyone with an interest in Black British history to read it. Also recommended are *Black England: A Forgotten Georgian History* by Gretchen Gerzina, *The Good Sharps: The Eighteenth-Century Family that Changed Britain* by Hester Grant and, on the life of an eighteenth-century prostitute, *The Covent Garden Ladies* by Hallie Rubenhold.

Turn the page for an exclusive extract from Louise Hare's atmospheric and compelling debut, *This Lovely City*.

1

The basement club spat Lawrie out into the dirty maze of Soho, a freezing mist settling over him like a damp jacket. He shivered and tightened his grip on the clarinet case in his right hand. He'd best hurry on home before the fog thickened into a 'pea-souper', as they called it round here. The hour was later than he'd have liked; the club had been packed and the manager always paid extra if the band stuck around, keeping the crowd drinking.

'Done for the night?' The doorman leaned against the wall by the entrance, waiting for the last stragglers to leave.

Lawrie nodded. He'd been invited to stop for a drink with the band after the last set but he had somewhere to be. The night's moonlighting had been a last-minute call-out. He'd already arranged to take Evie out to the pictures but he needed the money and his name was just getting known around town: *Mr Reliable. Able to fit in with any band at short notice. Call Lawrie Matthews, he's your man; he'll play anything for a shilling or two.*

It might be after three in the morning, but the street was still open for trade. Across the road a couple of girls loitered, hardly dressed for the March weather, their legs bare and their jackets open. They sheltered in a shop doorway, huddled together as they smoked. One of them called over to him but he pretended he hadn't heard. That sort of entertainment wasn't for him. A few minutes of pleasure taken in a dark piss-scented alleyway could not outweigh the guilt. This he knew.

Even back home in Jamaica, he'd never felt confident in himself, not like his older brother Bennie, but this city forced him even further inside himself. It was a chronic condition, like asthma or arthritis; he could go a day or so feeling perfectly normal and then just a word or a glance was enough to remind him that he didn't belong. He liked working the clubs because he could just play his clarinet and get lost in the music. His fellow musicians respected him; many of them even looked like him. He revelled in the applause that came when his name was shouted out and he stepped forward to give his small bow and a smile, just the right side of bashful. But as soon as he left the warmth of the club, things changed. People looked and decided what he was without knowing a single thing about him. Most of them were well-meaning. Somehow that was worse.

He walked swiftly down to Trafalgar Square, putting on a sprint as he saw his night bus approaching, leaping on the back just before it pulled away and clambering up the steps to the upper deck. He sat down, panting slightly through exertion and relief.

Settled, he looked out of the window at the desolate streets rolling by. The city appeared defeated beneath the weak glow of the late winter moon, which lazily cast its light down on the abandoned remnants of buildings that looked flimsy enough to blow over in the backdraught, if only the driver would put his foot down. Almost five years now since VE Day, almost two years since Lawrie had landed at Tilbury, and the city was still too poor to clean itself up. Austerity they called it, as if giving it a name made it more acceptable to those struggling to make ends meet.

The double-decker wound its lethargic way south of the river and Lawrie tried to stay awake. His eyes were heavy but the draught through the window kept him shivering enough that he didn't nod off. He'd be home just in time to change into his uniform and swallow down some breakfast before heading out again to his proper job.

Jumping off at the Town Hall stop in Brixton, the last passenger left on board, he tugged his scarf up over his chin to ward off a wind that felt like icy needles stabbing against his face. By the time he turned the corner of his street his face was already numb and his gloved hand felt stiff around the handle of the clarinet case. He wiggled his fingers and looked down, checking they were still there.

Home at last; a chip of grass green paint flaking away from the swollen wood of the gate as he swung it open, the rough edge catching his glove. He let himself in the front door, careful to close it quietly behind him. Everyone would still be asleep; he could hear Arthur's less than gentle snores through the thin wood of the door that led to what had been the front room before Mrs Ryan had to let it out for much-needed cash. He silently pulled off his shoes and shrugged off his coat, hanging it up by the door, his trilby next to it.

Upstairs in his bedroom he stowed the clarinet safely away at the back of his wardrobe. He trusted his fellow residents well enough, but his mother had always preached that temptation could befall the best of men. That stick of rosewood had been his father's before him. Irreplaceable. Maybe one day he would pass it on to a son or daughter himself. He'd dared to mention that dream to Evie only a few weeks ago, and her smile had given him hope.

It was a room that his mother would have been ashamed to offer her cook. Besides the wardrobe there was only space left for a narrow bed and just enough room on the floor for his friend Aston to sleep on when he was in town, which seemed to be less often in recent months. The small window, with a view from the back of the house, let in a little bit of light and a lot of draught. Lawrie had rolled up some newspaper and jammed it into the gap between the window and its frame, but that wasn't enough to stop the inside of the glass from frosting over.

His uniform was ready on its hanger, but the cold had stiffened his fingers and it was a slow process; shedding the suit of a professional musician and putting on his everyday postman's uniform. He blew on his hands, trying to get some warmth into them, but he already knew that only a hot mug of tea would work.

Down in the kitchen, he expertly lit the flame on the stove and stared out of the window as the kettle boiled. He fancied he could see the sky lighten slightly as the hour grew closer to dawn. The kettle began its low whistle, and Lawrie lifted it off the ring before it could wake anybody with a full screech. Mrs Ryan would be up early so he made a full pot, tugging the hand-knitted tea cosy around it so that she could have a hot cuppa as soon as she came down. He always let it sit a good long while. He'd never been a big tea drinker before meeting Mrs Ryan, so he'd become used to the way she brewed it. He kept one eye on the time as he clasped the mug, his fingers softening, the feeling returning, as he sat at the table and enjoyed the silence and warmth of the kitchen.

When the clock hands read half past four it was time to go. Lawrie wrapped up again in his heavy coat and the deep burgundy scarf that Evie had knitted him for Christmas. Reluctantly, he forwent his beloved lined leather gloves for the bobbled fingerless ones that did what they could to protect his precious hands against the elements while still allowing him to work easily. Pausing before unlatching the door, he took an extra few seconds to adjust his postman's cap on his brow before the long, age-speckled mirror, his forehead bisected by a crack in the glass, courtesy of a V-1 that had fallen in the next street in darker days.

'Oi!' Derek, Mrs Ryan's son, stood at the top of the stairs, just out of bed and wearing only an off-white vest and pants. His mother would have words if she saw the state of him. In his hand was a brown paper package. 'Take these over to Englewood, would you? Usual place.' He threw the package down and Lawrie caught it lightly, nodding his consent. More black-market stockings, he guessed. Rationing had made Derek a fortune. He tucked the package away in the hallway cupboard to collect after his shift.

The sorting office was only a ten-minute walk but Lawrie had to be early. He had to be the first to arrive. He glanced up at the house next door as he pulled the front door closed behind him, but Evie's window stayed dark. Not yet five and she'd be fast asleep. Last summer the early dawns had woken her, the sun rising to greet the city as he left for work. He'd pause and wait, turning when he heard the scrape of her sash window opening up. They'd never speak – she'd hold a finger to her lips and smile down at him worried that her mother would hear, even though she was unlikely to. Agnes Coleridge took sleeping pills and snored louder than any man Lawrie had heard, the rumble audible through the party wall. He'd smile back and Evie would blow him a kiss as she rubbed sleep from her eyes. And even though the dark mornings had put paid to this small joy, he couldn't help but pause for a moment beneath her window. Just in case.

'You!'

Lawrie stifled a groan. 'Sir?' He turned to face Eric Donovan who was waddling down the aisle in his direction, his creased shirt already coming untucked from trousers whose waistband looked to be on the verge of capitulation.

'Get a move on today, boy, you hear? Second lot's gone out late twice this week already.' The words were barked around an unlit Woodbine that perched on Donovan's narrow bottom lip; the slimmest part of him.

'Yessir.' Lawrie had never headed out late, but he'd learned there was nothing to be gained in talking back to the boss.

'And don't forget my order.' Donovan lowered his voice, Lawrie nodding to show he understood. Donovan's sweet tooth kept Lawrie in his good books, Derek supplying bags of white sugar to maintain Donovan's addiction.

Lawrie put his head down and got on with the sorting while his fellow postmen straggled in, the air filling with a cacophony of male voices. Joining in with the general banter cheered him up by the time he'd got his bag packed, hefting it across his back and adjusting his stance to accommodate the weight. His walk took him back down his own street – past Evie's house – so he didn't complain, despite it being one of the heavier routes.

Evie answered the door when he knocked at the Coleridges', a round of toast in one hand and a shy smile on her face that brightened his mood in an instant. He didn't deserve a girl this beautiful, not after what he'd done, and yet here she was.

'Anything for me this morning, Mr Postman?'

'Always.' He leaned forward and kissed her lightly on the lips, one eye checking over her shoulder in case her mother made a sudden appearance. He didn't take it personally that he was forbidden to cross the threshold. He was sure that Mrs Coleridge would have said as much to any man who was wooing Evie. After all, his skin was barely a shade darker than her own daughter's. Evie's father had returned to wherever he'd come from without knowing he had a baby on the way, leaving Agnes Coleridge holding a mulatto child. No wonder she had a disposition as bitter as quinine.

'Evie! Shut that door, will you? D'you want me to catch my death?' The kitchen door slammed.

'Don't mind her.' Evie pulled the door to behind her and wrapped her arms around her body, a flimsy protection against the cold, standing there in a plain blue cotton dress, navy jumper and her house slippers. 'You got time for a cuppa? I can bring it out.'

Lawrie adjusted his bag across his back so that there was space for her in his arms, pulling her off the step and holding her tight to keep warm. 'Not today.'

'Is it Donovan? You should tell him what's what.' Evie fussed with his scarf, making sure his tender skin was protected.

'I can manage him just fine.' Lawrie stole another kiss before letting her go. 'Just one letter today, ma'am.' She laughed and took it, pressing the palm of her other hand to his cheek. 'I'll call round tonight when you're home from work. You have a good day now.'

She leaned against the doorframe and watched as he made his way up the street, pushing envelopes into letterboxes, just as she did every day, whatever the weather. It was a miracle she'd never caught a cold, but Mrs Ryan reckoned that love did something strange to a body – that if it could be bottled or turned into pills it would make penicillin look like an old wives' remedy. At the corner, he turned back to wave and blow a kiss. She never went inside until he was out of sight.

Towards the end of the day, as he sat in the police station, he would wonder if in this moment he'd jinxed himself – walking around with that stupid grin on his face as if he were the luckiest man alive.

The morning followed its familiar rhythm. First man back at the sorting office, first back out with the next delivery, smirking at the look of disappointment on Donovan's face. He had a little gossip with Mrs Harwood as he gave her a hand carrying her shopping bags home and thanked Mr Thomson for a racing tip that he wouldn't use himself but would pass on to Sonny who loved a little gamble. Lawrie clocked off in the early afternoon, declining the offer to join the others in the pub down the street. He tried to go with them once or twice a week, but only because he felt he should. He liked a game of snooker or dominoes but he really didn't have a lot in common with these men: mainly married, mainly ex-servicemen, all white. Besides, he still had Derek's delivery to make.

He made a short detour home to pick up his bicycle and the package. Englewood Road was on the south side of Clapham Common, a place that was close to home; that green expanse of open land beneath which he had spent his first few nights in England. He remembered arriving there, that summer of 1948, and wondering how the sun could be so bright and yet so chill. And then they'd led him into the deep-level shelter, laughing at his terror at being underground, and fed him tasteless sandwiches along with the rest of the *Windrush* passengers who were unfortunate enough to have nowhere else to go.

The south side of the Common was busy with traffic, those famous red buses no longer a sight that thrilled him. At weekends the paths that cut across the Common would be much busier: couples strolling, children playing, fathers teaching their sons to sail boats on the ponds or feed the ducks. This was where he'd first set eyes on Evie, and where they'd had their first real kiss the summer before, sitting in the deep grass on a long hot Saturday afternoon. In better weather the air would be full of the shrieks of young children playing games, the chatter of their mothers as they exchanged gossip and pushed their progeny in huge Silver Cross prams that forced Lawrie from the path and onto the grass.

On this cold March afternoon, only the odd dog walker had ventured out. At this time of day he often saw these middle-aged women with their precious pets emerging from the large houses that surrounded the Common to walk their pampered animals in circles. Their children were grown and their housework managed by a housekeeper or a charlady, someone like Mrs Coleridge who did for a family over on the north side. They came striding along with an entitlement that Lawrie would never possess, letting their dogs off the leash and looking the other way as their beloveds squatted and left the mess for someone else to step in. Just before he reached Eagle Pond, Lawrie looked up and saw one such woman coming towards him, veering to one side as she walked briskly down the centre of the path; there was a Jack Russell trotting along at her heels, and if Lawrie had learned anything in his postal career it was to watch out for those little bastards. The woman stared as he rode past, and he knew that if he looked back she'd be watching him. Making sure he kept moving and didn't hang around like a bad smell.

The lady who answered the door at Englewood Road was no better. Barely two words to say to him, neither of them wasted on thanks, but the money felt comforting in his pocket. Lawrie's cut was twenty per cent, bargained up from ten the year before. Derek needed a trusted delivery man, he'd argued. Someone who didn't look suspicious knocking on a door and handing over a brown paper package. Who better than the local postman?

Maybe he should take Evie out, he mused. Not just to the pictures. The boss of the club where he'd played the night before, he'd mentioned a few times that he'd get Lawrie a good table if he wanted to bring his girl along. Lawrie always smiled back and thanked him for the offer, said that he'd let him know. He wasn't sure what he was wary of. There was no shame in playing music for a living. It wasn't as though Evie didn't know what he did but he liked that she was separate from all that. The women who frequented the club, not all of them but a few, they reminded him of his mistakes. They reminded him of Rose.

He cycled back the way he'd come, recognising the woman he'd seen with the terrier as he drew close to Eagle Pond, but the dog was nowhere to be seen. There was something strange about the way she was moving, and he found himself slowing down. She was pacing up and down in front of the pond, looking for something. Her gait was lopsided and, when she drew closer, he saw that her face was wet from tears that were blinding her. She didn't notice Lawrie until the last moment, suddenly aiming towards him and coming up short as she took him in properly. She held herself rigid, her mouth gasping for air that her lungs didn't seem to want to accept.

'Ma'am?' Lawrie swung his leg and dismounted, making his movements slow so that she didn't spook. 'You all right? Can I help you?'

She looked over her shoulder but turned back to him, fixing her eyes on his uniform. Whatever she'd seen was more frightening than one skinny black man. And there was no one else in sight. 'You – you're… a postman?' Her tongue tripped as she spoke.

'Yes, ma'am. Do you need help?'

She nodded and pointed in the direction she'd come from, a ragged sob creasing her body.

He couldn't see anything out of the ordinary at first. There was the pond, and there he spied the terrier. The small dog was soaked through. Barking urgently at him, it ran back towards the water.

'The pond.' The woman squeezed out the words and he noticed now that her hands were filthy, her coat spattered with mud.

'There's something in the pond?'

It was useless. She had begun to shiver, her teeth actually chattering as shock took hold. Lawrie laid his bike down on the grass and headed towards the pond on foot. The dog was still barking in a fury, running laps between the edge of the pond and the path.

'What you got, boy?'

The dog splashed into the water, checking back to make sure he was being followed. There was a bundle there, a dirty blanket that once had been white. Lawrie crouched by the edge next to a smaller set of footprints that must have belonged to the woman. It didn't look like much, this wad of sodden wool, but that didn't stop fear from squeezing his chest tight as he reached out with his right hand, the palm of his left sinking into freezing mud as he tried to keep his balance.

He strained his arm and caught an inch of fabric between two fingers. Pulling gently, the bundle moved closer and he grabbed a tighter hold. The wool was heavy with water. White and yellow embroidered flowers peeked out from beneath the pond filth. Daisies. When he lifted it the bundle was heavier than he'd anticipated, but it wasn't the weight that sent him crashing to the ground – only sheer luck landing him onto the bank rather than into the water. His heart pounded his ribs so hard that he glanced down at his chest, expecting to see it burst out through his coat, scattering buttons onto the ground.

The blanket lay there on the grass, the bundle coming apart. A baby's arm had escaped, along with a shock of dark curly hair and a glimpse of a cheek. It could have been a doll, but one touch had been enough to convince him that it wasn't. The hand was frozen stiff but the skin gave as his fingers had brushed against it.

Someone had left a baby in the pond to die. A baby whose skin was as dark as Lawrie's.

Don't miss Louise Hare's utterly glamorous and clever murder mystery duology *Miss Aldridge Regrets* and *Harlem After Midnight*.

Lena Aldridge, a struggling singer in 1930s London, is thrust into a dangerous game of intrigue and murder when she is offered a chance of a lifetime: a starring on Broadway and a first-class ticket to New York. But when death follows her aboard the Queen Mary, Lena's new life becomes a deadly performance.

ONE PLACE. MANY STORIES

Bold, innovative and empowering publishing.

FOLLOW US ON:

@HQStories